DOWN DEEP

MIKE CROFT

ALMA BOOKS

ALMA BOOKS LTD
London House
243–253 Lower Mortlake Road
Richmond
Surrey TW9 2LL
United Kingdom
www.almabooks.com

Down Deep first published by Alma Books Limited in 2008
Copyright © Mike Croft, 2008

Mike Croft asserts his moral right to be identified as the author of this work in
accordance with the Copyright, Designs and Patents Act 1988

This is a work of fiction. Names, characters, places and incidents either
are the product of the author's imagination or are used fictitiously, and any
resemblance to actual persons, living or dead, business establishments, events
or locales is entirely coincidental.

Printed in Great Britain by CPI Cox & Wyman, Reading, RG1 8EX

ISBN: 978-1-84688-058-2

To Daniel and Tanya Watkins

DOWN DEEP

Prologue

Blackfin had waited for darkness to fall before surfacing so close to the beach. It was a warm August night, but rain was falling steadily, and the moon was hiding behind dense cloud. The sea, filthy in this place, washed over his great back. He floated unseen in the water, resisting the outgoing tide. To the right of him a strange structure – Brighton Pier – stuck out of the land, poking the stomach of the sea, and he watched the humans who were on top of it. He had no notion of what a fairground was, but he sensed that the humans were playing. The lights they seemed to like so much flashed and dazzled, bouncing off the rain-stippled sea, and the noises they enjoyed being inside – searing rhythms, clanging bells, screaming sirens – cascaded over the edge of the pier and attacked the atmosphere. The humans shrieked and whooped as they were whirled around by their demented machines.

There had been a time when Blackfin used to play. He had been young then. Migrating to the cold waters for the first time with the rest of his bachelor herd, he had passed the sunsets in mock-fighting, chasing, lob-tailing, playing dead and showing off. They had raced through the water, just under the surface, then launched themselves into the air and breached spectacularly. Or, deep in the fecund polar seas, they had transmitted misleading messages to each other: gorging himself on scores of comatose squid, he would signal the scarcity of prey. But that had happened half a life ago, and the time for playing was over.

Blackfin was a mature bull sperm whale, huge and battle-scarred. With age had arrived the urge for solitude. He lived alone near the poles of the planet, and surrendered himself to an ancient rhythm: dive, feed, ascend, surface, breathe; dive, feed, ascend, surface, breathe. He liked it this way. Once a year, perhaps once in two years, he made the journey to the warm waters to mate. He would find a family group of twenty or so – two or three old females, five or six mature females, a dozen young – and stay with them from one moon to the next. For a while it was pleasant to be pestered by the young whales, and he would teach them about migratory routes, feeding grounds and hunting techniques. But it was seldom long before he hankered after an immensity of solitude.

What had impelled him to leave his rich, lonely depths for the unknown shallow waters?

He had been travelling for several weeks. At daybreak he had arrived at the end of the world. He had entered a shallow, dirty sea that lay between two land masses. Swimming in it was like navigating a fetid tunnel. Human presence was everywhere – boats of all sizes, underwater cables and pipelines, nets to be avoided, filth on the sea bed, in the water – and there was noise, unrelenting noise, polluting the sound waves until his mind ached. But he had endured it all, reaching his destination towards the middle of the day. Then he had waited.

Waiting still, and the night half gone, Blackfin's acute sense of sound was assaulted by a different din. At the end of the pier a nightclub had opened. The hypnotic music inside the club cooked itself to a hot high, reverberated through the structure, was caught by the thousand metal struts supporting the pier, and broadcast to an uncomprehending underwater world. From the far end of the beach, too, the clamour increased. Pubs and clubs under the esplanade filled up, and the drunken shouts of men and women rolled down the shore and made themselves heard over the rain and the sea's long sighs.

It was almost dawn when Blackfin ended his vigil. The pier, at last, was deserted, its lights turned off, and the night-clubbers under the esplanade had been ejected from the clubs. There had been an hour when this strange human world had wound down: men and women had pushed one another up against dark brick walls, grunting, then departed for separate homes; groups of lads had finished the last greasy remnants of their kebabs and burgers, and thrown the wrappings on the beach; and two men had given up fighting each other because they were too drunk to do anything but stagger around in the shingle, hugging. When all the varieties of human behaviour were completed, a sort of silence descended on the Brighton shoreline.

Blackfin blew, and five cubic metres of gas from his hot lungs struck the air, condensing into a cool cloud of vapour. His tail flukes, flat and mighty, struck the sea. He attacked the water with conviction, and within a few seconds was swimming at speed. The water sheared off his sides and formed a churning wake behind him, his great tail forcing the sea to let him past. He felt strong. He felt distance rushing past him, and the land came towards him faster than he could think about it.

On the beach there was only a stray dog to see him coming; the hound leapt into the air with a pathetic yelp as the great living thing launched itself from the black like some improbable monster. Slamming into the land, Blackfin felt his mass shudder and strain as a tall spray of pebbles exploded into the air. The dog loped away unsteadily as the pebbles cascaded down on him.

Now Blackfin's life force was becalmed. All his power was transmuted into helplessness, and his infinite water world had been swapped for a stony stretch of land. He felt empty of all feelings, of the despair that had driven him to such an act, and of the terrible fear that he would succeed in nothing but death.

Inside The Grand Hotel, which stood on the front at Brighton and looked out over the sea from behind a pompous Victorian façade, they knew nothing. The guests slept in their beds, the night staff dozed and bickered in windowless rooms, as a whale tried to save the world.

Part One

1

"You moved to Clacton-on-Sea from *California*?" Roddy asked.

"Yeah, that's what I said," Joe Farelli answered.

Roddy locked the door of his car and looked at the little American guy sceptically, the wrinkles at the corners of his eyes in full wry-amusement mode. He and Joe had met only a minute or two before, after Roddy had eased his clapped-out car to a halt on Clacton's promenade, but their conversation was already proving to be confrontational.

"And this is where you decided to set up WhaleWorld? A million-dollar investment, here? In Clacton?"

"Great," Joe muttered, "a smartass asshole on his dirty-ass day."

"Erm…" Roddy said, after a pause, wondering how to respond to the insult. But Joe, his bald crown glinting under the early morning sun, his ludicrous grey ponytail swishing around, was already launching into a complicated defence of his decision to open a dolphinarium in a rundown English seaside resort. Roddy nodded, simultaneously amused and annoyed, as the expletive-rich explanation flooded out.

"What, you never made a mistake?" Joe was pleading at the end, holding out his hands with the palms up. "Now I gotta crazy killer whale over there, Dr Bigshot, that's why I contacted you – let's take a look."

They tramped along with the sea to the left and the town to the right. Two men could scarcely be so physically different: Roddy had height, hair (in need of a cut) and a face that was attractive, despite an overly prominent chin and the exhaustion imprinted around the steady eyes; he was lean enough to look like he needed a good meal, and scruffy enough to suggest that his clothes needed urgent attention – mending, or washing, or ironing, or throwing away; Joe was short, chubby, bald, dressed like an A-lister and as ugly as a lemon-biting camel.

"This institute you run, the Marine Mammals Institute—"

"Yes?"

"Are you sure you're the Director?" Joe asked.

"Sorry?"

"The janitor wouldn't drive that heap of crap," Joe said, turning back to point at the elderly vehicle. "Do you get off on the humiliation?"

Something like that, Roddy thought – the Marine Mammals Institute had been founded by a Victorian philanthropist and was subject to all kinds of outdated eccentricities in organization and governance, including amongst many other indignities a salary of only £16,000 a year for the Director... Even so, he decided he had to counter Joe's aggression somehow as he came to a halt at the tatty entrance to Clacton Pier. He took in the desperate FREE ENTRY! sign, the wooden façade with its peeling white paint, the fish and chip shop.

"Mr Farelli—"

"Joe."

"Joe, forgive my bluntness, but I've driven here at the crack of dawn, following an unsolicited telephone call, to do you a favour, unpaid, despite the fact that you're a complete stranger to me—"

"Yeah."

"—so I'm not in the mood to be ridiculed by someone who makes a living from five dolphins in a swimming pool."

"Yeah yeah," sighed Joe, "you've got it ass-backwards. They make a living out of me."

Roddy tried to hang on to his indignation, but it ebbed away. *Ass-backwards?* It was impossible to dislike someone who could do so much with the word ass. And anyway, Roddy decided, there's no point quibbling with him: I'm forty-three years of age, no wife, no child, no house, fewer possessions than an impoverished student, and I spend more time with whales than people. It's not his fault for thinking that I must be crazy.

"Hey, don't take my crap personally Doc, I'm full of it – better out than in, right? I appreciate you coming here, really. I contacted you because they say you've got this creative, unconventional approach."

They certainly do, Roddy thought; "they" – other marine biologists, academics and whale experts – said a lot more besides. Some of them said he was a genius, others that he was an irresponsible maverick. However, none of them would have disputed his unconventionality.

"A year ago there weren't any killers in the UK," Joe said, digging his hands deep into his pockets as they resumed their walk along the wooden boards of the pier, past the Hall of Laughter and an empty amusement arcade. "That's why I brought Attila the Killer over – I thought I'd make so much money, my ass would itch for joy. What did I know." He scratched at his groin and winced. "You know, I'm from New York, so I thought I knew everything there was to know about feeling like a big piece of shit in the shittest shit shop in Shit-town, got it?"

"Er, got it."

"Right. But I hate England, I loathe this town, I really detest this pier, I truly and entirely and absolutely without qualification *despise* Whale-fucking-World..." – they were passing through the doors of his enterprise, and he pointed at the 'WHALEWORLD' sign as they went in – "...and now, my biggest attraction, my killer whale..." – he stopped in his tracks and put his head in his hands insanely – "...my killer whale is having a nervous fucking breakdown!"

After passing the ticket office and a big board that read "ATTILA THE KILLER, THE WORLD'S BIGGEST THRILLER", Joe guided Roddy through a small warren of corridors, up a flight of stairs, and out through a fire escape into the open air once more. Roddy found himself standing at the top of a tier of dilapidated concrete seating. Other tiers led down to a partitioned section of pool, a meagre blue rectangle containing four bottlenose dolphins... God, he moaned in his mind, what a depressing, miserable scenario. Those poor animals.

There was a teenage boy working at the pool's edge, disconsolately gathering dolphin crap with a large net. The dolphins were listlessly following his progress around the perimeter.

"Hi Mr Farelli," the boy called.

"Hey Jason."

I wish I hadn't come here, Roddy realized – fun-loving, sophisticated mammals like these, creatures of the open seas, confined in such miserable conditions... horrible. Doesn't Joe understand the complexity of their natural environment? The rich social hierarchies of dolphin society? And it'll be even worse for the killer whale, three times the size and without a companion of her own species.

"You're gonna get Animal Rights on me, right?" Joe growled, watching him.

Roddy sighed.

"Well, what did you expect? But you know, what really strikes me is how odd this is. A small cube of water with dolphins in it, suspended above the sea."

"I don't get you."

"Sometimes there'll be whales and dolphins out there, in the sea, completely unaware of your animals swimming above them. It's surreal."

"Oh, they're aware of each other. Sometimes you can hear them calling to each other. A few days ago we heard a killer calling to Attila."

"That's incredible."

"I know. Kinda heartbreaking."

"You feel sorry for them? Do you think they're happy?"

"Happy?" Joe sighed. "What's happy? Am I happy? Are you happy? These animals were captive-bred in California, they wouldn't survive in the wild. Listen, I feed them well, I give them medical care, I keep the water clean and well pumped and at the right temperature, I keep them exercised, I give them activities... It's like they're in prison, sure, but there's good prisons and there's bad prisons, and this is a good prison. It's an ass-breaker, but I do the best I can."

They descended the concrete tiers and skirted the pool. Roddy walked towards the screen that divided the dolphins' pool from that of the killer, passed it and – a word breathed in his mind, inadequate to his surprise: *Oh...*

The killer whale – technically a species of dolphin like the bottlenoses, despite her name – was floating belly-up. She wasn't moving. Not the faintest ripple was disturbing the surface of the pool. Her beautiful pure white underside, edged by the black of her flanks, shimmered in the water, gorgeous but shocking against the bright blue of the pool walls. Her black, paddle-shaped fins stuck out of her sides like stubby wings. The dorsal fin, four feet long and sticking straight down in the water, was casting a sleek triangular shadow over the bottom of the pool.

"So there it is," Joe said slowly, "that's what she's doing. She won't eat, she won't do the shows and she's not moving – just floating upside-down like that. Pretty weird."

"So strange," Roddy murmured to himself, crouching down in an effort to look the creature in the eye.

"I've worked with killers for over ten years in the States, in three different Sea Worlds, and I never saw an animal do this."

"You say she's not eating?"

"Not for three days."

"How would you describe her overall health?"

"Pretty good. She had a low-grade infection a few weeks ago, but it was nothing serious. We had her on two-hundred-and-forty capsules of tetracycline twice a day, two-fifty mils in a capsule."

"Any side effects?"

"None."

"Do you have a specialist vet here?"

"Not exactly. I've found a local vet who's really enthusiastic. He's studying the subject pretty hard, but until he's up to scratch, we kind of work things out together with Sweeney's *Handbook of Marine Mammal Medicine*."

"That's not exactly ideal, is it. I have to be frank with you, Joe, I just don't agree with this situation. You confine highly intelligent creatures in minuscule pools, they get ill – well there's a surprise – and you don't even have a qualified marine veterinarian to treat them. I think it stinks."

"So I guess we'll have to agree to disagree."

"I suppose we will."

Roddy turned away from him. He walked around the pool slowly. He could hear the sea lapping at the unseen struts of the pier beneath him; from the amusement arcade came the tinny strains of an inane melody.

Attila rolled over. She exhaled as soon as her blowhole hit the surface, her salty spray rising low and wide. Roddy could smell it. He watched the water running down the animal's dorsal fin. The pool smoothed itself out. Attila took in a breath and exhaled again. Even now that she was the right way up, she didn't move. She took another breath. Over on the other side of the pool, Joe was looking at his watch.

"She takes three breaths, then goes back under."

"You're timing her?"

"Six, five, four, three, two, one."

The dolphin rolled back over, her dorsal fin slapping the surface.

"She comes up for exactly twenty-eight seconds, and goes under for twenty-two minutes and forty seconds, give or take one or two seconds."

Roddy plunged his hands in his pockets and, deep in thought, walked back to Joe's side of the pool.

"I suppose you've done diagnostic tests?"

"Well, there's the problem. I mean, there's nothing I'd like better than to do a sed rate or a serum check, maybe get a sample of the bacterial culture around the blowhole to send away for analysis, but if she won't cooperate, then what can I do?"

"How do you usually get the samples?"

"In the bad old days we would have drained the pool to get at her, but then we realized the stress inducement was just too high. We started training the whales to help us out. Attila's trained to present her underside for blood samples and her tongue and blowhole for scrapings. And she can piss on demand. But as long as she's imitating a log I can't get at her."

"Has it occurred to you that she could be severely depressed?"

"Yeah, like, maybe, but she could do that the right way up. Like, I'm depressed as well – much too depressed to stand on my head, right?" Roddy smiled as he pondered this remark. "Listen," Joe continued, "this is a whale doing something really weird in a very deliberate way. Now maybe to you I seem like nothing but a bad businessman who exploits nice animals, but I know killer whales and I know the captive-killer industry. I've been in the game a long time, and this behaviour has no parallel."

Roddy nodded, then turned around to climb up the tiers of seating. He sat down on the top row and rested his hands on his knees. Joe followed. They sat next to each other and said nothing for a while. Joe sighed a lot. Below them, Attila in her pool looked like a painting by Salvador Dalí. From somewhere they could hear Jason murdering the melody of a pop song in an out of tune falsetto:

> *you can buy ma body,*
> *you can buy ma body,*
> *you can buy ma body*
> *but ma soul ain't up for sale*

"I wouldn't give him ten bucks for both," Joe muttered.

"Can you tell me about Attila's routines? When she's performing?"

"It's the regular kind of stuff – jumps, tail-slapping, water soccer, flipper-waving, breaches."

"What about riding?"

"Uh-uh. That's sorta frowned on nowadays. There's a place in Spain where they still do it, but waddaya expect in a country where the national sport is to wave a red blanket at a bull and then stick a spear in its ass?"

Joe issued a few cynical snickers. In the background Jason was still singing. Roddy's mind struggled to come up with a reason for Attila's behaviour: is depression definitely out? Yeah, Joe's right: depression doesn't manifest itself like this. He nibbled on his lower lip, concentrating intently. An idea was forming. After a while Joe touched his arm hopefully and smiled an awkward smile, as though being nice, no matter how insincerely, could influence the situation.

"C'mon Doc, you got any ideas?"

"Not exactly, at least, nothing concrete."

"Shit."

"On the other hand, my fabled creativity and so on…"

"Yeah?"

"Some of my colleagues complain that I have a tendency to anthropomorphize cetacean behaviours…"

"Yeah?"

"You remember what you said before, about standing on your head?"

"Huh?"

"It was very thought-provoking."

"I said something about standing on my head?"

"I mean, if this dolphin were a human, I'd say its behaviour was absolutely bizarre, way off the scale of usual behaviours – just as bizarre, in fact, as a man who chose to stand on his head continually."

"OK," said Joe, in a dubious tone.

"Attila can't talk to you and your staff here, but she's a highly intelligent, sociable being, and you're the only contacts she's got. So, making an anthropomorphic analogy, she's like a person who lives in a prison-like environment, who can't communicate anything more complex than her most elemental needs and feelings – hunger, sadness – who suddenly decides to withdraw from even basic contact in order to stand on her head all day long."

"OK…"

"If you were that person, what would you be conveying?"

"That I'm a crazy sonuvabitch?"

Roddy smiled.

"Well, maybe. I'm thinking, perhaps it's more like a protest. When people can't get what they want, or if they feel that no one is listening to them, or if they feel just – I don't know –

absolutely powerless, then they can end up doing something apparently illogical and striking, something that you just can't ignore."

"Like what?"

"You know – rooftop protests, publicity stunts, hunger strikes, setting fire to themselves, sewing their lips together."

"You think this is why my whale is floating upside down? She wants to be in the news?"

"Perhaps she wants to be heard… Joe, I don't know, it's just a thought."

"So what is she saying? How do I hear her?"

"I don't know that either."

There was a silence, during which Joe was hoping that Roddy would have another thought, markedly better than the first one. He rubbed his eyes for a moment.

"Roddy, my six-year-old niece could feed me better bullshit than that."

Roddy's mobile phone started to ring as he shrugged his shoulders without apology.

"Yes, hello? Derek, hi! How are—"

His friend Derek Petersen, also a whale expert, fellow of Clare College, Cambridge, and head of a research laboratory, didn't let Roddy finish his sentence: "Where are you?"

"I'm far too ashamed to tell you."

"Can you get to a television? As in, immediately?"

"I don't know, what's going on? Joe, I need a television."

"You wanna watch TV now?"

"Have you got one or not?"

"In the office," Joe said, pointing wearily.

Joe's office was gloomy and cluttered. An ancient desk sagged beneath a weight of junk. Ashtrays full of cigar butts spilt over onto various papers and documents. Files and boxes were piled up against the walls, and strange objects – a broken oar, at least seven obsolete computers in various states of disrepair, and a stuffed giant crab – were spread across the floor. There was a small black-and-white television mounted on the wall in the corner, which Roddy, still with his mobile glued to his ear, switched on.

"Channel?"

"Four. Take a look. A sperm whale on Brighton beach."

"Don't be absurd!" Roddy exclaimed automatically; he knew that sperm whales don't beach, not in Brighton. But there it was, on the screen. A young reporter was standing next to the animal, resting his hand proprietorially on its great flank.

"…still not sure what kind of whale it is and why it's stranded itself," the reporter was saying, as smirking teenagers shuffled into shot behind him. "Was this a desperate bid to commit suicide, a death wish, or has it simply lost its way? Perhaps we'll never know. For the moment, until some kind of rescue operation is mounted, Brighton has a unique new tourist attraction. This is Andrew Griffiths for the Biggest Breakfast News."

The camera panned down the animal's body, past its tail, and looked out to sea.

"Do you see what I see?" Derek's voice breathed in Roddy's ear. "There's a furrow in the shingle."

"But – that's astonishing."

"Unprecedented."

The beached whale was replaced by an item on cooking. Roddy flicked off the television and sat down heavily in Joe's chair. There was silence between him and Derek for a moment.

"So what's the big mystery?" Joe asked from the doorway.

Roddy didn't answer. He told Derek that he would try to get to Brighton within three hours, and he asked his friend to inform the police, the RSPCA and the Coastguard that he was on his way. He also gave some instructions as to what equipment he would want waiting for him on his arrival: medicines, anaesthetics, kits for sample-taking, a camera with plenty of film, measuring equipment, a ladder, a CD player, and Yo-Yo Ma's recording of Bach's *Cello Suites*. Roddy had dealt with a dozen major beachings over the years, and he had established certain techniques. Then he left Joe's office and within half a minute was striding back down the pier as Joe struggled to hurry after him.

"What's the big deal?" Joe was asking.

"It's a sperm whale – extremely rare for a deep-water species such as a sperm to beach at all, but to do so from out of a shallow sea like the English Channel is just unbelievable. Also, when a whale becomes beached, it generally drifts in slowly, gets stranded in low water, tips to one side a bit when it tries to free itself and, more often than not, ends up pointing in a random direction, not head on with the land. But this one—" he shook his head, and his eyes shone with excitement. "It was perfectly upright, facing straight ahead, and then there was that big furrow behind it."

"So?" Joe asked, panting slightly – he was not in good shape, and he was now jogging in an effort to keep up with Roddy's long, purposeful strides. But Roddy, pulling away, didn't respond. Joe gave up the chase, stopping at the entrance to the pier.

"What about Attila?" he called, mournfully.

* * *

Sitting in his clapped-out Ford Escort, Roddy swore as the ignition failed. He tried the key for the third time and listened to the starter motor groaning. His mobile phone rang again.

"Yes?"

"It's Whitaker, the RSPCA are on the line, there's a dirty great—"

"Fuck–ing–*hell*!"

"I beg your pardon?"

"Sorry. I'm on my way but the car won't start."

"Ah," said Whitaker gravely, "'Twas ever thus."

Whitaker was a research assistant at the Marine Mammals Institute. His real name was Peter Grant, but everyone except his family called him Whitaker because of a supposed resemblance to the film star Forest Whitaker. He had traced a curious academic path through three undergraduate degrees – literature, psychology and zoology – before starting a Ph.D. under Roddy's supervision at the age of thirty-two. He had ended up being Roddy's unofficial PA as well as a researcher, his meagre wages paid from a series of expense fiddles.

"Is there anything I can do?" Whitaker asked.

"Yeah, beam me up from here and put me down in Brighton. Wait, OK, I'm away. OK Whitaker, I've already asked Derek to organize things, but there's some stuff I forgot to tell him. I need you to phone the police at Brighton and have them put a thirty-metre cordon around the whale."

"Yep."

"And I need sea water rained down on the animal as soon as possible, that's really vital, I don't care how – ring the fire brigade."

"Yep."

"And, er, I don't know, use your initiative."

"Whoa there."

"Wait, tides. Find out about the tides for the next few days."

"No problem."

"Thanks. OK, I want to think now. I'll speak to you later."

"Can I bunk off and come to Brighton?"

"I think it's better if you stay in the office so that—"

"Can I bunk off and come to Brighton?"

"I'd prefer it if—"

"Can I bunk off and come to Brighton?"

"Whitaker!"

"Roddy, it's a sperm whale!"

"OK, OK, do what you like."

The car, rust-pocked and clanking, phut-phutted out of Clacton-on-Sea.

2

Sixty miles away in London, Tony Rattigan was sitting in the back of his chauffeur-driven Bentley. The car was stuck in rush-hour traffic on the Strand. Motorcycle couriers weaved in and out of the gaps and black-cab drivers swore out of open windows. The still air, preparing itself for a hot and sticky August day, was already clogging up with noxious emissions. But Rattigan was unaffected by the noise, the heavy stench of exhaust fumes, and even the snail's pace of the traffic. The Bentley was primarily a working environment. Air-conditioned and air-purified, virtually soundproof, and equipped to enable him to run his multifarious shipping interests, he often preferred it to his offices. It was more private, and it contained everything he needed, from a fax machine and a paper shredder to an Internet connection, satellite TV and, sitting in front, a new PA. A new PA, he considered, who doesn't seem to like me very much. Just like the last one.

Reflecting on this fact transfixed him for a moment: why the hell should I care? He looked in the mirror, his gaze ranging over his own aspect thoughtfully. His build was huge. The mirror could hardly contain his face. His hair was still jet-black, even though he was in his mid-forties; impressive, he thought. He wore it close-cropped. The short cut exposed a double crown. He was plump rather than fat, and yet, looking at the thick, padded cheeks of his face, he knew that he somehow gave the impression of being obese – as if all his presence and muscle, once so irresistible, had degenerated into something off-putting. Is my appearance the problem? Do I disgust her?

Now that he was no longer young, there was much about his face to dislike instantly – the heavy features, the dissatisfied set of his mouth, the sweat that always seemed to be glistening around a nose with large, far-apart pores – and yet there were his eyes. He had once heard a theory: a face may spend a lifetime proving that a person is no good, yet the eyes even of the worst man alive show only the goodness of which he was capable.

Rattigan's eyes were dark, and deep, and strange, and powerful. He knew that. And as he thought about it, his mind made an abrupt announcement: I'm still capable of *more* extraordinary goodness. I am.

"Three minutes, Mr Rattigan."

"What?" he said, startled by the PA's disembodied voice.

"Three minutes to eight o'clock."

"Good. Thanks."

In the past few years he had been exploiting a high-risk, high-yield operation with the Russians, and now it was nearly time to listen in on a telephone conversation that had been set up on an encrypted line between one of his intermediaries and a functionary in Moscow. He dialled a number and waited.

On the hour the line crackled into life. A crisp English voice made an anodyne health enquiry; a stammering Russian answered with the correct formula. It was obvious that the Russian, a delegate for a fringe neo-nationalist party in the Russian State Duma, was terrified. So he should be, Rattigan decided: one hand clinging to the coat tails of the Russian mafia, the other one lying, limp and sweaty, in the menacing grip of very big, utterly cynical military players – and his balls in the grip of kleptocrats. In short, a classic parasite of the new Russia that had succeeded the Soviet implosion. Rattigan almost felt sorry for him.

"We congratulate you on *The Vegas*," the English voice enunciated slowly. "The ship is scheduled to make the drop within the next day or two. I have some information concerning the ship after *The Vegas*. She will arrive in Murmansk in nine days. Her name will be *Jasmine*... *Jasmine*, J-A-S-M-I-N-E... She will have come from Malmö and she will have a cargo of cement bound for a new meteorological observation station that is being constructed near Olenegorsk. The port safety inspectors have been bribed. They will examine *Jasmine* and pronounce that the condition of her pumping equipment makes her unseaworthy. She will remain impounded for three days while repairs are carried out. Do you understand?... There are three days to get the consignment to her. The captain of the ship will be an American called Schwarzkop. The code phrase he will be expecting to hear is 'Are your parents or your grandparents German perhaps?' The consignment should be concealed by delivering it with a second-hand reconditioned pump engine. After three days the vessel will receive a certificate of seaworthiness and she will leave Murmansk, with documentation proving that she is behind schedule and due in Bergen to pick up a cargo of paper bales bound for Reykjavík. That is everything. Is there anything I have said that you do not understand? ...Good... No... Yes."

Excellent. The mechanics of the procedure had been handled well. Assuming his people had chosen the vessel well – and they had always done so to date – then another consignment would be going out shortly. And another substantial payment from the Russians would be wired to a newly set up offshore account. Rattigan threw his encryption mobile onto the seat.

The Bentley was stationary in the heavy traffic. Glancing outside, he saw a little boy who seemed to be lost. The child, only five or six years old, was standing by himself on the pavement as people hurried to work. The small, innocent face crumpled into tears. Rattigan lifted a hand in some kind of gesture, though he was completely invisible behind the one-way glass, but just then the boy's relieved mother arrived. In the back of the Bentley, Rattigan grunted in relief. His mind drifted to another time, when he had been that age.

My life, he thought... what a journey. The children's home, the contempt of the staff: "You're useless, pathetic, nothing". Why did they pick on me, why didn't they *like* me? Was it random? And then, as I got a bit older, the assistant manager of the home, the things he made me do...

Rattigan shook his head uneasily; even now he couldn't think about those events in any depth. It was too dangerous to his fragile equilibrium... Every adult I came into contact with thought I was nothing, assumed that I barely existed. But I did exist. And I worked – Christ, how I worked – to get the scholarship. To *Oxford*, he congratulated himself, savouring the two syllables in his mind. Only – he wrinkled his nose childishly – the bastards. Utter bastards. Oxford was just the children's home all over again. More subtle, but I was still the scumbag, the outsider. Well, now look at me. I'm probably wealthier then my entire college and all its living alumni put together. And how many people in this world have given away – anonymously – almost a *hundred* million pounds to charitable causes?

As a major shareholder in a merchant shipping line whose fleet comprised container ships, bulk-ore and chemical carriers, oil tankers and general cargo ships, Rattigan enjoyed substantial legitimate wealth. Within the industry he was perceived as a respectable, middle-ranking shipping man. But the source of his real wealth lay elsewhere, in the unregulated frenzy of the global shipping scene and the infinite opportunities it presented to amass money. The organizations responsible for policing the oceans –

the International Maritime Organization and the International Maritime Bureau – were underfunded, and struggled to cope with the system of multi-layered ship ownership generated by flags of convenience. One of his tankers, owned by a front company in New York, and flying a Liberian flag, might be financed from a bank in Hong Kong, registered by a classification office in Norway, operated by a second front company in Monte Carlo, be insured in London and administered from Singapore. It was possible to conceal awesome shipping assets – and awesome scams – in such a system.

Thinking about these things with some satisfaction, he scanned his email, and saw one from his daughter. Oh *shit*. He felt the dismay seeping through him. Please, don't let her have cancelled, he privately begged, as he clicked on it.

Daddy, change of venue: Bob's Caff on Stroud Green Road, Finsbury Park. See you later, Ally.

Bob's Caff? *Bob's Caff?* In Finsbury Park! What was wrong with the table he'd booked at The Richoux? But at least she hadn't cancelled. God, why was she so elusive these days? He didn't even have a telephone number for her. But – he sighed in relief – I'm meeting her, after all these months. I'm meeting her! The thought of it consumed him with anticipation: my darling Ally.

If someone could have seen him then, wallowing in his love for her, they might have liked him. And that is all he had ever really wanted.

* * *

The traffic in the centre of Brighton was bumper to bumper. In his eagerness to get to the sea front, Roddy was going for gaps that were hardly there.

"Damn it, come on."

The car radio was on. He caught something about food scares – "This time, is it the fish in the sea we should be worried about?" – but stopped listening when the car ahead of him stalled in front of a green light.

"No no no," Roddy pleaded, "don't do that."

It took him fifteen minutes to get to the top of West Street. He abandoned his car in Queen Square, which would later cost him a parking ticket, and trotted briskly down to the front. There he stood above the esplanade and looked along the shore in both directions. It wasn't difficult to spot where the beaching had occurred. Some three hundred yards to his right, overlooked by the mournful structure of the abandoned West Pier, he could see a sizeable crowd clustered in a horseshoe formation on the lower ridge of the beach. Above them a jet of water rose and descended.

Roddy jogged along the sea front until he was level with the crowd, then descended to the beach. His feet sank into the shingle as he walked along the ridges and skidded down the slopes.

"Mummy, it's so ugly," he overheard a little girl say disapprovingly as he pushed through the onlookers, and he smiled: it was true that sperm whales, with their lumps and bumps and off-putting skin, their small eyes and their down-turned mouths and their truly monumental heads, wouldn't win any prizes in a Cetacean Beauty Contest. He reached the front and – just stared. Still staring, he stepped over the orange cordon where a policeman was standing.

"I'm Roddy Ormond, Dr Roderick Ormond," he said, not looking at the man but at the whale. "A colleague will have phoned ahead, I'm the Director of the Marine Mammals Institute in London, I'll probably be directing things here, if you can just, er..."

He fumbled for some ID and handed it over. The constable scanned the ID and mumbled into his radio incomprehensibly.

"Very good sir," he said at last. "There's another whale person waiting for you over there."

Roddy prised his eyes from the whale and saw a small, trim woman, of Asian origin, about forty years old. She was wearing a light-blue T-shirt, dark-blue jeans and green wellingtons. Huddled with a police officer and a fireman, she was engaged in earnest discussion. As Roddy scrunched through the shingle to join the group, voices shouted out: "Sir, can we ask who you are sir?" – "Sir, would you like to make a comment to the press?" Roddy looked behind him and saw three or four journalists pushing at the cordon. He noticed, too, that there were two television crews, and both cameras were trained on him. He frowned in distaste.

"Dr Ormond?"

"Yeah," he said.

"Kamala Mohandhas, Senior Vet with the Cetology Conservation Trust." She smiled and shook his hand.

"Oh, you're Kamala Mohandhas, of course – I've seen you around at a conference or two."

"That's right, in fact I was at York when you delivered that paper about the oil companies infringing on the North Atlantic Frontier."

"It's good to know you. The CCT's campaign against the lifting of the moratorium on hunting whales is absolutely inspirational."

"Well you're no slouches yourselves at the MMI—"

"Thanks."

"OK," Kamala said, "let me introduce you to Superintendent Peter Shires—"

"Hello."

"Hello there."

"—of the Brighton Police and to, er, I'm sorry, I didn't catch your…"

"I'm a fireman," said the fireman, grinning as he gestured towards his black-and-yellow uniform. "Jonathan Edgar."

"Hi," Roddy said, shaking the man's hand. "Fine, fine. Right…" He gazed around him for a few moments. "Can I assume I'm officially in charge of the welfare of the whale?" he asked. "Because as I remember, overall responsibility has to be cleared with the environmental department of the local authority."

"Yes you are," the superintendent confirmed, "the environmental officers have been down here and it's all done and dusted."

"OK, in that case, there are one or two things we can do straight away. I'd like the crowd back a further ten metres," he told the superintendent. "I know I specified thirty metres, but it's a big crowd and a big whale."

"No problem."

"Now," Roddy continued, turning to the fireman, "John?"

"Jonathan."

"Jonathan, the water—"

"Yeah, pump's over there," he said, pointing to a section of the crowd, "behind that lot."

"I want it moved further away. If possible I want it moved much further away, it's too noisy. I want peace and quiet for this animal."

"I understand."

Roddy scrutinized the water descending on the whale's back.

"I suppose you can change the what-do-you-call-it, the way the water comes out of the hose?"

"We can almost make it loop the loop if you like."

"I want the water a lot finer, at the moment it's almost spattering off his back—"

"Mm."

"—I don't want it bouncing off him like that. We need a fine spray misting over every part of him. Is that possible?"

"Done in three minutes."

"Thanks."

The fireman trudged away.

"Quite a sight," Kamala said, nodding at the sperm whale.

"God yes. I think I'll go and say hello to him. Did you get together everything I requested?"

"I've got industrial quantities of everything, don't worry about that. But are you sure that it's necessary to notch him?"

Surprised, he raised an eyebrow, thinking, of course it's necessary – it's standard scientific procedure. In order to avoid answering the question, he smiled at her and headed for the whale. The crowd watched him with interest as he approached. He walked up to it slowly and from the side, so that it could see him coming.

"All right now, old boy," he murmured, "OK."

Christ almighty… I've never seen a fully mature sperm whale out of the water, it's unbelievably huge…

The creature's eye was unmoving above its low, three-metre-long jaw. The two different beings held each other's gaze intensely. You wonderful, beautiful creature, Roddy found himself thinking. He broke eye contact first, walking away towards the tail. It took him twenty-six paces to reach it; that's about nineteen or twenty metres, he calculated. Probably weighs in at around fifty tonnes. Oh my. Fifty *thousand* kilograms of matter combining to form just one life… It was certainly a mature bull; the size alone proved that, but also the long white scars raking across the head suggested the usual breeding disputes with other bulls. Standing next to the tail, he examined the furrow in the shingle that lay between the whale and the sea. Wow.

Circling the tail, which was seven metres across, he walked back up the beach towards the animal's head, trailing his hand along the distinctive skin. Dark-grey and, like a tyre, wrinkled in a design that reduced hydrodynamic drag, it covered massive blocks of muscle, the great natural engines powering the mighty tail flukes. Undulating "knuckles" lay along the ridge of the animal's back, between the tail and the stunted dorsal fin. The flippers were short and stubby, and in front of them, the head... Huge and square, with a great blunt snout and a single, asymmetrical nostril on top, it comprised more than a third of the length of the entire body, and contained a brain that in terms of cortical size, degree of folding and cellular organization, was the most complex and evolved in the animal kingdom. It also contained the spermaceti organ, a unique structure full of oil that acted as an acoustic lens to direct sound beams for ultra-distance echolocation. As an instrument of communication and location, it was so powerful as to make a submarine's sonar systems seem on a par with two empty cans of beans connected by a piece of string; and as a source of one of the finest known natural lubricants, an oil that could retain its viscosity under extremes of heat and temperature, it had been so profitable to whalers in the nineteenth century that they had decimated the species. As Roddy had once bellowed through a megaphone at the Norwegian delegation to the International Whaling Commission, how would they feel if nine out of ten Norwegians were slaughtered for their ear wax?

Roddy stopped directly in front of the sperm whale's unblinking eye. The seawater raining down on them both tailed off, then came back a few moments later in a fine mist.

"You hit this beach as fast as you could swim," he whispered. "It could have killed you. Why would you do that?"

Blackfin looked back at him, and neither understood much about the other, but Blackfin knew this: he had seen this man before, many seasons ago, when both of them had been young.

* * *

In London, in St James's Park, the ornamental lake glimmered greenly under an atmosphere that had developed into something sunless and muggy. The bloated birdlife on the water could hardly be bothered to collect the food offered to it by the tourists. A group of scruffy teenagers was standing at the centre of the bridge, throwing sticks at one of the famous St James pelicans; there was hilarity on finally making a hit, and the bird clattered away over the water.

Not far away from the bridge, sitting on a park bench with another man, Rattigan surveyed the scene impassively.

"How accurate is this information?" he asked; in his inside pocket was an eight-week schedule of Royal Naval patrols in the North Atlantic.

"Three of them are pretty much a hundred per cent, I've marked them. The rest I'd put at between eighty and ninety per cent. The further on in time, obviously, the more liable to alteration."

"Any talk of recent zone infringements?"

"Not that I know of," replied the man, scratching at his beard. "Frankly, I don't think those in the know care that much. There's plenty of talk about this other business though."

Rattigan's companion, named Jenkins, was a civil servant. He held the position of Secretary within Fleet Support at the Ministry of Defence. He was earning five thousand pounds every time he gave Rattigan information that, although formally classified as a matter of national security, was in practical terms about as secret as the Great Wall of China.

It had all begun at a chance meeting at a Lloyds function – that is, Jenkins had thought it was a chance meeting, and continued to think so, although the reality was that he had been carefully selected as a candidate susceptible to an approach. Given an encouraging prompt, he had readily imparted some information to Rattigan about Royal Naval deployments in the South China Sea. The information had been so innocuous that a half-sober journalist could have uncovered it with a couple of phone calls to the Press Office of the MoD; and yet technically it was confidential, and he had disclosed it. Rattigan had expressed a wish to thank him "quantitatively"; the offer had not been rejected. A few days later, an intermediary had invited Jenkins to offer occasional information about Royal Naval patrols "on a need-to-know basis". And Jenkins had accepted, as Rattigan had suspected he would.

Jenkins's usefulness to Rattigan centred on his access to information concerning Naval Special Operations, and in particular an obscure, 225-square-mile patch of the North Atlantic Ocean known as SONAZ – Special Operations No Access Zone. SONAZ was an archaic legacy of World War Two, when Britain, as one of the victorious Allies, had grabbed exclusive access to the zone, ostensibly for the purposes of submersible research and development. It was an ill-kept secret, since acknowledged by the British government, that underwater nuclear tests were carried out at the site in the 1950s. Despite her own assurances that the area was now completely safe, and in the face of international protest, Britain had maintained her exclusive control into the modern era. She nominally patrolled its invisible borders. Technically, no surface vessel could go into SONAZ without making an application to the Deputy Chief of Defence Staff (Special Operations), and few applications were successful. In reality, some vessels did infringe on the zone and, though logged, were not challenged. Ocean exploration, however, was completely banned, while any form of submersible intrusion would have risked an international incident.

"Well?" Rattigan prompted, waiting to hear what Jenkins meant by "other business".

"You know. This rather peculiar question of whales around SONAZ."

"Oh that. Our fat friends in the sea, nudging the ships. Naughty."

Rattigan smirked.

"It seems to be increasing. Every month I take the minutes of a joint Defence-Fisheries meeting with top-level officials at the Ministry, they're keeping an eye on this situation. And now it seems that some Icelandic trawlers which work the perimeters of SONAZ are having strange experiences with whales. There have been several communications made to our Fisheries people about a large number of whales – dozens and dozens of them – following the trawlers..."

No response.

"One trawler encountered a large number of whales which actually, you know—"

"What?" Rattigan asked, frowning.

"Engaged with the vessel."

"What shit."

"Well, yes. It's not corroborated. But minutes of the meeting have been sent to senior civil servants within the Environment and Defence Departments. Well, of course, *they'll* do nothing with them, but, well, it's hard to deny that, for whatever reasons, there's a slow accumulation of attention gathering around SONAZ."

The man suspected Rattigan of some kind of illegal dumping. Why else would someone go to such lengths to send ships to that godforsaken and neglected patch of ocean? But he also suspected that Whitehall wouldn't care to confront this activity even if it knew; the rumour was that Britain had herself used the place as a marine dustbin for years, and until relatively recent times – no wonder she wasn't overly keen on exposing the infringements of others.

"Well, that's useful to know," Rattigan said, with heavy irony.

"But you're discounting it?"

Rattigan eyed him, with no particular effort to hide his disdain.

"Sorry," said Jenkins. "Not really my business."

Rattigan closed his eyes and sighed. Go away now, he thought, you clown, and let me think about my daughter...

He's actually really rather scary, Jenkins realized for the first time, looking at the great chest rising and falling; there's the potential to... what? Jenkins didn't know, and decided he didn't want to know. He looked away quickly when Rattigan's eyelids opened to reveal an implacable stare, as deep and dark as a coal mine.

3

The Bentley pulled up outside Bob's Caff. Rattigan peered through the darkened windscreen: what a cesspit, surely Ally didn't mean this dump? He got out of the car when the chauffeur opened the door, jiggling his shoulders to get the lie of his suit correct, and checked his watch: twenty minutes early. Scanning up and down the street with exaggerated distaste, he saw everything that drove him mad: tatty shops, single mothers dragging snot-nosed children, third-world driving and parking, designer dropout youths, druggies and no-hopers and mental cases clogging up the pavement: oh, Ally's been a silly girl to ask me to come here. But she's young. I forgive her. I'd forgive her almost anything.

Ally had gone up to Oxford nearly two years before to study, at his suggestion, Politics, Philosophy and Economics. He saw PPE as the degree read by those who wished to signal early their intention to be someone. He was desperately proud of her, but her absence from his life was hard to bear. Their father-daughter relationship had always been, he considered, an especially close one. Even at the age of fourteen or fifteen she had regularly sat on his knee – so exquisite, so innocent. Rattigan straightened his tie, using the black mirror of the car windows to guide him. He sometimes wondered if his wife, Theresa, suspected him of being too intense with his girl. He sniffed impatiently. How could she think that? After what I went through as a child, and after all the things I've done, the money I've given, the projects I've funded?

When Theresa had been young and beautiful, with that grace and tenderness of spirit which he admired so much, then he had hungered for her. And he had thought she was happy in the marriage, enjoying his success. And then, and then... and then she ruined everything by trying to leave him. He could still remember the shock, the sense of betrayal, the *panic* in his heart at the sense of abandonment. "You're in love with money, not me," she had said. But – Rattigan clenched a fist – it was all right for her, she'd never been without it...

He hadn't let her leave – and he shook his head now at the memory of the ruthless way he'd prevented her from doing so. Since then, she seemed to live in fear of him. When Ally used to come home for her vacations, he thought, then the pair of us could at least pretend, but this summer, with Ally disappearing on some hare-brained student expedition somewhere, something to do with landmines, artificial limbs, saving the world... He remembered the times when he had hit Theresa: twice, three times? That mustn't happen again. That has to stop.

He shambled through the door of the café. It took a suspension of disdain to force himself to sit down on one of the greasy plastic chairs, rest his elbows on the greasy formica table, and order a cup of tea from the man in the greasy apron who was looking at him dubiously from behind the counter. Rattigan winced.

The smell of bacon fat was overpowering. By the window was a care-in-the-community case, rocking backwards and forwards over an empty mug, mouthing incomprehensible obscenities. Nearby, an old woman noisily sucked for life on a boiled sweet. To the side two workmen had stopped attending to their all-day breakfasts and their *Suns* in order to look at him suspiciously. One of them held a fork in the air on which was pronged a whole sausage. Two or three tables away, but sitting directly opposite, was an example of the worst kind of scum, a female hippyish alternative type, a lowlife white girl with her hair in ludicrous dreadlocks, who had a ring through her—

He blanched.

She stood up, walked across the café and sat down at his table.

"Hello Daddy."

In his shock he swallowed a mouthful of air, and the resulting coughing fit left him gasping for breath.

"Jesus—" he hissed, as his eyes fixed on the ring through her nose, on her skin – which seemed sallow and dirty – and on the rigid hanks of twisted hair, tied up with string, that protruded from her head at all angles...

"Daddy, it's OK."

He reached for his tea and gulped at the vile stuff. That ring in her nose, *Christ*.

"Daddy—"

He stood up, grabbing her by the wrist and wrenching her away from the table. She screamed in surprise. His cup of tea went flying. One of the workmen got to his feet and started to say something about calming down, mate. Rattigan, still grasping Ally's arm tightly, pushed the man back down into his seat. With the veins on his neck bulging and his breath coming in short, dangerous gasps, he dragged his daughter out of the café and towards the Bentley.

"You dumb, you stupid, stupid... Get in!"

He pushed her into the back of the Bentley, only to watch her scramble across the seat and get out of the car at the other side. He almost yelped in rage, but then this rage seemed to fizzle out. His frame collapsed and sagged. He had to cling on to the car for some seconds. They faced each other over the roof of the vehicle. Tears streaked Ally's face.

"You hurt me."

He held out his hands to her, palms up.

"Ally," he whispered, "what have you done?"

"I came to tell you something."

"I'm sorry," he moaned, "I'm sorry I hurt you, baby..."

"You don't just, you don't just – drag people out of places!" she screamed, her eyes flashing.

"Ally, you can't go back to Oxford like that, not like that, sweetheart..."

She breathed out hard, her gaze fixed on the set of his mouth, its despair, thinking: he doesn't understand anything, he's so damn blind...

"I'm not going back to Oxford like this, I'm not—"

"Ally, I—"

"Daddy, that's what I'm telling you, I'm not going back at all, I haven't been there for nearly a year – I dropped out, Daddy."

Ally shook her head in wild frustration; he can't make any sense of other people's wishes, the words won't give him a meaning he approves of, he's just gaping, and blowing, and denying.

"But you *are* at Oxford," he insisted, smiling hopefully.

"I've been *lying*. I dropped out, ages ago. Get it into your head, *I dropped out.*"

"But where do you live?"

"In a squat."

"Where? Why? Why?"

"Daddy, I've got my own life now. Oxford was just crap, absolute crap – don't you understand there's more meaning to life than mixing with morons and squeezing out every last drop of unfair privilege just to, to, I don't know – I mean, for what?"

"I—"

"To be 'successful' and rich. To consume a hundred times more of the earth's resources than anyone needs or wants. It's *pathetic*!"

Blinking furiously, Rattigan became aware of people looking on: the bastards, the dirty lowlifes, the filthy no-hopers, watching Ally do this to me, I want to kill them.

"What are you doing with yourself?" he asked weakly.

"I'm a protester, against roads and development, against the consumer society."

"You little idiot," he whispered helplessly.

"Daddy, don't try and find me."

She was off, racing down the street faster than he could hope to follow, and within a few seconds veering off down a side street. Rattigan's mouth clamped shut. He slumped into the car and slammed the door, screaming to his chauffeur to follow her. The car didn't move.

"Move this car! Why aren't you moving? Go!"

Nothing happened, and he slapped his hands against the sides of his head. By the time he had realized that the intercom wasn't on, it was already hopeless. She had gone.

* * *

The crowd at Brighton had swollen into the thousands. Pushed back up the beach a further ten metres on Roddy's instructions, people were mostly following his pleas to avoid making any unnecessary noise, as was the press – for now. There was an

41

unusual atmosphere. It was something to do with geometry: the whale, immense in the centre of a horseshoe of people, while a graceful jet of water arced overhead. But it was also down to the music. Yo-Yo Ma's tender interpretations of Bach's cello suites were being relayed from loud speakers, massaging the sound frequencies.

Humming along, Roddy was standing by the whale and stroking it just behind the eye.

"I always wondered what he'd be like," Kamala Mohandhas said in a low voice to Roddy's assistant, Whitaker, who had arrived from London. They were watching Roddy. "Everyone in the field has seen all that fiery footage from years ago, when he was a famous activist, in the little Greenpeace dinghies confronting the whaling ships. But now he seems to keep such a low profile."

"Hates the press and the limelight."

"He seems very *unconventional*," she added, after a pause.

Er, yes, Whitaker thought.

"I mean, playing music to a whale? Seems a bit odd."

"Ever heard the song of the humpbacked whale?" he asked her.

"Who's it by?"

"It's by a humpbacked whale."

"Oh, I see what you mean, well, obviously I've heard about it, but I haven't actually got round to listening to it."

"Very complex, very beautiful. The recording of it has sold in the hundreds of thousands. You must know that doctors and therapists recommend it for depression because it's so uplifting?"

"Is this another bad joke?"

In the half hour they had been chatting, Kamala had already been the victim of several ridiculous wind-ups. It was starting to get on her nerves.

42

"This is one hundred per cent true."

"So how does this relate to Bach?"

"Well, you'll already be aware of how vital it is to keep stranded whales as relaxed as possible, to extend the time they can stay out of the water, and improve their chances of survival once they are successfully refloated – their music seems to relax us, and our music seems to relax them."

She pondered this for a few moments.

"But why Bach?"

"Your whales, on balance, aren't very big on Guns N' Roses."

A world away from human dialogue, Roddy was alone with Blackfin. He was soaked to the skin, and his eyes were red and stinging from the permanent mist of seawater, but he continued to stroke the animal. He was trying to establish a bond of trust. Already he could tell that stress levels had decreased. He murmured gentle words, and consciously projected positive, friendly thoughts.

"OK then," he said at last, "are we ready?"

It was time to get on with some science. He needed a skin sample for analysis in the lab. He knew that the skin of sperm whales is sloughed off continually, as a biological mechanism to protect against infection. So he walked down the length of the whale's body, looking for a patch of skin that was ready to be pulled away. He located two possible areas, one just behind the left flipper and one further along and higher up, near the ridge of the back. As he was deciding between the two, he saw something that he'd missed earlier. There was a black mark on the rounded hump that comprised the dorsal fin. A frown of concentration formed on his forehead.

Whitaker and Kamala didn't notice Roddy's intense interest in the whale's dorsal fin. Whitaker was by now talking about his love life, a subject he was prone to raise with anyone who'd listen.

"So you understand what I'm trying to say here?" he checked.

"Oh, absolutely," she replied, bemused that he was confiding in a complete stranger.

"I mean, it's a question of statistics, that's how I look at it."

She nodded blandly. He seemed to expect her to say something.

"So, erm…" she tried, "well… What would you say is the main reason why you can't seem to, er, well, you know… find anyone?"

"Well I'd say there are two main reasons," Whitaker answered gratefully, plunging his hands into his pockets, "the first being that I'm a short, tubby, impoverished, over-educated thirty-two-year-old perpetual student with no security and no prospects who bears an unfortunate resemblance to Forest Whitaker in his least flattering roles. I'm talking Idi Amin here, by the way."

"Oh no, honestly, that's not true," Kamala murmured, embarrassed.

"Please," Whitaker stopped her, raising a hand, "spare me your sympathy. We come to my second reason." He was enjoying himself hugely. "As I mentioned before, this is a matter of statistics—"

"Statistics."

"—in that I tend to go for tall, skinny, gorgeous, successful, unusually brainy women who like short, tubby, impoverished, over-educated thirty-two-year-old perpetual et cetera et cetera et cetera."

"Ah."

"You see?"

"I think I do."

"It whittles down my options… Oops – something's up."

Roddy was walking towards them with a very purposeful stride. As he came nearer, a reporter broke the bar on shouting, and instantly they were all at it, seven or eight of them, yelling out their questions.

"Dr Ormond!"

"Sir, a word!"

"Sir, will you make a comment to the press?"

"When is the whale going back?"

Roddy diverged from his path and went up to the journalists, his expression grim.

"Oh dear," Whitaker said. "He's not very good at this side of things."

"What do you mean?" Kamala asked.

"He's not on the best of terms with journalists. One time he agreed to be profiled – it was for a series of interviews with prominent campaigners. So he had this hack in his life for two days, and he's spilling out his history and ideals, and the hack's as sweet as pie and in full sympathy with green issues, but of course, when the article comes out, Roddy's painted as a cross between Pol Pot and the Animal Liberation Front, and all the issues he raised are distorted and made to look barmy."

"Surely he can take a bit of rough and tumble from the media? They're trying to sell products, that's all, you've got to accept that and fight just as dirty to get what you want out of them."

"That's what I told him once. He was so angry with me, he just went mute."

"Mm. That doesn't add up, getting as angry as that. There must be something else to this journalism thing. Something more hurtful, from way back."

"Yeah," Whitaker said, "that's what I think."

"You're not very discreet, are you?"

"No," he confirmed, complacently.

Over by the journalists, Roddy was articulating his displeasure by means of a blunt plea.

45

"Please shut up. Every time you start yelling you induce unnecessary stress in the whale, so please, *stop*. I'll talk to you when I can, but the whale comes first, and that's not an unreasonable position, it's the only position."

He stomped away, towards Whitaker and Kamala.

"It's vital to keep the public informed!" a voice shouted after him.

Roddy turned around and sought out the owner of the voice. There she was, thrusting herself to the front of the pack. The glare he fixed her with faltered a little when the memory of someone else flashed into his mind; she bore a resemblance to someone he once knew. He saw bright, determined eyes, and a frown of concentration that made her pretty, slightly oriental-looking face seem appealingly comical. But he discarded the image from the past. How could this woman be so obtuse?

"This is just intolerable," he muttered.

"I'll talk to the superintendent," Whitaker said, "try and get them under control."

"Please, anything."

"How about if I give an interview to the press?" Kamala suggested. "It might get them off your back."

"Yeah, good idea, do it – if you can bear it." He exhaled a long, controlled breath. "They drive me nuts. They always have. OK, listen, Whitaker, I came over here for a reason. I want you to ring the Institute and get them to track down a file for me. It's very old, from my postgrad years, and it concerns the beaching of a bachelor herd of juvenile sperm whales in Canada, OK?"

"OK."

"I don't know where it is and I don't know what it's filed under, but I want it here, I want it now, so tell everyone, and I mean everyone, to drop everything until it's found."

"I get you."

Roddy spun on his heel and walked back to the whale. He immediately caused a sensation by climbing onto it. The shutters and flashes of hundreds of cameras and phone-cameras went off. He straddled the base of the tailstock, then carefully worked himself up the ridge of the back until he was sitting just behind the dorsal fin. The black mark was about the size of a dinner plate. He scrutinized it minutely, then shook his head. Damn it. I'm not sure...

Back on the ground, he tried not to think about it. There were blood samples to take and biopsy materials to gather. After accomplishing this, he took photographs of the sperm whale from every angle. Then he and Whitaker recorded all the measurements before Roddy prepared to do the notching.

Half an hour after the anaesthetic had been administered, the crowd looked on in confusion as Roddy, holding a large saw, stood next to the whale's tail. First he levered up the end of one of the tail flukes and rested it on Kamala's medical box, so that a part of it hung over the edge. Then he picked his spot on the trailing edge of the fluke and without any fuss began to saw into the flesh, efficiently moving the blade back and forth as though sawing through timber. He cut into the tail a depth of three inches, wiping away the blood with a sterile sponge. A shout made him look up. A few people in the watching crowd were booing, and a man yelled, "Shame!"

Roddy pulled a face as he worked. Why do people make judgements on issues they know nothing about, he wondered? It's standard procedure to cut a notch into a beached whale's tail, then photograph it: painless, harmless and immensely useful...

Blackfin blew, and the fishy odour of the vapour was dispersed by the light breeze. He felt calmed by this man who clambered about him, and who made such gentle friendly noises. He could divine the goodwill being directed to him from these many, many humans. And yet the dominant feeling was one of helplessness. How could he let the humans know what was happening in the world of water? How could he tell them that his beaching was an act of deliberate desperation, a hopeless act of hope, an attempt to communicate catastrophe?

4

The Secretary of State for Defence, the Right Honourable Victoria Adlington MP, arrived at the Ministry of Defence straight from Heathrow, having attended an assembly of European Defence Ministers in Strasbourg. She was meeting with her Permanent Secretary before chairing a Cabinet subcommittee.

Her driver held the door open for her, marvelling at how long it took the ministerial arse to extract itself from the ministerial car. Yeah, she's a fat old tart, he conceded to himself, as Adlington placed her feet on the pavement, grasped the door with her right hand, and eased her gargantuan bottom to the edge of the seat.

She stared at the pavement dubiously, as though preparing for a bungee jump, then hauled herself out of the car. Not only was she fat, she was tall, almost six feet tall. She dwarfed the driver. Her monumental but shapeless bosom, which could not be concealed by any amount of ingenious clothing, alarmed him: you ugly old trout, he thought.

"Have a good day, Minister."

"Thanks Jim. And you."

The first woman to hold the macho post of Defence Secretary, Adlington was at the top of a hierarchy comprising thousands upon thousands of men more than usually disposed to discriminate against women. Her size was the daily butt of hundreds of jokes throughout the MoD, Whitehall,

Westminster and the Armed Forces. She had been awarded enough nicknames to fill a small reference book, ranging from the puerile DP, short for Don't Point, short for Don't Point Those Things at Me Madam, to the vicious Torpedo Bay – a reference to the supposed capacity of her vagina. But the most popular of her nicknames, and one tended to be used with a certain amount of affection, was Hattie, after the generously sized Carry On actress Hattie Jacques.

She walked – slowly – towards a set of double doors, which were opened by a porter long before she reached them. She disappeared into the Ministry of Defence with the dispatch of a horse-drawn canal barge entering a tunnel.

She had no idea that the first faint stirrings of a crisis were inside, one that would envelop her Department.

* * *

In the North Atlantic, near the southernmost part of the Denmark Strait, and two hours away from a position consistent with the deepest area of the Irminger Basin, an elderly chemicals carrier was progressing North-north-west at ten knots. The sea was calm, conditions good but icy cold. She was three hundred miles due west of the tip of Greenland, while five hundred miles to the North-east-east was the ragged western coast of Iceland. She was a listing rust bucket called *The Vegas*, and she was one of the two ships mentioned in the telephone conversation that Rattigan had listened into.

Captain Isaksson was unaware that the vessel he commanded belonged, via a labyrinthine network of companies, leases and legal entities, to Rattigan. Captain Isaksson hadn't heard of Rattigan, and he never would. He had been hired in Norway to skipper a ship he had never seen before, and it was his fervent hope that he would never see it again. He could endure a poor vessel with a good crew, and he could endure a good vessel with a poor crew, but an appalling vessel with an appalling crew scared seven shades of shit out of him.

The Captain was stretched out on his bed in his tatty suite. In two hours he would have to oversee the disposal of the cargo, because *The Vegas* was approaching its specified position. This scared him even more. He tried closing his eyes, but knew it was futile to try for sleep. There was too much on his mind. It wasn't just the cargo, that thing, that whatever-it-was in the dry cargo hold; the extent of more practical problems was almost as frightening. The gyrocompass wasn't working, there was a worrying acrid smell behind the bridge, there were collapsed mooring winches and docking, there was a leak in the exhaust-gas system, one of the water-supply pumps in the engine room had given out, and the other was teetering on the edge. Of his meagre crew of sixteen, four were out of action. His first (and only competent) engineer had persistent, virulent amoebic diarrhoea. The pump man and the relief pump man had consigned each other to the sick bay by means of a vicious fight. As for the third mate, he was clinically depressed and refusing to come out of his cabin.

A ship as old as *The Vegas*, and in such a state of dilapidation, required a crew of great competence, men who were not only effective while on duty, but who spent half their off-duty hours tinkering in an expert fashion with machinery that was continually failing. But the Captain rated barely five of his crew as adequate; and in an uncomfortable chamber of his mind was the knowledge that he was not among that number.

The ship he skippered was probably an accurate reflection of his currency as a captain. In the 1980s, he had been in the first rank of Finnish skippers, but somehow his career had gone into a spiralling decline. Problems mounted, he suffered bad debts, his marriage broke down – and as for his consumption of alcohol,

it was enormous even by the standards of his countrymen...
What am I doing here, he now thought, in this floating tomb,
on course for some godforsaken spot in order to commit who
knows what criminal act? For there was no doubt that the task
with which he had been charged was illegal. A man isn't paid
ten times the going rate to deliver a box of chocolates to the
fishes. That little zone of ocean over the Irminger, where he was
heading, that fifteen miles by fifteen miles of water, that 0.000007
per cent of the mighty Atlantic, was out of bounds to merchant
shipping, and had been for as long as anyone remembered.
Everyone knew about the nuclear tests by the British, but that
was long ago; there was thought to be some other hush-hush
mystery about it. Some said it was to do with the Second World
War, or submarine research projects, or an unresolved fisheries
dispute between the UK and the northern nations. But whatever
the reason, he thought, never again – never again will I allow
myself to sink so low. If I survive this journey, I shall take it
as a message from God that he is granting me a final chance. I
will reform my life. I will banish the drink – the cause of all my
misfortune – and regain my dignity, and I will devote myself to
my career with diligence until I am a skipper of the first rank
once more, commanding modern vessels, legal cargoes, and first-
rate, clean-cut, well-paid American crews... Captain Isaksson
sat up on his bed, suddenly enthusiastic about the future feats
of seamanship he would undertake. He took a comb out of his
back pocket and began to comb his thinning hair.

The first mate, the helmsman and the lookout – an Italian
and two Bangladeshis – were in the wheelhouse on the bridge.
The Italian first mate was ashamed to be associated with
Bangladeshi crew: they had no boots, no warm clothes, nothing!
The north fucking Atlantic, he marvelled, below fucking zero,
and they were loping about with their feet tied up in bundles of
newspaper in plastic bags! What a ship! Never again!

"No seeing," the lookout said, passing the binoculars over. "All gone."

For over an hour a convoy of whales had been accompanying *The Vegas*. The first mate had never seen anything like it; first dozens, then scores, then hundreds of whales, swimming alongside the ship and criss-crossing in front of it. It had been fine entertainment. Some of the off-duty crew had braved the icy elements and made their way to the bow to watch. But it looked like the show was over. The whales had been thinning out for ten or twenty minutes, and now – the little Bangladeshi was right – the whales seemed to have gone.

As the first mate continued to scan the ocean with the binoculars, the helmsman tapped him on the shoulder and pointed down to the ship's deck. Another Bangladeshi crew member was running along it towards them. The first mate was amused. Which one was it? Khalil? What was the lunatic doing?

Khalil stopped to wave at them frantically. Getting no response from the bemused crew on the bridge, he set off again, clambering over the obstacle course that was the deck – a rusting jumble of hose derricks, breakwaters, pipelines for loading and discharging, cargo hatches and fire hydrants.

There was little the first mate could do but wait for Khalil to arrive; he could hardly leave the bridge to meet him halfway, and unfortunately it seemed the man had been too stupid to utilize the telephone sited at the bow. He rang the second mate, rousing him from an exhausted slumber, and told him to come to the bridge immediately. Then he waited. It took a further two minutes for Khalil to cover a hundred and fifty metres of deck and climb up the five storeys of the superstructure to the bridge. He burst into the wheelhouse and bent over double, resting his hands on his knees as he sucked oxygen into his depleted lungs with high-pitched gasps. A bit of spittle dangled from his lower lip, then landed on the mess of torn plastic bag and papier mâché encasing his left foot.

"You coming sir, whales!" he managed to hiss, still bent double. "These bad whales, sir! You coming!"

* * *

In the Captain's suite, the consequence of a poor decision was manifesting itself. The Captain had elected to watch the video recording of his daughter's wedding again. He had been unable to attend the ceremony – marital problems, mental exhaustion and a three-day bender had seen to that – and in fact he hadn't seen his daughter for nearly five years. He had never even met his only grandson...

When the telephone next to his bed announced its shrill and unwelcome ring, his daughter was walking up the aisle, the Captain was weeping, and a bottle of vodka that stood next to the telephone was three-quarters empty.

"Yes, what is it?... I'm very busy!... I know of these whales already... No! Yes! Fukkit!"

What else, thought Captain Isaksson, what now, what next? He struggled to focus on the difficult task of putting on his boots.

* * *

Twelve hundred miles south of *The Vegas*, off the Bay of Biscay, there was another curious constellation of whales and alcohol. *Alyson* was making sedate progress on the back of a gentle northerly. She was a Swan 41, built to the highest specification, a nimble and elegant yacht with the looks and speed of a racing boat and the finely finished interior of a cruiser. Her crew, Rupert and Ian, had been sailing companions for longer than either of them cared to remember. It had started during their school days, at Marlborough, when they had raced dinghies; in the many years since, while carving out their careers – Rupert had become a consultant urologist with a private practice in Harley Street, Ian a businessman and non-executive director of half a dozen companies – they had sailed together whenever circumstances allowed. In recent times, having both taken early retirement, they were out on the ocean two or three months in the year. They were presently making for Galway on the west coast of Ireland.

"Lovely and calm," said Rupert.

"Forecast still first-class," Ian answered.

"Bliss."

They had a system: if conditions were challenging, or forecast to be challenging, they both remained sober; if conditions were moderate, or forecast to be moderate, one of them remained sober; and if conditions were good, and forecast to remain so, then both of them got roundly slaughtered.

"Here's the first."

"Always the nicest."

They downed ample G&Ts. On the horizon towards Spain a trawler showed itself as a hazy black dot. A single cloud hung above it. *Alyson* bobbed in the whispering waves.

"Never been to Galway before."

"Been once. Wedding. Groom threw up."

"Threw up?"

"Nerves."

They sank a second gin twenty minutes later, and a third gin twenty minutes after the second. The sun was still high. The distant trawler was barely visible – it was difficult to tell whether it was really there or just seemed to be because it had been there before. Ian was reading a golfing magazine. Rupert stood at the helm. Between them they had already downed half a bottle of Gordons.

"Changing tack."

"Righto. Oops—" Ian lost his footing slightly as he stood up.

"Bit squiffy?"

"Completely blotto."

"FUCKING HELL!"

"Steady on."

"IAN!"

Rupert was pointing out to sea on the port side, the sleeve of his shirt flapping in the breeze. About fifty metres away, scores of whales were passing the boat. It was their speed that seemed so staggering, not just their number, and the way they were swimming so close together on the surface of the sea. The force of their ploughing through the water made a great churning noise, and a mighty wake fanned out behind them. It hit the boat, lurching the vessel up and over to a perilous angle. Ian half fell over, half sat down on his bottom. Rupert gripped the handrail tightly. Within a minute the whales were hundreds of metres away; within five minutes Rupert needed binoculars to track them.

"Knocked the bloody gin over," said Ian.

They made a situation report. It was picked up at the Coast Radio Station in Falmouth.

"Coastguard this is *Alyson*, over."

"Routine traffic, medium frequency 2182, proceed *Alyson*, over."

"Sitrep. Position is forty-six degrees twenty-eight points North, fourteen degrees seven points West, conditions calm, no problems, anchoring up, heading North-north-west a.m. for Galway, Ireland, over."

"Received and understood, over."

"Minor incident, fifteen hundred hours, hundreds of whales swimming hell-for-leather past the craft, over."

A pause.

"Communication not understood, please repeat, over."

"Hundreds of whales, swimming fast and in formation, passing the craft, over."

"Coastguard requests to know if crew of *Alyson* are inebriated, over."

Now it was Ian's turn to pause. He turned to Rupert.

"He thinks we're drunk."

"We are drunk."

"Well yes, but… Coastguard, this is *Alyson*, concede that we are not one hundred per cent sober but affirm that we are not hallucinating, over."

"Coastguard requests *Alyson* terminate sitrep and free up channel for other traffic, over."

"The buggers," Ian said indignantly.

* * *

Beneath the bow of *The Vegas* they were assembled into a giant wedge shape. Their huge bodies were packed as closely as tadpoles in a jam jar, with scores on the surface and who knows how many below, and – it was preposterous, unthinkable – they were pushing at the ship's hull, trying to halt her progress. Their tails whipped the sea until it foamed. The noise of their frenetic struggle hurt the ears. Captain Isaksson, drunk despite the sobering effect of the icy air, shivering despite his fur-lined leather coat, watched fatalistically. His urge was to climb over the rail and jump to his death in the best Finnish tradition. I am a bad man, he told himself, and this is my destiny. It is a scene from hell which wants me in it. Then blasts of logic whistled through his fuzzy and melancholic thinking: the ship was 92,128 tonnes, with an unladen displacement weight of 125,260 tonnes; she was 211 metres long with a beam of 30 metres; she had 22,000 h.p., and her momentum was such that many thousands of whales couldn't impede her. He gripped the handrail more tightly and glanced at four panicking Bangladeshis. He reminded himself that he was the captain of this vessel. Furthermore, he thought about his illustrious history within merchant shipping, and that of his father before him; finally, he remembered that he was a reformed man. It was important to be seen to be in control, and to do something – anything – to reassure his crew.

"Phone the bridge and establish our exact position," he instructed the second mate, a Turk.

"Phone not working, sir."

"Huh?"

"Not working."

The Captain's bubble of resolve popped. He gave a little whimper and knew that this was it, he'd had enough, he wasn't going to spend one more minute than was necessary on this cursed death trap of a ship. He no longer cared what their position was, how far or near they were from the drop zone; the cargo was going overboard, and the vessel was getting out of this hellish and forbidden stretch of water.

The container was in the dry-cargo hold. In keeping with the overall condition of *The Vegas*, this hold was little better than an on-board rubbish tip. Within, the cargo nestled on a stinking mess of rotting rope, a discarded mattress thrown over the top of it.

While the whales still thrashed at the bow of the ship, two Bangladeshis – bribed to the tune of US $600 dollars each, and from the Captain's pocket – reluctantly went into the dry cargo hold to recover the container. It was a small, heavy case of dull, dark-grey metal, as heavy as a man. It took the two seamen a quarter of an hour to manoeuvre the object out of the hold. They didn't know what it was, but it didn't take a genius to realize that it was something horrendous. A few minutes later it was pitched into the sea. It disappeared from view.

Within a short while the whales began to abandon their futile task. Sixteen minutes later, the metal container settled on the sea bed, some 2,400 metres down in the Irminger basin. It contained material so toxic that it could exterminate all the residents of New York.

5

"They had to trash the Institute to find it," Whitaker said, handing over the file Roddy had asked for.

Roddy was taking a break prior to a TV interview he had reluctantly agreed to do. He was sitting on a deckchair, a sandwich in his hand and a paper cup of coffee by his feet. Now he opened the file eagerly and riffled through the contents.

"Newfoundland," he said. "I was in the third year of my Ph.D. A guy called Professor Robinson – dead now – was investigating the effects of different types of fishing on humpbacked whales, and he needed a dogsbody. My supervisor let me bunk off to Canada for two months."

He handed a photograph to Whitaker: it showed two grinning men in very short shorts, arms around each other's shoulders, standing on a cliff top with a setting sun behind them. One was a cuddly-looking middle-aged guy, with a beaming Father Christmas face, right down to the shiny red cheeks and white beard. The other was a skinny, fresh-faced Roddy with a tragic haircut.

"It was the early Eighties," Roddy said defensively.

"Come on Roddy, it takes more than the passage of time to excuse a rug like that."

Roddy gave him another photo. It showed a cluster of whales stranded in three or four feet of water.

"Sperm whales in White Bay alongside Long Range Mountains," he said. "Juveniles. They swim up looking for easy pickings, and – in my opinion – adventure. Young bachelor herds of sperm whales can be incredibly curious and foolhardy. The ones at most danger are those that are doing it for the first time; they often get caught out by the speed of the outgoing tide. These guys here were lucky we were around, we had them back in the sea with the next tide. It was a pretty routine job, just a bit of equilibrium work."

Whitaker mused over the photograph, nodding.

"A completely different situation to this case then," he observed.

"Oh, completely. No common factors."

"So why were you so keen to access the file?"

Roddy was leafing through old field notes, charts, graphs, copies of articles, photographs and sketches. His brow wrinkled up as he extracted an envelope. He examined the handwriting of the address, then took out the old letter that was inside.

Dearest Roddy,
It's impossible to write this letter to you, but write it I must...

Watching him, Whitaker observed Roddy's whole face sagging into a state of wonder and – what? Grief?

"Well?" he asked, after a long silence.

Again, Roddy was thinking: the second reminder of her in a day, and this time a big one, the bloody letter telling me she was leaving. He shook his head.

"Just an old letter, not what I'm looking for."

The letter was slipped into his back pocket. He turned his attention back to the file and pulled out a dozen or so black-and-white photographs held together with a rubber band. He quickly flicked through them before finding what he wanted. Then he stood up and put his arm around his assistant's shoulder, smiling at some private joke.

"I want you to meet an old friend of mine."

"Who?" Whitaker asked, looking around.

Roddy led him over to the whale.

"Whitaker, this is Blackfin. Blackfin, this is Whitaker."

The improbable distance covered by Whitaker's eyebrows as they moved up his forehead indicated the extent of his scepticism. Roddy handed him the photograph. It was a close-up of a sperm whale's dorsal ridge. Half of the ridge was covered in an irregularly shaped black mark which, when compared to the black mark on the dorsal fin of the sperm whale in front of him, exactly corresponded.

"Shee-it."

* * *

"Oh," Roddy said abruptly, when the television producer led him over to the same young journalist who had so annoyed him earlier. "I'm not sure if I'm happy with this."

"Hey, I'm not so bad," said the woman, smiling. "What's the problem?"

The problem, Roddy considered: you yell out when I ask you not to, you ignore completely reasonable requests, and you bear a passing resemblance to the woman who broke my heart.

"You've been putting my whale through unnecessary stress."

Your whale, thought the journalist, Kate Gunning, but she nodded in a conciliatory fashion and held up a hand in supplication. "I'm really sorry about that, but we've been here all day and you haven't told us a thing. Look, people are interested in this magnificent animal, they want to know why it's here, they don't have a clue at the moment. No wonder they're getting frustrated."

"Yeah, well," he said, rather ungraciously, knowing it was a fair point.

Though he didn't say anything else, it was apparent that he wasn't going to back out of the interview. The producer, visibly relieved, took him aside to brief him. Kate scanned her interview notes, frowning: maybe he's right, maybe I shouldn't have been shouting out, but how else were we supposed to get him to notice us?

Kate was in love with her job. In an era when aspiring journalists needed MAs in Journalism Studies, and preferably a blood relation working in a senior media position, before they even had a hope of working in the canteen of the Bognor Regis Bugle, she had done it the old way. From the age of sixteen she had doggedly pestered editors all over the country; she had sent three ideas a day to different newspapers for seven months before her first piece had been commissioned. She possessed all the qualities of an investigative journalist, including the capacity never to give up, and an apparent absence of self-consciousness; and when, at the age of twenty, she had got her first big break – a job with the London Evening Standard – her progress had been rapid. Within a year she had been head-hunted, and within two years she was not only a junior member of an investigative team on one of the big Sunday papers, responsible for some minor but respected exposés, she was also doing a weekly TV spot for a regional cable news programme, South Coast News – or the M4 (Muggings, Mischiefs and Municipal Mishaps) as she privately called it.

It was her overwhelming ambition to go down in history in the manner of Carl Bernstein and other journalistic greats; to force light into hidden, horrible places, to add a celebrated exposé to the grand tradition of investigative journalism. If she had professional faults, they were the faults that went with being young and obsessed with an objective that seemed all-important. In the pursuit of people who deserved to be exposed she usually hit the target, but at times the collateral damage – innocent people impugned, excellent causes and projects damaged – had been significant. She had yet to start balancing up the gain and the pain of her actions. But now, at Brighton, she was pleased. This was an opportunity to raise her profile, and the higher her profile, the nearer she could get to the big stories. *An enormous quantity of blubber lolling around on a beach is not exactly Watergate,* she thought, *but it could still get my face on the Ten O'Clock News, if I handle it right.*

The interview was live. Roddy, in his sodden clothes, with clumps of damp hair clinging to his forehead, looked a mess standing next to Kate; and by the end of the interview it wasn't just his appearance that looked bad.

To Kate's hopeful prompt that the whale was trying to commit suicide, he gave an emphatic no. "Very ill whales sometimes drift ashore to die, but this isn't an ill whale, he's in excellent overall health."

Her second question had a hint of a suggestion that the scientific procedures he was undertaking were cruel and pointless – and that got to him. He heard the irritation rising in his voice as he said something about the tests being "an essential tool in understanding – and therefore helping to prevent and deal with – the beaching of whales."

"But isn't it vital to get this animal back into the water as soon as possible?" she challenged him.

"Not at all, the most vital thing is to maximize its chances of survival once it's refloated, and the way to do that is to keep the stress levels to a minimum – which isn't helped," he found himself saying in a pointed way, "by people shouting out indiscriminately." In the silence of her surprise he tried to turn the subject in a more promising direction. "Look, let me make this easier for all of us. The most newsworthy aspects of this case are *one*, the species of the whale, *two,* the fact that it swam through the shallow waters of the Dover Strait, *three,* the unprecedented manner in which it beached itself, and *four,* how the hell to get such a huge creature back in the water."

"But Dr Ormond, do you seriously maintain that it's acceptable to keep this magnificent animal virtually captive?"

"No one's keeping the whale captive, that's completely—"

"In which case why can't it go straight back in the—"

"I already told you."

"—sea, the world he knows?"

"The reason is—"

"But isn't it true that you've allowed the tide to come in without utilizing it, condemning the whale to an unnecessary and terrifying night on the beach?"

"No no, all my decisions about the welfare of this whale are based on its needs and on standard scientific procedure."

"Thank you very much Dr Ormond. From Brighton beach and the growing controversy about a magnificent visitor from the deep, this is Kate Gunning returning you to Gordon in the studio."

"What controversy?" Roddy asked her. "There's no controversy!"

Kate smiled and shrugged, turning to her producer. Roddy found Whitaker's hand on his arm, firmly pulling him away. Sod it, he chastised himself, thrashing through the shingle; I'm just genetically allergic to journalists.

"Well that went rather well," Whitaker said.

* * *

Ally and her boyfriend, Dave, lived in a squat in Worthing, a few miles from the Brighton coastline. Dave was another aspect of Ally's life which her father knew nothing about. She arrived back home in the late afternoon, psychologically drained by the showdown that had taken place in London earlier. She wanted a hot bath, for her commitment to looking grimy was superficial; she wanted toast and jam and all the comfort foods of her childhood; she wished she could call her mother, but her mother's attitude to Dave had caused a breakdown in communication some months before; most of all she wanted to burst into tears on Dave's shoulder. He had said he would be in, so it was bitterly disappointing that he wasn't. This wasn't the first time that he wasn't where he'd said he would be. She sat down on the sofa – a piece of furniture salvaged from a skip – and wondered what to do with herself.

She had met Dave while still a student at Oxford a year before. On her way into Blackwell's one Saturday afternoon, she had vaguely noticed a stall manned by scruffy-looking types, all of them wearing regulation Doc Martens and grubby, shapeless clothes; on her way out of the bookshop, lugging eighty pounds' worth of Adam Smith, Jeremy Bentham and Hobbes, she had been accosted by one of them. His unprepossessing image couldn't disguise striking good looks.

"Would you like to sign our petition?"

"What's it about?"

"Consumerism and the catastrophic environmental impact of airport expansions."

"All right."

She'd been a nineteen-year-old romping through a £50,000 annual allowance from her father; she owned a Mercedes SLK 230 for show and a Sunbeam Alpine for fun; she'd travelled on planes more often than she'd been on buses. But she signed the petition, solemnly protesting against the destruction of the environment via the reckless expansion of the airline industry.

He described himself as an eco-terrorist. Fifteen years older than her, a veteran of the protests at Manchester Airport, Twyford Down and the Birmingham Relief Road, in pursuit of his ideals he had tunnelled under the earth, slept in trees, chained himself to bulldozers, and been beaten up by security guards. They went for a coffee, and he had passionately condemned globalization, abuse of human rights by corporate power, third-world exploitation, consumerism gone mad, environmental degradation, unsustainable economic growth.

"But what do you do for money?" Ally had asked.

"I live on the social."

"Why should society have to bear the cost of your existence?" she asked, this aspect of his position striking her as typically hypocritical. "It's not fair on everybody else."

"I cost society £45 a week and I live in an environmentally responsible, socially equitable, carbon-neutral way. I think I'm bloody good value."

He had surprised her then; leaning over, he had picked up her left hand to examine the ring on her middle finger.

"Diamond?"

"Yes."

"How much did it cost?"

"You don't want to know. And I don't want to tell you."

"Know anything about working conditions and pay in the diamond mines of Africa?"

"Not really."

"Why are so many people in this world living like dogs to pay the huge price of *your* existence?"

After a couple of weeks they were going out together. A few months later, anxious that her family should know him, she had tested the water by introducing him to her mother. The meeting had been such a disaster – with Theresa apparently terrified of the scruffy weirdo presented to her – that Ally had refused to speak to her mother since. She didn't want to submit to what she saw as pure prejudice, not understanding that Theresa was trying to protect her from her father's fury.

In the living room of the squat, Ally got up from the sofa. She wandered around the tatty two-up, two-down terrace, so different from the luxury she had always known. In the kitchen there were five recycling boxes: one for scraps, one for paper, one for glass, one for metal and one for plastic. They used copious layers of clothes instead of central heating, slept on a futon home-made out of old pallets, and made love to the scent of smouldering joss sticks. On the walls of the bathroom Dave had painted a quotation from his "Bible", *Small is Beautiful*, E.F. Schumacher's call for real economics:

> *...since consumption is merely a means to human well-being, the aim should be to obtain the maximum of well-being with the minimum of consumption...*

Dave had added his own postscript:

> *...rather than the maximum of consumption with the minimum of well-being.*

There was a developing and not fully articulated system of values in Ally that did not wholly accept Dave's environmental fundamentalism. She felt that in time she would come to her own ideas. But for now, despite the clichés and the petunia oil, she was grateful that the unquestioning materialism of her upbringing had been smashed to pieces.

Still wandering around the house wearily, she ended up in the kitchen and saw the note:

> *Ally, I know I said I'd be here, but a big old whale has parked itself on Brighton beach – gone for a look! Come along! Love D.*

Roddy had hardly had time to think about the problem of how to get Blackfin back into the water, but that night, at the cheap guesthouse where he was staying, while Blackfin endured his stony open prison under the protection of the police and a hardcore of onlookers, he rang up his colleague Derek Petersen to talk the issue through.

"The immediate priorities are to keep him in good shape and to work out how to refloat him," he was explaining. "But I can't follow the usual procedures. The beach, as you probably know, is a pebble beach comprising steep ridges. Because of the speed he came in at, he's actually crested the first ridge."

"Incredible."

"Fortunately he beached at low tide, or as near as damnit, OK?"

"Ah-ha."

"High tide tomorrow raises the water level by nine feet, but from looking at the high tide today it's clear that much of his mass will remain high and dry. I mean, obviously, if it were just the mechanics of the job that was problematic, we could get him into the water easy – we could winch him out using tugs for example – but the problem is how to do it without injuring him."

"So what are your ideas?"

There was a long pause. Lying on the sagging single bed, whose sheets were quaintly darned, Roddy wiggled his toes; I haven't got any ideas, he thought. Breaking the silence, Derek started talking about a colleague of theirs in New Zealand who had recently refloated a school of pilot whales.

"...had fourteen of the damn things to deal with," Derek was exclaiming.

Not very relevant, Roddy found himself thinking. He stroked his face. During the day's endeavours it had burnt in the sun, and the landlady of the guesthouse had given him some cream for it. His fingers rubbed up and down his cheek, gliding over the greasy film of cream. His other hand was hanging over the edge of the bed, fiddling with the corner of a bean bag.

"...trouble being that it was a completely different situation – a flat, sandy beach..."

The bean bag was filled with tens of thousands of tiny polystyrene balls. He rolled some of them around between his fingers, under the fabric. I'm damned if I know how to get this whale back in the water, it really is an *impossible* beaching.

"God, it'd be easier to launch a ship," Derek complained.

"A ship..."

It all came together in an instant. As one part of his mind conjured up the image of a huge steel ship gliding slowly down a launch-ramp, another part of his mind linked the polystyrene balls between his fingers to the shingle of the beach, the slippery cream on his face to vast quantities of oil...

"Ball bearings!" he blurted, absurdly.

"Sorry?"

"We'll douse the pebbles in oil, no, not oil, something water-soluble, and dermatologically neutral, a detergent – and they'll be like ball bearings in grease: then the whale can glide down the ridge!"

There was silence from the other end of the line; whether this denoted admiration or scepticism was impossible to know, until Derek said, "That's, er, quite a concept Roddy. It's worth thinking about. Ball bearings in grease?"

"The shingle's perfect for it."

"You're a mad bugger. Where did you get an idea like that?"

"From a bottle of skin cream and a bean bag."

"What?"

Over the course of the next ten minutes they took the main

stages of the raw concept and mapped out an entirely original technique for refloating beached whales.

"Hope it works," Roddy muttered towards the end, suddenly anxious.

"I can't see any reason why it shouldn't, assuming we haven't missed anything."

"If it doesn't work, the press will chew me up and spit me out, as usual. Did you see what that woman did to me on the news?"

"I wasn't going to mention it unless you did. Can I give you some advice about it?"

"Go ahead."

"You got turned over because you didn't play the game."

"I got turned over because she wasn't interested in the facts!"

"But one of the reasons for that is that you didn't abide by the rules—"

"I hate the fucking rules."

"—the number-one rule being that you give them the message you want to get across at the earliest opportunity."

"I didn't have a message, it would have suited me to ignore them completely."

"Well exactly, you kept them hanging around all day. Tomorrow, my advice is to start the day off with a short press conference."

"Well, maybe I should, but I'm not going to. I've already decided not to get involved with them any more."

"Well it's your funeral."

"Who's that I can hear? Lizzie?"

"Yeah, she wants me to help with her homework – all right sweetheart!" he called.

"How is she, Derek?"

"She's… good. Her last skin graft is turning out nicely. I think she's beginning to accept what happened to her."

"And you?"

A pause.

"I'll never accept it in my heart."

Eighteen months previously, Derek's teenage daughter had been playing with her three-year-old nephew in the kitchen. They had been sitting down on the floor. There was a pan of hot soup on the stove, on the near hob, with the handle sticking over the edge; this was something Derek would never forgive himself for. The little boy had stood up and pulled on the handle of the pan for support. Still clutching the handle, he had fallen back down on his bottom. The near-boiling contents had missed him, but not Lizzie. The horrendous sound of her screams still echoed in Derek's dreams.

"She's a tough kid," Roddy said. He knew from the silence which met this comment that Derek was struggling with tears. "She'll survive this, Derek. And prosper."

"She's getting very upset about boys," came the hoarse reply.

"I know."

"I'd better go. Tonight it's the French Revolution."

"I thought that ended more than two centuries ago. Kiss her for me, will you?"

"I will. And hey, Roddy—"

"Yes?"

"Good luck tomorrow."

6

Securing the necessary support and funding for his innovative refloating plan – from the local authority, the police, the Environmental Protection Agency – proved to be a frustrating experience. It took up much of the night and most of the morning to force the concept past key officials.

"Detergent? Are you serious?" was one of the typically bemused responses. "Do you normally ask for thousands of litres of Fairy Liquid when a whale beaches itself?"

"Normally we wait for the tide to come in and then we give the beast a bloody big shove," Roddy had said, "but normally it wouldn't weigh fifty tonnes, normally it wouldn't hit the beach like a torpedo and go above the tide line, normally – well, look – if you want to deal with this situation normally, go ahead, then see how normal Brighton beach is with a fifty-thousand-kilogram carcass stinking out the town."

Once he had won backing for the scheme, organizing the practical details of its implementation took up more precious hours. High tide was due by mid-afternoon, and there was a small army of volunteers to be selected and briefed. Way behind schedule, Roddy delegated this task to Whitaker. And on top of every other hassle was the press. Whenever he looked up, went near them or scratched his nose, they started yelling.

"Sir! Sir!"

"Dr Ormond!"

"Dr Ormond, please, sir!"

"A word with the BBC."

"Daniel Houghton of ITN—"

"Is it true that the whale is dying?"

The only sanctuary was with Blackfin. As Roddy walked towards him – probably the calmest animal on the beach, he thought to himself – the descending mist of seawater enveloped him. The sun's rays were refracted and reflected by the water droplets, and for a moment Roddy was blessed with the vision of a perfect rainbow. Hello old friend, he murmured in his mind, you're going home today. Back to the wide deep ocean. I wish I could go with you, just for a day, just to know what it's like to be you.

Blackfin understands that the people are striving to return him to the sea. Why else do they send this man to him, his saviour from seasons ago? And yet the knowledge gives him no relief. He feels as helpless as he did in those first moments after the beaching, when the weight of his own body settled on him for the first time; for how can humans and whales learn to signal to each other, across the mysteries of their foreign minds?

Stroking Blackfin, unconsciously voicing curious thoughts, Roddy lost track of the time somewhat. Whitaker interrupted him.

"Roddy, there's only forty-five minutes to go before we mobilize the volunteers, and your detergent people are here, wondering what the hell to do."

"Yes. Yes…"

Roddy almost regretted that the time was near. He could sense, but he could not articulate, some reason, feeling or truth, deeper than himself, that urged consideration. It was almost as if it were emanating from the deep chambers of Blackfin's unknowability, and Roddy found himself thinking, he's here for a reason, he's trying to tell me something…

"Roddy. Roddy!"

"Yep."

He briefed the two operators responsible for pumping the detergent. Their first task would be to douse the shingle in front of Blackfin immediately prior to high tide; but their critical role would come in towards the end of the equilibrium work, and for that hundreds of volunteers were needed.

The volunteers were standing together, each holding a raffle ticket issued by Whitaker. When Roddy saw them, a weary, faintly incredulous expression settled on his face. He looked across at Whitaker, who studiously avoided his gaze.

"Oh Whitaker… Oh Whitaker, you're a sad man."

"What?"

"Thanks. I mean, just – thanks. This is going to look great. Fantastic. Excellent."

"All chosen on merit," Whitaker protested.

At least three-quarters of the volunteers were young women. Shaking his head in disbelief, Roddy approached the group and gave them his spiel.

"First, thanks for helping out," he called. "I know this is going to be an interesting adventure for all of us. You're probably wondering why I need so many volunteers. The reason is this: we're going to rock the whale from side to side for ten minutes before he goes back into the water."

Four hundred uncomprehending people stared at him.

"Why?" somebody asked.

"Because otherwise the whale might boomerang, which means that once we float him, he might just swim in a big circle and beach himself again. This was a feature of rescue attempts in the past, and it led to the myth that whales have a death-wish. In fact, they lose their sense of balance and coordination when stranded on land, a result of lying at an angle. In this particular case the whale is almost completely upright – very unusual – so maybe his sense of balance is fine. On the other hand, why take the risk? All right, any other questions?"

"It's… big," someone said, to nervous laughter.

"He's massive. Rocking him will be very hard work. We're not doing this for fun. If anyone has any health problems, I'd advise them to give it a miss. Another thing: try not to lose your footing, or you could become a human chapatti. OK?"

Hesitant nods.

"When we're ready to go, approach the whale slowly and quietly, in single file. My assistant and I will be standing by the whale, one at each eye. Line up along each side of the whale and, er, think nice thoughts. I mean it. I personally believe that even when they don't understand our actions, they can sense our intentions. OK, more questions?... Great. Please wait here with my assistant until we're ready. Thanks again."

As he turned away, someone called out: "Why have you picked so many women?"

"Good question!" Roddy said. "My assistant will explain," and he winked at Whitaker. As he tramped off, a familiar face among the volunteers had him wondering where he knew her from. She was young, very striking, and her hair was crazily knotted and tangled. It's the eyes I recognize, he decided – they're so intense.

But there was no time for idle reflection. He went over to the pump operators and issued some last-minute instructions. Then he and Whitaker went to Blackfin, stood one at each eye and murmured reassuring words and sounds. Five minutes later they supervised the placing of the volunteers.

There were now seven television crews covering the event, and the crowd had swollen to over five thousand. With the tide lapping at the animal's tail, and only minutes to go, Roddy stood stock-still and took it all in: the people, the media, the tangible expectation, the volunteers, and Blackfin, so mighty, so mysterious, stranded in the middle of everyone's anticipation like a god who had lost his powers... Excitement laced with panic raked through Roddy's insides. He signalled for the operation to commence.

He had not exaggerated when telling the volunteers what hard work it would be. Within a few minutes they were gasping for breath. It was a surreal sight. Blackfin was shifting minutely, left, right, left, right. The sea now covered the animal's tail flukes. With five minutes to high water, Roddy had the detergent turned on. The two operators doused the shingle in front of the whale. They pumped out eight hundred litres, and then came the critical part of their task; the volunteers were urged to rock the whale even more vigorously, and detergent was pumped under him, first on one side, then on the other. A girl slipped but scrambled to her feet, quickly followed by another. Oh God, this is too risky, Roddy suddenly agonized, someone could get hurt… But the event had its own momentum now, and the volunteers weren't stopping for anyone. High water was only two minutes away. Blackfin's position up the beach was, surely – wasn't it? – changing, and then at last he started to slither down the ridge of shingle, picking up speed and entering the sea. A peculiar image came into Roddy's mind, of a glistening, newborn calf flopping out of an exhausted cow. The crowd was cheering, the press broke through their cordon and charged, volunteers were hugging each other, falling over, slithering down the shingle in Blackfin's wake, as a sperm whale turned away from the land and glided slowly through the water.

* * *

After the police had rescued Roddy from the mob of the press, he spent some minutes watching Blackfin disappear. Then he started to walk slowly up the beach; he had agreed to do some interviews, and the journalists, corralled in their pen once more, were shouting to him desperately.

"Erm, excuse me – congratulations."

It was the girl he had recognized earlier among the volunteers.

"Oh, thanks. And congratulations to you as well."

"That was amazing."

She walked alongside him, and he took a good hard look at her. This was going to sound like a pick-up line, but…

"Do I know you from somewhere?"

"Me? I don't think so."

"I haven't taught you or anything?"

"No."

"Do you mind if I ask your name?"

"It's Ally Rattigan."

He stopped walking abruptly... of course, those eyes, they were like preposterous jewels. Like her father's. My God.

"*Do* you know me?" she asked him, looking uneasy and confused.

"I knew your mother."

"My *mother?*" The screams of the press were almost deranged now, but they went unheard. "How did you know my mother? Did you know her well?"

Did I know her well...

He smiled, not answering; he was thinking about a particular place, far away, and a particular time, long ago.

* * *

He was nineteen years old. He was lying down on the summit of Dun Caan, on the small Inner Hebridean island of Raasay. It was one of those rare days in the Hebrides when the weather did everything right: the sun was beating down, but there was a moderate breeze to keep the notorious midges at bay. Roddy, his head resting on a rolled-up jacket, closed his eyes, enjoying the feel of the sun's heat on his eyelids. Lying beside him was his girlfriend, Theresa. Her long hair, brown and completely straight, was flapping in the breeze, until she sat up and secured it behind her head to reveal a pretty face, bright, honest eyes, and beautiful skin. Close by to the east, across the sparkling Sound of Sleat, was the Scottish mainland; to the west was the Isle of Skye under its purple hat, the heather-covered Cuillin mountain range.

Biology students at Warwick University, they were on a two-week field trip, camping at a farm with twenty other students. They worked in the field all day, drank in Raasay's single pub all evening, and made love half the night every night, in the cramped and comical confines of a one-and-a-half-person tent. During those nights, feeling her slim body against his, the weight of her head on his chest, he would sometimes wake up from a surfeit of contentment.

In the second week of their field trip another party of students arrived on the Isle of Raasay, geologists from Oxford. The two groups got to know each other in the pub. Roddy and Theresa played dominoes with three generically witty and self-assured young men, an Alistair and two Peters.

During a break in play, Roddy noticed an Oxford student standing by himself at the bar. The student was built on a scale that seemed a good twenty per cent larger than the norm, though he also managed to seem gaunt and spare. His attitude was hesitant, even diffident, and yet he was staring at Theresa with large, unblinking, compellingly dark eyes. Frowning a little, Roddy turned back to his table, where a new round of dominoes was about to get underway. Fresh drinks had arrived, banter was resumed, and the first tiles had been put down when the intense-looking Oxford student approached.

"Bugger it," Roddy heard one of his companions murmur.

"Dominoes?" asked the new arrival.

No one seemed to know how to respond to this less than inspired question. There was an awkward pause. Theresa noted the slight flinch of the newcomer's nostrils as he tried to conceal a sense of being snubbed. His startling eyes somehow seemed to plead with her to help him.

"Do you want to play?" she asked.

The smile that surged over his face was oddly touching. He grabbed a stool with childish, greedy eagerness, and somehow contrived to wedge it between Roddy and Theresa. Roddy felt the student's great thighs pressing against his own. Theresa discreetly shifted her chair. Just as the game was about to recommence, the new arrival leapt to his feet.

"*Who wants a drink?*"

"*I've just got a round in,*" *Alistair pointed out.*

"*I'll get another.*"

"*That's all right*" – "*No thanks*" – "*Not yet*" – *came the replies.*

Rattigan swallowed and paused, as though gathering to himself all available dignity. "*I have enough money,*" *he said, and strode away to the bar.*

"*Oh Christ,*" *said one of the Peters,* "*that's the evening straight down the toilet now Five Degrees is tagging along.*"

"*Five Degrees?*" *Theresa asked.*

"*Five Degrees Rattigan.*"

"*Because he's always five degrees off the mark,*" *Alistair explained, to laughter.*

"*Ninety degrees is more like it.*"

"*A hundred and eighty.*"

"*If he'd only do the full three-sixty then he'd go off the scale of nuttiness and reappear on the other side.*"

"*Is he as bad as that?*" *Roddy asked.*

"*He'd be perfectly all right if he didn't have so many chips on his shoulder.*"

"*He'd be perfectly all right if he had some chips in his stomach, you mean,*" *one of the Peters said.* "*His only source of income is a small scholarship; he doesn't get a grant because no Local Education Authority will admit responsibility for him – some giant bureaucratic cock-up – and he's got no parents I think… so basically he doesn't eat. And he's so sensitive about being perceived as poor that he spends what little he has in totally inappropriate ways, like now.*"

"*Do you dislike him?*" *Theresa asked.*

Peter hesitated. "*It's not that I dislike him, but he won't let himself be liked, he just puts too many barriers in the way. I mean, I know he's clever, and interesting, but he's just not very…*"

"*Matey,*" someone interjected.

"*He thinks everyone hates him,*" Peter said.

"*So…*" said the second Peter.

"*So everyone does!*" Alistair finished, again to laughter. "*No, really, I shouldn't have said that, it's not true. Actually, he's an incredible geologist. Very focused. Bound to get a first.*"

The new round of drinks started arriving. Six pints and a set of dominoes were already on the table, and there was barely enough room for the six new glasses. Rattigan clumsily rearranged the table. Beer sloshed over the surface. There was a general reluctance now to continue the game, but Rattigan, true to his nickname, failed to tune into the feeling. He chided them to carry on. Not wanting to offend him, they did so. Conversation became desultory, witticisms weak. Roddy observed the scene with an almost morbid fascination for the newcomer's ability to demolish an atmosphere. Rattigan was extremely involved in the game, as though winning at dominoes would prove something. Then Roddy noticed that whenever Theresa picked up her glass, Rattigan picked up his; at the exact moment when the base of her glass touched the table again, so did Rattigan's. Was it deliberate or unconscious? Roddy didn't know, but he found himself struggling not to laugh. At that moment he had the misfortune to catch Alistair's eye, and instantly the two of them were helplessly hunched over their pints, eyes down, shoulders shaking.

"*Your go,*" Rattigan said to Roddy.

Roddy and Alistair snorted into laughter, and within moments everyone was at it, hooting and wheezing and gasping. Everyone except Rattigan, who smiled uneasily. He seemed baffled, and then, horribly, he joined in with them: a big, hearty, "*ha-ha-ha!*" kind of laugh. It shut everyone up instantly, and lingered in the air by itself. In the uncomfortable silence that followed, Roddy felt sorry for him, thinking: *he's cursed, he can't get anything right.*

The two Peters started mumbling about long days and early rises. The group broke up..

"What did you make of the big guy?" Roddy said to Theresa during their dark, damp trek back to the camp site.

"Weird. Interesting. Eyes like a god. And I thought you were very mean to him."

"Me?"

"Laughing like that."

"I couldn't help it!"

"Neither could I!"

"Heh heh…"

From the very next day, Rattigan contrived to be with them. They tried to be kind to him. He was easier to be with in one-to-one contexts. On those occasions when he succeeded in escaping from the straitjacket of his own awkwardness, he could become a dynamo of arguments and original ideas. He seemed to have an obsession with accruing great wealth from a business career and "doing something useful with it", although he resisted all attempts to make him say what that useful something might be.

"Why are you studying Geology?" Theresa had asked him one time.

"Rocks."

Theresa had pushed and probed, curious to discover what motivated him. Rattigan had struggled to articulate himself, searching deep within his uncharted self until, his face screwed up, the answer came.

"Rocks are, just, rocks are definitely there. They were there first. Do you see?"

"I'm not – maybe. Well, not quite. I—"

"No one can deny the existence of rocks. That's all."

One evening, Roddy returned in a state of great excitement from a solitary walk to the barren northern strip of the island.

He had been admiring the view when he had seen a dark shape appear in the water, less than a hundred yards away. His exhilaration, when he had looked through the binoculars and seen a whale blowing, was difficult to describe, but describe it he did, again and again, until Theresa, laughing, hugged him.

"I've never seen anything like it!" he exclaimed into her hair.

"I know! You said!"

"It arched its back, its tail – you should have seen it, it was massive – rose up into the air, and then it disappeared from view with hardly a ripple."

"Wow!"

He made extravagant claims about his future career: he would do an M.Sc. in some aspect of Marine Biology, then he would go on to do a Ph.D. – definitely to do with whales – and become an authority in Cetology.

"But last week you were going to go into molecular biology, and a month before that you were going to work for a pharmaceutical company for reasons which I forget but found pretty baffling – and anyway you never do a scrap of work, so how do you expect to do any of these things?"

"No no, this is it, the whale changes everything."

After he had calmed down a little, Theresa said, "I saw a large and mysterious animal myself earlier."

"What was that?"

"Five Degrees came round,"

"Did he? He's certainly very sure about what he wants from life."

"It's amazing, the fact that he knows already, that he's already working towards it. Might be something to do with his background. Did you know he was brought up in a children's home? Seems to be ashamed of it. I told him it's pretty glamorous really."

"What did he say to that?"

"Got very emotional. Went red. Cleared his throat. Nearly started to cry, then kissed me on the cheek."

"Bloody hell."

"And then he asked me out."

"He did what?!"

"I pointed out that there was no vacancy."

"How did he take it?"

"Not very well. Stormed off."

"Bloody hell."

"I've decided something about his eyes."

"The sneaky sod."

"It's as though they belong to a beast that's been in terrible danger so often, it knows it's going to survive, even though it's still... I don't know... utterly terrified."

For the remainder of the week, Rattigan fluctuated between high dudgeon and slavish attentiveness. Theresa spent a few half-hours with him, went on a couple of walks, and each time reported back to Roddy some new manifestation of her admirer's character.

On the final day, Rattigan told her that he loved her. The more she asked him to stop, the more determined he became to make her understand, and she found his eyes were fixed on her own like limpets on a treasure chest. His ever more lavish protestations eventually made her lose her temper, and she had pushed him away and told him to leave her alone. Later, feeling exceptionally cruel but unable to stop themselves, she and Roddy had laughed about it until their stomachs hurt. They left the Isle of Raasay in the morning without saying goodbye to him. That seemed to be that.

Back in Warwick they resumed their old lives. One day she said, "You'll never guess what – I've got a letter from Five Degrees Rattigan. He's got a thumping great first in his degree.

He's got a job with some oil-exploration outfit." He took to writing letters to her, one a week, which seemed strange at first, but she grew to appreciate them. A few months later she said, "Five Degrees says he has to come to Warwick on Monday. We're meeting for lunch, do you want to come?"

Rattigan was patient. From beginning to end the process took three years. At no point did Roddy, now obsessed with his studies in marine biology, realize what was happening. When he went away to Canada for several months on a field trip, Rattigan stepped up the pace and the pressure of his attentiveness to Theresa. It was in Canada, towards the end of the field trip, that Roddy received the letter:

Dearest Roddy,
It's impossible to write this letter to you, but write it I must. I can't think how to say what I have to say in any form which will make it less hurtful to you, so I had better just come out with it. Roddy, I'm sorry. I want to end our relationship. I have developed feelings for Tony…

Tony, Roddy had though – who's Tony?

He realized, too late, that they had been growing apart and taking each other for granted – but even so, he couldn't begin to understand how she had fallen for Five Degrees Rattigan. Back in England there were long, tearful evenings, in which she claimed that she was as surprised as anyone, but that when the issue was brought out into the open, she felt more for Tony than Roddy.

She begged him to remain her friend, but he couldn't do it. It wasn't that he didn't want to, but he felt broken, soul-scorched and alone, and he knew that he could only recover by cutting all ties. A year after their final meeting, he heard that she had married.

He got a new girlfriend. Then another. He moved in with some-
one for three years. They split up over his lack of commitment.
The next girlfriend became pregnant, and he was very excited. She
had a miscarriage, and he realized that he was glad. Soon she was
accusing him of being too distant and uncaring, even arrogant.
She left him. She was the last serious relationship he had.

7

Blackfin cruises the surface, echo-locating at short intervals
with a steady clicking. Being returned to that puny sliver of sea,
the English Channel, does not cause him to feel that he is back
where he belongs. The sea bed is only sixty metres down, and
it reveals thick sludge, wrecked boats, tangles of net, dumped
rubbish. The vileness of the swilling waters, however, isn't the
reason why he longs for the deepness; the water is too shallow
here for long-distance communication. When he is a thousand
metres down, with a planet of water pressing on him, his
signals will travel at five times the speed of sound, and then he
will be able to pick up the signals of other sperm whales from
thousands of miles away.

He swims steadily. Two or three pleasure craft are tracking
him but he is barely aware of them. He will go to the deep waters
and feed. He will signal the outcome of his solitary action to all
the sperm whales of all the oceans. And then he will return to
this shallow, slimy sea, and he will beach himself again, in the
same place, in the same way. Confounding the humans is his
only hope of making them think.

As he heads south-west into the widening Channel, something
puzzles him. Sightseers in his escort of small boats clap their
hands in delight to see his huge tail flukes rise into the air, and
his body sink vertically down only metres away.

On the murky sea bed he is astonished to receive signals – there are other sperm whales in this shallow sea. Their reverberating clicks, arranged in a series of complex codas, convey the momentous news: man has stained the sea again; the *badbright* is expanding; and the whales are ready to die, as Blackfin had been ready to die, on the edge of the human world.

Blackfin's spirit soars. He sends out a stream of data. Then he rises to the surface. The sightseers exclaim in excitement when he appears, but wonder why he doesn't resume his journey. They edge their boats close to him. Blackfin doesn't notice them. He waits for his brothers and sisters.

* * *

The reports had been coming in for some hours. All along the shores of southern England, from Falmouth to the Solent, the Maritime Rescue Centres of Her Majesty's Coastguard were awash with confusion. Initial reaction had been irritation; the Channel was one of the busiest sea lanes in the world, and the last thing which HMCG needed was a practical joker clogging up the frequencies. But as more reports arrived, from sources so diverse as to preclude a hoax – a car ferry, a trawler, a bulk carrier – the front-line Coastguard personnel wondered what the hell to make of it, and consulted their supervisors.

Phil Bibby was Southern Regional Controller. It was two hours into the "situation", as Watch Officers were calling it, when he was pulled out of a meeting with the RAF about a revised search-and-rescue procedure to be implemented in the new year. He had been pulled out of a meeting only once before, when a supertanker carrying ethyl acetate had started taking in water two miles off Portland Bill. The unenviable task of informing him about the whales belonged to his deputy, Heather Mahoney.

"This'd better be good," he grumbled, lighting a cigarette outside the entrance to the building.

"Well, we've got a big bunch of whales swimming up the Channel."

He looked at her with an underwhelmed expression.

"At speed," she added desperately. "New reports are coming in every few minutes and no one knows what to do."

Phil scowled as he blew out a plume of smoke.

"Nothing!"

"I'm sorry?"

"So there's whales in the sea!" he exploded, jabbing his cigarette in the air. "I can't believe you've pulled me out of a meeting just to – for pity's sake, Heather, there's trout in the Thames and seals in the Solent, who gives a toss?"

"Phil, I know how it must seem, but please, just read these transcripts."

She thrust them under his nose. He exhaled in an exaggerated display of annoyance, but took the papers from her. 15.38, from the skipper of a trawler: *at least fifty whales overtaking vessel starboard...* 15.45, from a pleasure craft: *sea like a foam bath...* 15.59, from a small yacht: *craft capsized, repeat capsized, by the wake of a large group of whales swimming at great speed on surface, crew safe, vessel now secure...*

Phil flicked through some more, shaking his head.

"There are over twenty reports now," Heather told him, "and they're coming in every six minutes on average."

He flicked ash from his cigarette and watched it fall to the pavement.

"Fucking hell," he complained; he had no idea what he was supposed to do, if anything. In order to meet his responsibilities as Southern Regional Controller, he had available to him the facilities of the Maritime Rescue Coordination Centres, the RAF Rescue Coordination Centres, the Coast Earth and

Radio Stations, the International Maritime Satellite facility and the Intelligence Department of Lloyds of London; in the case of shore-based incidents he could call on the police, the local authority, the fire brigade, the ambulance service and the lifeguard; he could launch RNLI lifeboats, request helicopters from the RAF and search aircraft and ships from the Royal Navy; in short, he could call on every imaginable resource, and frequently did, in order to deal with the thousands of incidents that occurred annually. And he knew that in the previous year, the statistical distribution of incidents was this: shore search-and-distress 31.5%, pleasure craft 25%, cliff and tide rescues 19%, commercial fishing 8.5%, medical assistance to shipping 8%, dinghies and inflatables 5%, merchant shipping 3%, rampaging hordes of crazed whales, nil.

"I've never heard anything like it," he moaned.

"That's been the chorus from the beginning, that's why it's come all the way up to you. I mean, it can't really go any further, operationally."

She was right. Above him were the Chief Coastguard and the Chief Executive of the whole caboodle, but in terms of operational responsibility, Phil was the biggest banana in the bunch.

"Tremendous."

* * *

The little girl started screaming. Everyone in the ten or so pleasure craft that now surrounded Blackfin turned their attention from him and—

"Oh my God!"

"Look out!"

"Daddy!"

Blackfin dived, but no one noticed him now, as dozens of whales sped past the small flotilla. There were screams and wails as the boats rocked and clattered into one another. A sleek motorboat overturned, tipping out its crew, and four people from other craft were also pitched into the water; the rest managed to cling on during the brief ferment. As the whales swam away, Blackfin among them, those overboard were pulled out of the sea. A man had banged his head and a boy had cut his foot, but no one was seriously injured. A new round of reports was transmitted to H.M. Coastguard.

* * *

Phil Bibby was tracing the progress of the whales on a chart. His senior staff were assembled around him. Every couple of minutes the Radio Officer received a new report, and the position of the whales was replotted.

A member of his team had been dispatched to track down the very first report of the whales, and had come back with a sitrep from the previous afternoon, made by "two drunken old farts" in the Bay of Biscay. Other early reports, regarded as one-offs at the time, clearly demonstrated that the whales had swum three hundred miles in twenty-four hours.

"What about this beached sperm whale on Brighton beach?" someone asked.

"What about it?" Phil rapped out; he felt desperate for a cigarette.

"Er, I don't know. Just thought I'd throw it in the pot."

"The pot's plenty full enough, thanks very much."

For the hundredth time he looked at the chart and went through the same thought process: the whales *could* be heading for Brighton, but it's just plain silly to assume that they *will*. They'll probably pass through the Channel and emerge in the

North Sea; even if they beach, they could beach anywhere – Sandown Bay, Bognor Regis, a deserted shore. The chances of it being Brighton are negligible. Aren't they?

He had already put out a warning about the whales on the shipping forecast, and that had been embarrassing enough. But what if they do attack Brighton beach? Phil asked himself – then caught himself thinking, for Christ's sake, *attack?* They're whales, not amphibious assault vessels. But if, just if, they were going to beach themselves there, they'd arrive in twenty minutes, maybe less...

Every ten minutes he had been rushing outside to smoke for one minute, and his packet of Marlboro had emptied its contents at a frightening rate; I've only got three left, he remembered in a panic, as he tried to work out how to play the situation. He pulled one of the three from the packet, and tapped it on the chart table. My dilemma, he articulated to himself with some disgust, is this: if I don't make the call to Brighton police, and whales hurl themselves out of the sea, then I'll lose my job, and in the subsequent film of the book of the true-life-story I'll be cast as an indecisive toe-rag; but if I do make the call to Brighton, and the bloody whales don't show, then I'll make an absolute, unmitigated arse of myself. Cobblers, knickers, bollocks and – just for good measure, he decided – fuck it. Then his cigarette snapped in two – *shit!*

"Get Brighton police on the line."

* * *

The beach was nearly back to normal. Where Blackfin had been stranded, a group of rubber-clad workers were cleaning up as much of the lubricant as possible, and a few onlookers remained, unwilling to acknowledge that the excitement was over. Tourists and day trippers had fanned out along the beach, laying out their mats and erecting their deckchairs. The TV crews had packed up and gone, taking footage of a triumphalist Roddy with them, but a fair number of print journalists were still occupying Roddy's time.

Whitaker and Ally were sitting cross-legged in the shingle, waiting. Despite a dip in the sea, fully clothed, to wash off the gunge from the refloating, they looked like sea birds pulled from an oil slick. Whitaker had no idea who Ally was nor what her link to Roddy might be, but he knew that the two of them had arranged to go for a coffee. He was enjoying her company, and she seemed to be enjoying his. She had forced him to confess that he was personally responsible for the "young women" recruitment policy for the volunteers, an admission that she found simultaneously appalling and hilarious.

"OK," Whitaker said after a pause in the conversation, "so you're Roddy's long-lost love child?"

"No."

"A distant cousin?"

"No."

"A distinguished academic colleague?"

"Hardly."

"Not his girlfriend?"

"Doesn't he have a partner?" Ally asked.

"No. Hasn't had one in years and years, I think."

"How come?"

"I don't know. He doesn't seem to mind, or at least, he's so absorbed in work and whales that he doesn't seem to notice."

Ally didn't get chance to reflect on this.

"Sorry to keep you waiting," Roddy said, sliding down the ridge of pebbles above them.

"That's OK."

"Shall we take that coffee?" he asked, smiling at Ally. "Or do you need to get off home and clean up?"

Whitaker watched them clamber up the shingle towards the promenade. He felt abruptly melancholic, wishing he'd had the guts to ask for her mobile number. He turned around and stumped down to the sea.

Crunching the shingle underfoot, Roddy felt painfully shy and couldn't cobble up any conversation. Perhaps Ally was experiencing similar feelings. They walked in silence, with their heads down.

This is Theresa's daughter, Roddy marvelled. Theresa – what is she doing now? What is she like? Would I even recognize her, after more than twenty years? Damn, it all seems like a different life ago, in a different world… He imagined Theresa in a variety of contexts – as an academic in a provincial university, as an author of textbooks, as an Open-University student, as a translator, as a mother of five children – and felt desolation steal over his heart.

"There's the whale fella," someone said. Ally glanced across at Roddy, and smiled.

And what the hell am I going to say to this girl now, he worried: "So, you're a student / a topless model / a trainee manager at Marks & Spencer… how interesting, and by the way, I adored your mother…"

Suddenly a helicopter was overhead, flying so low and fast that as soon as they heard it, it was hurting their ears, and as soon as they saw it, they instinctively ducked.

"Christ!"

Children all along the beach bawled their terror as the small police helicopter flew out to sea.

"What's that all about?" Ally asked.

"God knows."

They had nearly got to the top of the beach when they heard the wail of the first siren. Police vans came screeching down the esplanade. One stopped directly above them, police men and women bursting out of the back of it. The other vans were stopping further along. Loudspeakers blared out:

"THIS IS AN EMERGENCY, LEAVE THE BEACH NOW, THIS IS AN EMERGENCY, LEAVE THE BEACH NOW."

Roddy and Ally gave each other incredulous looks. The police were sprinting past them towards the sea, shouting at everyone to run. Women started screaming, and when Roddy looked out to sea he saw a localized area of churning water, dense with dark shapes, that looked something like a miniature storm about to break on the beach.

"Whitaker!" he yelled.

Whitaker doesn't hear Roddy's cry. One moment he is using the toe of his shoe to poke at an empty Coke can on the tide's edge; the next, he is looking up at a boiling tempest of sea creatures surging towards the land, already nearly on it.

"Christ," he pants.

He feels nothing but the focus that terror brings. He tries to scrabble up the shingle ridge, his feet powering into it, his hands pawing and scooping it under his body. But under him the round pebbles roll and shift; he can't run fast enough.

Blackfin is swimming just under the surface. The water shears off his body, channelled by the patterned ridges on his skin. He has never swum so fast nor with such exhilaration. The sea is getting shallower, on each side of him are the dark shapes of his brothers and sisters, packed close and travelling swiftly; he scatters – shatters – a shoal of fish, passes over a staved-in rowing boat, then impulsively swerves up and out of the water, sees for the briefest moment the approaching beach, so close, the humans scrambling up it, then he is back in the water, skimming along the bottom. The surface gets closer, lighter, closer, lighter, his great bulk furrows the surface, the waters roar, another whale crashes into his flank, pebbles sear into his underside and with ecstatic pain he slams into the land.

A dark and mighty shape shoots past Whitaker, just to his right, occluding his vision on that side, and there is the ear-rending crunch of shingle being crushed, and the knowledge, the sight briefly glimpsed but forever registered, the awful truth of a human being disappearing underneath that juggernaut of living flesh; and Whitaker, still scrabbling hysterically up the ridge, has a moment to know what is going to happen to him before it happens to him, as the unseen creature behind him bears down.

* * *

It couldn't have lasted more than half a minute. To Roddy and Ally, from their position at the top of the beach, it seemed much longer. Roddy's mind dealt as best as it could with a spectacle it considered to be technically impossible. What he saw were whales, fifty, sixty, maybe eighty whales, of many species, hurling themselves onto the land, sending showers of pebbles into the air which fell back down to earth like lethal hailstones. What he heard was a continuous rasping noise as thousands of tonnes of whale simultaneously broke up great swathes of shingle. What he witnessed were people dying. Voiceless in terror or screaming without cease, panting or crying, emitting non-sensible animal sounds, whether on two feet or scrambling on all fours, there were some few people who did not make the safety of the second ridge.

It's over, Roddy announced to himself. The soft and rhythmic sea reclaimed the sound waves. Dozens of whales lay motionless and massive, looking unlikely, impossible, and as harmless as abandoned monoliths in a desert.

A stillness settled on the horror. It was a time to force the brain to accept the data fed to it. Spectators, police officers, Roddy, stared. Men, women and children who had scrabbled to safety lay quietly, resembling exhausted shipwreck survivors washed up on the shore. Then came the cries of an injured man, and a whale blew; it seemed to set off the next stage of the aftermath, for then many whales blew, their mighty breaths sounding like some kind of industrial process or the exclamations of archaic gods.

He realized that Ally had been gripping his arm only when she let go of it. With many others, he started to walk down the shingle to the whales. He went past the first whale almost without looking at it. For some reason he needed to be in the middle of them. When he was there... it was like being lost in some unthinkable maze. He walked along the side of a mature pilot whale, stepping over a long, slender, sickle-shaped flipper. Rounding the head, he found himself face to face with a man. They looked at each and moved on. Now Roddy's way was blocked by a colossal rorqual – ugly, undeniably ugly, and as barnacled as the keel of an old ship.

The wounded were beginning to receive attention from the police and other individuals. Their cries were drowned out by the louder, mechanical wailings of speeding ambulances. For some witnesses, for some reason, this seemed to be the prompt that pushed them back into their selves. But Roddy was still deep inside an unpleasant, shock-induced stupor. Perhaps his superior knowledge of whales, what they do and what they don't do, wouldn't allow him to accept what had occurred. And something was nagging at his brain, some dreadful anxiety or awful responsibility – what is it, he asked himself; there's something I should be doing – but he couldn't pin it down as he passed randomly among the great creatures. A pulverized corpse brought him to a halt. Only the blood-soaked clothes could indicate which parts of the body had been which, and that, together, they had comprised a woman. A whale had ridden directly over her. He remembered the image he had used when briefing the volunteers an hour, a history, a different world ago: human chapatti.

Now many hundreds of people were among the whales, looking for the injured or simply gawping. A short while passed – was it a few moments or a few minutes? – and Roddy was walking up a furrow that led from the sea to the tail flukes of a sperm whale. He saw, without the faintest trace of surprise or interest, a neat, V-shaped notch, the wound still raw and red; Blackfin's identity card.

"Dr Ormond – Dr Ormond."

I needed that, he noticed himself think, I needed someone to speak to me to get me out of this – and when Roddy answered "Yes?" he heard the sound of his own voice with relief.

"I've been sent to locate you and be your link to the rescue operation," said a young police officer. "Obviously the priority is care of the injured, but my superior wants to know if we should be doing anything for the whales."

"Tugs."

"Sir?"

"Arrange for some tugs to anchor off shore and spray water over the whole scene."

"I'll tell them. I don't think they can do that until all the injured are removed from the scene."

"I saw a dead woman," Roddy said. "Over there."

The policeman nodded. Both of them looked around. There were now many police, paramedics and firemen in situ, all doing as best they could in an unprecedented situation. Ghoulish sightseers had swelled in numbers, exclaiming and shouting.

"These people have to be got out of here," Roddy said.

"They will be, as soon as the manpower is sufficient."

An appalling weight was still oppressing Roddy's mind, as heavy as guilt.

"Sir," the young police officer said, "Sir, how could this

happen?" and he made a vague gesture with his hand, which was somehow supposed to signify the magnitude of the incident.

"It couldn't," Roddy answered.

"Sir," the man tried again, looking so young, like a boy scout, "I think—"

He never got the opportunity to tell Roddy what he thought, because at that moment the last element of Roddy's trance-like state shifted and dislodged.

"My assistant – oh shit my assistant, he was here—"

"Is he a black guy?"

"Yes he's—"

"I'm sorry, but if it's the same person, then I think he's one of the casualties—"

"Oh Jesus."

"If it's the same person, then he's over in that direction."

8

Rattigan's chauffeur and new PA were bored. For nearly an hour the Bentley had been parked outside a modern, undistinguished building in Southwark, near the tube station. A small, discreet sign revealed that the building was called Dewdrop House.

"What is this place anyway?" asked the PA.

"Dunno."

"It looks like a new hall of residence for students, but without any students."

"Does it?" the chauffeur answered, wearily. He had little knowledge of student life, and less interest.

"But why is he just sitting in the back, doing nothing?"

"Dunno. Does it from time to time in a few places. You better get used to it."

"What kind of places?"

"Dunno. All pretty much like this one."

In the back, Rattigan was staring resolutely out of the window at the entrance to Dewdrop House. He had Radio 4 playing low, but he wasn't listening to it. After the shock of the encounter with Ally, he had come here almost instinctively. For self-validation. Scattered on the seat were some well-read books and documents: *Dewdrop House, Annual Report*; *Case Studies in Child Abuse*; *Children's Rights – Reality or Rhetoric?*, and an estimate by a construction firm for the building of a new wing.

No one at Dewdrop House, a residential care centre for abused and vulnerable children, knew who he was. He had never met any of the staff or the children. But he was the centre's prime architect. He had conceived it, funded it, overseen its construction, approved its management. It had cost five million to build, and the running costs were currently set at two million per annum. Every penny came out of his pocket, via an anonymous trust fund he had founded some fifteen years before.

The centre's front door opened. From over the low wall and the neat, narrow lawn, Rattigan watched as a boy about ten years old came outside. The boy sat down on a bench, arms folded, head down, and scuffed his shoes together. I wonder which one that is, Rattigan found himself thinking, and what hell he has survived... The poor little sod. The poor little bastard. He's just a kid... Rattigan knew the backgrounds of all the children in Dewdrop House, as well as those of all the children in the other three centres he had set up.

There was a rage in Rattigan about certain injustices: one of them was that children could be so easily abused by adults; another was that he had been one of those children. It was an unpalatable fact, one he preferred not to analyse or even understand. It was so much easier to help children now than to understand the child he had been. If Ally knew about all this, he reflected sadly, perhaps she wouldn't accuse me of being rich and useless; Theresa too. But then, if they knew about all this, then they'd know all about me. I don't want anyone to know about me.

Like the child he had been, he still blamed himself.

The boy had lit a cigarette. He was blowing smoke rings. Rattigan couldn't help smiling at this defiant display. As he watched, he became aware of the radio. The tone of the broadcast had changed – there might even have been an announcement along the lines of "We interrupt this programme..." – and he listened, half disbelieving, as an excited reporter gabbled about whales killing people on Brighton beach. Then disbelief turned to incredulity when the reporter said something about "Dr Roderick Ormond, who had been supervising the refloating of a beached whale..." Ormond? Why was he cropping up like this? The man my wife loved more than me.

"Take me home," he barked into the intercom.

* * *

The Rattigans lived on the multi-millionaires' row of The Bishops Avenue, near Hampstead Heath. The neo-Georgian pile was protected by high walls, electronic gates, CCTV, manned patrols and guard dogs. Rather than a house in a community, it resembled a semi-autonomous state which had declared independence from the nation of ordinary life.

Theresa was in her hobbies room. It was the only room in the house where she felt reasonably safe from her husband's relentless psychological oppression and occasional violence. Rattigan had taken to calling it the "sticky-back-plastic room". In the past she had followed intellectual interests: botany, languages, astronomy. But it seemed that Tony, who had been so proud of her in the early years of their marriage, had come to feel threatened by her accomplishments. She had tried cultivating an interest in geology, so that they would have a shared pursuit, but for some reason this had made him edgy. For long years now he had been more or less derisory about anything she did. These days she only felt capable of messing around with paint and glue.

What a waste, she tormented herself – what a dreadful waste of love, and lives. His life, mine.

Her latest hobby was decoupage. Frowning in concentration, she applied a pale yellow wash to a copy of a Victorian line-drawing of a basket of flowers, then hung up the piece of paper to dry on a string that ran along one wall. A dozen other such pictures were hanging from the string, all waiting to be trimmed and then glued to an old wooden clock she had bought. She took down one of the dry pieces of paper, a picture of a puppy that had already been washed brown, and began to paint its eyes. She tried not to notice the slight tremor of her hand. A few minutes previously, she had heard the Bentley rolling down the drive, the slam of the car door as Tony got out, then the car disappearing into the underground car park. Nerves, it's just nerves; all I need is to sink into the rhythm of the physical task... Her tongue protruded from her teeth as, with the concentration of a small child writing a big word, she painted a red collar on the puppy.

The muscles of her slender wrist contracted and released. Her fingers were long and slim and still young-looking, the nails unpainted; she only wore make-up when he told her to. But nowadays he seldom did.

Sometimes she admired herself in the mirror. Not bad, she would think hesitantly, for a woman over forty. I can pass for thirty-five after I pluck out the grey hairs, I've still got good skin, cheekbones, dimples. I have a nice face, she would think, but I'm way too thin, all collar bone and angular hip and jutting rib. I haven't eaten properly for years.

The puppy was finished, resplendent in his red collar and blue bonnet. She hung him up to dry next to the basket of flowers, and managed to emit a small sigh of satisfaction. And then a harsh ringing noise made her jump.

There was a buzzer installed in the hobbies room, so that he could summon her. That kind of thing had begun soon after she had tried to leave him, ten years ago. Trying to leave him had been the second biggest mistake of her life; the first had been marrying him. After a day or two of frightening rage, and a beating, he had sat her down in his office and explained in chilling detail exactly which methods he would use, legal and illegal, to ensure that she would never see Ally again. So she had stayed with him, locked into a marriage that was instantly ten times worse than the one she had been trying to escape. And every trait and tendency of his that she disliked had intensified from that point on. His pursuit of wealth became absolutely all-consuming and compulsive; his business deals, often leaning towards a dubious connection with the law, lurched sharply into criminality; his treatment of her became abusive; while his relationship with Ally seemed unhealthily intense.

She sat still for a few moments, trying to calm herself down. She grabbed some pills from a bowl and threw them in her mouth. Then she went downstairs. He was in the living area that they called Ally's room, for the simple reason that Ally had always preferred it to the bigger, better appointed room that was formally the main lounge.

"Look at this," said her husband; he was slumped in a black-leather armchair, watching television.

"What is it?" she asked, in as neutral a voice as she could contrive.

"Obviously it's the news!" he lashed out, exasperated.

She sat down nervously on the edge of a settee. The voice of the presenter took some moments to filter through:

"...astonishing incident... three dead and twenty-six injured... five people are in critical condition... many species..."

"Seventy-eight whales!" exclaimed Rattigan. "Launching themselves at the land in a pack!"

She watched the screen, intrigued, as he flicked between the channels. He seemed to be searching for something: "...by analysis of the furrows, it is thought that scientists will be able to calculate the speed at which..." – "...twenty-nine minke, nineteen pilot, twelve sperm, six fin, five sei, three killer and..." – "...no exaggeration to suggest this is the most newsworthy event since..."

Rattigan continued to change channels impatiently.

"...Prime Minister expressed deep sympathy for the victims' families, and promised to spare no effort in dealing with..." – "...no clear consensus among marine biologists as to..." – "...Dr Roderick Ormond, seen here leaving Royal Sussex County Hospital after visiting his assistant, who is believed to have been critically injured in the incident."

Theresa blanched. *Roddy*... Roddy, what is he doing, he's going grey – he looks like his father, how is he, I can't believe it... She saw him striding out of the hospital at a furious pace, only to be engulfed by journalists.

"Sir, how is your assistant, sir?"

"No comment."

"Can you explain what happened today?"

"No one can explain what happened today."

"Is it true that—"

"Dr Ormond, has there ever been an instance before in which whales have killed people like this?"

"No."

"Dr Ormond, is it true that you may sit on an Emergency Committee appointed by the Government and the Local Authority?"

"That's the first I've heard of that, so I can't answer."

"What about—"

"Excuse me, but that's all I want to say for now."

"Sir!"

"Sir, sir!"

"Dr Ormond!"

He was shown fighting his way through the press pack, making little headway until the police stepped in to assist him.

Rattigan turned to his wife, eyebrows raised.

"First love?" he murmured.

She knew that his contempt was fuelled by feelings of being threatened, but she shrivelled in its blast even so. She wouldn't meet his gaze. I'm nothing now, she told herself, I barely feel alive any more. He's assessing me, as though I'm an item of defective merchandise... Just concentrate on getting out of this room.

"You're pathetic," he stated, wearily. "Go to bed. I'll be up later."

It was eight o'clock in the evening. She went, walking cautiously on legs that felt as weak as pipe cleaners.

"Go on! Wear the pink thing," he growled as an after-thought.

He watched her skinny backside exiting the room, and felt a painful surge of guilt – she looks like a malnourished zombie. Did I do that to her? Is it my fault? She shouldn't be frightened of me. I tried to give her everything. If she liked me, then she wouldn't be frightened. That's the one thing she can't understand.

Does she still love Ormond?

He stretched out his heavy legs, one ankle resting on the other. Ormond, a marine biologist, an expert on whales... why? Where was his money and power? What good did he do anyone? Why are people so incomprehensible? And – his face contorted – why do I feel so jealous? Why was I never like him, them, everyone?

His thoughts became caught up in the old cycle of bitterness, in which he perceived himself to be randomly disliked; as a child, as a student, as a husband, and now, yes, even as a father...

The images on the TV screen related exclusively to the whale situation: lingering shots of huge beached forms; rent-a-quote MPs who intoned gravely on the imperative of returning the animals to the sea; the brother of a victim, mad with grief, shouting that the whales should be put down in the same way as with dogs that maul children; recorded footage of Dr Roddy Ormond being made to look foolish in Kate Gunning's original interview. Rattigan smirked at this, then slammed his fist down on the arm of his chair in frustration. He needed release. He considered his options and found them tedious. His wife's wary expression came into his mind.

Now on the television was a piece about all the foreign news crews descending on Brighton. Grave Scandinavians, philosophical Frenchmen and excitable Italians were featured. Two Japanese were shown debating furiously, chopping the air with their hands. Bloody Japs, Rattigan mused; such a fanatical people.

He wasn't sure how or when his outrageous idea arrived. It must have been something to do with seeing the two Japanese television presenters. It must have crystallized in his mind, until, as he rubbed his nose in a cupped hand, he became aware of its existence. The idea was ingenious. It was so outrageous as to be unthinkable. But he had thought it, and the more he thought about it, the more it electrified him. But can it be done? He found that his palms were sweating. He rubbed his hands across his thighs...

He had found not release, but distraction. Now he watched the television reports with an avid professional interest, making notes. He was fizzing with excitement. I can see it, he recited to himself, I can see so much money in this...

He watched the TV news for hours. At quarter-past midnight the formation of two bodies was announced: a small Whale

103

Crisis Coordination Team, and a larger Emergency Response Committee. The former was to consist of whale experts and was charged with looking after the beached whales and investigating why they had left the sea in such an unprecedented manner. The latter, composed mainly of representatives from the Local Authority and from the emergency services, was to direct the mobilization and deployment of the personnel, equipment and practical expertise needed in any rescue plan proposed by the Whale Crisis Coordination Team.

At two in the morning it was announced that Dr Roderick Ormond was the leader of the Whale Crisis Coordination Team, and that he had appointed Dr Derek Petersen and Ms Kamala Mohandhas as the other members. Rattigan's eyes widened in wonder; an inevitable function of the success of his idea would be the absolute destruction of whoever was responsible for the whales. He paused a moment to imagine a ruined, desolate, reviled Roddy Ormond, and – convinced that his wife was in love with the man, even after so many years – could only find it a deeply satisfying fantasy.

Before going upstairs he made a phone call to one of his intermediaries, instructing him to phone Tokyo; he financed a front office there which could come in useful. Then he heaved himself to his feet, winced at a stab of indigestion and lumbered upstairs to his wife.

* * *

Theresa was in bed. When she had first lain down she had felt dizzy; memories of Roddy had flooded her mind. He appeared to her as in old photographs: sleeping in a rocking chair, standing proudly next to a pan of inedible stew, and peering from under a duvet with one eye closed. And he appeared to her as he had at their last ever meeting, when she had begged him to be her friend. But he had shaken his head, said sorry, said that he wasn't strong enough to do that. And left her life.

She tossed and turned in bed. The cocktail of anti-depressants she had taken had put her into an unpleasant state of consciousness. Perhaps she was slightly feverish. When Ally came into her mind she began to sob, not knowing that she was doing so. I was trying to *protect* you, she argued to herself hopelessly; what was the name of the boy? John. Don. Dave. A nice boy, a silly boy. God knows what would have happened to that boy if Tony had found out about him. Ally, you don't know such things, you don't know anything. I've lost you.

The door opened and the light went on.

"I *told* you to wear the pink thing," he said grimly.

"I forgot," Theresa whispered, shocked – she cowered away from him as he strode across to the bed.

9

4:30 a.m. A nearly full moon hung over the seventy-eight unmoving whales. Light glinted in cool shades of blue from smooth, dark skins. The beach was silent but for the sea and the mighty inhalations of the animals. The crowd had shrunk to a quarter of its previous size, and the police had taken the opportunity to move it back a full hundred metres. Helicopters, which had been such a nuisance earlier, hovering above the whales for aerial footage, had been seen off with a court injunction; and TV crews, which had persistently flouted requests not to illuminate the scene with dazzling artificial light, had finally fallen into line when a Brazilian film crew was arrested and hauled off for a night in the cells.

Roddy and his old friend Derek Petersen were standing side by side in front of the whales. The two men were waiting for the veterinarian Kamala Mohandhas, who was doing checks among the animals. Derek had only just arrived. He stared at the whales in silence. With his feet set rather far apart, and his hands linked together behind his back, he looked like a mariner contemplating unusual seas. The impression was further emphasized by his neat white beard. Derek was in his middle fifties. Twenty years earlier, as the supervisor of Roddy's Ph.D., he had described his student as "immensely talented, very sloppy, and generally infuriating". They were firm friends.

"You haven't told me about your assistant," Derek said finally, breaking the silence.

Roddy shook his head. He could still hardly believe everything that had happened, or that he was in charge of an operation that the entire world was watching. He felt that his life had been turned upside down.

"They were assessing him when I was there, the Glasgow coma test or something. They wouldn't let me see him. It doesn't look good."

"I'm sorry. What a mess."

From the crowd came a loud, unexplained whoop. It lingered in the air. From even further away, Roddy heard the shriek of a car being put through a wheel spin. His face, ghostly-looking in the moonlight, was spattered with water from the two tugs anchored off shore; droplets hung from the tip of his nose.

"Derek—"

"Yes?"

"Derek, we've got an aggressive, coordinated, multi-species beaching of whales, and that in itself represents a unique event in nature with far-reaching implications."

"Well, quite."

Roddy shook his head vigorously, to get rid of the water, then smoothed his fingers through his hair. "But it's somehow more than that too, it challenges everything we think we know. It's the day when the relationship between man and animals was changed for ever, the whole damn picture ripped up, thrown away and redrawn – *by the animals*."

Derek nodded slowly, but didn't answer. He looked up as a woman emerged from the stranded whales in front of them. She clambered up a ridge of shingle, breathing hard, water dripping from her yellow waterproofs, and stretched her arm out to Derek.

"Are you Derek? Hello there, I'm Kamala Mohandhas."

"Hi. How are they doing?"

"They're in remarkably good physical shape, considering. I've had a look at six, all of different species. Heart rates are nearly normal, no obvious signs of distress. Of course I've got samples to send off to the lab – blood sugar levels may be a concern, given that they aren't getting any food inside them – but so far they seem as well as could be expected, if not better."

"Lack of food shouldn't be a problem for a while," Roddy said. "Most species can go weeks without food."

Kamala nodded. A silence occurred, not so much awkward as symbolic, as though it summed up the three of them hesitating at the edge of their task.

"Look," Roddy said, "in less than two hours we'll be in a meeting with this Emergency Response Committee. I've already been in long discussions with various Local Authority people, but there's a lot more to do. If it's OK with you two, I'll brief you here and now on what I've done so far, and get your input on what has to be done next."

"OK."

Roddy paused for a moment, to collect his thoughts.

"All local authorities have County Emergency Planning Units. I didn't know anything about them twelve hours ago, but now I know rather a lot. They're geared up to deal with any imaginable emergency, from burst water pipes in an old people's home to nuclear winters across an entire region. But this emergency, obviously, is one they hadn't imagined. Frankly they haven't got a clue about whales. So although our team is small in number, strategy really is down to us. They can mobilize, deploy and direct resources and personnel, but only around the decisions I make, with your guidance. I've been talking to Margaret Gilchrist – she's the Chief Executive of the Local Authority, very capable lady – and Harry Giles, who's the County Emergency Planning Officer. We've decided to set up an Operations Centre right here on the beach – that's the Portakabins going up at the top of the beach there – and she's insisted on a Media Centre too, which I understand will be in the gymnasium of a local leisure centre. But what we need to do now is thrash out an initial strategy for the whales."

"Put 'em back in the water pronto," Derek said. "That much is obvious, isn't it?"

"Not necessarily."

They looked at him.

"When I put the original whale back in the water, he returned with seventy-seven friends."

"Sure, but, I mean," Derek said, spluttering rather, "what's the alternative?"

"I think that putting them back in the water tomorrow – I mean, today – is not only the wrong decision, but technically impossible. It would require sixteen thousand volunteers and four hundred thousand litres of detergent. The beach would require weeks of cleaning up, and frankly I think there'd be casualties; yesterday I was lucky. But in three days there's a spring tide. Understand? It will do the job for us. It raises the sea level by eighteen feet over the low water the whales came in on. We can easily keep them in good condition for three days, and there'll be the opportunity to do a battery of tests, and a lot of thinking."

"It's not a bad idea, per se," Kamala admitted, though with a measure of reluctance in her intonation. "It has its merits."

"But?"

"Well, I'm wondering how it would go down with the public and the media... they might not like it very much."

"To be honest," Roddy said, "that doesn't bother me. In the few short hours of the crisis so far the media have been completely irresponsible. We've had more than twenty helicopters here during the night, despite our desperate pleas for cooperation, and intrusive floodlighting. So I say, bollocks to the media – they're impossible to satisfy, so why waste our time trying? I personally don't intend to go near this Media Centre."

"You're not going to do press conferences and stuff?"

"No."

"That's bonkers," Kamala said bluntly, "if only because they'll crucify you."

"They'll crucify me whatever happens. Anyway, we're moving off the point – the point is, are you with me on this high-tide idea in three days? Actually, I really don't think there's any option... how can we possibly shift seventy-eight whales stranded high up a ridged shingle beach without a high tide?"

"I suppose that's right," Derek said.

"And you see," Roddy continued, "it's not only our job to return the whales to the sea. We have to understand why they left it. In three days we can do a hell of a lot of tests, and a hell of a lot of thinking."

"It makes sense," Kamala conceded.

"Great, so that's what we'll instruct the Committee. In the three-day period we can take thousands of biopsy samples. And I want each whale to have a team of mentors, to stay by each animal and help to keep it calm, like I did with the original animal. But the other big idea I've got, well..."

Something in the tone of his voice signalled that he was going to say something that would surprise them, while the apologetic grimace on his face told them that, whatever it might be, it wasn't pretty.

"I've considered this long and hard – I believe it has to be done."

"Well?" Derek prompted.

"Necropsies."

Kamala Mohandhas gave a little gasp of disbelief.

"You can't be serious!" she blurted, at the same time as Derek asked, "How many, exactly?"

"Six."

"You want to kill six of the whales?" Kamala rapped.

"I want to understand this unprecedented event in which people were killed and dozens of whales have imperilled themselves, so that I can stop it from happening again. So I don't *want* to 'kill' them, no – but do I reluctantly feel that six should be put down, humanely, so that we can conduct necropsies."

"What's the difference?" Kamala cried, appalled. "Have you any idea how depleted whale populations are?"

"Of course I do," Roddy responded testily, "I've dedicated my life to—"

"Well how's it going to look if a seasoned whale-conservation campaigner like you is seen to be killing whales? Imagine how the whaling nations will use that bit of propaganda. They could turn over the IWC's moratorium on hunting with it!"

"I'm not suggesting it isn't an unpleasant option with a lot of downsides, not least for myself, but it's not about how it looks, it's – listen, you're just thinking of this as an ordinary beaching, and I feel you're responding in an ordinary way. It isn't an ordinary beaching, it's extraordinary, it's alarming, one must surely suspect that it's indicative of something grossly wrong out there in the oceans, because it's clearly a deliberate, preconceived action. We simply must have every available clue to come to an understanding of all this, or who's to say it won't happen again?"

"Why should it happen again? It's never happened before!"

"Kamala, it happened yesterday!"

They were facing off now, like boxers with a history of bad feeling. I'm never going to bring her round on this one, Roddy realized, and he found himself regretting that he had appointed her to his team. But he'd needed a vet with expertise in whales, she had been the closest thing to one in the UK, and in the interests of speed he had decided it was best to go for her rather than waste a day or more flying someone across from the States.

"I won't support the killing of whales for research," Kamala announced.

"OK. At least that's clear. Derek?"

His old friend looked between the two of them uneasily.

"There are arguments for and against on both sides," he began. "It's a dilemma, and dilemmas, by their very nature, don't allow for easy answers."

He rocked on his heels, and showed no signs of continuing.

"And?" Roddy prompted.

"On balance, I support your interpretation."

Kamala snorted in derision.

"Great, the old boys' club," she said bitterly. "Well, don't expect me to keep my mouth shut in the committee meeting."

She stormed away.

"Oh dear," Derek said.

"You said it."

Derek turned back to the whales.

"Where's Blackfin?"

"Over there," Roddy answered, pointing. "Come on, I'll show you."

"I'd love to know what he was thinking."

"That's what we have to find out."

Derek gave a little laugh, which he quickly reined in after realizing that Roddy was being serious.

* * *

Rattigan hummed and snorted in the bath, scooping up pawfuls of water and sloshing them over himself. His body, layered in fleshy rolls and yet curiously firm, like that of a Sumo wrestler, glistened in the wetness. When he submerged himself completely, in an sudden surge of high spirits, excess water sloshed over the sides.

His first objective – to confirm that there would be interest in his idea – had already been met. He had several operations in Japan, ranging from a one-man commodity broker to an interest in a traditional fishing fleet to ownership, via the usual complicated channels, of a variety of vessels. The kite he had flown among these contacts, through protective layers of intermediaries, had indicated that interest would be frenzied. This was all the encouragement he needed.

His bath completed, he spent the rest of the morning by the television, listening to the pundits and formulating a strategy. Elements of the scheme were so audacious as to make it seem almost impossible to bring off, he realized – at least, not without heavy-duty pressure, at certain stages, on certain people. The kind of pressure I prefer not to use if I can help it – he thought – for human beings, when subject to intolerable pressure, can do the most unpredictable things.

Ormond appeared on the TV. A commentator revealed that, after the 6 a.m. meeting, the leader of the Whale Crisis Coordination Team was expected to spend much of the day on the beach, where a prefabricated Operations Centre was being set up.

Rattigan winced; that bastard. Unbidden, unconnected, his daughter's words to him – "Daddy, don't try and find me" – played back in his memory, a major wound to grieve over. Then, as though in revenge for this hurt, violent fantasies flickered across the darkness of his thoughts, in which Roddy Ormond was seen beaten up, bloody and humiliated.

* * *

In China a major earthquake had claimed three hundred lives; in Iraq two huge bombs had levelled a mosque and killed scores; and in Hollywood a $10-million-per-movie film star had hanged himself after being caught having sex with a minor. None of these stories could make the first page. The beaching of the whales had become a global obsession within minutes of occurring. Assembled outside The Grand Hotel in Brighton, where the Whale Crisis Coordination Team and the Emergency Response Committee were in session, were more than twelve hundred journalists.

Inside a meeting room of the hotel, Dr Malcolm Gillie, Deputy Chief Scientist with the Defence Scientific Staff at the Ministry of Defence, was listening to the proceedings with great interest in his role as government observer on the Emergency Response Committee. The small bottle of Malvern mineral water in front of him remained untouched. The three-day "delay" in refloating the whales had been questioned by some members, but most, including himself, could see that it was a sensible solution to a difficult problem. Roddy Ormond had outlined some of the procedures that would be undertaken during the three days – mainly the gathering of different kinds of biopsy samples – and Margaret Gilchrist, Chief Executive of the local authority and the chairperson of the Emergency Response Committee, had suggested some ways in which operational support could be provided. But the idea of putting down six whales was more contentious. Gillie noted with interest that Dr Ormond had a rebel within his team.

"Japan and Norway already kill several hundred minkes each year," Kamala Mohandhas was declaiming, passionately. "They're currently trying to get the go-ahead for 'scientific whaling' to be extended to species that have enjoyed protection for twenty or thirty years, such as the sperm whale. This strategy sends absolutely the wrong message to the whaling nations."

"I know it's an unpleasant prospect," Roddy admitted, "but—"

"Unpleasant? It's barbaric!"

"—but what we have to take on board is that this incident is not merely a beaching. The issues are much bigger and more complex. Everything about it, all its exceptional characteristics, suggests that we must conceptualize whales in a new and radical way, we need a different mindset. It's not merely our job to return those whales to the ocean: we need to find out *why they did it*—" he held his hands out, as though making a plea "—if we are to learn anything at all."

"But what's wrong with just taking samples?" someone asked.

Why they did it, Malcolm Gillie repeated in his mind... Because of his position within the Ministry of Defence, there was a vague idea in his head as to the cause of the beaching. It was unlikely, wasn't it? Something of an imaginative leap... He scribbled the idea down, on a whim, and looked at it on the page dispassionately.

"...is that samples only provide a fraction of the data that necropsies give on, say, disease and toxicity," Roddy was arguing. "The data we gather could well save many more whales in the long run and..."

Malcolm Gillie doodled on his note, framing certain words

while listening to Kamala Mohandhas's angry response. Shall I pipe up with it? he wondered. No. Maybe I'll have a quiet word with someone else at the MoD first. The minutes passed. His thoughts kept returning to his idea, so that he only took in half of what was going on.

Margaret Gilchrist, severe-looking in a Margaret Thatcher-style blue suit, was explaining how she would work on a provisional schedule that prioritized the main tasks, and then delegate small working groups of the committee members to implement them. She broke off mid-speech, cocking her head to listen to something. Gillie realized that there was some kind of disturbance going on outside, the sounds swelling into a single block of indeterminate protest. On the other side of the horse-shoe arrangement of desks, Roddy frowned, wondering what was going on. He couldn't know that, somehow, the massed ranks of the world's media had just learnt of his decision not to deal with them, and were venting their indignation and contempt.

* * *

The operations centre was up and running by 9 a.m., and Roddy was installed in it by 9:30, hunched over a small desk in one of the forty compact stalls and clattering away on a laptop. His mobile phone – configured, like everyone else's, to an Overload Control Network that gave precedence over all other users – was ringing every few minutes, and rang again now.

"Roddy Ormond... Hello there... You're joking."

He got up and threaded his way between the stalls, each one occupied by someone on the phone, to stand at the entrance to the Portakabin and look out to sea.

"Unbelievable," he muttered into his mobile.

Many pleasure craft were anchored just off the beach, as close to the whales as they could get, and even as he watched two power boats were noisily approaching the scene.

"There must be fifty of them!" Roddy said.

The person on the other end of the line was the Deputy Chief Constable of Brighton Police. He revealed how a reconnaissance flight by the police helicopter had established that hundreds of yachts, dinghies and power boats were heading for Brighton from every marina and harbour along the south coast.

"What next?" Roddy asked. "Parachutists?"

It was quickly agreed that the pleasure craft had to be removed and prevented from returning. Roddy terminated the call and went back to his desk, shaking his head in frustration that people could be so stupid. Just before he sat down, he peered out of a small window at the massive crowds.

"Unreal."

Earlier Roddy had requested that the whole of the beach between the two piers should be off-limits to spectators, but the police had been unable to comply; there was nowhere else to put so many people. They were in their hundreds of thousands, ranged around the cordon in a colossal, radiating arc of bodies; above the beach the esplanade was similarly packed.

Roddy sat down and got back to work. He was writing guidelines for mentors. There were to be two mentors for each whale, who would work alternate four-hour shifts. The main task of the mentors was to be with the whales and reduce their tension levels, much as Roddy had tried to do with Blackfin. The mentors were mainly students from university marine-biology departments and veterinary colleges, as well as trainee RSPCA officers. Many of them were already arriving and were being assigned to their whales.

Ten seconds after Roddy had sat down his phone rang again.

"Roddy Ormond."

"It's Derek."

"What's up?"

"I need to talk to you... where will you be in five minutes?"

"I'm in the Operations Centre."

As soon as he put the phone down it was ringing with another call; Harry Giles, the County Emergency Planning Officer, had information on how the Women's Institute would be up and running with large-scale catering for the hundreds of volunteer helpers by lunchtime. Roddy was talking to Harry about a different issue, while simultaneously finishing off his guidelines for mentors, when Derek arrived.

Derek looked at his friend with some concern; Roddy was looking grubby – God, he stinks, Derek noticed, and he looks completely exhausted, with his neck sunk into hunched shoulder blades, and sweat drenching his shirt...

"So what's the problem?" Roddy asked just then, coming off the phone.

"It's this media problem."

"We don't have a media problem."

"Well, I've been getting an earful from the Media Liaison chap, and I'm convinced that he's right in what he says."

"Which is?"

"He says the press are already against us because of your refusal to deal with them directly, and that public concern is growing about the whales not being returned to the sea, and that those two things mixed together is like putting a flame to tinder."

"They've been out of the water less than a day! How can anyone get uppity about that?"

"I know that, you know that, but the concern is simply that some of your strategies seem pretty radical at first glance, and if you don't present them properly – I mean, the three-day delay, if we don't get on the case media-wise, we'll get crucified, and as for the necropsies—"

"Look Derek, forgive me, but I thought we'd covered this. And my understanding was that you're presently supposed to be working out a schedule for the collection, analysis and results of seventy-eight blow-hole cultures?"

"Well yes, but when the Media Liaison guy rang I—"

"Look, all I'm thinking about is whales, only whales, nothing else. We've got enough to worry about without trying to satisfy the media or the general public, so please, don't allow yourself to be waylaid like that again. OK?"

Derek raised his eyebrows. Roddy attempted a brisk smile, but was too irritated to do much better than a grimace. I'm absolutely exhausted, he was thinking, I've got an impossible number of things to accomplish in a limited timescale, and I just don't want Derek laying this kind of irrelevant shit on me.

Roddy turned back to his computer, leaving Derek to slope away. The bugger, Derek thought... I'm only trying to help. I know he's worn out, but treating me like that, lecturing me as though I were a school kid...

By mid-morning, Roddy's head was hurting from fatigue. He decided to go outside and spend a few minutes among the whales. He stood next to a thirty-tonne sei whale, as spray from the tugs offshore spattered off the big "A1" – his emergency identity code – on the back of his bright orange council-issue waterproof. He stroked the big guy's skin, and lost himself in abstract speculation. What goes on in the mind of a whale? What went on in Blackfin's mind when he led these animals out of their own habitat? What processes? How can I, a man, understand? He rubbed at his unshaven chin. The whole world is watching me, I can't scratch my nose without a thousand pundits expending a million words to a billion viewers on the significance of the action.

He walked deeper into the whales, where he was hidden from the crowds and the television cameras. Is it really only a night ago that these visitors arrived? Is it only forty-eight hours since Blackfin came here, alone, like some kind of scout from the deep?

His gaze ranged across the bold black-and-white flank of a killer whale nearby; a young man, one of the new mentors, was standing next to the whale's head, stroking it and talking softly.

Everything is in place, Roddy encouraged himself. Mentors are hitting the ground running, institutions and research centres all over Europe have been raided for equipment. This afternoon the whales will be relaxed enough for the science to commence; there are now over fifty specialists in situ to conduct the procedures. Once it's underway, I'll visit Whitaker for half an hour at the hospital, grab two or three hours' rest at the hotel, and then, and then... and the night will come, and I'll put down six whales. How intolerably vile that will be.

"Dr Ormond."

"Huh?" Roddy said, looking round to see the mentor gazing at him anxiously from under the hood of a fluorescent waterproof.

"Dr Ormond, is the rumour true?"

"What rumour?"

"That some of the whales have to be killed?"

He was young, maybe nineteen or twenty. His tone of voice was curiously pitched between accusation and sympathy. Roddy took in the fresh face, still barely capable of sprouting bristles worth shaving off of a morning, and tried to think of a way to explain it.

"No one's putting my whale down," the boy said grimly.

Then Roddy's phone rang.

"Excuse me," he said, glad to have an excuse to avoid replying.

10

Theresa felt so oppressed, so wretched, that it had been difficult to get out of bed. The smallest activity – taking her tablets, washing the wound on her cheek – involved such an exertion of effort over will that within half an hour of rising she felt mentally exhausted. This is what it's like, she now understood, when the last drop of hope is squeezed out of your life, and all you have left is your body and your misery.

She sat in front of the dressing table and examined her face. He had used the back of his hand. The bruise, livid as meat, stretched up the right cheek and surrounded her eye, which was partially closed. On the point of the cheekbone was a small, deep cut. His wedding ring had done that.

There was no sanctuary for the pitiable fragments of her self-esteem: he's demolished me. I want Ally, she moaned in her mind, I need her, how can I survive this without her?

For a few seconds she found herself thinking of paracetamol and alcohol, of leaving her blighted existence behind like a dirty old coat, and putting on a new world of nothingness, forever. But this grim escapist fantasy was superseded by something better: I don't have to endure this, she realized: Ally's abandoned us anyway, he can't use her as a threat against me, there's nothing to hold me here but his tyranny. I can just *go*.

The only thing that can stop me this time is me.

It was mid-morning when she tried to sneak out of the house. She knew how ludicrous she looked under the scarf tied peasant-style, the dark glasses. She tiptoed down the stairs with not a single item of luggage, just her handbag containing money, credit cards, car keys. At the bottom of the staircase she could hear him on the phone, not the words but the tone beneath them, which sounded curiously amiable.

There was just the cool marble of the great hall to cross. She padded across like a cat burglar in a bank, intent on reaching the front door without setting off any alarms. Her fingers closed around the handle. Rattigan's voice was still rumbling, rumbling in the hinterland of her concentration, then came out into the open with the word "Ormond". She hesitated, suspended between the future and the past; she released the door handle and moved across the hall.

"Not even near," he was saying, "...No, not three hundred, think again... No... Don't forget we're talking about a speciality, effectively off the market for a long period..." Something made him cackle with delight. "...No no... All right, a single stake costs eight hundred dollars... Yes... Eight hundred dollars!"

Theresa didn't take much in. Her mind was focused on the word Ormond. She drifted further away from any comprehension of his speech, listening for the word, longing for escape. Then "Ormond", once, twice, and her mind attached itself to the present.

"Well put it this way, the consequences will destroy him, they represent his worst nightmare..."

Theresa moved away from the doorway, walking backwards. A sense of numbness enveloped her as she retraced her steps up the stairs. She passed through her bedroom to the bathroom, where she locked the door and sat down on the toilet. The wound on her face throbbed. I've got to stay and find out what's going on, she thought. God knows how I'll do it, he never lets me get near his work, but I won't let him destroy Roddy.

I won't let him do it, she vowed, because I did it myself, years ago.

* * *

"Hey," Whitaker said in a feeble voice.

"How are you?"

121

In the hospital room, Roddy tried to make the question sound ordinary, but it was difficult not to cry with relief.

"I feel tired. Bits of me hurt, other bits I can't feel. And such a sore head, God, you can't imagine."

Roddy blinked back some tears. His friend was flat out on his back, one of his legs suspended in some kind of sci-fi metal structure, all pins and screws.

"You thought it was all over for me?" Whitaker asked.

"When I came here yesterday, I was told they were sticking pins into your heels but getting no response from you. I'm just – so glad you're OK."

"I was out because of the pebble. I remember it hitting me on the head, then nothing. Probably a good thing, given that a whale came along and broke my leg with its fin. God. Can you believe it? Can you truly, really believe what happened on that beach?"

Roddy smiled grimly. His face looked like someone had wrung out the energy from him.

"You look like shit, Roddy."

"I know."

"You're getting a lot of flak," Whitaker said, gesturing to the TV at the end of the bed.

"So I'm told. It'll get a lot worse. I'm doing necropsies. Six whales."

"People won't like that."

"People are a problem, but not the one I'm worried about."

"So what is it?"

"Whitaker, I'm sorry, you're in no condition to—"

"It's OK."

Roddy sighed.

"Look, I can put the whales back in the sea, I've got it all worked out, the process, but… it's not enough. It's not enough. No one's interested, not even Derek or the other whale people, but surely it's imperative to work out *why they did it*, or how do we know they won't do it again?"

"Why do you think they did it?" A wave of weariness had just swamped Whitaker, and he was struggling to conceal it.

"I'm thinking, maybe, environmental degradation."

"I don't get it."

"Remember those two whales that washed up dead on the Belgian coast a while back? They had so much crap in their systems that the authorities there had to classify them as toxic waste."

Whitaker issued a croaky sigh and closed his eyes. Roddy didn't seem to notice.

"What if," he said, "what if the whales have just had enough? All the organochlorins, all the toxins, the reduction of phytoplankton because of ozone depletion, the polychlorinated biphenyls, the overfishing of their prey, the oil installations, the dumping, the low-level nuclear waste, the obliteration of their sound frequencies by shipping, the billions of human turds pumped straight into the sea every fucking day – I mean, what if life is just becoming insupportable and they're trying to let us know?"

It was a struggle for Whitaker to open his eyes again. He did it eyelid by eyelid.

"You're assuming," he whispered, "that they can reason and communicate like us."

"Not like us," Roddy answered, neurotically hunched over in his chair with his hands clutched together in front of him. "That's what we've always wanted, the homocentric fantasy – but yes, what if they can reason and communicate and plan and execute intentions?"

Whitaker made a final exertion. His voice was thin and shaky.

"If they can do all that, why haven't they beached like this before? In the Sixties, when seventy thousand whales were slaughtered in a single year? Or in the nineteenth century, when the blue whale was reduced to one per cent of one per cent of its population?"

"I don't know. I don't know."

"I'm feeling… not good now, Roddy."

"I'm sorry. I'll go now."

"Roddy – Roddy, trust me, don't do necropsies, you'll get – lynched."

Whitaker was asleep instantly.

The hospital room seemed neat and orderly. The walls were blue, the sheets were white, the apparatus high-tech and impressive. His friend was getting better. Self-pity swamped him. He felt tired beyond endurance, and wished that he could find his own hospital room to sleep in. But sleep wasn't far away. He just had to return to the beach to check on the progress of the stat-taking, the medical tests, the preparations for the night's ordeal; then he could go to his hotel for a few hours' rest.

* * *

He didn't know where he was and a phone was ringing. Heart pounding, he picked up the receiver and put it to his ear the wrong way up.

"Hnnuuh."

A faint voice said into his mouth, "Your wake up call Dr Ormond, it's five fifty-five p.m."

Having been wrenched from an ocean-deep sleep, he felt worse than before. He fumbled for the bedside light, and discovered that he was in a hotel room. The Grand, he remembered.

After leaving the hospital and going to the beach, he had been unable to get away until three-thirty in the afternoon because of a mini-protest by some of the vets who had been brought in. They had objected to the notching of the whales, and it had taken Roddy and Derek a good forty minutes to deal with their concerns. This meant that he hadn't collapsed into bed until four o'clock. He had been sleeping for less than two hours.

He swung his legs out of the bed and sat with his head in his hands. His nose wrinkled up involuntarily. An extraordinary smell emanated from his armpits, and it wasn't good. I need a shower, he thought, a shave, then I'll be ready for what lies ahead. But on the way to the bathroom he switched on the TV.

The self-confident face of Kate Gunning filled the screen. Turn it off, he told himself, *turn it off* – but it was impossible not to look at her and think about Theresa; the shape of the eyes, the facial mannerisms. Twenty years, he marvelled, and I can still remember the most minute ways in which she moved.

"So the usual pattern indicated by your research is what?" the newscaster was asking Kate Gunning.

"I have established from other experts that the usual pattern is for a single sick animal to beach by itself. It emits distress calls, and it's these distress calls which bring in other whales, members of its immediate family pod. The new whales get beached, they emit distress calls too, and before you know it an entire herd can be stranded."

"But are you saying," asked her interviewer, "that this typical beaching pattern, as you termed it earlier, bears any relation at all to what happened on Brighton beach yesterday? Because on the face of it there would seem to be little similarity."

Roddy, watching, nodded emphatically: no similarity *whatsoever*.

"Well perhaps the crucial similarity," Kate Gunning said, holding up a hand in emphasis, "is that initially there was a *single animal*, a single animal beached itself first. You see, the research I have undertaken during the course of today shows that the best method of dealing with a single beached whale when other whales are close by is to dispatch it humanely."

"Kill it, you mean?"

"Yes."

"Why?"

"One, it's probably dying anyway, that's why it's beached itself or why it's been washed ashore, but two, and most importantly, if it's dead then it can't emit distress signals, in which case its herd isn't drawn in."

"Kate, let's be clear about this – this is very serious, because the implications of what you are saying would appear to cast a lot of doubt on the actions of the Emergency Coordinator, Dr Roddy Ormond."

"Indeed Peter – and the question now is whether Dr Ormond made a very grave error in not killing the original sperm whale that beached itself two days ago. If he had followed the usual procedure, then it's possible that the subsequent mass beaching would not have occurred, and the three people who died today in such tragic circumstances would still be alive."

"Well, Kate, Kate Gunning, thank you. A startling suggestion there from the journalist Kate Gunning, and here to consider it is—"

Aghast, Roddy sat back down on the bed. No, *no*, that's *disgraceful* – the crudeness, the banality, the pathetic wrong-headedness of the allegation… This is a beaching so unparalleled – aggressive, purposive, multi-species – that it's a *joke* to apply the sick-whale paradigm to it. How do broadcasters have the right to broadcast such *crap*? When she says she's been researching the subject for a day, a single day, doesn't that ring alarm bells with anyone? It beggars belief…

He leapt to his feet and stomped across his room a couple of times, swearing. He ended up near the window, pressing his forehead hard against the window frame. From here he could see the whole scene: the sea, the beach, the whales, the crowds, the press. Along the esplanade were television-production lorries parked bumper to bumper, one after the other, each sprouting florets of satellite dishes. What a circus, Roddy brooded: a few days ago I was looking down a microscope at a saliva sample from a pantropical spotted dolphin; my biggest worry was justifying escalating domestic postal expenses to the Board of the Marine Mammals Institute; now I'm not only in charge of an incident in which people have been killed and nature upended, but it seems I'm *to blame* for it too. Christ, I've got no one to talk to, no one to confide in... His CV of ex-partners scrolled down his thoughts, as it often did when he was unhappy. You dumb sod, he accused himself, why couldn't you have just made a go of it with one of them? Like a normal person?

He clenched his eyes tight shut, until they hurt. Momentarily the responsibilities he had taken on just seemed too much, he wanted to throw the towel in. All right, he would say, I resign – put that renowned authority Kate Gunning in charge, let her announce that there will be no three-day "delay", no scientific investigation, no notching, no collection and collation of data, no necropsies, no interest at all in why it happened; let her put the whales in the sea now, let her tow them down the shingle with tugs, with cranes, with Chinook helicopters; then let her explain why seventy-eight traumatized whales are dying in the water. And finally, he thought to himself, going into the bathroom and slamming the door on the television and its imbecile pundits, let her account for herself should a second mass beaching occur.

* * *

The Bentley glided through the hinterland of King's Cross, its glinting paintwork and chrome incongruous against such drab environs. To Rattigan, the appeal of the area was linked to his own interior landscape, which in itself was only half understood. It was something to do with the mouldering

Victorian warehouses and the bleak expanses of wasteland that
still outlived the regeneration going on, it was the gas tanks
and the lorries and the little people who worked there, dossed
there, died there. I'm like a dog returning to its own vomit, he
found himself thinking; half the boys from my children's home
ended up in low streets like these, as criminals or beggars or
addicts, or all three, or dead.

As the Bentley, with arrogant languor, slowly passed a group
of staring workmen, Rattigan had a mobile pressed to his ear.

"But this is disappointing... I see... I was hoping there'd be
something vile in his life... there is in everyone else's... Wait. I'll
be a minute, don't hang up."

He had spotted a prostitute outside. She couldn't have been
more than fifteen years old, and so desperate for a fix that she
was exposing her breasts to him in broad daylight. He had
the car stopped. His breathing quickened. For fully twenty
seconds he looked at her through the one-way glass. Then the
window glided down. The multi-millionaire scrutinized the
child prostitute and thought: she's got the face of a victim, of
a mental patient, of an angel. Horrible visions from the past
forced their way through the self-imposed filters he had set up:
he was about thirteen years old, and having sex with a girl of
similar age, some serially abused sex-slave of the state care
system, while his care worker watched, egged them on... The
filmy sheen of sweat that habitually coated Rattigan's brow was
forming into beads. He blinked rapidly.

"Want some business?" said the young girl.

He didn't answer. His eyes roved up and down her.

"Got a fix?" she tried.

"Were you in care?" he asked.

No answer. He took his wallet out and extracted a twenty-
pound note. She took the money gingerly from his outstretched
hand. The light in her eyes died another death as she made to

open the door of the car. Rattigan prevented her from opening it. Now from his wallet he took a card: Dewdrop House, Independent Care for Vulnerable Children.

"Use that money for a black cab and go to this place," Rattigan said, "run away from your pimp, now, don't spend it on crack, go to that place, now. *Now!* They'll look after you, they'll sort you out, no one will abuse you or let you down or exploit you. Tell them your age, tell them you're an addict, tell them you're a prostitute. Get some help or you'll be dead in a year." The car was moving on. "Don't mess it up," he pleaded, sticking his head through the window and looking back at her scantily clad form and her dull, uncomprehending eyes.

With a low moan he slumped back in his seat, then wiped his face with a handkerchief and picked up the mobile, thinking, horrible, banish it, get rid it of it, gone.

"I'm back... Mm... as dirt goes it isn't very dirty, but if that's all there is... I want it leaked, carefully... use that journalist... Kate Gunning... she seems to have it in for our friend..."

He looked at his watch; the leak might make the late television news.

"The other issue is more fundamental... Persuading this character Derek Petersen to come on board... I don't like using that kind of pressure, I'm not the Mafia... Oh, our man, I know he's persuasive, but academics are strange people, it may prove problematic... I doubt money will work, but make sure he's offered plenty, and if that doesn't do it... and the photos have been taken?... Excellent... Christ no, I don't want to see them."

With the phone call completed, he immediately switched the television on; news about the beaching was moving fast, and he wanted to keep up with it.

"A sense of disgust is the prevailing mood," a reporter on the beach was reporting back to his studio. "Much of the enormous crowd here was booing and jeering as the so-called 'notching' of the whales took place, and there were isolated incidents of people trying to breach the cordon."

"James, the argument for the notching is presumably that it will aid scientists in future incidents. Why do you think people are reacting so strongly to what is said to be, in the final analysis, a fairly harmless scientific procedure?"

"Harmless is not how they see it, Richard, and I have to say that scientific procedures aren't cutting much ice on the beach. Scientists taking hacksaws to whales is not what the crowd wants to see."

"Well, I think we know what they want to see."

"Yes indeed, and that's the immediate return of the whales to the ocean."

"But we understand this isn't possible until the spring tide in two days' time."

"If that really is the case, then the next forty-eight hours are going to be extremely testing for the police, for the local authority here in Brighton, and of course for the man at the centre of all this, Dr Roddy Ormond."

"And presumably the task of maintaining order isn't helped by Dr Ormond's stance over the media, which has been described as eccentric at best?"

"Well exactly. The official line is that the Media Centre is providing sufficient information, but their bulletins are fairly anodyne, and the centre isn't denying the fact that Dr Ormond himself has had no direct contact with them. This has led to a vacuum of reliable, up-to-the-minute information, which is contributing to the impression of a problem turning into a crisis. Rumours of conflict between the whale experts are rife: we already know that even some of the vets who performed the notchings staged a mini-rebellion over it beforehand, and then there are the damaging allegations of incompetence made earlier today by a journalist called Kate Gunning, which swept through the huge crowds here like a bush fire. While all this is going on, it's understood that Dr Ormond has spent most of the afternoon asleep in his hotel room."

Rattigan switched the television off and examined his fingernails, marvelling that Ormond had lost control of the situation already; rather reminiscent, Rattigan realized, of events twenty years earlier, when I separated Theresa from him without his even knowing about it until it was done. A smile, of sorts, arrived slowly on Rattigan's face; this feels good, to see the whole plan coming together with such – he took his time to find the right description – with such remorseless elegance. And he knew that, given a little luck, Gunning would hit the news that night with an interesting little exposé. Very soon indeed, the farce of Ormond's leadership would turn into ruinous disgrace.

* * *

Feeling much better after a shower, Roddy emerged from his hotel room at half-past six in the evening. Four police officers were waiting for him outside.

"Hullo," he said, puzzled.

"I'm Detective Sergeant Gray, sir."

"Yes?"

"These are Detective Constables Morrow, Watkins, Carter and Flower."

"Yes?"

"We're your PPU, sir."

"My what?"

"Personal Protection Unit."

Roddy shook his head in disbelief.

"We'll be accompanying you at all times until 6 a.m., when we will be relieved by a second unit."

"I don't need police protection!"

"I'm sorry sir, but I'm afraid you're wrong. Death threats have been received by the Media Centre and by several newspapers. They're probably from cranks, but given the strong feelings you seem to be generating at the moment, we have to take them seriously."

A cold feeling came over him as he digested the information. *Death threats?* This is starting to get completely out of hand. He turned away furiously, striding down the corridor.

Five police officers rushed after him.

11

It was at night when the beach was at its most eerie. The moon, almost full and set in cloudless dark, bounced light on the rolling curves of the sea, on the whales. The stars were pinpricks in the black fabric of the galaxy, through which could be glimpsed the infinite light beyond. Such beauty; and so utterly unlike what was about to happen.

Workmen came tramping down the shingle, carrying large screens. Roddy and Derek watched as the men began to erect the screens around selected whales. The crowd didn't like it; odd, swelling rumbles of disquiet pulsed through the massed people. In the press pens, journalists made mystified reports to camera.

"How do you feel?" Derek asked.

"Awful."

"Do you really want to do this?"

"Of course I don't want to do it," Roddy snapped.

"I see." I can't seem to do anything right at the moment, Derek thought.

"Look, Derek, I'm sorry, I'm tired, but..." Can't he see what

I'm going through, he asked himself, acutely irritated; I've been delivered here under armed guard, I have to put down some whales, and he asks me if I "want" to do it. "Look, I'm sorry, the pressure's getting to me. I don't want to do it, of course I don't – I'd rather do it to myself – but that's not the point. It's a skilled task, it's got to be done, and I'm the only one who's done it before."

"I know."

Roddy thought about his experience of putting down whales. There was the sick Bryde's whale two years ago, in Sri Lanka – turned out she'd had three kilos of worm infestation in her inner ear, must have been in agony – and then the fin whale that was basically dying of old age; that one must have been at least ten years ago. Both experiences had been horrible.

Dazzling light appeared from the top of one of the newly erected structures. Roddy went inside, blinking before the powerful flood lamps, and took in the defenceless minke stranded there: poor bloody minke, looks cruelly exposed in this lighting. What a beautiful creature. Look at the white of her underside that sweeps up her flanks and graduates to a dark grey; and at her throat grooves, so abstract, so beautiful, starting under the mouth like that and stretching under her for a full three metres, all the way to her slender flippers. Her black flippers…

It was Derek who, earlier in the day, had observed that, of the twenty-nine beached minkes, five didn't have white bands on their flippers. White bands signified that a minke was from the North Atlantic; their absence meant that it belonged to a southern hemisphere population. It was mind-blowing to think that whales from both populations had travelled from opposite ends of the planet, implying cooperation across vast distances. On the back of this fact, it made perfect sense to Roddy to increase the number of necropsies from six to seven, so that two specimens of the same species but of confirmed different geographical habitats could be examined. He remembered with regret his spectacular lack of diplomacy earlier, when trying to convince Kamala Mohandhas of the need to put down this extra whale; "This is a fantastic opportunity," he had managed to say. Kamala's hostility had set like cement: "It might be a fantastic opportunity to you. To me it's an obscenity." You bloody idiot, Roddy thought, of himself. Then he patted the flank of the animal he was going to kill, its hard, hot bulk: I don't, I *don't* want to do this.

He span round; six men wearing white rubber overalls and white wellingtons were pushing into the enclosure. Roddy nodded to them. The butchers; what a job… Taking this whale to pieces will be like demolishing a building filled with blood. Not that this lot will lose any sleep over it – pretty ironic that we have to import Norwegian whalers.

Kamala Mohandhas came in with Derek, her face hard under the unforgiving floodlights. She looked at the Norwegians as though they were convicted muggers. Roddy attempted to give her a sombre smile.

"You're really going to go through with it?"

"I am."

She shook her head in sorrow, or disgust. One of the Norwegians had unwrapped a long bundle of tarpaulin and extracted a six-foot-long lance. "Jesus," Kamala whispered as the instrument was passed to Roddy, who took it awkwardly. When he closed his fingers around it, he truly remembered the nastiness of his task. The metal felt so cold.

Kamala walked out. A chant was starting up from the promenade: "Leave the whales alone, leave the whales alone!" The crowds had been in a tense mood all evening. Very quickly they were bawling at the tops of their voices. Roddy waited for it to subside, but it didn't. The night before, he would have been angry; the racket they were making would make the whales anxious. Now his primary emotion was… what? Fear, he realized, uneasily. He looked to Derek for support.

"I'm doing the right thing, aren't I?"

"Roddy..." Derek struggled to find the words. "I don't know. I don't know if it's right or not any more. It has to be your decision."

Great, he thought. He looked at his watch. 10 p.m. If I'm going to do it, it's time to get on with it. He crouched down on one knee, about a metre in front of the massive, helpless animal. OK. Thank God her eyes are on the sides of her head; couldn't do this if she were looking at me. He manoeuvred the tip of the lance under the whale's throat. Close-up, the throat grooves had a pinkish tinge to them. I didn't know that, he thought, and he chose his spot. The lance rested against the whale's skin lightly. This was a skilled task. If he were to be out by much more than an inch, he would succeed only in causing acute suffering to the creature; but if he got it right, pain would be minimal, and death would follow in minutes.

He paused. How could he not? Derek watched, fascinated. "Leave the whales alone, leave the whales alone!" The chant was relentless, it held Roddy back, he couldn't blank it from his mind. He thought, everyone hates me, and then, I'd better do this now, now, for Christ's sake do it now. But the tip of the lance, as lethal as a shard of glass, didn't move. The slaughter men waited impassively. He thought, what if I'm wrong? But before the doubt was complete, he had done it, thrust the lance in with controlled strength and delicacy, through the skin and blubber and muscle, deep into the jugular. For a fraction of a second, long enough to think, *huh?*, nothing happened; then the blood spurted from the puncture with such force that he scrambled backwards to avoid its jet. Standing now, he looked down at red, red everywhere, and *Jesus*, Roddy's mind repeated over and over, *Jesus...*

How could the crowd have sensed the critical moment? They did. As Roddy watched the dance of the blood bubbling from the minke's jugular, the chants gave way to jeers.

The Norwegians took over. Each man held an instrument of butchery. One of them walked down the entire length of the dead animal, opening her up from flipper to tail; near-white blubber sagged down over the lip of the incision, oozing scarlet. Sickened, Roddy stumbled out. As soon as he emerged, the crowd went almost berserk, screaming abuse. He looked in the direction of the noise, frightened, and hurried to the next set of screens.

It didn't get any easier after the second whale had been killed, or the third. He ceased to feel human. Blood soaked his trousers from the knees down, stained his shirt, his neck. He walked towards the next one mechanically, not even remembering what species of whale lay behind it. There was a rhythm now: nod to the team, kneel down, choose the spot, brace the lance, plunge...

"Roddy. Roddy!"

"Hmm?"

"Kate Gunning's been on the news," Derek said, crashing through the shingle, his sea captain's face flushed red with exertion and anxiety, "somehow she's got hold of that business from years back about you faking research on whale populations."

Roddy stopped and stared incredulously.

"What?"

"It's all over the news, it's absolutely absurd, they're presenting it like some kind of scandal, like you're a fraud."

"Oh, fuck it! Fuck it! Fuck everyone!" He went half mad briefly, capable of nothing but expressing his frustration. "I'm just trying to do a job!"

"They're calling for you to go, and there's something else, I'm sorry: Kamala Mohandhas has resigned. She says she's going to issue a statement explaining why she can't support you."

Derek observed the shock on his friend's expression. That's

right Roddy, he thought, Kamala's bailed out, very, very publicly, and if you don't start getting a grip on the media, you'll be removed from your position, and then what will you have achieved? Why won't you see sense?

"Roddy, listen to me," he said, trying one last time, "you have to wise up, you have to deal with the press, do it on their terms, do you see? How else can they understand your side of the story? You have to explain *everything*, and you *can* explain everything: why we're waiting for the high tide, your reasons for the necropsies, the circumstances of the faked research. I'm begging you, it's your last chance."

What's wrong with everyone? Roddy raged internally. *My* last chance? What does *my* last chance matter, what does the media matter? The whales matter, only the whales. Why am I the only person who can see that? He was so angry, it was as much as he could do to stop himself from yelling at Derek. Instead, he uttered a curt rebuttal.

"I won't waste one minute justifying myself to them."

Derek shook his head and turned away, making some inadequate gesture with his hand that could have meant "I give up". He walked up the beach, leaving Roddy behind, alone, and still with four whales to get through.

* * *

3 a.m. The seven animals had been dispatched. Two of them were already butchered and in the freezer lorries parked along the esplanade, one for each animal. It had proved impossible to protect the crowds from the goriness. Men in blood-smeared overalls were working in groups to heave huge chunks of plastic-sheeted carcass onto trailers.

Roddy left the beach at 3:30 a.m. His mind was like jelly. The cumulative exhaustion, the horror of putting the whales down, and the hostility of the crowds had all taken their toll. He stopped off at the operations centre to ring Derek, desperate to apologize. The phone rang and rang, but Derek didn't respond. Wearily he delivered himself to his Personal Protection Unit for the difficult manoeuvre of negotiating a way through the angry crowds. The five police officers packed around him tightly to form a human shield. As they neared the protesters, the deafening, hate-filled chant that had been in Roddy's head for so long became even louder: "ORDMOND OUT, ORDMOND OUT!" Ahead, scores of policemen were trying to make a passage through the bodies. People pushed and screamed, press photographers called out angrily, and the television cameras bore witness to the chaos.

Detective Sergeant Gray took a firm grip of the collar on Roddy's waterproof.

"Walk quickly, don't look up, don't respond to provocation," he shouted.

Then Roddy was being manhandled through.

"Ormond you fucker!"

"You fucking murderer!"

"You piece of shit!"

The lines of police struggled to hold the protesters back. Something wet hit Roddy's face.

"Spit on the bastard!"

It rained down, on him and the police officers around him. It stank. He tried to wipe his face on his sleeve, but his arms were being held by policemen hustling him through.

An area directly in front of The Grand had been sectioned off much earlier. They burst through into its open space. The shouting and abuse were vicious, and Roddy, walking unsteadily to the hotel while the flash bulbs went off and the obscenities were called, looked around, bewildered: so many faces, so much hatred and fury. And all for him.

12

The Secretary of State for Defence got up at her usual time of 4:30 a.m. She fed the cat and set the table for a six-thirty breakfast with her husband, putting out the bread, jam, fruit, cereal, and preparing the coffee percolator. Then she disappeared into her study.

5 a.m. to 6.30 was her private time. For an hour and a half each day, she could be one hundred per cent sure – well, eight-five per cent sure – of peace and quiet and the opportunity to think things through. She sat down at her desk, arranging her hefty haunches across the long-suffering seat of the chair, and started to leaf through the newspapers: whale crisis, whale crisis, more on the whale crisis, and then the whale crisis, she noted. This Ormond fellow is being vilified on virtually every page – how thoroughly unfortunate; at any other time I could have expected to see myself on the front pages, not buried in the middle:

ADLINGTON PUSHES FOR FURTHER RUSSIAN CW REDUCTIONS

The Secretary of State for Defence, Victoria Adlington, has brokered further three-way deals between Russia, the US and the EU in the disposal of chemical weapons from the former Soviet Union.

In a meeting of European Defence Ministers in Strasbourg, and in private sessions later with the Russian Deputy-Premier B.V. Kucherov and the US Secretary of State for Foreign Affairs Don Ferny, it was agreed in principle that the United States would put in an extra three US dollars for every two extra dollars contributed by the EU, up to a maximum of US $100 million.

Mrs Adlington hopes that EU Finance Ministers will allocate a further US $66 million, an amount which would capitalize on the American offer.

The money being pumped into the dismantling of the former Soviet Union's chemical defence programme is substantial. The Russians themselves pledged three billion roubles in 1999, although how much of that sum has so far been spent where it was committed is disputed. The new agreement, should it go ahead, takes the United States' commitment over ten years to beyond the US $500 million mark. Europe has so far put in US $338 million, of which the UK's share is equivalent to £70 million.

The sums are so huge because of the astronomical expense of rendering safe such complex and deadly compounds as sarin, soman and the so-called V-agents, in particular the nerve agent VX. The only internationally monitored CW disposal facility capable of doing the job is on the St Johnston Atoll in the South Pacific.

Mrs Adlington has been a consistent advocate of assisting Russia to dispose of its dubious CW legacy. She cites the volatile politics of the country and the sophistication of international terrorism as reasons why the issue is more pressing than ever.

Upon announcing the new plan to the House of Commons yesterday, Mrs Adlington defended it from accusations that taxpayers' money could be better spent. "We can't afford not to take this opportunity of making the world a safer place," she argued.

Adlington nodded with a certain degree of satisfaction. *The Times* had got it just right, for a change, and her instrumental role had been properly emphasized.

She checked out the other newspapers before turning her attention, reluctantly, to six boxes stacked up on the desk. They contained classified files about SONAZ, the Special Operations No Access Zone in the North Atlantic, ranging back over forty years. On the topmost box was a printed-out email, the latest irritant to this festering sore:

Colin,

This is private. As you know, I'm the government observer on the Emergency Response Committee for this whale problem. An off-the-wall thought I want to run by you, informally and confidentially: given that both the MoD and DEFRA have received puzzling reports of whales engaging in abnormal behaviours in or around SONAZ (barging into trawlers, etc.), and given that the mass beaching at Brighton is clearly an abnormal behaviour, could the two be linked?

Obviously I have no particular insight into SONAZ, and certainly none into whales, so this is pure speculation.

Don't hold back from telling me I'm entering the realms of science fiction. But if you're not immediately reduced to tears of laughter, any ideas on what I should do with the notion? All contributions gratefully received. SONAZ seems to be a pretty sensitive subject, so I hesitate to raise the idea to the committee without clearance from Hattie.

Yours, Malcolm

"Hattie" tapped her teeth with her thumbnail. How strange to be publicly lauded for reducing the Russian chemical-weapons threat one moment, while having to step over this home-grown banana skin – not entirely unconnected to the issue of chemical weapons – the next. But politics was characterized by such awkward oppositions.

Her Second Permanent Secretary had annotated the email with the identities of the sender and the recipient: Malcolm, the author of the note, was Malcolm Gillie; Colin, the recipient, was Colin Nye; and both were Deputy Chief Scientists with the

Defence Scientific Staff. Next to the nickname "Hattie", the civil servant had written: *Sorry about this, Minister*.

But a link between whales at Brighton and whales around SONAZ, Adlington pondered – is that possible? Surely not. And yet, let's just suppose for a moment that there were a link – the consequence would be media interest in that beastly patch of ocean. Which would be highly unwelcome.

When she had first come to office, she hadn't understood the unique problems posed by SONAZ; she had been minded to abandon Britain's exclusive rights over the area. It was well known that the nuclear testing conducted there in the Fifties had been on a small scale, and an investigation in 1961 had established that the limited radioactivity it produced had dispersed within three years. The very concept of maintaining, in the face of the protests of other nations, an exclusive "special operations" zone, decades after the special operations had ceased, seemed too old-fashioned and ludicrous for words. But on becoming Defence Secretary, Adlington had discovered that SONAZ was not quite so simple.

She flicked through the top inch of papers from the topmost box of files; this wedge of documents represented her own contribution to the problem, which she knew didn't differ substantially from that of every other Defence Secretary since 1966. Indeed, as one of them had written in the late Eighties – a laconic scrawl in the margin of a Permanent Secretary's memorandum – *I'm damned if we should offer our arses up for a whipping just because an administration from thirty years ago was smoking behind the bicycle shed.* She tended to agree. SONAZ was a scandal, but it was a scandal of someone else's making. The horse had bolted, and other such clichés. Administrations generated enough disasters of their own without actively hunting for more.

She extracted a blank index card from her desk tidy and

wrote: "Malcolm Gillie to submit confidential memo to Hawksley, deadline two weeks, expanding on his ideas of a link". Two weeks seemed just about right. Gillie would think that he had been given something to do; at the end of that time, there would be no Emergency Response Committee to which he could reveal the notion; and asking him to submit the memo to Hawksley, one of her junior ministers, rather than herself, would prevent him from forming an impression that the issue was important.

She paper-clipped the index card to the note. And what about these necropsies, she wondered. Her colleague Clive Manners, Secretary of State for the Environment, was the member of the Cabinet to whom Gillie was reporting. Manners had explained in Cabinet the kind of information these animal autopsies provide. Well, Adlington mused, perhaps MoD-linked laboratory facilities might be best placed to undertake this work; just for that extra control. It might be worth phoning Manners this morning, just to explain the advantages of such a move.

* * *

Rattigan felt vaguely disconcerted. He could barely remember the last time Theresa had voluntarily sat down to breakfast with him, but here she was, sipping orange juice. He took another furtive glance at the bruise on the side of her face, and asked himself, why is she here? Trying to make me feel guilty? Trying to improve things between us? It doesn't make any sense.

"Why have you got so many newspapers today?" she asked, her voice so quiet that he strained to hear it.

"Well er…" He hesitated; the answer was obvious. Public loathing of Roddy Ormond had found full expression in the press, and this was something he could enjoy on a very simple level. Ordinarily he wouldn't have felt much compunction in telling her so. But today, with that livid bruise reproaching him, he wasn't in the mood for gloating. "Extraordinary stories coming from that beach."

He managed to give a little grimace, intended to be a minute smile of conciliation. If she noticed it, she didn't register it.

"How are you going to destroy Roddy?" That's what she wanted to say, but didn't dare. She had no illusions about her mental strength. It was fragmentary, battered, and she couldn't risk provoking confrontation. Just to be in the same room as him, in the hope of gleaning some information, was about as much as she could manage.

After scrutinizing her with some puzzlement, he turned back to the newspapers. The coverage of Roddy Ormond, whether tabloid or broadsheet, was unfettered in its ferocity. Among the more striking of the front pages was the *Daily Mail*'s. The paper had managed to secure an image of Roddy plunging the lance into one of the whales. The photograph had been taken through a gap in the screening, from a boat out at sea. Though blurry, there was no mistaking the elemental ugliness of the act. MURDERER! shrieked the headline.

He flicked through other papers. They were similarly hysterical. A headline WHALES OF ANGUISH accompanied an image of slabs of carcass waiting to be loaded into a refrigerated lorry. DODGY DOCTOR ORMOND AND THE MYSTERY OF THE MINKES was how *The Independent* led on the revelation that the Emergency Coordinator of the Whale Crisis Coordination Team was guilty of faking research results. "How has the government contrived to appoint a man who was known to be an unstable maverick and an irresponsible cheat?" Rattigan read.

Theresa looked at the headlines of the papers spread all over the kitchen table: BLOOD AND GORE; IS THIS MAN SANE?; KEY COMMITTEE MEMBER RESIGNS IN DISGUST; ORMOND MUST GO...

How has Tony done this, she agonized, not knowing that her husband had barely started. How can I find out? Heart thumping in distress, she grabbed one of the papers to hide behind. It was *The Sun*. The front page was almost entirely given over to a crystal-clear image of Roddy in the most abject, pathetic circumstances. It showed him standing outside The Grand Hotel after the police had hustled him through a mob. Blood, spit and egg covered his face, his neck, and hung, for ever, in a sticky trail from his chin. In the background, foreshortened by the long lens, was a collage of fists, placards, angry faces. In the foreground Roddy's eyes, wide and fearful and looking to the extreme left, resembled a wild animal's at the moment of capture. FAKE RESEARCH, FAKE EXPERT, FACE OFF! *The Sun* pronounced.

She didn't look up from the article. She sensed the curiosity and unease of her husband, and that his deep eyes were boring into the newspaper, as though trying to see through it, and through her, into her purpose beyond.

* * *

Derek Petersen was sitting on his bed in his hotel room. He had been sitting there for some four hours, gazing at nothing in particular from a line of vision obscured by blood and tears. He was fifty-six years old, and the only issue which had made him cry in the previous thirty years had been his daughter's accident with the pan of hot soup.

In the night, arriving back at his hotel, he had become aware of a man walking closely behind him in the corridor. Still reliving in his mind the awkward incident with Roddy, he hadn't given it much thought. But when he went into his room and made to shut the door—

"Dr Petersen."

145

"Yes?" he answered, startled to see the man standing in the doorway with a curious smile that was half sympathetic, half ingratiating.

"Will you permit me to enter?"

Though the greeting was, perhaps, a little old-fashioned in tone, it was not obviously threatening; and yet Derek's overriding feeling was a desire that the man would go away. Small and nondescript and probably in his fifties, the stranger had dark-grey hair on a balding head, cut short and neat. He wore a grey suit which seemed outdated, although in what way Derek couldn't quite pin down, and he carried a battered, brown-leather briefcase. His face was forgettable; even afterwards Derek struggled to recall it properly. It fronted the head without distinction, as memorable as a beige cushion on a beige settee.

"Who are you?"

"It doesn't matter. Call me, I don't know, Barlow."

Lunatic, Derek thought, and he tried to close the door.

"Barlow it is then," Barlow said, forcing it open before it could lock shut, "and I apologize sincerely for my intrusion."

The smile hadn't left his face. His foot was planted firmly between the door and the doorframe.

"You're not from the press?"

Barlow smiled and marched in. Derek moved aside as though by the power of the man's self-confidence, not finding his anger until the deed was done.

"Excuse me?" he said indignantly, following him into his own room.

Barlow reached into his jacket and took out a pistol, which he aimed at Derek's head. Derek stared into the barrel of it blankly.

"What's that?"

Barlow gave a little shake of the head, as though not wanting to embarrass his host by answering such a superfluous question.

146

"Will you sit there please?" He wagged the pistol helpfully in the general direction of a chair. The dull sheen of its metal persuaded Derek to do as he was told. Barlow took a turn around the room, deep in thought. "Dr Petersen," he began, "this is my job, but I am not at my happiest at the moment. You see, as a rule, the people I point guns at are the vermin of the earth. You, on the other hand, are a decent man." His aim didn't waver, but he laid a comforting hand on Derek's shoulder, and squeezed. "Believe me, Dr Petersen, I am pained."

Fear had now swamped Derek, so that he was forced to pause and gulp in some air, but it came to its own decision and caused him to try and stand up.

"Gun or no gun, I'll be damned if I sit here while you—"

It was like a punch, but there was a pistol butt at the end of Barlow's arm instead of a fist. Derek slumped back into the chair, groaning. Blood oozed out of his forehead, dividing at the bridge of his nose into two channels that raced down his cheeks and rejoined at his chin.

The man sat down on Derek's bed and used a handkerchief to carefully wipe the blood from the pistol.

"I have a client, and my client has a request to make of you."

Derek pressed a fold of his jumper to his head. A moment's interval, then he felt the pistol's tip being pressed gently against his ear.

"Oh – don't," he whispered involuntarily.

Something else touched Derek lightly on his other ear. He only realized it was Barlow's lips when he heard words whispered in his ear – not many words, less than a dozen, but forming a proposition so huge and ugly, so impossible that from under the crushing weight of his terror Derek thought, he's got to be joking.

The mouth of the gun and the mouth of the man moved away.

"Please look up, Dr Petersen."

Cautiously, Derek raised his head from his knees and lowered his jumper from his eyes. Barlow was standing by the bed, gesturing towards a briefcase open on the bed. It was crammed with banknotes. It represented a sight so unexpected and silly that Derek actually smiled at its corniness.

"I'm not brave," he said, in a nearly inaudible voice, "I'm terrified, but you must realize... you can't make me do this thing."

Barlow's face fell with theatrical emphasis.

"That's very disappointing. And foolish. Dr Petersen, my client rewards cooperation amply: this is a considerable amount of money. And clearly, when Ormond goes, you'll replace him. Won't you reconsider?"

Derek shook his head.

"I see. How unfortunate."

"If you kill me," Derek said, "then..."

"You can't do the task. Impeccable logic. What penetrating intellect." Barlow sighed. He pulled an envelope from his inside pocket. "This is very regrettable, but I must ask you to look at these photographs of my clients' associates."

They were photographs of dead people. Most of them had been shot in the centre of the forehead. They sprawled in death's ungainly postures, each surrounded by the requisite pool of blood. Derek flicked slowly through the pictures. The pictures were real and he wondered if he would faint, or throw up, but...

"I told you," he uttered hoarsely, "I'm not brave, but I won't do this."

"All I ask is that you keep looking at the pictures, Dr Petersen."

An old man at a desk, his head resting on the surface, one of his hands still holding a pen over a half-written letter; a young

148

man sprawled on his back in the street, legs splayed, blood coating his entire head; a very, very fat man at the bottom of a flight of stairs; a young girl...

Derek felt life go from his body temporarily, leaving him panting and hopeless. He was holding a photograph of Lizzie, his daughter. She was walking out of a clothes shop with a friend, running a hand through her hair and looking back over her shoulder. She was laughing.

There was a long silence.

"I understand your feelings," Barlow responded, generously. "Take your time to come to terms with this. Have a look at some more."

"You keep away from my daughter," Derek pleaded. "She's just a child."

The photographs of Lizzie, now smeared with blood, slipped from his fingers.

13

Roddy typed the words quickly, jabbing at the keys with the middle fingers of each hand:

A personal statement by Dr Roderick Ormond, Emergency Coordinator of the Whale Crisis Coordination Team...

From outside there came a ragged cheer by the protesters which made him look up briefly. It was approaching midnight. Eighteen hours had passed since the police had forced him through the howling mob, through obscenities and spit and hatred. Since then the events of the day, and his own handling of things, had left him feeling much better and more secure, although – God knows, he cautioned himself – I'm not out of the woods yet.

There had been a period of abject despair and anguish. He had never felt lonelier than he had in the previous night, after he had put down the seven whales and been escorted back to the hotel. Standing in the shower, allowing hot water to blast off the disgusting substances that coated his skin, his hair, he had felt as though his resolve was imploding in slow motion. No one can be expected to endure such abuse, he had agonized; no one can lead a situation like this in the face of such vitriolic criticism. And without anyone to talk to, not even Whitaker and now not even Derek... Utterly alone...

But there was a mantra in his mind that reflected more accurately his true state of mind: I won't resign because I'm right, I won't resign because I'm right... I might have made all manner of minor mistakes, I might have completely mismanaged the media, I might be receiving death threats from half the nutters in Britain, but on the core issues, on the whales, I won't resign because I'm *right*. He had emerged from that shower not just clean, but chastened by his mistakes and determined to make amends. Derek's advice – he had realized – had been right all along. So he acted on it, no matter how belatedly.

The day on the beach had been arduous: not just getting on with the job – though drilling two thousand soldiers in refloating the whales wasn't easy – but consciously taking time out to be interviewed for television and for newspapers, explaining everything a dozen times to scores of hostile journalists, eating slice after slice of humble pie. And yet the media are still baying for my blood, he thought; the crowds are still so antagonistic that I need police protection; and the support I'm getting from the committees is, well, lukewarm at best. As for Derek, still refusing to speak to me, not even looking me in the eye...

To the tune of Rod Stewart's *I Am Sailing*, the protesters on the esplanade outside The Grand Hotel had started singing "Stop this whal-ing... Stop this whal-ing... Stick your sci-ence... Up your bum...". A half smile crept across Roddy's face. Despite all the difficulties facing him, he still felt optimistic that, when the soldiers refloated the whales on the back of the big tide tomorrow, there would be a change in public opinion. Until then, he was hoping that his written personal statement would help allay some of the bad feeling. He tapped at the keyboard swiftly:

> *During the course of the past three days, I – and my decisions – have been subject to an intense level of criticism. I now believe that some of this criticism has been justified. Likewise, some of it has not. I have thus decided to write a detailed personal statement, both to apologize, without qualification, for the mistakes I have made, and to explain clearly those aspects of my situation which have been misunderstood...*

* * *

Derek was standing on the beach near the battered and rickety West Pier. His wound throbbed under its dressing. Further up the beach the "Stop this whaling" ditty was being belted out by thousands, but he didn't register it. He stared sightlessly out to sea, thinking.

I've never been brave. I know that. Gathering enough courage to do something worthwhile and dangerous must be difficult; but to gather enough courage to do something evil and unjustifiable? How can I do it? But then, how can I not?

He turned around to look along the shore at the whales. Those mighty helpless innocents.

Cloud obscured the moon. It was just as well, given what was going to happen.

* * *

That I faked the results of some academic research is true...

Roddy wrote on, supremely unaware of the irrelevance of his efforts...

...It occurred when the International Whaling Commission was under pressure to lift the moratorium on the hunting of minkes. The whaling nations had promised to adhere to a voluntary code that would guard against over-exploitation, but no one with any knowledge of their history believed this. These nations had hunted first the sperm, then the blue, then the fin, then the sei to the brink of extinction. As each species became so depleted as to make hunting it uneconomic, they simply switched to the next biggest whale. Well, the minke is the next biggest whale, and the only one of the great whales that still exists in sizeable populations. In a bid to protect the minke from decimation, I temporarily sacrificed something very precious to me: my academic integrity. I manipulated ongoing research into the population of minkes in the North Atlantic, providing an estimate to the IWC that was thirty per cent below the true likely figure. I do not deny that this was a proactive, political act. And I do not regret that it contributed to the defeat of the lifting of the moratorium. Six months later, my deception was exposed. That I had been technically in the wrong can be seen by the fact that I was suspended from my post as Director of the Marine Mammals Institute; that I had been morally right can be seen in the fact that I was reappointed only three weeks later, after receiving widespread expressions of sympathy and support from many sectors of the whale-research fraternity...

* * *

Head bowed, feet dragging across the shingle, and carrying a shoulder bag heavy with large, loaded syringes, Derek had made his way along the shore to the site of the mass beaching. A couple of whale mentors tried to engage him in conversation, and he did his best to respond to them appropriately – yes, the whales were going back in the water tomorrow; no, there would be no more whales put down – but his low, flat voice and dead eyes gave them the creeps. They did not persist with their questions. Derek nodded to them and walked between their two animals – a sei and a minke – towards the tails. He stopped to bend down and tie his shoelace. From his bag he drew a syringe.

Like everyone who works in the field of cetology, he knew that of the untold differences between whales and humans, one of the most fundamental lies in the respiratory system. Whereas humans inhale and exhale unconsciously, even in their sleep, whales have to decide when to breathe. An unconscious whale can't remember to do so, and will die.

He intended to render the animals unconscious.

It took about ten seconds to inject the sei. He put the empty syringe back into his pocket. He felt filthy with shame. But then he thought of Barlow. Then he thought of Lizzie. And then his hand closed on the next syringe.

Later, Blackfin becomes aware of a human near his tail. For another darkness he is helplessly stranded on the edge of the human world, and yet he is neither panicked nor impatient. He and his brothers and sisters have determined to stay where they are, even when the great tide comes and lifts them from their pebble prison. They will stay on the land from one moon to the next and beyond, if it persuades the humans to see what has to be seen.

Blackfin feels nothing when the long needle penetrates his blubber and enters the tissue beneath.

* * *

1 a.m., and for the first time since Blackfin's arrival in Brighton, Roddy was looking forward to going to bed in a reasonable frame of mind. His personal statement ran to five pages. It explained how waiting for the spring tide was the only realistic way of attempting to get so many whales into the water without inducing stress levels that would kill them. It comprehensively demonstrated the absurdity of Kate Gunning's allegation that he was to blame for the mass beaching. Not everyone would agree with the arguments it made for performing seven necropsies, but at least an open-minded person now had the opportunity to come to a measured view. Perhaps most importantly, the statement contained an admission that he had been mistaken in his handling of the media, and he had apologized without reservation.

Reading the text through, he felt a great weight being lifted from his mind. He did a spell-check and made a couple of small alterations before emailing it to the Media Liaison Officer at the Media Centre, for immediate release. Then he stood at the window, in contravention of the instructions of his Police Protection Unit – two of whose members were stationed just outside his door – and looked out at the beach.

It was a dark night. The crowd, about a quarter of its daytime size, was blurrily visible. They lay in their sleeping bags, or huddled together in groups, keeping vigil, ready to do battle with the police again should any new horror be perpetrated on the whales. Several fires had been lit, and round these fires Roddy could make out more protesters. Beyond the people, visibility was poor, but he could just make out the large, dark, rounded shapes of the whales. He turned away from the window, yawning and unbuttoning his shirt.

* * *

4:45 in the morning. From the distant planet of his sleep, Roddy became aware of an insistent ringing. When he managed to croak a "Yes?" into the receiver, Margaret Gilchrist, chairperson of the Emergency Response Committee, didn't bother with small talk. She just stated what had happened.

"What?"

She repeated it. The marrow in his bones seemed to petrify.

"Do you understand?" Margaret Gilchrist said.

He made a noise of assent. She put the phone down. Roddy stared at the receiver in his hand, pleading with God... Please, for pity's sake, let this be a mistake, a hoax, a nightmare I can wake up from...

When Roddy crashed down the beach minutes later – the sun was waiting to rise, sleepy protesters were wriggling out of their sleeping bags – the whales didn't look any different. Wild hope surged through him. He ran past the Operations Centre, gasping for breath, then doubled back on himself and rushed in through the door.

"...how does one dispose of five thousand *tonnes* of dead whale?" Margaret Gilchrist was saying bleakly.

The room fell silent. There were five or six people from the committee present, and about twenty others. Various night staff looked at him. Derek was sitting by himself on a plastic chair, holding his head in his hands. Two vets were standing together at the back of the room; their intense discussion abruptly ended. No one moved or spoke.

"It isn't true, is it?" he said at last, with an intonation so curious, so desperate, that no one in that room would ever forget it.

A long moment passed, during which Roddy felt savaged by grief and guilt.

"What happened?" Roddy howled. "Derek, what happened?"

His old friend looked up slowly, but shook his head.

"One of the mentors noticed his whale hadn't breathed for a long time," a member of the night staff said, her voice flat and heavy. "I rushed down, and... I realized that none of them was breathing."

"They're all dead," Margaret Gilchrist said in an icy tone.

Roddy span round, running out of the Portakabin to the scene of the tragedy. Mentors were standing around in disconsolate groups. Roddy came to a halt in front of a couple of young women. He walked past them slowly, unable to return their gaze. He approached a sei whale. How could it be dead, this fantastic creature, this celebration of life? Its wet skin was shiny, it is *not* dead, Roddy insisted to himself. But when he examined the open eye he saw the tell-tale filmy sheen. He jabbed his finger straight towards it, and nothing happened. He touched the eye with his finger, but the animal didn't flinch, couldn't flinch.

The light of the sun was beginning to nudge at the horizon. At that moment, the water that had been misting down for days, pumped from the sea by a tug, tailed away. Roddy looked around desperately. Who had authorized that? It was too soon. He ran up to another whale, a pilot whale, and gazed into its eye, but all he saw was that same filmy sheen of death.

He was scrabbling around in the shingle. He hurled himself against the flank of one of the sperm whales, this one's alive, let it be alive! Against the sunrise, deranged and disbelieving, he shuttled madly between the huge, stranded corpses, like a child in a game of musical chairs who refuses to accept that he is out. Sperm whales, pilot whales, a killer, another sei. They were all dead.

The crowds, hearing his shouts and noticing that the water

had been switched off, became uneasy. Wolf whistles and jeers sounded.

Margaret Gilchrist had followed him down. Accompanied by half a dozen of the redundant mentors, she went looking for him. She found him next to a pilot whale. He was sitting in the shingle, resting the side of his head pathetically against the dead animal's flank. When they approached him he looked up, tears flooding his eyes.

"I think you'd better leave before the crowd realizes what's going on. Your police officers are waiting for you in the Operations Centre. Dr Ormond..."

She held out her hand, almost tenderly. Roddy took it, and stood up. He allowed himself to be led away, threading a route through the lifeless giants of the sea.

Interlude

The four Japanese freezer ships worked in close proximity to one another; so close that the crew of one could shout good-humoured abuse at the crew of another. There was a rolling sea. Accompanying the mournful cries of the ocean came the moaning of a motor. A great chain, whose links were half a metre long, began to wind its way up the floating ramp of one of the vessels. The open stern resembled the jaws of some sea monster waiting to close on its prey; the ramp that stuck out of it shifted up and down on the surface of the sea, like a greedy, salivating tongue.

So far six carcasses had been hauled aboard the four craft, and men had set about dismantling them in preparation for freezing. But there were dozens more whales to haul in. On the instructions of Dr Derek Petersen, the new leader of the Whale Crisis Coordination Team, the unfortunate creatures that died on Brighton beach had been towed far out to sea and abandoned. This would avoid a huge health hazard on land, he had said during a press conference, and was the most environmentally responsible method of disposal.

The dead animals, tied loosely together, rose and fell on the ocean, ghastly in their lifelessness, the flotsam and jetsam of giants. Two workers in a small boat were attaching a chain around the tail of one of them. They were laughing about something, something to do with the wife of one of their

161

colleagues, her propensity to open her legs to all and sundry. Still roaring with laughter, they secured the attachment and signalled to their mother ship. Another motor started up, the slack of the chain was taken up, and then the whale was being dragged through the water. The chain snaked up the ramp of the waiting freezer ship.

For hours, Blackfin has been swirling in a lost and unknown world, passing in and out of dark hallucinations in which oceans vaporize, whale skeletons stack up on a dry sea bed. At times he sees a flickering light, and longs for it; when he goes nearer, it intensifies, becomes so beautiful that he wants to disappear inside… But then he hears strange codas, such as he has never experienced before, telling him to live, live. The light grows distant again, there is the feeling of a real world waiting for him to be in it, he hears a thump-thump-thump and an awful groaning, and when his mind comes back to him, when his lungs explode into life, his tailstock is being hauled up a metal ramp into the bowels of a freezing vessel.

Half in and half out of the water, he lurches mightily, provoking screams of panic from the four or five Japanese who wait at the top of the ramp for what they had believed to be his corpse. The winding motor rasps in protest at the new force being exerted on it. With all the strength available to him, Blackfin thrashes his tail. The chain whips into the air, then comes lashing down onto the metal ramp. But still the motor, now whinnying in protest, is powering him up the ramp. He lies still, empty of energy. The Japanese crew are enraged. Absurdly, one of them jumps down onto the ramp and starts to beat Blackfin's tail flukes with a stick, all the while shrieking unintelligibly. The men on the other ships shout and gesture. Blackfin feels his jaw clunk against metal. Something on the ramp, a loose rivet or some twisted metal, rakes into his blubber. He sees the flickering light again, it needs him, it glows with beauty, but the coda is still there, to live, live, and his great body spasms with elemental rage. The chain whips up a second time, instantly knocking the screams, and the life, out of the man on the ramp. For a moment Blackfin lies like before, helpless, still attached. But a high-pitched ping announces the breaking of one of the links of the chain. To the maddened shouts of the crew, he finds himself slithering down the ramp.

Part Two

1

It was a Thursday morning, some days after the death of the whales. In the bedroom of their squat in Worthing, Ally and Dave were dozing. The radio was on low and playing Radiohead. Dave turned over, woke up, made to put his arm around Ally, then stopped himself. Oh yeah, he remembered: no physical contact. Once again he wished that he hadn't started anything with the girl who had come on strong to him; then there wouldn't have been an indiscretion to admit to Ally; and then he and Ally could have carried on as before.

Outside, a car zoomed past, drowning out the best efforts of a valiant urban blackbird. Quiet, rather sweet snores emanated from Ally. Dave wanted to stroke the back of her neck, but didn't dare. He decided, in theory, to get up, then found in practice that he wasn't quite ready for it. His thoughts drifted to the crazy, interlinking topics that become sleep: a bird singing; a bird with a human face; a bird with a human face standing on his shoulder and issuing a long, toneless trill...

Shit, the doorbell... He got out of bed and padded to the window.

"Who is it?" Ally murmured. "Your other woman?"

"Ally," he said plaintively, exasperated with her continuing punishment of him. "It is a woman, though, reminds me of your mother."

Another long blast of the doorbell, then a voice wafted up the stairs from the letter box.

"Ally? Ally, are you there?"

"My God, it is my mother!" Ally exclaimed, sitting up in bed.

"Ally! Ally darling!" came the call.

Half a minute later, Ally was leaning out of the front door and looking down the street at her mother's retreating, hunched-over figure. She hesitated a moment: if she thinks I'm just going to forget about what happened, the way she rejected Dave...

"Mummy! *Mummy!*" she called.

Theresa turned back and came running, sobbing, into her arms. It was impossible not to respond. "Oh Mummy," Ally cried, blinking back tears of her own. She hugged her, hard.

Dave appeared in the hall.

"Er, oh," he said. "Um... I'll make some tea."

He went into the kitchen. Ally pulled her mother into the house, and saw her face. She breathed in sharply, dismayed by the yellow-purple pattern that disfigured one side.

"Mummy, what happened?"

Theresa broke down again, her skinny body shuddering in Ally's arms.

* * *

Tanya Grant put two cups of tea on top of the chest of drawers, one for her brother, Whitaker – or Peter, as he was known at home – and one for Roddy. She cast a disapproving eye over the two men. Whitaker was prone on his bed, playing *Tomb Raider VI* on his computer. He was wearing nothing but a plaster cast and a pair of boxers that sported the slogan *Oo-er!* on the front. Roddy was slumped in the room's only chair, his eyes half-closed, firmly clutching a bottle of Scotch in one hand, a glass in the other.

"Dr Ormond, there are journalists and television crews all over the garden," she said, "and some kind of lunatic who wants to shoot you."

"He'll need a gun to do that," Whitaker pointed out.

"He's got an air rifle."

"Ah." Then "Oooooooh!" Whitaker cried, as the game yielded him a meaningful underwater shot of Lara Croft.

"Dr Ormond, I appreciate your problems at the moment, but my brother needs peace and quiet to recuperate."

Roddy nodded, but did not prise his eyelids open any further.

"Peter," Tanya tried, "I know he's your friend, I know we said he could stay here for a *short* while, but, but…"

"But what?"

"But he can't! Mum's going hysterical."

"If he goes, I go," Whitaker said.

For the hundredth time, a journalist yelled up to the second floor flat from the communal garden below.

"Dr Ormond! Just a word please! Dr Ormond!"

"This is ridiculous!" Tanya exclaimed, and she slammed the door shut on them.

Whitaker continued with his game, zapping and being zapped. Roddy poured another inch of scotch into his glass, then drank half of it.

"Do you think," he said, "that a whale could deliberately kill itself by deciding not to breathe? Do you think they decided the beaching wasn't working, and so they deliberately committed mass suicide? As the ultimate protest against something?"

He's got to cut this out, Whitaker thought, he'll go mad.

"Roddy, listen, you've got to stop going over and over things like this – and I don't want to nag, but you have to stop drinking. Your larynx sounds like it's lined with gravel."

Stop drinking? Roddy repeated to himself.

On the day the whales had died he had sought refuge at the Marine Mammals Institute in London. He hadn't had anywhere else to go. The police had driven him there in the kind of secure-transit vehicle normally used to shuttle high-profile criminals between the courtroom and the prison. He remembered how appalling it had been: helicopters transmitting live coverage on TV, paparazzi on motorbikes, behind them a convoy of cars and vans crammed with journalists, and thousands of rioting protesters waiting for him there. Then, inside the Institute, he had been told that he was no longer the Director, and that the Institute was no longer his home. The kindly Detective Inspector in charge of him had suggested a police cell. For the love of God, Roddy marvelled, how did I come to spend three days as a voluntary inmate of Holborn police station? And yet in many ways it had turned out to be the perfect sanctuary: protected from hacks, sending out for pizzas, and all day with nothing to do but think...

I've been thinking, and thinking, and thinking, and I'm still no nearer to understanding how it happened.

Whitaker put down his joystick and looked across at that baffled, pained face. It had hurt like hell when his friend had ended up in a police cell. There had been nothing Whitaker could do until being discharged from hospital, when he had insisted that Roddy should stay with him at his mum's place in north London. But he hadn't anticipated the scale of the media hounding that would follow.

Though the whales were dead, the story was still very much alive. An almighty, multi-faceted media frenzy was going on. It was much more than rabid reporters pursuing Roddy from one hiding place to another, offering him outlandish amounts of cash and opprobrium. Their newspapers ran daily pull-outs such as 'The Complete and True Story of the Whales' and 'The Biggest Event in History'. The television news programmes had whales as their first, second and third items. Lavishly funded foreign news teams overran Brighton and London, seeking answers. The big Hollywood film companies were at loggerheads, each trying to find an angle by which it could claim the event as its own intellectual property; a similar war was going on between the video-gaming companies; and the huge, soulless factories of China were already churning out cheap plastic whales for sale in western markets.

At least it can't possibly get any freakier, Whitaker told himself.

And then came the convoy.

* * *

V.A. Apukkatan was an illegal immigrant from Tamil Nadu in southern India. To support his wife, two boys and in-laws back home he plied a minicab in the Tottenham area. He worked fourteen hours a day, six days a week, experiencing friendliness, racism, fare-dodging, hilarity and in-car vomiting with supreme equanimity. By night he studied for an HND in Information Technology at an adult-education college. On Saturday evenings he went to bed in the dingy room he shared with four other illegal immigrants, all Moroccans, and slept without cease for twenty-four hours. It was his ambition to achieve citizenship, get a good job as a computer programmer, and settle his family in Britain.

While Roddy was drinking whisky in Whitaker's bedroom, Apu was doing one of his easiest and most lucrative jobs. Every Thursday morning he ferried an elderly Jewish lady from her house in Highgate to John Lewis on Oxford Street – where she had her hair set – before taking her on to friends in Marylebone where she enjoyed her weekly fix of bridge.

Apu turned his ageing Passat into the A400. The route was as busy as he had ever seen it.

"After all," his passenger was saying, "whales aren't supposed to go on land, no wonder they all died, if I spent three days in the sea I'd die."

"Oh yes Mrs C."

"That's just common sense as far as I'm concerned."

Apu changed down into first; the traffic was crawling.

"Apu, why is it so busy today? I'll be late."

"Mrs C, I'm not knowing."

Apu's car didn't budge for some minutes.

"Can't we do something?"

"Traffic is halted Mrs C."

After a further ten minutes it became clear that the jam was something out of the ordinary; even the horn blasters gave up. Drivers were getting out of their cars and talking to each other. Some people were even leaving their cars and walking down the road.

"Find out what's going on, Apu."

He got out of the car and, standing on tiptoe, peered down over the jam.

"So many people Mrs C, oh my God."

"But I'm late for my hair," his passenger pleaded.

"Mrs C, I'll be going and looking."

He persuaded her to lock herself in, and he told her he would be back in a few minutes. Then he set off down the gap between the two rows of cars, following a steady stream of people. Some of them were holding transistors to their ears; others were collecting around cars in which radio news bulletins were playing loudly. He heard snatches of broadcast: "...Second major incident in a week..." – "...Government assuring us that there is no threat to people's safety..."

Apu reached the edge of a mass of people. It was difficult to know why they were gathered exactly there, but they were in an excitable state. The worst English crush was as nothing to Apu, and he burrowed into the crowd expertly. After a few minutes he was near to the front. With a bit more shoving and pushing and wriggling, he levered his thin body between two men of Indian origin – Gujaratis, he noted automatically – and found himself peering into the showroom of a television shop.

"Look at that, my friend," said one of the men.

On the large, state-of-the-art, flat-screen television that lay just behind the window, was a slightly wobbly aerial shot of an expanse of water.

"God is angry with us," one of Gujaratis said, as Apu gaped.

* * *

In a quiet voice, looking down at the bare and dirty floorboards of her daughter's squat, Theresa was explaining how the injury to her face had happened. How it wasn't the first time. How she couldn't cope any longer. Ally stared at her, sickened.

"Why?" she whispered, almost angrily. "Why did you never tell me?"

"I was – I wanted to protect you. Ally, this boy, Dave – I don't mind about him, as long as you're happy, but I was scared for you."

Ally's face screwed up in confusion and pain.

"Surely Daddy wouldn't hurt Dave?"

Then she looked at her mother's face, and the ugly bruising contradicted her.

"Oh Mummy… Why did you never *tell* me?" On the word "tell", Ally's face creased into rage and guilt.

"There was no point when you were young, believe me."

"So why are you telling me now?"

Theresa's voice became surprisingly resolute.

"I think Daddy's done something really dreadful. I need your help."

"My help?"

There was a pause. Ally waited. Strangely, Theresa smiled.

"Ally, a long time ago I was in love with a man who... he's been in the news a lot lately—

"Roddy Ormond?"

Theresa breathed in quickly.

"How on earth?"

"I was a volunteer on the beach at Brighton and he seemed to recognize me. When he found out my name, he virtually went into shock."

"He loved me. He loved me very much."

"I know."

"He told you that?"

"No, he just said, 'I knew your mother'. It was the way he said it."

Theresa's eyes half-closed. Her pale fingers stopped moving and, when she spoke, her voice was half an octave lower. Ally thought she was going to say something about Roddy, but:

"Your father is as damaged as a person can be. There's no way back for him, he won't be helped."

"Oh Mummy."

"That's why I had to come here. Ally, he seems to be involved in this whale thing, I heard him say he was going to *destroy* Roddy, and..." She gestured with futile incredulity. "I believe he has."

"What do you mean?

"I know he's done something to Roddy, I'm not sure what, but... damn!" – Ally flinched at the quiet vehemence – "Ally, come home—"

"What?"

"You're the only one with any power over him, the only one who isn't afraid of him. I want you to come home with me and find out what he's done."

Ally nodded. She couldn't help it, but a part of her was thinking it would be a good idea anyway, if only to look after her mother; if only to get away from Dave for a while. Or longer.

The door opened.

"Er…" Dave said.

Ally shook her head at him furiously, but Theresa beckoned to him to come in.

"Look," Dave said, "I know you've got something heavy going on, but I've just heard something on the radio, I think we should put the telly on."

"For God's sake Dave!"

He switched it on anyway. It was an elderly set, of a type whose sound arrives long before the picture forms.

"…Now swimming past Purfleet," said a voice, vaguely reminiscent in tone of the commentaries of great state occasions, "in single file, in stately progression, with an escort of police patrol boats… an extraordinary scene…"

"What's going on?" Ally said.

The picture formed.

* * *

Tanya Grant rushed into her brother's bedroom.

"Whoa!" she blurted.

Roddy was standing in the middle of the room with nothing on.

"He's going for a shower," Whitaker explained, handing Roddy a dressing gown.

"There's another whale thing going on," Tanya announced flatly.

Roddy looked up slowly.

"They've done it again?" he asked.

"Not exactly. It's on TV."

Pulling the dressing gown on, he strode past her and out of the room.

Downstairs, Whitaker's mother screamed.

"I don't want no undressed white man in this room!"

Roddy crouched down in front of the television and put his fingers to his temples, trying to sober up and think straight... But it was difficult, when the screen showed hundreds of killer whales swimming up the river Thames to London.

"That – is – just – unbelievable."

He scanned the screen hungrily. People on the banks were holding up their camera-phones and snapping pictures; the gleaming jet-black backs of the killers reflected the flashlights going off. To Roddy the creatures gave the impression of being calm and purposeful, but he knew that they must be enduring acute discomfort – leaving the sea for the murky fresh-water of the Thames would be intolerable for any length of time.

Tanya let him digest the scene for some minutes before speaking to him again.

"Dr Ormond, there's something else, a message for you on the answerphone from Derek Petersen. It sounds urgent."

"Can I ring him? Is there somewhere private?"

"The phone's in Mum's room," she said.

"No!" Mrs Grant wailed. "Not in me bedroom!"

Mrs Grant's bedroom was full of flowers: fresh flowers in vases, artificial flowers in elaborate arrangements, dried flowers hanging on the wall, and printed flowers everywhere – the duvet, the valance, the wallpaper, the ornaments, the curtains. Roddy scanned the room, without success, for the phone.

"There," Tanya said from the doorway, pointing at something not entirely dissimilar to a large, flowery tea cosy. He whipped it off and picked up the phone.

There was no answer from Derek's home number, work

number or mobile number, so Roddy tried the emergency number that Derek had been assigned at the start of the crisis.

"Derek, it's me."

There was a long pause. It was their first contact with each other since Roddy's dismissal and disgrace.

"You've seen?" Derek asked.

"The killers? Yes."

Another long pause. And then, to Roddy's inexpressible dismay, Derek burst into tears – not the swallowed gulps of ordinary male distress, but racking sobs.

"It's all my fault," he was gasping between breaths. "My – my fault."

"Derek—"

"I can't take it any more Roddy, they're watching me."

"Who are?"

"Roddy… Roddy, they're suppressing the results, they—"

The sobs took hold of him again.

"What results, Derek?" No answer. "Derek, what results…"

"The necropsies…"

"What do they show?"

"I'm frightened, Roddy, I don't want to lose her."

"Lose who?"

"I can't take – I just, I can't, I can't take it – I'm sorry, always remember I didn't get a choice."

The line went dead.

"Derek!"

Roddy sat stock-still, looking up at Tanya Grant, as the press pounded at the front door in a desperate effort to learn what the ex-Emergency Coordinator of the Whale Crisis Coordination Team thought about a convoy of killer whales swimming up the river Thames.

2

Apu had managed to take Mrs C back to her home and her television, and then had headed back towards the city via a different route, caught up in the growing hysteria about the convoy of killer whales. He was soon stuck once more – parts of central London were gridlocked. Drivers were abandoning their cars, many of them joining the throngs of people walking towards the river. He was soon walking amongst them. An ambition had formed in his mind. On his monthly telephone call to India, he wanted to be able to say, "Wife, I was there, I saw all these whales in the river Thames of London, a topmost-quality first-class viewing."

The only way to get to the river was on foot. It had become known that the killer-whale convoy had halted in the heart of London, between the Waterloo and Golden Jubilee bridges. He made good progress at first, but the last mile of his journey was very difficult. The police, caught on the hop and desperately under strength, were trying to turn people back at every entry point. It had taken him a good half-hour to find a way of breaching their barrier, and beyond it the crowds were so dense as to impede almost all movement. But he was determined. He pushed and shoved, wriggled and writhed, ignoring the shouts of protest. By the early evening he was within a hundred metres of the Thames, suffocating with ten thousand other people in the bottleneck of Villiers Street. It took him an hour to make that last hundred metres, but finally he emerged on to Victoria Embankment. He was confident that he could wriggle his way right to the front, but looking up and to the right, he saw the gleaming walkway of the Golden Jubilee bridge; the bridge, that was the place to get a great viewing. So he struggled to the stairs that led up to the walkway. Here the people were packed so densely that he regretted his decision. But he noticed how some nimble and fearless youths had scaled up the outside of the structure. His only thought was to see the whales. He fought his way across to an appropriate point, grabbed hold of a metal strut and started to haul himself up.

* * *

A few hundred metres away, Rattigan was being escorted into a suite at the Savoy; he was still shaking his head at the size of the inducement required to "free-up" a riverside suite. It had been a trying few hours. He was not used to inconvenience. He had been in the Bentley, engaged in a complicated telephone call with the solicitor who acted as his executor in his charity work, when he had first realized that traffic hadn't moved for a long time. The telephone discussion had concerned a project he was developing: university scholarships for children who had been brought up in care. He was considering allocating ten million pounds to the scheme. Since Ally had "left" him, he had found himself thinking about such issues even more than before.

When the call was completed, and it was clear that SW7 was completely gridlocked, he had abandoned his chauffeur to look after the car. He had pushed through the common hordes to the nearest building that had a helipad, from where he had arranged to be picked up by helicopter and flown to the Savoy.

He flopped into an armchair with relief, a glass of gin in his hand, and turned the television on. The image that appeared on the screen was one he would be able to see for himself as soon as he chose to step out onto the balcony.

"…The atmosphere like down by the river?" a studio presenter was asking.

"John, from my vantage point here on top of the Shell building I can see people, people, people, they're thronging Victoria Embankment below me, they're absolutely teeming on the walkways of the South Bank centre opposite, the trees on each side of the river are festooned with them, the bridges bulging. Far below me on the floating Bateau restaurant and on the Savoy Hotel's private pier there are exclusive parties taking place, and noisy toasts being made to the whales which are only metres away – frankly it's surreal, extraordinary, unthinkable."

"Is there any sign of Dr Derek Petersen and the people in charge of the *last* whale crisis?"

"None. As we know, Dr Petersen was reported as suffering from stress yesterday, and that was before this latest development. The Whale Crisis Coordination Team seems to have disintegrated."

"Now tell us about the whales—"

"Yes."

"We can see the pictures here, but what does it feel like there, looking at them with your own eyes?"

"Words can't render this sight, but let me at least try to describe it. The police have illuminated the entire section of river with powerful flood lamps and, as you can see, the whales are slowly milling around in the middle. There are two hundred and forty-four of them, large, graceful, with that exquisite black-and-white coloration. Police patrol boats are lined up under the two bridges, as well as SBS craft – that's the Special Boat Service, the marine equivalent of the SAS – and they're keeping out sightseers on boats. The effect is of an immense, four-sided arena, filled with – no matter how many times I say it, it doesn't become any less incredible – killer whales, whales which I and a million other people can't take our eyes off."

"Any ideas as to what the whales may do?"

"There are all sorts of predictions being discussed here from the obvious to the ludicrous, from the whales turning around and swimming back to the ocean, to their mounting an assault on the Houses of Parliament—"

"Good heavens!"

"—but the bottom line is that no one knows why the whales are doing this, no one knows what they are going to do next."

"Well thank you Ian. That's Ian Hudson there, on top of the Shell building overlooking the Thames. Well now we turn to—"

Rattigan grunted as he got to his feet. He finished off his gin and opened the door to his balcony, stepping out onto his own private viewing platform.

* * *

When Big Ben, just a short distance along the river, started to chime midnight, no one could know that the incident was about to reach its climax. Apu, like scores of foolhardy sightseers, was clinging to the walkway of the Golden Jubilee Bridge – on the wrong side of the barrier. Beneath him the river flowed, silent and black.

"They're moving!" the man next to Apu shouted.

From the bridges and the riversides came the noise of a million people exclaiming, a great roar punctuated by the chimes of Big Ben. The whales had started to mill around much more urgently, dipping their heads in the water and then coming up again. News channels suspended studio discussions and switched to live coverage. Big Ben chimed the eighth, ninth, tenth stroke.

Apu hung over the river, open-mouthed at the scene below. The whales were now swimming around in a frenzy, churning up the black waters. There seemed to be no pattern to their movements. They swam so fast that it seemed incredible that they didn't collide with one another.

On the twelfth stroke of midnight the whales stopped swimming and came together in a big knot. They did something that no one – not the watching crowds, not the reporters and journalists, not the experts corralled in TV studios, not the police – had anticipated. They called.

The noise was a collective, high-pitched, eerie squeal that could be felt in the atmosphere, akin to a thousand people scraping their fingernails down blackboards. The shrill stridency assaulted the ear like guilt strikes at the heart, but the crowds only heard it for a second or two: triggered by the decibel level and the peculiar oscillations of the frequency, many of the windows in the surrounding buildings exploded, every car alarm within a quarter-mile went off, and the whole of London started screaming.

Along hundreds of metres of riverside buildings the windows were shattering simultaneously. A sheet of lethal shards crashed down into the massed, helpless crowds on the South Bank and on the Embankment. The noise of the crashing glass, the vicious, ear-splitting wails of the car alarms and the shrieks of tens of thousands had Rattigan swearing and stepping back into his suite, crunching over the remains of an exploded French window, holding his hands to his ears. He rushed across the suite and out into the corridor, where other guests, crying and shouting, were assembling.

Outside, stupefied, the crowds cowered and bled, trampled and were trampled on. On the narrow and packed walkway of the Golden Jubilee Bridge there were stampedes at each end. Hundreds tumbled down the steps, and as for those clinging to the barrier over the river...

"They're dropping off the bridge, they're dropping off the bridge!" the man from the BBC was screaming insanely.

Apu was in a crouching position, each foot wedged against the outside of the barrier, hands holding on to the handrail. Instinctively he clung on through the pain of his eardrums, but his hands were being struck by the frenzied, stampeding people. One of his feet lost its purchase. He tried to swing his leg back up, but as he did so his other foot slipped down too, and he found himself hanging merely by his hands. He screamed and yelled, but no one heard him. Everyone was screaming and yelling. Something slammed onto his left hand so hard that it felt like his fingers had been sliced off. Now his hands were slipping fractionally down the handrail, and then he was plummeting down, looking ludicrously across at a teenage boy who had lost his grip at the same moment, both of them pedalling the air.

He hit the water feet first while thinking only this: I can't swim. As soon as he went under, his body was twisted by the notorious undertow of the Thames, and though his limbs flailed in an imitation of swimming, he knew he was a dead man. He couldn't even control, or know, which way up he was, as the current continued to play with him. His eyes were open and bulging out of their sockets, while his lungs, desperate for oxygen, forced him to try to breathe – the dirty river gushed down his throat. He wished only for the agony to be replaced by death, and then he found himself above the surface of the river. Choking, regurgitating the Thames, he seemed to roll down back into the water, but as soon as he went under he was pushed back up again. Without knowing what he was doing, his hands wrapped around something and clung on grimly. It was the dorsal fin of a killer whale.

Police and SBS boats were on the scene and hauling people out of the river. As people all over the country and beyond watched the incident unfolding on television, it became clear what was happening: there were dozens of people in the water, and the killer whales were keeping them afloat.

3

Early the following morning, only two journalists were still waiting outside Whitaker's mother's flat for a chance to doorstep the ex-leader of the Whale Crisis Coordination Team. They looked forlorn. Roddy's currency as news had slid dramatically during the night. The focus of the media was now on London, and on the killer whales that were making their way back down the Thames to the sea. After nudging to safety all the people in the water, and while the capital city was still lost in panic and confusion, the killers had turned back towards their home. All through the night they had swum down the river, past Canning Town and Creekmouth, past Dartford and Tilbury. Soon they would be approaching Canvey Island. Police boats escorted them before and behind, training powerful searchlights on the black-and-white bodies in the dark, glinting water. The whales were no longer swimming in the unnatural formation they had used when they had travelled up the river, on the surface and in single file; now they were in loose pods, sometime on and sometimes under the river's surface. Crowds were still turning out on the banks of the river to witness them, sullen, almost silent. Nobody knew what to think.

Inside the flat, Roddy, hung-over but sober, was listening on his mobile to all the voicemail messages that he had failed to attend to earlier in the week. Several things had combined to lever him out of his self-pitying apathy. First there had been Whitaker's low-key, rather sarcastic encouragement; secondly there had been the alarming conversation with Derek; but most of all it had been the convoy, and its devastating finale. It would have taken a coma to suppress his fascination with that. He had been watching the killers making for the open sea for most of the night, torturing himself with speculations: whales beaching in Brighton, whales swimming up the Thames and shattering much of the glass in every surrounding building – Christ, what were the whales going to do next?

"Hello Dr Ormond, my name is David Green and I'm a reporter from the US working with *The Enquirer*, I understand you may be feeling the pressure right now, but I can promise you a sympathetic and indeed a highly *lucrative* hearing with…"

Say goodbye, Roddy thought, and he scratched the message…

"This is Gillian Hendry, I'm ringing on behalf of *Newsnight* on BBC2…"

…and goodbye to you as well.

He was sitting at the kitchen table, eating a foraged breakfast. Tanya and her mother were in the lounge, watching television as the killer whales left the Thames estuary for the open sea. Everyone in the flat had been up all night.

"They're now saying two hundred and forty people were killed by falling glass or by being crushed in stampedes," Tanya said, walking in, "well over a thousand injured, and a couple of murders out of the city."

"Murders?"

"People freaking out, going nuts, lashing out."

"Bloody hell."

"But over eighty people fell into the river, and the whales saved every one of them. Amazing."

With his mobile to his ear – he had already scrubbed twenty messages from journalists – Roddy nodded.

"Martin Grange, Chief Executive of Radio Brighton, and I'm making this call myself Dr Ormond to emphasize how much we want to…"

Another message bit the dust.

"Dr Ormond, this is Kate Gunning, if you get this message, don't hang up, this is too important…"

Kate *Gunning*? You've got to be joking.

"...I've found something out, something big, it's to do with the whales, and I think you'd better hear it, can you please—"

Delete. He reckoned Kate Gunning's half-baked theories on whales had caused him enough grief.

"So what are you planning to do?" Tanya asked.

"I want to find Derek Petersen and talk to him."

As he was speaking his mobile rang.

"Hello?"

"Roddy?"

"Who is it?"

"At last! It's Joe!"

"Joe who?"

"Joe Farelli, WhaleWorld Joe. Do you realize how many messages I've left for you since those killers did a Pied Piper of London routine? Too fucking many, that's how many."

"I'm listening to them right now, haven't got to yours yet."

"I heard you tried to hang yourself with a pair of black cotton socks."

"Don't believe everything you read in the newspapers."

"Well I'm glad you survived because I want you to come over here – I think the convoy and Attila are connected."

"What do you mean?"

"I can't explain it over the phone, you have to see for yourself."

Roddy hesitated.

"You'd be better off informing the people in charge. I'm not involved any more."

"I know that – I believe that much from the newspapers, even if I don't believe you murdered seventy-eight whales with your bare hands. But this new guy, Petersen, he's AWOL, no one's in charge anymore, I've contacted everyone I can think of from the council to the government, no one's listening. Someone has to get over here – trust me, you'll be glad you did.

* * *

Even the two remaining journalists had given up by the time Roddy left the flat. It was a coolish summer day, dry but overcast. Inside his car he turned the key and listened grimly to the whirring starter motor.

A black, soft-top BMW turned into the road a couple of hundred metres away. Inside, Kate Gunning scanned the houses left and right. She parked outside the flats, in front of a battered Ford Escort. No journalists, she noted in relief: OK, how am I going to do this?

Half crouched down in the seat of the Escort, as though being nearer to the ignition might persuade it to fire, Roddy gave the key another fruitless turn. Hopeless. He gave up in frustration, sitting back in his seat. He saw Kate Gunning at exactly the same moment that she saw him.

"Oh hell."

With a sinking feeling, he watched her get out and walk towards him. He resumed his dealings with the ignition. Come on, he prayed, I'm begging, start, just start, do it…

There was a tap at the window, and a muffled voice:

"If you're not careful you'll make the battery go flat. Dr Ormond, can I talk to you? It's incredibly important."

"Absolutely not," he barked.

"Dr Ormond—"

Roddy wound the window down frenziedly.

"Have you any idea," he said, "any idea at all, how damaging, how wrong, some of your reporting was? Do you seriously believe I caused all those whales to beach?"

"Yes to the first question," Kate said. "No to the second. I'm sorry. It was an appalling mistake on my part, I admit it. I got carried away."

He blinked, not expecting such an admission. She was looking at him with an expression pitched between apology and hope. He turned the ignition once more and swore furiously as the battery gave up.

"What do you want?" he complained. "There's no blood left to suck." He got out of the car and slammed the door shut. She hurried after him as he strode away towards the flats.

"Look," she said to his retreating back, "I've discovered something about the whales, please let me tell you what is!" But he grabbed hold of the front-door handle, yanked at it. Kate, with an inspiration born of despair, yelled, "I've got a car that works!"

He paused on the threshold, his back to her.

"I'll drive you anywhere you want to go, just name the place, and on the way I'll tell you my information. If you don't believe it or anything, you can just ignore it. Come on, what have you got to lose?"

"Nothing," he said fiercely, spinning round. "That's the point."

"Have we got a deal?" she said into the silence. No answer. "Where are you going?" she tried.

"Clacton-on-Sea."

"Is that a joke?"

"Do I look like I'm telling you a joke?"

* * *

Ally held the receiver of the public phone box to her ear; it rang five times before her father's deep voice said, "Who's there?"

"Daddy?"

"*Ally?*"

"Daddy, where are you?"

"I'm in the car. Why, what…"

He was exhausted by a sleepless night, disconcerted by the turn of events, and he had things on his mind. The convoy of killer whales had strengthened his feeling that the whale phenomenon was in danger of compromising his Russian operation. He'd only just stopped talking to his Moscow intermediary, who felt the same. But although *The Vegas* had successfully accomplished her voyage, the next vessel, *Jasmine*, was in the North Atlantic with the cargo aboard. She had to complete, and then he would close the operation down.

"Where are you?"

"I'm in London, Daddy."

"Ally... Ally..."

"Yes Daddy?"

"I'm so glad you rang me, I want to see you, can I see you? Ally? Oh, don't cry!"

"I'm sorry. Daddy, I'm really really sorry."

"It's OK baby, it's OK, where are you Ally?"

"Tottenham Court Road. I'm next to a shop called Computers Unlimited."

"I'm coming to get you, OK? Baby?"

"Come and get me Daddy, please, now."

"I'll be there in minutes."

Immediately after hanging up, Ally made a second call.

"Mum? I've done it."

A few minutes later, the Bentley passed slowly down Tottenham Court Road. He looked for her in her weird alternative rags: there's the shop, but where is she, where *is* she?

The chauffeur parked by the side of the road. Rattigan felt hot tears filling his eyes. He didn't see her until she opened the car door.

"Ally!"

Clean, shiny hair in a pony tail, a white shirt, a dark, knee-length skirt. My little girl is back, he exulted, and looking how she should always look.

Cobbling up more theatrical ability than she had thought she was capable of, Ally burst into tears again and flung herself at her father.

"I'm so sorry Daddy!"

"It's OK, it's OK."

He clutched her to him, pressed her face into his shoulder, and stroked her hair.

* * *

"Months and months ago," Kate was saying, driving fast, "there was a rumour about a mutated fish that was caught in the extreme North Atlantic, have you heard about it?"

"No," Roddy replied tersely.

"There's a zone out there called SONAZ, Special Operations No Access Zone, or the Forbidden Zone. It was a British nuclear test site in the Fifties. It's kind of a mystery now, because although the government has always claimed that it's one hundred percent safe, they won't abandon this exclusive-access thing. There's an admiral at Whitehall who has to authorize access."

"What reasons do they give?" Roddy asked, failing miserably to do as he had intended, which was to remain virtually mute for the duration of the journey.

"Well, we're talking about the military here, they're not big on giving reasons. Most people think there must be some hush-hush research going on, boys-with-toys or something. Who knows. What I do know is that there's a link with the whales."

She swung into the outer lane of the North Circular and accelerated sharply.

"Do you remember the day the first sperm whale beached?" she asked.

"What do you think?"

"That day, after months of pushing, I managed to get a small report out on regional radio about this mutated fish. You see, the Icelandic skipper of the trawler that caught the fish originally made a big thing of it, and the fish was supposedly sent off to a government lab. Then it was suggested that he'd been fishing near SONAZ—"

"This 'Forbidden Zone' place."

"Exactly. It wasn't clear if pressure had been put on him, and if so, by whom, but he got cold feet. Said it wasn't a mutated fish, just a mutilated one. Said he'd thrown it back into the sea. It wasn't much of a story, but, I don't know… I pushed and pushed, and I got a piece out, along the lines of, why would this skipper say one thing one minute, another the next? Where is the fish he caught? Where, precisely, did he catch it? Is there a cover-up, and if so, what is it? Are our fish safe to eat? To be honest, it was an absolute vest of a story—"

"A what?"

"More holes than string, but the idea was to generate interest and flush something out, from somewhere, from someone."

"But what's the link with the whales?"

"Well, yesterday I received an anonymous letter from Iceland. It's from a British crew member of a trawler in the Icelandic fishing fleet. The guy heard my radio report when it was repeated on the World Service. Basically, he supplies the link between whales and SONAZ."

"And the link is?"

"You can read the letter, it's in my briefcase on the back seat."

"Can I open it up?" he asked, lugging the heavy case onto his knee.

"Feel free."

Badly crammed with papers and miscellaneous junk, it ejected its contents all over his lap.

"How am I supposed to find it in this lot?"

"Airmail envelope. Smells of fish."

He sifted through the papers. A photograph of a sleekly handsome middle-aged man slithered off his lap and into the gap between their seats. Roddy picked it up and looked at it.

"Your father," he guessed.

"Just some bastard who broke my heart."

He tried not to show his surprise as he slotted the photograph back into her papers, suppressing the urge to ask her if a road drill had been involved.

"He ran off with a younger woman," Kate added.

"Younger than *you*?"

"Found it yet?"

"No... Is this it?"

"Yeah. From the way he writes, I sort of got the feeling he's a Geordie, but I might be wrong."

He extracted the letter: an A4 ruled sheet, torn out of an exercise book, slightly wrinkled. Black ink in a bold but messy hand.

Dear Miss Gunning

Im in my fifties Ive worked the north Atlantic fisheries for thirty years Im not a skipper on account of I like my drink but I dont touch a drop out at sea and Im as good a trawlerman as any. I heard your program on the radio the other night Im writing this in my bunk on the trawler weve been at sea seven days.

I cant give my name. These are hard men Miss and some of them would make short work of a grass its our livelyhoods. But the fisheries are getting queer and its time someone spoke out so use this information well.

The fact is weve had problems with deformed fish for some years now its an open secret in the industry Miss. The skipper who spoke out broke the code and he was threatened very bad had a blade against his windpipe that's why he changed his tune.

Twenty years ago we used to fish SONAZ illegal weed just slip in and lay the nets regardless. Then we started hauling in too many baduns thats what we call these fish baduns. The last few years weve put a five mile buffer round SONAZ and that keeps the baduns to an OK level but there's always a couple. Every catch we make they're sifted out and chucked back in the sea. Theyre horrible looking things really you wouldnt think it possible.

Well Miss its got worse steadily. I told you Ive been at sea thirty years and I've seen a fair few whales like any seaman but lately I've seen things I still cant believe. For the last few months any trawler that goes near SONAZ gets hassled by the whales and theres lots of them different sizes different types seen a couple of big blues and a lot of minkes and sperms too. My skipper puts a ten mile buffer round SONAZ now and the reason is we were pushed backwards by twenty odd whales just a couple of weeks ago and I tell you Miss I'm seen as a tough man but I was frightened because its not natural. Its happening to a lot of trawlers and some trawlermen I've spoken to on land say there boats were charged and rammed so theres something wrong. Likely as not theres something nasty on the sea bed but the owners of the boats want to keep it quiet well they would wouldnt they.

Well miss it's back on land tonight Ill be posting this tomorrow and I hope it reaches you and I hope you get something going but as I say I wont give my name and Ill be obliged if you dont track me down personally. Yours,
a trawlerman

He read it through quickly as the BMW whizzed in and out of the traffic, his heart rate quickening when he came to the bit about the whales. When he got to the end he went back to the beginning and pretended to read it again, so that he had time to think. I knew it, he was thinking; right from the beginning, right from the moment Blackfin hurled himself at that shore, I knew there was something very big and bad going on, and here's the proof. We've got whales beaching en masse, we've got whales swimming up rivers, and now we've got the same kind of aggressive behaviour out at sea. This guy's hypothesis, what is it – *likely as not theres something nasty on the sea bed* – is a bloody good starting point.

"Well?" Kate asked.

Roddy made a non-committal noise. His mind was racing about the "baduns", the mutated fish. Endemic congenital mutation in a fixed location, as this seemed to be, suggested long-term population exposure to an agent – God knows what it could be – that was both persistent and concentrated. That meant the agent, too, had to be fixed in the same location, possibly entering the submarine ecosystem constantly over a long period of time, otherwise the effects of the exposure wouldn't be so severe and localized. Christ… what an incredible twenty-four hours, first the killers swimming up the river, then the phone call with Derek, now this.

"What do you propose doing with this information?" he asked.

She hesitated.

"Can I be honest with you?"

"I don't know – can you?"

She smiled sourly but didn't complain.

"I could do a story now and there'd be a lot of interest, and that could lead to more substantial facts coming out. I could make my name on this one right now, you know? But I want to get it right this time. I've learnt a lot from the past few days, honestly. And I think this thing is big, really big. I mean, if there's stuff in the sea that's mutating the fish and making the whales aggressive, then your mind naturally comes up with two hypotheses: large-scale dumping of toxic industrial waste, or large-scale dumping of toxic military waste."

"Well you can't assume that yet, you have to—"

"I'm not saying I'm assuming it, but it's the most likely scenario, and in that case you're dealing with people who have a lot of power and can get seriously nasty. And I want to do this right. I want the truth and I want all of it. The danger in just going to press now is that the big players get the chance to cover their tracks.

"That's why I've come to you. I thought we could, kind of, link up."

"You can't be serious…"

"I'm completely serious. I know how you must feel about me, but what I'm trying to get across is that I've come to realize that this whole whale thing is not just a media story, this time it's more important than that. Look, I'm really sorry for treating you badly previously. And I'm sure you must be desperate to vindicate yourself. After all, what did you really do wrong except leave the whales on the beach so long that they died?"

"But they shouldn't have died," he blurted out, exasperated.

"That's another mystery that needs clearing up. Why is no one asking how they died? Why didn't Derek Petersen ask it when he was appointed? Why weren't the dead whales investigated? The government just towed them out to sea to rot!"

"I hadn't thought of that."

For a moment he was tempted to tell her about Derek's phone call, the necropsy reports, but something held him back.

"Work with me," she asked him directly.

He shook his head, and to hide his confusion he switched the radio on.

195

"...been announced that Dr Derek Petersen has stood down as Emergency Coordinator of the Whale Crisis Coordination Team..."

"Whoa," Kate exclaimed.

"...not clear whether Dr Petersen resigned or was forced out, but it is known that he had been suffering stress and depression since being appointed to the post left vacant by the previous leader of the team, Dr Roddy Ormond, the man widely blamed for the disastrous handling of the Brighton beaching. Since Dr Ormond's departure, efforts to deal with the situation have been seen as ineffective. The convoy of killer whales that yesterday..."

"It's chaos now," Kate said. "Total chaos."

4

Twelve hours after the midnight madness of the killer whales, London was still struggling to come to terms. In St James's Park, a few hundred metres away from the river, there was a feeling of unreality. Many people who had been in London throughout the night were sleeping off their exhaustion, prone on the grass under a half-overcast sky. Others milled along the paths and around the small lake, bleary-eyed and numb.

Rattigan was sitting on the park bench he normally used when meeting with Jenkins, his MoD contact. This time they were talking by mobile phone. Rattigan could see Jenkins quite clearly across the water. He was taking this precaution because Ally was with him. He didn't want her to know anything of his business. He could watch her sauntering across the bridge while she waited for him to complete his call.

"...the possibility of an explicit link between the Brighton whales and the SONAZ whales is being actively considered within the MoD," Jenkins was revealing. "The other way that the MoD is involved is with the necropsies. These have quietly been taken over by military laboratories, but it's only a matter of time before the newspapers get hold of that. I mean, anything to do with whales is going to get enormous attention at the moment, obviously."

"And there's still funny stuff going on in SONAZ?"

"There are a few unconfirmed reports and rumours flying around, different kinds of things, but all concerning whales doing odd things to boats near SONAZ."

Rattigan yawned. He was aware of how his attention was switching on and off in irregular bursts. He was exhausted by his sleepless night, anxious about the ship from Russia that would soon be accessing SONAZ, elated by Ally's return. *She's so pretty,* Rattigan mused, his eye following her. *I don't like men looking at her, she's just a child.* Her gaze met his own and she smiled, so that his heart skipped a beat.

Ally got to the end of the bridge and started walking along the lake. She was carrying a newspaper, inside which was a letter. When she had got into her father's Bentley earlier there had been depressingly little evidence of his work; she had always thought he cruised around under mountains of paperwork. It was as though he had cleared it all away, out of sight, before meeting her. But there had been one document caught under the folding arm rest. When they had got out of the car, she had taken the opportunity to spirit it away.

"Hullo?" a voice was saying into Rattigan's ear. "Hullo? Are you still there?"

"Yeah I'm still here." He forced himself back to the issue, it was important, he had to assess the risks. "What about infringements in SONAZ?"

"The trawlers are keeping well away now. A vessel called *The Vegas* was logged cutting straight across. But the government's in a tricky position. It doesn't want any attention brought to bear on SONAZ at all. So although it doesn't want boats going in, nor does it want boats that do go in to be apprehended – that would defeat the objective. It looks like they've decided that turning a blind eye is the least bad option."

"*The Vegas* was mine," Rattigan said gravely, aware, even as he spoke, that he was being uncharacteristically open. He felt slightly light-headed from fatigue and emotion. He wanted to put aside these worries and just be with Ally, but they had to be dealt with. His eye was drawn to the wildfowl in the lake, where a coot was chasing a moorhen.

"I kind of assumed so," said Jenkins.

Across the water, Ally sat down on the edge of a park bench and waved at her father. But he wasn't looking. She unfolded her newspaper and searched through the pages for the letter, hoping that it would give her some clue about what he was up to. Finding it, she smoothed it out and read the letterhead at the top. Her brow folded in puzzlement.

ChildrenChance

Mr Geoffrey Hardwright
Hadlyn Stemper Wertz Co.
Solicitors

Dear Mr Hardwright

I wish to apologize unreservedly for having offended your client. Please be assured that the fault lies with me and me only, and that it can be put down to exuberance. As I explained in my original letter, ChildrenChance has never before received a charitable donation of this magnitude. £5 million allows us to maintain and develop all our existing programmes, some of which had been under threat, and it allows us to extend our work and so protect and nurture more vulnerable children. It was pure joy that induced me to be less than rigorous with your strict instructions to avoid all manifestations of gratitude to the donor. I have never encountered a donor of your client's type before.

Following your letter, in which the terms of the donation are repeated with great clarity, I confirm that ChildrenChance will make no further attempt to express any gratitude through you to your client. I confirm that we shall give no publicity to the donation, nor draw undue attention to it, nor speculate upon its source, in any shape or form, so that your client's anonymity shall be inviolate. Let me assure you that, so far as is consistent with the law, we will give the donation the absolute minimum level of prominence in the accounts and elsewhere.

I hope this serves to reassure you that I note and accept all your client's objections to my previous letter. I repeat my most profound and unreserved apologies.

Yours sincerely,

Marilyn Frears

Chief Executive, ChildrenChance

Ally read the letter through again, shaking her head. What the hell?... She looked across the lake at him as she stood up to continue her walk, somehow seeing his shape, the outline of him against a backdrop of bench and grass, in a different way. Five million pounds...

"There's another one, soon," Rattigan was saying to Jenkins. "*Jasmine*. I'd like to stop it, the situation is becoming untenable, but I can't. It's too late. Will she be OK?"

"I'm just a small player," Jenkins said, "you know that. But in my opinion, for what it's worth, it should be OK. In the very short term, any illegal access into SONAZ is likely to be ignored. The unofficial line appears to be see no evil, hear no evil, think no evil. On the other hand, it's only a matter of time before this situation blows up. Then the ministers will totally reverse their position, they'll be desperate to be seen to be doing something. So as long as you can get *Jasmine* in and out quickly…"

Rattigan was taken by surprise when, looking up, he saw Ally walking past Jenkins's bench. He waited for her to move on before finishing off the discussion.

"That's the last vessel," he told Jenkins.

* * *

In Clacton-on-Sea it was raining heavily. The sky was as cheerful as worn tarmac. By the fish-and-chip shop at the entrance to the pier were four old ladies and one old man, all wearing transparent plastic macs and faces empty of hope, pleasure and expectation. Kate gave them a polite "Good morning" as she and Roddy passed by, but they didn't answer, staring at her implacably as though wondering what she meant.

"Charming," she muttered, walking along the pier stride for stride with Roddy. A short way in she pointed ahead. "What," she asked, "is that?"

A short, tubby man was hurrying down the pier towards them, his pink, bald head bobbing up and down, his grey ponytail flapping up and down.

"That's Joe."

"You came!" Joe called as he reached them, huffing and puffing.

"Hello Joe – this is Kate Gunning."

Joe looked between the two of them incredulously.

"I'm not even gonna ask. Thanks for getting your ass down here. Come on, let's go, you've got to see Attila."

"She's still upside down?"

"Oh no, no no no, she switched strategies."

"What's she doing?"

"I think you should see it for yourself."

He led them through the reception area of WhaleWorld and up a flight of stairs. As soon as Joe kicked open the emergency exit door to the rain-lashed outside—

"What is that *noise*?" Kate asked.

They were standing on the top tier of seating above the dolphins' pool. Directly below them, Joe's four dolphins were huddled together. And from somewhere came a piercing sequence of squeals, endlessly repeated. It didn't hurt the ear; rather, it pained something inside the human instinct. It was like listening to a baby crying but being unable to help. They descended and reached Attila's section. The animal swam straight at them, still emitting her ceaseless call. "Jesus!" Kate yelled, stepping back from the edge as Attila's huge head rode up the lip of the pool and, like a boat stuck half in and half out of the water, stayed there. There was no break in the squealing. Roddy looked down at her, transfixed. The word which came into his mind was "imploring" – she's imploring us, begging us, telling us to do something. But what?

"How long has she been doing this?"

"She started in the middle of the night."

"How do you know?"

"Cos I was at home watching TV while the killers in London were doing their little party-piece, and my phone goes, and the pier's kick-ass security guard, Hector – seventy-five years old and a hundred pounds of pure rheumatoid arthritis – is on the other end of the line squirting into his incontinence pads. He thought it was a ghost."

"She looks under-nourished, Joe."

"She looks like shit. She's stopped eating."

"The same thing, over and over again." Roddy crouched down and put his hand on Attila's snout. "What is it? I wish you could talk to me."

"What if she could?" Joe offered, after a pause.

"Could what?"

"Talk to you."

"What's that supposed to mean?" Roddy said, getting to his feet.

"She is talking to us."

"She's talking to us?" Kate repeated.

"What are you, deaf?" He turned away and stomped into his office, calling over his shoulder: "It's just that she's not making any sense. Come into the office, willya? We're getting wet."

Inside the filthy, soul-oppressing junkyard that was the office, Jason, Joe's young employee, was fast asleep on a swivel chair, a tabloid newspaper resting on his lap and open at the picture of a topless model.

"Wake up!" Joe shouted.

Jason got to his feet sleepily, then his eyes widened as he recognized Roddy.

"You're the guy who—"

"Yeah yeah, make us three coffees," Joe interrupted, bundling him out of the room, He sat down on the freshly vacated chair. "Take a seat, Roddy, Kate."

There was a moment's pause.

"Where?" Kate asked, surveying the cluttered, grubby surfaces.

"Anywhere. OK, Roddy, let's get serious now. You know that captive killers are trained to recognize elementary words, right?"

"Words?"

"Well, we use different kinds of whistles to represent different words. Like, one kind of whistle means 'fish', another means 'ball'."

202

"Oh I see. Yes, I know this."

"Dogs can do that," Kate chipped in.

"Certainly. Attila has a vocabulary of eleven words, OK? She knows the nouns 'fish', 'ball', 'whale', 'man' and 'water', she knows the verbs 'dive', 'get', 'leap' and 'roll', and she knows 'up' and 'down'."

Kate precariously lowered her behind onto a teetering pile of folders.

"A whale can't know what nouns and verbs are," she said, then looked at Roddy. "Can it?"

"Well, no, but that's neither here nor there, children of eighteen months don't know what nouns and verbs are but they can understand simple sentences."

"We put the different whistles together," Joe continued, "in a sequence of sounds to construct simple sentences which whales can interpret. If the trainer blows *whale-leap-roll,* Attila leaps in the air and does a roll. If he blows *whale-get-ball,* Attila gets the ball. You know this, right?"

"Yes," Roddy confirmed. He picked up a grubby piece of coral from the clutter of Joe's desk and turned it over in his hands. "It doesn't mean much. Humans always presume that an animal, to communicate intelligence, must show a linguistic facility comprehensible to us. The terms of reference are all wrong. Far from proving or disproving their intelligence one way or the other, it merely demonstrates our stupidity."

"And anyway," Kate added, "who's to say that the whales really interpret each part of the command? Maybe they just learn which combinations of sound are associated with which actions."

"Yeah yeah," Joe said dismissively, examining a cigar, "that's what people used to say. But then Hughie came along."

"Hughie?"

"Some crazy scientists in Santa Monica bought an adolescent killer from a Sea World in Canada." The cigar went into his mouth; there was a short interval while he lit it to his satisfaction. "They spent all day every day teaching this animal a bunch of tricks, all designed to find out how intelligent he was. Hughie learnt amazing routines, he could practically tie his own shoe laces, and he had a vocabulary of forty or fifty human words, much more than Attila or any other whale, but the big question was exactly like you said: was he understanding each part of the command and interpreting the whole – was he, in some way, manipulating an artificial language – or was he merely learning a pattern of noises associated with a particular action and reward, like a dog can?"

"And?" Kate asked, while Roddy moved around, picking things up, putting them down again.

"One day they'd told him to get the ball a hundred times. They threw it in, whistled *whale-get-ball*, and watched him bring it to the side. Hughie was bored, real bored. He stopped cooperating, but they keep on whistling the command, *whale-get-ball, whale-get-ball,* a hundred, a thousand times—"

"This is the kind of pseudo-science I particularly detest," Roddy announced abruptly, "it's on a par with inflating a frog with a bicycle pump, just to see it explode."

"But listen up Roddy: Hughie suddenly goes crazy, rushes around the pool, and whacks the ball clean out of the water with his tail. The scientists are all looking down at him, kinda puzzled. Then Hughie starts squealing, only it's not a regular killer call, not a clicking and squealing, it's something different, it's a repeated three-part phrase. It's an imitation of the whistle language. Understand? Hughie's talking to them."

"What do you mean, he's talking to them?" Roddy asked after a pause.

"He's talking to them!"

"What did he say?" Kate asked, standing up to move away from the clouds of noxious smoke that were rolling out of Joe's mouth.

"He said, *man-get-ball*. That's what he said. So the scientists start jumping up and down in excitement, one of them goes and gets the ball and puts it in the water, Hughie whacks it out again, and then he's telling *them* to get the ball a hundred times, and he's loving it. Then they put a trainer in the water, Hughie says *man-roll*, so the man rolls, Hughie says *man-dive*, so the man dives…"

"And Attila? Are you saying Attila is doing this?"

"You bet. Just started doing it, out of the blue, must've gotten bored of floating upside down all day and all night…"

They waited for Joe to continue, but he didn't.

"And?" Kate prompted.

"And what?"

"What's Attila saying, for God's sake?"

From behind his desk, Joe held his hands up apologetically.

"So you've heard the good part, OK? At the same time as two hundred and forty-four killers take a daytrip to London, my captive killer starts talking. I think that's pretty mind-blowing, don't you? I mean, I think someone in authority should listen to this. I think it's pretty damn relevant anyway you look at, agreed?"

"What's the whale saying, Joe?"

"It doesn't matter, it makes no sense."

"But what is it?"

"Here's the kid, c'mon kid, bring it in here. Roddy, coffee, Kate, here it is, take it."

"Joe!"

"All right, I know," Joe said, making space on his desk for the mugs; a loaded ashtray fell off the edge and smashed onto the floor. He stared at it for a few moments. "It's just weird, that's all. What she's saying, over and over, it's..." He picked up his coffee and sipped at it, shaking his head. "...A whole bunch of stuff about *man* and *fish* and *get* and *fish* and *man*, it's totally fucking incomprehensible."

"Tell me exactly," Roddy said. "I want the sequence."

"*man-get-man-fish, man-get-man-fish, man-get-man-fish.* Or maybe *fish-man-get-man, fish-man-get-man, fish-man-get-man.* Or how about *man-fish-man-get, man-fish-man-get, man-fish-man-get.* You work it out."

Roddy walked out of the office and back to Attila. She still had her head lodged on the lip of the pool; she was still emitting her mantra. He sat down cross-legged in front of her but slightly to one side, so that they could look at each other. Her eye swivelled in its socket, then locked onto his gaze: *...get-man-fish-man-get-man-fish-man-get-man-fish-man-get-man-fish-man-get-man-fish-man-get-man-fish-man...*

* * *

Whitaker was resting on the balcony of the flat. He dozed under a weak sun, wrapped up in blankets. His fractured leg was supported on one of his mother's prize possessions, a leather pouffe embroidered with silk roses. The balcony looked out onto a bowling green, whose hidden square of colour seemed surprising in such grey urban sprawl. Elderly men and women were engaging in a spot of mid-week practice in preparation for their Saturday league match. Whitaker had nodded off to the pleasant sound of bowls kissing.

"Whitaker... Whitaker."

"Mmm? Oh."

"How are you?"

"I'm OK Roddy. Leg's throbbing. Did you find Derek?"

"Not yet, that's next on the agenda. Something came up.

I ended up going to WhaleWorld, the place I went to before, where the freaked-out captive killer is."

Whitaker's eyes widened as Kate Gunning stepped onto the balcony.

"Hi!" she said. "Remember me?"

"Er, yes."

"How are you?"

"Erm, I'm OK."

Whitaker looked from Roddy to Kate, from Kate to Roddy.

"Roddy?" Whitaker asked, grimacing as he pushed himself up in his chair. "What's going on?"

"It's hard to explain," Roddy said weakly, grabbing two folding chairs and handing one to Kate; the morning's events and revelations had not so much overridden his history of bad feeling for Kate, as temporarily erased it from his memory. He unfolded his chair and sat on it. I never actually agreed that I would work with her, he defended himself hopelessly; it's just that, in all the excitement, I forgot to tell her I wouldn't...

"This is even weirder than the whales," Whitaker said. "Really, how can you two be—"

"Whitaker, believe me, this won't seem as interesting after we've told you what we're going to tell you. There's something extraordinary going on. I want us to brainstorm it. Listen to this..."

* * *

Half an hour later, Whitaker was stroking his chin as he looked down at some scribbled notes:

1. Sperm whale, deep-water animal, enters shallow sea and beaches itself in wholly atypical fashion on beach used by humans.

2. *Shortly after sperm whale refloated, 78 whales of different species beach themselves in same spot. Original sperm whale among them. Unprecedented incident. People killed.*

3. *All whales die mysteriously during course of one night. Derek Petersen appointed to replace Roddy. Corpses disposed of at sea (with indecent haste?) because of "public health hazard". Authorities not falling over themselves to establish cause of death.*

4. *Another unprecedented whale incident, 244 killer whales leaving the sea to swim up the river Thames to London.*

5. *Roddy receives call from Derek Petersen. Derek unstable. Derek mentions that the necropsy results are being suppressed.*

6. *Kate establishes likelihood of mutated fish being caught in area of North Atlantic known as SONAZ, above Irminger Basin; a source reports that whales regularly harass trawlers in this region.*

7. *WhaleWorld: a captive killer that had previously engaged in bizarre behaviour (potentially a protest?) now frantically emits a sequence of four "words", over and over again:*

	man-get-man-fish
OR	*get-man-fish-man ?*
OR	*man-fish-man-get ?*
OR	*fish-man-get-man ?*

On the bowling green a good joke elicited laughter from the old people. Further away, an ice-cream van played 'Greensleeves' through a crackling tannoy. Roddy and Kate sat on each side of Whitaker's chair, hunched forwards so that they could read the piece of paper too.

"It's all related," Whitaker said, thoughtfully. "Whatever the whales have done so far, whatever they try next, it's all related, it's all designed to achieve the same purpose, to tell us something."

"But tell us what?"

Whitaker's mother knocked on the glass of the French windows. She had interrupted their discussion several times, concerned that her son was over-taxing himself.

"Mum, stop it! I'm fine!"

Mrs Grant slid the door open.

"Mum, we're busy!"

"It's something for 'im," said Mrs Grant, nodding at Roddy as she handed him a package, "a motorcycle courier brought it. Now come inside son, you got to rest."

"I'm resting, I'm resting."

Mrs Grant slid the door shut testily.

Roddy had extracted a document from the envelope.

"What is it?" Kate asked, watching his expression.

"Wait." He scanned it intently, one hand raised to fend off any interruption. "We've got a breakthrough... This is from Derek... It seems to be a summary of one of the necropsies."

"Read it."

"Blood, lymphs and lymph nodes reveal unsustainable amounts of unstable by-products from the chlorophenoxy group, in particular: 2,3,7,8-tetrachlorodibenzo-para-dioxin; 2,4,5-trichlorophenoxy acetic acid; 2,4-D; picloram; and cacodylate. These chemicals also deposited in all major organs, muscles and fat, indicating serious long-term exposure. Also, gravely worrying, significant quantities of further complex chemicals. Among these, the organophosphate N,N-diisopropyl-2-aminoethyl chloride hydrochloride. Work continuing to establish if this organophosphate has caused

*imbalance of acetycholine in the brain. Of other complex
chemicals found, many <u>do not conform to known chemical
compounds</u>; seem to be <u>original products</u>. Preliminary biopsy
report on this issue suggests it's much too early to reach any
conclusions whatsoever, but makes tentative speculation
that these unknown chemicals could be result of unusual
and unknown chemical reactions occurring at very high
pressures, e.g., deep under the sea."*

Roddy and Whitaker stared at each other.

"Fucking hell," Whitaker said.

"What is it?" Kate pleaded. "What does it mean?"

Roddy didn't respond. He had turned his attention to the
second sheet of paper in the envelope.

"What is it?" Kate repeated, almost angrily.

"I don't know where to start," Whitaker said. "Have you
heard of Agent Orange?"

"Vietnam."

"Yeah, chemical weapon used by the Yanks. It contains
dioxin, which is thousands of times more toxic than all the
other poisons we've leached into the sea, and for a whale
to have significant amounts in its system implies a grave
contamination of its habitat, because whales are at the top of
the food chain."

"And the second bit?"

"I'm not sure what that massive great equation means, but
organophosphates in general are pesticides, I think. But that
stuff about chemicals not conforming to known compounds,
that's utterly mind-blowing. What do you think Roddy?"

Roddy, ashen-faced, couldn't answer. He put a hand to his
left temple, and gestured to his companions to read the second
document.

Dear Roddy,

I don't know if you'll get this.

Roddy, I killed the whales. I anaesthetized them and incapacitated their respiratory systems. I had no choice, Lizzie would have been killed. Perhaps this seems crazy to you, Roddy, just as I seem crazy to everyone at the moment. But don't make the mistake of not believing this. I don't know the identity of the person or group who forced me to do this, but I do know that they're merciless. I don't know why they wanted the whales dead, only that they wanted it badly.

Don't go public with this. If they know you're on to them they'll deal with you.

I've scribbled down what I remember of the key necropsy. The preliminary necropsy reports are being sat on at the highest levels because the implications are horrendous. We both know what 2,4,5-trichlorophenoxy acetic acid implies. The "unknown chemicals" are even more alarming.

I'm sorry. I don't know if I'll succeed in getting this to you, they're watching me. But I can't live with the knowledge of what I've done.

I can only think of one way of releasing Lizzie from the threat she's under.

Forgive me.

Your friend, Derek.

He killed the whales, Roddy was repeating to himself mechanically, in shock, someone forced him to kill them, who would do that, why? And – *Lizzie would have been killed...*

Suddenly he was fumbling for his phone and dialling Derek's mobile. It rang and rang.

At the window, Mrs Grant's anxious face appeared again. But something in the expressions of the three people sitting on her balcony persuaded her not to disturb them.

* * *

In London, a middle-aged man came out of Farringdon station. He passed slowly along Cowcross Street. The collar of his jacket was up, and the cap on his head was pulled down low. His eyes were fixed on the ground. He resembled a parody of someone who didn't want to be recognized – and despite his huge media profile during recent days, no one recognized him. Misery emanated from him, so much so that passers-by wanted nothing to do with him.

Tailing him were two younger men. They took little care to conceal their presence. For a week they or their colleagues had followed him everywhere. They had sat opposite him in a doctor's waiting room, while the man waited to see his doctor to get some anti-depressants. They had watched him cry, they had watched him pray, and on one instance they had watched him sit on a park bench and stare into space for over three hours. Then he had walked over to them and said, "Who are you working for?"

"We don't know stuff like that," had been the honest reply.

"Why are you following me?"

"Just keeping an eye on you. Don't want you doing anything silly, meeting any journalists, making mischief. All right?"

The man had nodded and walked away. They had fallen in behind him.

"Christ, he looks rough," said one of the tails now, as the man turned right into Farringdon Road.

"Not a happy bunny," the other agreed.

The man turned left into Saffron Street and approached a multi-storey car park. He went inside and walked up the concrete stairs of the first flight. The two tails speeded up a little. They clattered up the stairs noisily. The man was going all the way up to the top storey.

"Oi," shouted one of the tails, "what are you doing?"

Ignoring them, the man walked briskly across the concrete concourse. He reached the chest-high safety barrier.

The two tails sprinted after him but the man, without pausing for thought, without looking back, and with a memorable degree of agility for someone of his years, vaulted cleanly over the barrier. Soundlessly he plummeted down seven storeys and impacted in the narrow street below. The two men looked over the edge at the dead body of Derek Petersen. He was on his back, lying in an expanding pool of blood. In his pocket a phone started ringing.

5

There were several people in her office – her Parliamentary Private Secretary, the Minister of State for Defence Procurement, and a middle-ranking civil servant – when Victoria Adlington, Secretary of State for Defence, opened the confidential report on the findings of the necropsies performed on seven beached whales. Like many ministers, she processed in two minutes the labour of hundreds of hours. She speed-read the introduction, flicked through the 170 pages that followed and turned to the five-page summary at the end. Her eye was immediately drawn to a section titled: *Main Contaminants*. At the top of the list: *N,N-diisopropyl-2-aminoethyl chloride hydrochloride*.

She winced.

"Minister?"

Adlington met the anxious gaze of her PPS and smiled.

"I think I'll go for one of my walks," she announced.

Everyone knew that the Secretary of State for Defence reserved "one of her walks" – abstracted perambulations along obscure corridors of the MoD – for issues that were particularly problematic.

Once in an obscure enough corridor, Adlington looked down, her feet invisible to her under the great swell of her body, and began to waddle along the wall slowly. She allowed the problem to swarm into every nook and cranny of her thinking: N,N-diisowhatever-it-is-aminoethyl something hydrochloride; I can't remember the formula and I wish I didn't have to... This would seem to be worse than the worst-case-scenario I could have imagined; if the whales have got that stuff in their systems, then... As if we didn't have enough problems. Whales swimming up the Thames, Derek Petersen committing suicide, the voters asking why the government isn't in control, and now this comes along. What an almighty mess.

* * *

A freezing white blanket of sea fog lay over the unfathomable North Atlantic waters. It wrapped itself around the *Jasmine*, hugging the vessel as though it would never let go. The 4,000-ton cruiser pitched on a rolling sea that owed its liveliness to the fag end of a storm two hundred miles away. Visibility was less than fifty metres. From his position on the bridge, Captain Schwarzkop peered out of the window, his hand on the manual tiller. He couldn't even see to the bow of the ship. Only one of the ship's two masts was clearly visible on the deck below. Three men were working on or near this mast. The Captain checked his position once more, and looked at his watch. About an hour to go. He was glad he was on the bridge. This fog was bone-achingly cold.

Captain Schwarzkop was a thirty-eight-year-old dissipated American. In the twenty years of his adult life he had been thrown out of every institution he'd gone into, including the New York Jets, the US Marines, two reputable merchant shipping lines and three marriages. He had got through one court martial, three disciplinary hearings, one criminal trial, three good-looking wives, two proud parents and about as much whisky as could be transported by a medium-sized tanker. By his thirties, he had found a style of life that suited him: that of a skipper for hire, no questions asked. During the previous five years he had engaged in gun-running to Iraq, drug-trafficking out of Manila, and the smuggling of illegal immigrants from North Africa to Italy. In comparison to such exploits, crossing the Forbidden Zone seemed tame.

Jasmine had entered the fog three hours before, and had iced up rapidly. The deck was a glassy, treacherous plate. Ice coated the derricks, the fire hydrants. To touch the wet-cargo pipeline with your bare palm would be to fuse yourself to the ship.

The bosun out on the deck swore and bellyached as he worked, his curses immediately turning into miniature clouds of freezing vapour. With two other men, he was working on the mast by the cargo hatch, chipping the ice from the cargo boom. He was wearing thick mittens, underneath which were thin woollen gloves, but his hands felt colder than the ice he was attacking. His two subordinates were similarly fed up.

"Cargo winch clean, Mr Bosun sir," said Able Seaman Ravn hopefully. A young Dane with an obsessive love for his girl in Frederikshavn, he was intent on getting back to his cabin and writing another long love letter.

"Bullshit," growled the bosun.

Ravn cast a disconsolate look at his Polish workmate, Able Seaman Matejko. They both set to with their hammers once more. The cargo winch suspended from the cargo boom needed to be absolutely clean before it could be used.

Not for the first time, the bosun wondered what the hell he was doing standing on a small ship under a freezing fog, chipping at ice with a bloody hammer so that his captain could chuck something nasty into the sea... Other men had easy nine-to-five days, at the end of which they had sex with their wives; all he had to look forward to was a few hours of exhausted slumber in a dirty cabin, or a game of chess with the filthy-minded Chinese cook.

On the bridge, Captain Schwarzkop phoned the galley.

"Get some hot coffee to those boys on deck," he ordered.

Then he glanced at the ship's radar. There was nothing out there to indicate that he was going to experience any difficulties in accomplishing his mission. It was all rather dull. The phrase "money for nothing" came to mind.

* * *

1 p.m. at the British Library at King's Cross in London: Roddy, carrying a pile of photocopies, pushed open the door of the Science 2 reading room with his foot and made his way outside. Grief and purpose could be seen in the set of his mouth, which seemed harder, less mobile – as though, beneath the lips, his teeth were clenched together. His eyes shone with determination. Derek's suicide had appalled him, and the guilt had briefly threatened to crush him. But such feelings had been quickly overwhelmed by even stronger ones, of anger and injustice: there was some power out there so vile that it had killed not just the whales on Brighton beach, but his friend: he wanted to nail the wrongdoers' filthy hides to the wall.

In the crowded canteen opposite Humanities 1 he saw Kate hunched over her papers. He manoeuvred around a portly, bearded professor who was standing forlornly with a tray in his hands, looking for an empty table.

"Kate."

She didn't hear him. Her face was partially obscured by the chestnut hair dangling over it. She was supporting herself on her elbows, her shoulders hunched up. Roddy found himself looking into the V-neck of her top at the pale skin, an achingly beautiful collar bone, and the small curve at the top of her breast. He frowned. An image of Derek, jumping to his death only a mile or so away, came into his mind.

"Kate," he said, sitting down. "It's chemical weapons."

She jumped slightly, startled by the screech of his chair on the floor.

"I know. Agent Orange."

"Not that, I mean the organophosphate, the N,N-diisopropyl compound thing. It's the formula for VX nerve agent."

Kate stared.

"But... Whitaker said it was a pesticide."

"Yeah, well, in the same way that a five-hundred-pound bomb is a firework. There are four main nerve agents: tabun, soman, sarin and VX. Tabun is at least a hundred times more toxic than cyanide. Soman is ten times more toxic than tabun. Sarin is ten times more toxic than Soman. And VX is ten times more toxic than sarin."

"What does it do?"

"Messes up the neurotransmitters in the brain. You get convulsions and you die."

Kate nodded slowly.

"Which countries have it?"

"VX? We've got it, the Americans have got it, the Russians have got a couple of hundred thousand tonnes of it, everyone's got it. Who hasn't got it is an easier question."

"OK then, who would dump it at sea?"

Roddy shrugged but didn't answer.

"Are you OK?" Kate asked.

"It just depresses me to death that someone's chucking this stuff in the sea."

"I know. What about the Agent Orange thing?"

"Oh Christ, that's no better." He flicked through his pile of photocopies and handed her a few marked ones. "It's just about the best-known, most documented, and certainly most used chemical-warfare agent in history. All independent commentators are agreed that the US military machine dumped a disgusting amount of this filthy concoction on Vietnam – one estimate is seventeen million gallons—"

"How much?" Kate exclaimed loudly.

People around them paused and stared.

"Amazing isn't it. Between 1962 and 1971, 10% of the inland forests, 36% of the mangrove swamps, 3% of cultivated land and 5% of the rest of the land was cleared, killed, poisoned by the spraying of Agent Orange and other related compounds such as Agent Blue and Agent White."

"But if it was sprayed in those kinds of quantities," Kate said, thinking aloud, confused, "I mean, Whitaker said that dioxin was a thousand times more toxic than other poisons, so how could they possibly spray that amount of it?"

"Agent Orange is pretty nasty stuff in its own right, there's no doubt about that, but it's not dioxin. Dioxin is a chemical by-product which arises during the manufacture of 2,4,5-T, and 2,4-D, the active components of Agent Orange. When the Americans sprayed Vietnam with Agent Orange, they didn't know – or claimed they didn't know – what the dioxin by-products in the Agent Orange would do. It's the traces of dioxin in the minke whale which are really frightening. Dioxin wreaks havoc. Agent Orange poisons environments, whereas dioxin…"
– he extracted copies of pages from a medical journal, and handed them across to her.

She found herself looking at a photograph of a child. Its head was grossly bulbous and knobbly, the left eye all but hidden by the overhang of a congenital deformity; the nose appeared to have split from the pressure which the misshapen skull had applied, while the child's mouth was huge and monstrous, stretching across the entire width of what should have been a

218

face. A thin vent opened between Kate's own lips, to exhale a sound of pain.

"How could this have been allowed to happen?"

On the next page, the picture was of a woman with a sickening skin condition, her whole body covered in blisters and sores; there was an expression of unspeakable suffering in her eyes. Kate put the pages down, unwilling to look at them any more.

"Basically," Roddy said, "exposure to high levels of dioxin may cause metastases, sarcomas, liver and kidney failure, tumours and cancers of all kinds, as well as miscarriage, congenital defects, growth abnormalities and untreatable chloracne skin diseases. Note particularly, congenital defects and growth abnormalities... Makes you think of anything?"

"The mutated fish in SONAZ!"

"Exactly."

"So just where does this leave us, I mean—"

"We're on to something just incomprehensibly enormous. It's almost certain that Agent Orange has been dumped in this SONAZ place in the North Atlantic, in massive quantities, probably years and years ago for the dioxin to have worked its way up the ecosystem. VX could be more recent, it would show up immediately after contamination. Then we've got the infamous 'unknown compounds', as if things weren't bad enough. So we've got a melting pot of truly hideous toxins. Throw in the immense pressure that exists as the bottom of the sea and you very quickly get into uncharted ideas. I mean, under that kind of pressure, there could be all kinds of chemical reactions occurring that just aren't known to science, the contaminants could be reacting with one another, or with naturally occurring chemicals and minerals. I basically believe that the whales are doing what they're doing in order to warn us about ecological catastrophe. But the thing I don't understand is: Agent Orange is an American thing, so why are the whales targeting Britain? Is it just random or—"

"Maybe the Americans didn't dump this filth. Maybe we did."

"We dumped American chemical weapons?"

She pushed across a folder.

"I commissioned a search from the Press Association Library. It reveals that the first country to deploy an Agent Orange-like defoliant was us—"

"What?"

"—during the Malayan Emergency of 1948 to 1958. It was sprayed on the jungle, and on the communication lines of the communist insurgents. So it's my guess that the whales have got their geography correct. The chemical weapons were dumped by good old Britain."

* * *

On the *Jasmine*, cables extended into the depths of the hold from the winch on the cargo boom. Two crew members stood at each side, waiting to prevent the load from striking the edges of the hatch as it was winched up. They clapped their mittened hands together in a fruitless attempt to stave off the cold.

Captain Schwarzkop watched from the bridge. His men on the deck below looked like ghosts, the colour of their clothes whitened out by a fog which had developed into the worst he had ever experienced. It pressed down on the pitching sea, as heavy as grief, as cold as dread. It weighed down on the boat and made her crew long for their cabins.

On the elevated foredeck, the bosun steadied himself as he operated the control box for the winch. The sea wasn't particularly rough, but the surface of the foredeck was little better than a skating rink. He didn't want to go arse over tit in full view of the Captain and his subordinates.

A shout from the hold indicated that the cargo was attached.

The bosun pulled the joystick. An uneven whirring noise emanated from the winch, and within half a minute a metal container, one of five, emerged from the hold. Once it cleared the hatch without any problems, the two crew members stepped away. "St Johnston" was printed on it in Russian and English, skull-and-crossbones symbols underneath.

Captain Schwarzkop peered into the fog, and wondered what was inside the mysterious container now swinging from the cable of the cargo winch. Whatever it was, he'd feel a lot better about it when it was safely at the bottom of the Irminger basin.

What happened next is that no one knew what happened next. There was, perhaps, the smallest indication of something extraordinary, a rumble in the pitching sea that the brain sensed rather than the ear detected. One moment the Captain was raising his hand to acknowledge the bosun; the next, there was a sickening crunch, and the bow of the ship jerked up, virtually out of the sea. Captain Schwarzkop found himself on the floor as though he had been poleaxed. The legs of the crew buckled under them as the boat shot upwards, and then everyone collapsed on the deck as it made its way down again. The bosun was still on the foredeck, but only just. The blow to the ship had knocked him out of the small railed area; he was hanging over the port rail, winded. As the bow of the ship smashed back down into the sea, the impact dropped a blanket of water onto the deck. The bosun was flung from the rail of the foredeck and struck the deck below; the two other crew on deck were flailing helplessly in the rush of water that now swept from stern to fore. Attached to the cable of the winch, the cargo swung about like a conker on a string.

When Captain Schwarzkop struggled to his feet, he saw his bosun motionless, perhaps dead, below, and Matejko desperately hanging on to a fire hydrant as the remnant of the waters swilled away. From the cargo hold came the yells of Able

Seaman Ravn, who had been swept through the hatch by tens of thousands of litres of Atlantic Ocean.

"Fuck," mouthed the Captain soundlessly, "fuck."

He waited, as though it might happen again. Matejko began wailing and crying, "Help me, help me," but the Captain didn't register the noise. Was the boat taking in water? Were the rest of the crew OK? What about the engines? What the hell *was* that?

He turned to the small grey box attached to the bulkhead and flipped open the cover, cursing the fact that the ship's Global Maritime Distress and Safety System was only HF Digital Selective Calling. He punched in the code number, scrolled through to the distress menu, then slammed his hand down on the large red button labelled DISTRESS.

* * *

The Royal Naval Frigate HMS *Ascension* was eighty nautical miles due south of the *Jasmine*. The beeping of a distress signal immediately attracted the attention of the ship's Radio Officer. On his IMMARSAT-C screen the *Jasmine's* position and identity came up automatically. They'd known she was there.

The procedure was simple. First the Radio Officer would inform the bridge; then he would ring HM Coastguard at Falmouth via satellite telephone, and relay the information to the Watch Officer. Then he would contact the ship's Radar Officer to tell him of the incident: the Radar Officer would help the Coastguard to establish which was the nearest vessel to the *Jasmine*.

He made the call to the bridge and was about to contact the Coastguard when the bridge rang back.

"Aren't those coordinates inside SONAZ?" asked the Commander of HMS *Ascension*.

When this had been confirmed, an encrypted call was put

through not to the Coastguard, but to naval intelligence at Portsmouth.

* * *

It was a few minutes after the impact. One of the enginemen was dead, thrown into the engine block by the force of the impact and crushed under a piston. The Chinese cook couldn't be located. The rest of the *Jasmine's* crew were on the deck, half of them carrying injuries of one sort or another. The bosun was still unconscious. Able Seaman Ravn had been rescued from the cargo hold but was shivering uncontrollably, and Able Seaman Matejko had overcome a bout of hysteria, and was now standing listlessly by himself. The First Mate was directing the lowering of the lifeboat.

On the bridge were Captain Schwarzkop, the Chief Mate and the Chief Engineer.

"No water coming in," the Chief Engineer was emphasizing. "None. But no engine any more."

Captain Schwarzkop now found himself in an invidious position: his vessel disabled in restricted waters, an illegal cargo in his hold, and his ass on the line as comprehensively as it had ever been before. It was essential to dump the cargo before they were rescued.

The bridge telephone rang.

"Captain… What?… You'd better repeat that… how many?… I'll come see." He put the phone down. "The bridge is yours," he said to the Chief Mate.

"Where are you going?"

Down on the deck, the Captain exchanged a few words with the men lowering the lifeboat, and reassured the crew that they were not abandoning ship: it was merely a precaution. Then he made his way fore. At the bow, out of the fog, emerged the figures of two crew members. They were standing at the iced-up sea barrier, mittened hands clasping the rail, looking down at the sea. Captain Schwarzkop took his place beside them and looked down over the prow.

The North Atlantic swelled and bulged under its covering of fog. It was as though the planet had contracted, leaving only a small, moving expanse of water to be the world. But in that small expanse were three dark shapes. Two of them were towards the edge of visibility. They rose and descended with the sea, lifeless. The third was directly below and almost touching the ship's hull. That one, too, was dead.

"It must be thirty metres long!" the Captain said. "It's nearly a third of the length of the ship!"

No answer from the two men.

"What kind is it?"

"Blue whale."

The creature's head was staved in. The long snout and jaw were compacted backwards, almost as far as the eye socket. Everything in front of the eye socket was a grisly mess of shattered jawbone, crushed baleen, mangled skull: a sickening mosaic of white bone, dark-grey skin and bright-red gore. The eye itself had burst out of the animal's head. Still connected to the socket by torn tissue, it bobbed in the water next to the mighty corpse. Captain Schwarzkop struggled against a wave of nausea; the dead, free-floating eye was as big as a football, and seemed to be looking at him.

Two hundred metres below the *Jasmine*, little light penetrates. Eight adult blue whales are circling closely. They touch one another's throats with their long flippers. One of them turns over to allow a female to swim over his underside, and she moves over him, gently, slowly, the grooves under her throat touching the grooves of his. Then they roll together, still touching, over and over, displacing thousands of gallons of water. The six other blues form into a spoke-like formation, with the heads at the centre, and nuzzle each other with their long, blue-grey snouts.

Their species is the biggest ever to have lived on earth. Each animal eats forty million krill a day. The lightest weighs one hundred tonnes; the heaviest weighs one hundred and seventy tonnes. Two centuries previously, their population in the North Atlantic and Arctic Oceans was numbering hundreds of thousands; now it is merely in the hundreds. These eight whales are among the last of their kind, and they know they are about to die.

The eldest bull breaks away from the group and quickly accelerates, the power pack of his tail stock propelling him sleekly through the water. The other whales follow. They swim in a large circuit on a horizontal plane, building up speed, each thrust of the tail flukes pushing them ten metres forwards, their streamlined snouts cutting efficiently into the water mass. The bull signals, and all eight whales shear away from the circle and swim straight up. Despite their vast bulk, they are among the most hydrodynamic of all whales, and they shoot towards the surface in the manner of submarine-launched missiles, their combined tonnage equal to a third of the tonnage of the ship above. Converging together, they reach a speed of thirty-five kmph. Above, light frames the dark bulk of the hull of the *Jasmine*. They are only fifty metres away from the vessel...

Captain Schwarzkop was making his way back down the deck. He looked up at the metal case still suspended from the cargo winch, and gestured to his Chief Mate that they had to finish the drop.

...And the blue whales impact. They smash into the central section of the hull, the noise booming up, shuddering through the vessel's structure like some kind of underwater detonation. Schwarzkop's legs crumple under him; the fibulas shear away from the knee, ligaments snap, he doesn't feel or hear or understand the pop-pop of his femurs leaving their sockets in the pelvis.

Under the ship, seven dead whales, heads crumpled, brains mashed, are pushed outwards by the force of the ship as it collapses back into the sea; the eighth dead whale is impaled on a severed ice-breaker cable. The whales have ripped open the skin of the first hull, but not the skin of the second. Millions of gallons of water are rushing into the cavity, rivets come away, steel scantling explodes outwards. The left side of the ship takes in immense quantities of ocean at an exponential rate, and the vessel, badly listing within minutes, begins to keel over.

Some crew were already dead, others were nearly dead, few were conscious, and none were capable of helping themselves. As the *Jasmine* keeled, only Able Seaman Ravn was screaming. Men slid down the deck and wedged on the port sea rail. At forty-five degrees the ship's steady roll to the left became irresistible to the ocean, which sucked the vessel down with sudden eagerness, and her crew, and the five metal cases of her cargo. It had taken about six minutes.

6

The mighty tail flukes rise majestically above the dark ocean, and for a moment seem suspended in the air. No one is there to see a broken length of heavy-duty chain slide down the upended tail stock. The sperm whale slips soundlessly down.

With each thrust of his tail flukes, Blackfin swims deeper into the chilled, lightless depths. Twenty-five percent of his volume is the oxygen he has taken in at the surface; physiological mechanisms make the most efficient use of this most precious of resources. His heart rate drops dramatically, and blood supply to non-essential processes cuts off. The pressure at two hundred and fifty metres triggers his lungs and jointed rib cage to collapse neatly; from this point on, oxygen supply is boosted by the high density of myoglobin molecules in his muscles.

Blackfin sucks in cold water through his blowhole. The tonnes of waxy oil in his head, in the spermaceti organ, contract and become denser in the colder temperature, helping him to descend with the minimum of energy expenditure. Five hundred metres; this is the absolute limit for human divers. For them to descend to such a depth involves days of incarceration in special compression chambers, and the breathing of carefully contrived combinations of gases. But Blackfin goes deeper – seven hundred, eight hundred, a thousand metres. The lungs are now squashed flat.

Now he is in the deep sound channel, a depth at which the ocean acts like a sound wave duct. He can detect low-frequency sounds from immense distances: remote shipping; a storm on the east coast of Japan.

Blackfin starts clicking. The coda, trapped and funnelled by the deep sound duct, transmits itself halfway around the world at five times the speed of sound in the atmosphere, and is picked up by all the sperm whales swimming at a similar depth. The coda is clear, unambiguous, and repeated over and over. It is a call for action.

For twenty minutes it issues from the old bull sperm whale, down in the timelessness of the ocean, until the metabolic processes involved in being at such a depth are pushed to the point of breakdown. Knowing that a few more minutes will result in oxygen debt and a longer recovery time at the surface, Blackfin stops clicking. The tail flukes begin to propel him upwards. The chain locked around his tail chafes against raw flesh, but he ignores the pain of the metal on the bloodied tissue. At the surface he will replenish the expended oxygen. Then he will begin another descent, another call.

* * *

"Where do you live?" Kate asked, as she and Roddy stepped into the lift of her apartment building in Clerkenwell.

A Pavlovian response nearly had Roddy saying "The Marine Mammals Institute" – the Institute had been his home for some years – but he checked himself. "Actually I'm pretty much homeless at the moment. I lived where I worked. When the whales died I was sacked. So when I was sacked I lost my home as well as my job."

"Oh."

"It wasn't much," Roddy added as the lift doors opened on to Kate's floor. "It was only a box room. But it was my box room."

Kate nodded as she unlocked the door to her apartment and ushered him in to the open space of a luxuriously furnished, Manhattan-loft-style apartment, with a wide-windowed view over the village-like vista of Clerkenwell, and to the city of London beyond.

"I guess everyone needs their own box room," she said.

"Yeah," he said, staring around. "I suppose they do." He walked over to the huge windows. This place must have cost a million or more, he reflected; she can't be much older than twenty-five or twenty-six...

"I'll make some coffee," Kate said, and bustled off to the kitchen. "Then we'll get down to business," she called out after a few seconds.

They had come to Kate's apartment to decide what to do next. In a very short time they had become party to a lot of startling information. It was simultaneously soul-destroying and exhilarating. And it was hard to know where to start. Roddy looked down at Clerkenwell Green, wondering if the name had once referred to a real green and, if so, when it had been paved over to make way for a gridwork of parking bays. Greens that weren't greens... a surreal image came into his head of oceans with no ocean in them: the Atlantic Ocean tarmacked over, the Pacific Ocean a giant shopping arcade on a thousand levels.

Kate came back into the lounge and set empty mugs on a table. She went over to her answerphone.

"Beep... Gerry here, you're not here, you should be here, why aren't you here, I'm here, call me here. Beep... Gerry here, I called you—"

"My boss," Kate explained, grimacing.

"—half a dozen times yesterday, I know you got the messages because this morning they were wiped, so for Christ's sake put me in the picture. Beep... OK, it's now 3:30 p.m. and you've been AWOL for thirty-six hours and you are NOT Kirsty Wark, phone me. Beep... Kate, this is Gerry, if you're dead or something then that's fine by me, but if you're not, you're fired. Beeeeeeep."

She sat down on the edge of a modern divan and smiled in an almost apologetic manner. Roddy regarded her with interest: the pale cheeks now slightly flushed, the mouth slightly open as she hesitated over what to say.

"Let's get on with it."

She jumped up to get the coffee pot from the kitchen. Was that a glint of excitement in her eye? Of relief, even?

"You seem to be taking it very well."

She paused on her way to the kitchen.

"I don't know. Actually, I could ring up Gerry right now and get my job back by delivering the biggest scoop he's ever had his hands on."

"But you're not going to do that, are you."

"No."

"Why?"

Kate sat down on the arm of a settee, considering.

"Maybe I feel relief that the job's not in the way any more. I'm probably making a big career mistake, but if I took this story to my paper now they'd run with it as it is – but it's still only half a story, and from now on I'm not doing that: I don't want half the truth and the rest conjecture, I want *all* the truth. I just…" She gestured vaguely during the struggle to find the right words. "This story isn't a scoop to me any more. I want to get the truth and help the situation more than I want a pat on the back. Does that dynamic make any sense to you at all?"

That dynamic has always made sense to me, Roddy thought.

* * *

Rattigan was suffering from a cold. It had hinted at itself during the night, and developed during the day largely unheeded until coming out into the open at last. It battered his temples, assaulted his sinuses and eyes. The bad news, he realized, had goaded it. He sneezed spectacularly into a sodden handkerchief.

There's no need for panic, he assured himself. But this was bad. *Jasmine* sinking, sending out a distress signal picked up by the Royal Navy…

He was alone in the Bentley, having dropped Ally off at home earlier. He had enjoyed seeing her entering the house, his house, their home. Perhaps things can be as they used to be, he thought – it's easier when Ally's at home. With Theresa. I get less… angry.

The car was doing a stately circuit of St James's Park. It went along Birdcage Walk and turned left into Horse Guards Road, passing within a hundred metres of Ten Downing Street. At the top of Horse Guards Road the Bentley turned into the wide, red, ramrod-straight Mall, and made its way in the middle of a convoy of black cabs towards the Queen Victoria Memorial.

Someone has fucked up, Rattigan complained to himself. He pressed a Havana-cigar-thick index finger against his throbbing temple. These vessels aren't supposed to have sophisticated distress alert equipment. If they go down, they should go down without trace.

In St James's Park, on the grass, green-and-white striped deckchairs were scattered around, bearing the weight of middle-aged tourists. He could see two youngsters lying under a tree, canoodling. He'd always felt uneasy about kissing, it seemed needlessly unhygienic. The Bentley quietly moved on, reaching the memorial and circling it. He slumped down, his arms stretched out on the seat, his hands palms up, and his muscly, fat stomach rising above his frame like a midden.

"Stop panicking," he said aloud. "This isn't meltdown. The ship sank. Dead men don't tell tales."

According to Jenkins, a Royal Naval vessel would have had up to a dozen men on it who would have been aware of the distress alert, but that's all they would have known. On terra firma, due to the sensitive provenance of the distress alert, it would had come encrypted to the Vice-Admiral responsible for SONAZ. And he, by all accounts, would want the incident hushed up.

* * *

Ally was stroking her mother's hair. She pressed her fingers lightly down the back of Theresa's head, then rested them at the base of the neck. The two women were in the hobbies room, surrounded by the fruits of past labours: embroidered cushion covers, decorated ceramics, papier mâché models, batiks, origami figures, wicker sculptures.

"I'm sorry," Theresa said quietly. "Drawing you into all this."

"Shush."

"Five million?" Theresa said the words as though they were straight out of the oven, too hot to hold in the mouth. "What on earth is going on?"

But as she allowed Ally to massage her shoulders, she knew that her question was rhetorical. Though it was amazing to learn that her husband was the benefactor of a children's charity, it also made a strange kind of sense. For years there had been something missing in her understanding of him, a gap she could see but not fill with an answer. She thought of his upbringing in a children's home: he never talked about it. And she thought of his curious involvement in bringing up their own daughter, how his attitude to her had been so wholly unreal, as though the child was a perfect being to worship rather than a real, delightful but often maddening human being. Have there been other donations? Is this what he does with all the money he makes? Why did he never tell me? And how can someone capable of such goodness be the same man to hit me, scorn my existence?

Ally put her hands on her mother's cheeks and pulled her up, so that she could look directly into her infinitely sad eyes. I didn't know anything, she tortured herself, as her arms pressed around her mother; how could I have blithely grown up and left home and not realized how desolate and terrorized she was?

"How do you feel about him now?"

"Odd."

"I want you to leave him."

"He'd kill me if he found me," Theresa said. "It's the one power I possess that terrifies him. He needs me to be his, utterly, even as he hates me."

Ally waited for her mother to say something else, but nothing came. "Do you still love Roddy?" she found herself saying after a long, painful pause. "Is that why you're doing this?"

"I didn't do it because I still love him. I did it because it isn't fair; he's a good man whom I abandoned. One day I want him to know that I was still his friend."

"So you'll leave Daddy?"

"Where shall I go?" she asked.

"Wherever you want to go."

"I've got no passport."

"Why not?"

"He keeps it locked up somewhere."

"Christ Mummy."

From outside they heard the Bentley sweep across the gravel of the drive, a door slam as Rattigan got out, and then the car being driven into the underground garage. The front door banged shut. Theresa's face took on an anxious expression.

"Start thinking of somewhere in the UK," Ally told her, kissing her and standing up.

Going into her own bedroom, she stood in front of the full-length mirror and appraised her appearance: knee-length green skirt, dark green stockings, white blouse. She waited ten minutes, then went downstairs. Padding across the hall, she quietly opened the door to the living area known as her room, Ally's room, and peered through a narrow crack.

He was slumped in a leather armchair, sniffing continually. There appeared to be some papers on his lap. Ally pushed the door further open and slipped inside. Her father's cold was absolutely streaming, forcing him to blow his nose and rub his eyes every few moments. She moved nearer to him, creeping up on him from behind. Her tongue poked through her teeth. She edged up to the back of his chair. When she was only a metre away, she squinted and stared. What was the heading on the top piece of paper? She leant further forwards, inches away from the back of her father's head. There was a musky smell, not wholly pleasant.

He let out a huge sneeze, his whole body pulsing with the spasm, his head lurching forwards and then rocking back so far that it almost struck Ally's own. She held her position, frightened to move or breathe, as Rattigan sighed in irritation at his condition. OK, all I have to do is get a little bit closer, a little bit closer... and just... lean forwards... and... just... decipher those words and—

"Jesus!"

He jolted as though an electric charge had gone through him. The papers on his lap fell on the floor.

"Daddy!" Ally exclaimed, flinging her arms around his neck and hugging him from behind.

"You nearly gave me a heart attack!"

"Sorry, Daddy." Heart pounding and face flushed red, Ally concealed her confusion by nuzzling her face into the side of his neck and hanging on grimly. "Oh Daddy, I've got something to tell you," she trilled.

"What is it?"

"I spent five hundred pounds!" she gabbled, making it up, "in Harvey Nicks! In an hour!"

"You naughty girl," Rattigan said.

He pushed her arms away from his neck. She took the opportunity to stoop down and pick up the scattered papers, saying, "What are these Daddy?"

"Nothing for you to worry about, sweetheart."

As she handed them to him, she scanned the top sheet desperately. It was just figures, column after column of figures, with not a hint of what they related to. She stood in front of him and pretended to be angry.

"Why are you worried all the time, Daddy? What's the matter?"

"It's just business, Ally, all very boring."

"Tell me about it."

"I had a little project going, very profitable, but it's all gone horribly wrong. I'm just trying to... mop up the mess."

"What project?"

He pulled her on to his knee, smiling sadly.

"How can I help you if you won't trust me?" she cooed.

"Ally," he rumbled.

His arms wrapped around her, and she found herself enfolded in his large chest. His fingers toyed with her ponytail. She made a half-hearted attempt to get free, but he held on. Her ear, her nose was pressed against his flesh. She could smell soap, sweat, man. She was already struggling with a surge of disgust when he sneezed again; she felt his lungs expand and collapse against her body.

"Daddy," she said, struggling to surface from his clasp.

"Sweetheart."

He wasn't releasing her. His hands moved down her back. One stopped halfway down, softly patting her; the other, slowly, cautiously, went down to her bottom and cupped it. It rested there. Ally didn't move. Her heart had momentarily stopped. She sat there, petrified, wondering what to do. Rattigan seemed to be in crisis, until the trill of the phone released them from the unhappy spell. As Ally lurched to her feet, Rattigan grabbed at the phone besides the armchair.

"What?"

Straightening her skirt, Ally left the room. She stood outside the door, breathing hard, trying to control herself enough to listen to her father on the phone, all the time thinking Jesus, *Jesus.*

* * *

A dark-blue Ford Fiesta, about four years old and in need of a good wash, passed through the village of Minton Brag, half an hour's drive from Plymouth. At the wheel was a radio officer in the Royal Navy, and it was his intention to make a call from a public phone box. Naturally there were public phone boxes in Plymouth, where he was stationed, but he wasn't taking any chances; he didn't want to be spotted by any colleagues.

He drove past a sweetshop and an off-licence and pulled in just beyond an old-fashioned red telephone box. Fumbling in his pocket for his cigarettes, he got out of the car and went into the phone box. After lighting up, he exhaled a double-plumed cloud of smoke into the confines of the little cabin. Out of his pocket he pulled a scrap of paper with a telephone number of a daily broadsheet on it. A quick look up and down the street, and a one-pound coin clunked through the slot.

"UK Media Group, Good afternoon, this is Amanda speaking, how may I help you?"

"Um…"

He wasn't exactly sure how to do it.

"Hello?"

"Yeh, um, I want to speak to someone."

"Who do you want to speak to, sir?"

"Um, I don't know." He exhaled further clouds of smoke and ran his free hand through short, cropped hair. "You're a newspaper. I've got some news."

"I understand. Can you tell me what field of information it is?"

"Er, naval."

"So you want to speak to someone who deals with defence issues?"

"Yeah yeah, defence issues, but an expert, all right? Someone who knows about the navy."

"Let's see if we can get hold of the Defence Correspondent. Please give me a minute or two, don't hang up. May I take your number in case of difficulty?"

"No."

"Please wait a moment."

The wait was three or four minutes long. The man drew on his cigarette almost continually.

"Hello, are you there?"

"Yes."

"I'm Giselle Kilcroft, Defence Correspondent." The voice was low, slow, and confident. "You have some interesting information?"

"That's right."

"Are you serving in the navy?"

"That's right."

He paused, but she was waiting for him to come out with it. Licking his lips nervously, he said, "Do you know what SONAZ is? In the North Atlantic?"

"A patch of ocean out of bounds to shipping."

"What would you say if someone told you about a serious incident in SONAZ that was being covered up?"

A pause. He got the impression that she was weighing her words.

"Is this about the fish?"

"What?"

"It's not about the fish?"

"It's about the bloody navy – would you be interested or not?"

"If it's interesting, I'll be interested."

The casual phone call from his colleague on HMS *Ascension*, during which he had been told about the distress signal from a vessel called the *Jasmine*, hadn't struck him as particularly interesting at first; but later, when he realized that the information about the incident had been encrypted before reaching London, he had smelt an opportunity. He had debts; his house was under threat of repossession; his wife was threatening to leave him, which wasn't a problem except that she'd take the kids.

"Twenty-thousand-pounds interested?"

"Well now... That would depend on the nature of the incident and the quality of the information. Can you give me an idea?"

"I'm not being greedy. I just need twenty thousand pounds."

"Tell me about the incident."

"There was a merchant ship. A frigate discovered she was in SONAZ when she sent out a distress alert. But the frigate didn't assist, just notified London. So she almost certainly sank. London's sitting on it."

"Why is London sitting on it?"

"I don't know. That's your job, isn't it?"

"Have you got the name of the vessel, timings, proof?"

"Have you got twenty thousand quid?"

"Perhaps a meeting would be fruitful for both of us," Giselle Kilcroft ventured.

* * *

Roddy and Kate were at loggerheads about what they should do.

"Look," Roddy was saying, "the point is, we know a hell of a lot, all we have to do is reveal what we know to the authorities, stand back, and—"

"Wrong."

"—watch the fallout."

"Wrong, we know some things, but without a hint of who the bad guys are, exposure would be disaster. Look Roddy, you're a marine biologist, you know about seaweed and shrimps, fine, but I'm a journalist, I know about the real pond life, and sometimes when you don't have a suspect it's vital not to reveal what you know – otherwise you alert the bad guys that you're on to the scent and you give them the time and opportunity to cover their tracks."

"We've got testimony that a North Atlantic Minke has

OD-ed on dioxin and VX nerve agent!" he exclaimed. "From an Emergency Coordinator who has committed suicide! All we have to do is tell the government!"

"Someone in the government already knows! Do you think those necropsies could have been quietly sidelined without influence from the very highest level?"

Roddy went to the window and looked down at Clerkenwell Green: two cars competing for the same parking space, a mother crouching down by her baby's pram to alter an item of clothing. There was no evidence down there that the world had changed, that it was now a place in which whales landed on crowded beaches, in which whales swam up rivers to astonish cities and then calmly swam back again to disappear into mother nature. But the world has changed, he reflected. And I have lost my work, my reputation, my friend, all my certainties...

Kate came to the window too, and they stood side by side, looking at the view.

"You were telling me earlier how, in an ideal world, you'd like to analyse footage of the killer-whale convoy," she said.

"Well, yeah. I could find out a lot from it."

"Let's at least do that first, OK? You need a video-editing suite for that kind of work. Let me fix something up with one of my contacts from my TV job."

"You don't have a TV job," he pointed out, with a hint of grim satisfaction.

"Do you still detest me?" she suddenly asked into a pause.

His eyebrows went up as he considered the question.

"Somewhat to my amazement, given how I felt about you twenty-four hours ago, no. Which isn't to say you didn't turn me over inexcusably—"

"I wouldn't go as far as that."

"—but a lot of strange things have happened in the last couple of weeks. Almost nothing would surprise me anymore."

For some reason, she was staring at him pretty intensely. He waited for her to speak, but she didn't. He felt himself grow embarrassed. He picked up an artefact by the window.

"What's this?"

"A sculpture by Daniel De Trouville."

"But it's three pieces of scrunched-up paper hanging in a cage made from chicken wire."

"Depends how you look at it."

"Right…" He gazed at her, shaking his head. "We make a pretty odd team."

The ringing of his mobile phone prevented her from responding.

"Yes?… Yes… Of course I remember you… I'm OK… Yes, despite everything… Whitaker? Multiple fractures of the leg, but he's going to be all right… I will, I'll tell him you said so… Yes… How did you get this number?… I see… Well actually… It's not really… the problem is that I've got a lot on my plate right now… well I'd like to meet up, I just don't have the time to… No… No… It is?… How important?… Give me a moment."

He covered the mouthpiece with his hand, wondering how on earth Ally could be involved with the whales.

"It's Ally Rattigan."

"Who's she?"

"Daughter of the shipping magnate Tony Rattigan," Roddy explained, keeping to himself any further information. "She says she's got something on the whales. She wants to see us."

"Let's go and see her immediately."

"It has to be late tonight, she can't get away otherwise."

"Well, whatever, we'll fix up to analyse the footage of the convoy first and meet her later."

"All right… Hello, Ally?… Yeah… That late?… Well look, there's that pub near Smithfield Meat Market that's open until really late, do you know that one?… All right… Around one-ish then?... Any problem, give me a ring... OK then... Yes... Yeah. Bye."

He put the phone down, frowning, the name Rattigan repeating itself in his mind.

7

"But this is the whale guy, right?" Geoff said, looking Roddy up and down dubiously. He was a vision man with Videosupersonics, a production company that had a contract with Kate's ex-TV company. "You didn't say anything about the whale guy, Kate. It's one thing to sneak you in for half an hour, but you didn't say anything about turning up here with the whale guy. I mean, for maximum secrecy why not bring the fucking Pope?"

"Relax, what difference does it make?" Kate said. "And his name is Roddy. Roddy, meet Geoff – Geoff, meet Roddy."

Geoff was in his mid-thirties and affected the curious combination of studied scruffiness and cutting-edge fashion that went with working in the media, having enough money, and worrying about his age. He wore £500 glasses on parcel string around his neck; he was proud of that string: it was his own idea to subvert its non-fashion status into a statement.

"I'll give you twenty minutes. Tim's going to be very pissed off if he finds out."

"Stop whingeing and let's get on with it Geoff – you're moaning like an OAP."

"Yeah yeah."

The video-editing suite comprised a windowless den, tatty furniture – benches improvised from planks, free-standing units from MFI – and £400,000 worth of kit, arrayed in banks of black boxes around three walls. Three TV screens were set into one of the walls.

"OK, sit there," Geoff said, gesturing towards two orange plastic chairs. "Give me the tape. OK, we'll use Flame. Basically this is a visual effects enhancement thing. You can do anything on a bit of kit like this, just tell me what you want."

Roddy watched the killer whales flicker into life on two of the screens. The background hum of a million wondering voices filled the room. The whales milled around between the two bridges in the way he remembered. He leant forwards, frowning.

"Does he speak?" Geoff asked, after a minute. "Does he want me to do anything at all?"

"Roddy? What are you looking at?"

"I'm trying to determine the group dynamic, which bulls are dominant, whether all the whales are in it together or whether the dominant males are directing things."

"Why shouldn't the females be dominant?"

"Well, the cows aren't dominant in the ordinary course of events, so it seems unlikely. Then again," he said, turning to her, "this is hardly the ordinary course of events. OK, can we go forwards? To a few minutes before midnight?"

"Noooo problem."

"They're gearing up now," Kate said.

"Can we follow just one whale close in?" Roddy asked.

"Sure. Which one?"

"Er, this one?"

"Sure, OK, hooked it."

"A bull," Roddy informed them.

They all fell silent as they watched the animal weave in and out of its companions, getting faster and faster as midnight approached.

"Two minutes till the shit hits the fan," Geoff announced.

The crowd, excited by the motion in the river, were getting noisier and noisier.

"Found anything out?" Kate asked Roddy after a while, watching him watch the single killer whale.

"Nope."

"You want to pan out now?" Geoff asked. "See the stampedes and the guys dropping off the bridge? Man that was cool. We're thirty seconds away."

"No, it's OK, stick with this whale if you would."

Big Ben struck. The killer whale was now swimming in a frenzied fashion. Roddy strained to decipher some telling detail: there must be *something* in its behaviour that I can work out…

Big Ben struck the twelfth chime.

"Fuck, sorry!" Geoff called, as they all clapped their hands to their ears: the screams, the shattering glass. He stopped the tape. "I'm not a sound man, I didn't realize it was going to be that loud."

"Can I see it again?"

"Yeah. As I say, I'm not a sound man, but I'll put it through a high pass filter on the mixing desk. I'll roll off ten decibels at one kilohertz."

"Are you making that up Geoff?" Kate asked.

"It'll take out the car alarms and most of the crowd noises."

The tape played again, now eerily quiet, even the chimes of Big Ben muted and dull. I'll follow this whale through the whole sequence, Roddy decided, I'll watch what it does when there are people in the water. Then the twelfth chime struck and—

"Fucking hell!" Geoff called, lunging for the mixing desk.

"Leave it!" Roddy yelled, grabbing his wrist, as the eerie squeals of the whales, now separated from the noise of the panicked crowd, the car alarms and the shattering glass, sounded loud and clear.

man-get-man-fish-man-get-man-fish-man-

"Roddy!" Kate gasped, grabbing his arm.

-get-man-fish-man-get-man-fish-man-get-man-fish-man-get-man-fish-man-get-man-fish-man-get-man-fish-man-get-man-fish-man-get-man-fish-man-get-man-fish-

"Let me turn it down!" Geoff shouted, pulling his wrist free as Roddy and Kate looked at each other ecstatically. The volume came down to a low level. "Christ, do want to make us all deaf?"

"The same call!" Kate exclaimed. "How can *wild* killers possibly know that artificial language? I mean, shit, has Joe been going out in an open boat training them?"

"It's not Joe who's taught them, it's Attila! Don't you get it? Wild whales must have been swimming under the pier at Clacton and communicating with Attila."

"But why should they want us to know what Attila is saying?"

"No, you don't get it. They want us to know what *they're* saying. It's their message, Attila's language." Roddy's eyes bore into hers, huge and bright, alarming in their intensity. "It's a code."

* * *

An hour later, after an unsuccessful brainstorm on the meaning of the killers' message, they were entering the pub to meet with Ally Rattigan when Roddy's mobile rang.

"Yes?... Whitaker, hi!"

"You sound cheery."

"Well, not exactly, not in the circumstances, but we're making progress."

In the living room of his mother's flat, Whitaker used a hand to shift the position of his aching leg on the sofa.

"Joe Farelli's just been on the phone looking for you, he wants to know how you're getting on."

"I don't have time to ring Joe Farelli."

"I'm just relaying the message. What are you doing?"

"I'm just about to see Ally Rattigan for some mysterious reason that I can't even guess at."

"Really?" Whitaker sat up on the sofa. "Excellent. Tell her I said, er, hello. Or something. Tell her to come and visit me and write on my plaster."

"She asked me to give you her regards and wish you luck."

"She did? Honest? You're not winding me up?"

"Whitaker, I've got more pressing things to do than bait a man with a broken leg."

"I suppose so. You must be tired. Do you want to sleep here tonight? You can turn up any time, four in the morning or anything."

"Thanks but I'm sleeping at Kate's." He regretted the words as soon as he said them.

"Attaboy tiger."

"Oh Christ."

"You're sleeping with Kate Gunning?"

"Good night Whitaker," Roddy said, ending the call.

The pub was roomy and gloomy and ornate, all dark wood and pillars and cornices. Clusters of men from the meat market stood at the bar, talking in low voices, and drinking swiftly.

Ally was sitting by herself at a table and looking morosely into a nearly empty glass of lemonade. She looked up with undisguised relief.

"Hi."

"Hi."

"What happened to the dreadlocks?"

"It's a long story."

Roddy didn't press her. She looked a little fragile.

"Ally, this is Kate Gunning, the journalist. We're working together now."

Ally's eyebrows went up in surprise.

"Wow... Roddy, no offence, but I didn't know you'd be bringing someone with you. What I have to say is very personal."

Roddy's heart sank. He wasn't here to talk about Theresa.

"You said it was to do with the whales."

"Well it is. But it's very personal too.

"Look, I'll, er, leave you both for a while," Kate said.

"Oh, well, it's OK," Ally answered. "If you're really working on this together, then you'll both need to know. You'd better get a drink, the barman's looking a bit unfriendly."

"I'll go," Kate said, rising. "It's Scotch for me. Roddy?"

"The same."

"What about you Ally?"

"Anything. Lemonade."

"You really don't look well," Roddy told Ally, after Kate had gone to the bar.

She didn't answer. They waited in silence. This is really odd, Roddy told himself: I can't imagine that she can know anything of significance about the whales... He drummed his fingers on the table top, waiting.

"I'm sorry," Kate said, coming back from the bar, "but I'm absolutely starving and they do food here for the night shift workers, so I've ordered myself something. Does anyone else want anything?

"God, not at this hour," Roddy said, and Ally shook her head.

Ally took a gulp of lemonade and a deep breath.

"I better get this over with. My mother came to me a few days ago. She asked me to come home and try and find out what my father was up to. I'm the only person he cares about, I'm the only one he lets near him. She'd overheard him on the phone. It was a conversation about the whales, he seemed to be involved in some way. Heavily involved. It was while you were still, you know, in charge. Of the whale thing. And my father was talking about you." Her eyes – so reminiscent, in their startling depth and intensity, of Rattigan's – soaked up his gaze. "Well, to get to the point, whatever he's up to, he wants to destroy you. Mummy heard him say something like that about you."

Roddy leant back in his seat, shaking his head.

"Me? Why?"

"I guess it's personal."

"Well, don't you think he's a bit late? The job's done."

"I've tried to uncover what's going on, but I haven't got very far and I can't do it any more. Something happened today to put me off."

"What happened?"

"To be honest I'd rather not say. Something that means I can't go on. All I can do is tell you what I know. My mother didn't pick up much, but a couple of times he was talking about a single stake being eight hundred dollars."

"A single stake in what?"

"I don't know. I thought you might. And the other thing is, does the word 'jasmine' mean anything to you?"

"Jasmine?"

"It's relevant. I don't know why."

"That's it?"

"That's all I know," Ally said apologetically.

They all looked at each other.

"Here's one steak I'd pay eight hundred dollars for," Kate said feebly as her steak sandwich arrived.

She put a corner of the sandwich in her mouth, bit on it, and then froze as Roddy gave her the weirdest look she'd ever seen. The features of his face had arranged themselves into an expression of the utmost disgust and dismay.

"What's wrong with you?" she said, with her mouth full.

"Steak…" he said. "Steak as in S-T-E-A-K, not stake as in S-T-A-K-E."

"So what?"

"In restaurants in Tokyo you can ask for 'special' meat, and if they've got any they'll serve up minke or pilot for a couple of hundred dollars. It's the loophole in the moratorium on whaling that allows them to hunt those species in limited numbers…"

"You don't – you think Rattigan has – you think he's gone and—"

"Meat from a fin, or a sperm, or a sei… Well, it's totally illegal to hunt those animals in any circumstances, no one will have eaten it for twenty years, the premium would be *astronomical*…"

The three of them sat staring at each other in silence. Roddy looked as though he might be physically sick.

* * *

It was only ten minutes, through the deserted London streets, from the pub to Kate's apartment in Clerkenwell. Kate tried pressing Roddy about Rattigan, his connection to the man, but Roddy was uncommunicative. They walked briskly. She held his arm, but doubted that he noticed she was doing so. He was walking with a mechanically regular rhythm, his eyes fixed on the ground. The news that Rattigan was out to get him, and that the whales might have been killed for profit, seemed to have winded him.

She swung open the door to her apartment and sent her shoes skimming across the marble floor.

"I like doing that," she said, making small talk, then slumped into a chair.

Roddy stood half in and half out of the doorway, frowning.

"Let's have a drink," Kate said.

He shook his head. He shut the door and padded across to the window in order to take in the nightscape. He pressed his forehead to the cool glass; the gesture surprised her. It made him seem especially vulnerable. The poor guy's virtually in shock, she realized.

"Roddy, tell me about Rattigan. Please."

She thought he wasn't going to answer. He kept his forehead pressed to the glass, his attention on the dead scene outside: parked cars, a flickering lamppost. She watched him with a sense of the moments passing, accumulating, becoming minutes, and had long ceased expecting his answer when he blurted it out.

"We loved the same woman. She married Rattigan. End of story."

A silent, theatrical "Oooooh" sounded in Kate's mind. She waited for more detail, but none came.

"Well..." she asked at last. "When, how, why, what happened?"

When, how, why, what happened... Roddy mulled over the questions half-heartedly, but soon left them behind for more immediate preoccupations. It was frightening that Rattigan could hate him so much. And that a man so full of hate should be married to Theresa... With a sense of shame he realized how, with the ordinary surfaces of his life ripped away – the job, the home, the satisfaction achieved so laboriously in strictly compartmentalized aspects of living – there was exposed underneath the same raw hurt and loneliness that had settled on him twenty years ago. The truth is, he confessed to himself, I never moved on – not really or, at least, not enough...

"We'll nail him, Roddy."

He looked at her and nodded. Then he turned back to the window and suddenly banged his head against it, hard, three times.

"Jesus!" she shouted, leaping up and dragging him away.

He collapsed on her sofa.

"Are you OK?"

249

"Yeah."

"I'm giving you some kava kava and then you're going to bed."

"What's kava kava?"

"A herbal medicine, calms you down.

"If you say so."

"Come to bed," she heard herself say.

He looked up, slowly and incredulously.

"What?"

"Not like that. I just mean, come to bed. With me. To sleep."

"I can sleep on the sofa."

"I know. You can, if you want. I just think – you're desolate tonight. You need someone by your side. That's all anyone needs, isn't it?"

"I'll be fine in the morning, it's just the shock of it, what he's done."

"I know. Come on."

He followed her into the bedroom, feeling, with some gratitude, as though he had been relieved of the responsibility to make decisions for himself. He sat down on the bed, and did nothing else for a while but continue to sit there. Kate had gone back out and was bustling around doing something. After a few minutes he realized she was handing him a glass.

"What is it?"

"Orange juice and kava kava."

"What does it taste like?"

"Dishwater."

He knocked it back, wincing, then without further fuss started undressing. Kate did the same on the other side of the bed. There was a brief glimpse of her nearly naked form disappearing into an over-sized T-shirt, but he was about as interested in it as a fish is interested in mountain air. He slipped under the covers. Kate went to brush her teeth in the bathroom. He heard the familiar noises, the scrubbing of the nylon bristles, the brief gurgle of the tap, and knew that he was far too unhappy to even attempt such a task.

A few minutes later, after Kate got into bed, they both lay on their backs, with a respectable avenue of mattress between them, listening to the night.

"How's the kava kava doing?"

"I don't think it's doing anything. I think I should sleep on the sofa. If I stay here I'll stop you from sleeping. At this moment I can't imagine ever losing consciousness again."

Five minutes later he was fast asleep. A few hours after that, he woke up to find Kate fitting snugly into his side, her face against his neck, her arm thrown over his chest. He felt the overwhelming peace of physical contact with another human being. Theresa used to lie with me like this, he thought, our bodies interacting just so. Then sleep washed over him again.

8

The moon is obscured by cloud cover. The ocean is dark at the surface. A thousand metres down, where a sperm whale cruises the sea bed, it is darker than dark. Blackfin is echo-locating for squid. He is hungry and exhausted. For a day and a night and a day he has been calling to the whales of all waters: diving, calling, rising, breathing; diving, calling, rising, breathing. The weight of the chain on his tailstock is unbearable, but he bears it. The flesh is rubbed raw all the way around and is now in the early stages of infection. This agony must be endured. Whales are responding from all the oceans and the seas, from coastal areas and the immense landless south, from the two cold waters and the warm places. They will join him, and he will lead them. He must live.

His clicks bounce back to him from a soft mass of flailing,

living tissue. In a few seconds his jaws snap shut on a deep-water squid. Not much bigger than a few humans, it presents no difficulties. The peg-like teeth of his lower mandible grind it against his upper jaw, and within a few seconds, dead and mutilated, it slips down the immense gullet.

More clicks are bouncing back to him. When he alters the range and direction of his echo-location, even to an improbable degree, the clicks still come back to him: a big squid, a huge squid, the kind he used to enjoy pitting himself against. The marks of such contests still scar his head, livid looping lines, caused by the fearsome suckers on the squids' tentacles. Now he is too old, too weak and too tired. He should avoid this adversary, which is a creature fully a third longer than his own body, but fatigue and exhaustion cause him to make a foolish judgement. Like a ship whose momentum makes stopping problematic, he glides into the slightly luminous, gigantic pulpy mess, jaws snapping.

The squid's tentacles, clutching and pulsing, fasten on him. They grip like white-hot wire. Blackfin's massive head is enfolded in formlessness; the small mouth of the beast locks onto his snout, over his blowhole. He thrashes, enraged, lifting the squid up and then lowering it onto the sea bed, swimming furiously to grind the animal into serrated rocks. All the time he is trying to close his own jaws on the giant squid's vulnerable zones – an eye, a section of soft brain – but he is entirely enclosed. The squid's tentacles fasten tighter, and its mouth pulsates on Blackfin's flesh, working its way into the nostril. Blackfin is losing this battle but cannot lose; he is dying and yet he has to live. From his blowhole he expels virtually every ounce of compressed oxygen that his body can offer up. The air jets out forcefully. There is nowhere for it to go but inside the squid, whose mouth is locked and airtight over the single nostril. The oxygen astonishes the animal's biology. Blackfin stops thrashing. It takes some moments for the suckers of the tentacles to release their grip, but they fall away, one by one, working in from the tentacle tips to the base. Finally the mouth goes slack. Blackfin twists back and forth, and the squid falls away.

Now Blackfin is without oxygen, a thousand metres down. He feels giddy. The muscles of his tailstock, deprived of myoglobin, feel as effective as drifting seaweed. His eyes throb, and strange explosions of light cluster before his vision. There is nothing now but the force of his own will and a primeval lust for oxygen that can persuade him to swim. The chain drags down on him and he is sightless with pain as he nudges, metre by metre, to the surface of the sea, and to the task before him.

* * *

Rattigan's upper lip twitched. Small beads of sweat formed a shiny film over the permanent five o'clock shadow. As for the thick hairs that stuck out of his nose, there was the suggestion of them retracting and protruding, retracting and protruding, keeping a rhythm to the beat of his anxiety.

It was 6:30 a.m. He was in the kitchen. The housekeeper had been and gone, neither seeing nor being seen, as he liked it. She had left a pot of coffee on the hot plate and an English breakfast in a warm oven. But the food and drink would go unconsumed, and five hours later the housekeeper would return to the kitchen to find a desiccated fry-up in the oven and, more mysteriously still, the remains of a fire on top of the breakfast bar.

Rattigan was sitting on a tall stool, a broadsheet newspaper in front of him open at page four. Ship Goes Down In "Forbidden Zone", said the headline to the two-column story. The subheading was *Silence from MoD as questions are asked, by our Defence Correspondent Giselle Kilcroft*.

What have I done wrong, he asked himself, to be faced with such a total mess? What were the chances of someone leaking it to the press? He forced himself to think straight: don't panic, it lacks any substantial detail, there's no accurate suggestion as to what *Jasmine* was doing there. And that's the way it will stay. It would take ten lawyers ten years to sift through the layers of legal chicanery and prove a link from that ship to me. But still… Some retrospective action was necessary, just to be on the safe side.

"Fuck."

Abruptly passing from weariness to fury, he gathered the pages of the newspaper to him and scrunched them up. His fist pounded on the ball of paper. But this was an unproductive way of destroying a newspaper. He lurched to his feet and fumbled in a kitchen drawer for some matches. The rasp of the match head on the sandpaper, the lick of the flame at a corner, and the newspaper was ablaze on top of the breakfast bar, hot black fragments ascending the mini airstreams of the kitchen.

"Fucking journalists," he breathed.

But he'd set fire to his mail.

"Shit!" he cursed when he noticed, picking the letters up at one corner and dropping them into the sink before turning the tap on. Miserably, he picked out the damp, singed envelopes. On one of them he recognized Theresa's handwriting. Why had his own wife written him a letter? For that matter, where the hell was she? He hadn't laid eyes on her for the best part of two days.

Tony, I have left. Theresa.

* * *

Trying not to look, the chauffeur shut the door on the fascinating movement of the Minister's elephantine haunches. Inside, the Secretary of State for Defence greeted the soft clunk of the lock with relief. She retreated into the leather of the Jaguar XJ's seats and watched Downing Street recede. Summoned to Number 10 to explain the MoD's alleged cover-up of a ship sinking while the Royal Navy stood by, she had just passed the least comfortable hour of her political career.

"Incandescent," she thought; that's the word the broadsheets used when describing the upper range of Prime Ministerial anger. Totally inaccurate, she reflected, pondering his moody civility. She remembered his expression becoming grimmer and grimmer as she had outlined the full extent of her fears and suspicions. The sinking of an unknown vessel had focused unwelcome attention on a sensitive area, but it was small fry in comparison to the related issues. There was the hypothesis by scientists that dioxin in the whales showed a causal link between the whale crisis and Britain's former dumping ground, SONAZ. There was the frightening necropsy evidence of VX exposure in the whales, with all the attendant ecological consequences. And worst of all, at least politically, there was the ghastly notion that Russia, with her vast stocks of chemical weapons, her crumbling storage facilities and her political instability, was by far the most likely source of the VX. Adlington winced. She recalled the moment when the PM had fully digested the indigestible: that Britain, which had led the EU and the US into funding the dismantling of the Russian chemical-weapons project, may have succeeded only in funding a politico-criminal network to dump much of it at sea...

The figures were as astronomical as the concept was horrendous. It cost well over $1,000,000 to render safe just one tonne of VX at the internationally monitored disposal plant located on the St Johnston atoll in the South Pacific, but to throw one tonne in the sea would cost how much, Adlington mused... $50,000? Someone was making an awful lot of money. It was the kind of scandal that felled administrations.

They had agreed that, as neither she nor the government were directly culpable for anything but bad luck and perhaps naivety, there was no merit or use to admitting to the problem. The aid to Russia would be quietly dropped; the latest initiative to increase participation by the US and the EU would be shunted down the sidings of bureaucracy... But all that effort and work and hope, Adlington mourned – all that abuse from cynical men who had lambasted her attempts to make the world safer as the misplaced idealism of a childless woman – disaster...

Her own position within the cabinet was, paradoxically, rock-solid. The Prime Minister couldn't risk jettisoning her without awkward questions being asked as to why she had to go. But that was of little comfort.

* * *

Thin shafts of sunlight breached the defences of the heavy curtains, picking out random things and illuminating them brilliantly: the door handle; Kate's foot sticking out of the covers, the blue-painted toenails glinting. By one side of the bed, a small television was on with the sound turned down low. The images danced and flickered, casting an inconsistent glow over Roddy's face as – still in bed – he watched. He turned away from the screen for a moment and glanced down at Kate's back. It lightly rose and fell as she slept on. There was the faint suggestion that the burbling noises she was making were on the verge of developing into full-blown snores. He rubbed at his eyes and turned his attention back to the old black-and-white Western he was watching.

"White man kill everything he see," an impossibly noble Red Indian was saying.

The night's aftermath lay on top of him as warm and as real as the quilt. It was pleasant to lie in bed while a beautiful young woman next to him slept on. He knew he should be getting up and facing all the questions and problems, but... just a little longer, he promised himself. And anyway, the wails of grief coming from the television demanded his attention; the old Apache chief was dying.

Years of living by himself had presented the opportunity and inclination to see hundreds of bad films. When it came to Westerns, he had a natural empathy with the Indians in their futile attempts to save their world. And he'd seen this film at least half a dozen times. In sync with the actor, Roddy mouthed the old man's dying words from memory:

"In a dead land, only dead men live."

Kate groaned.

"Huh?"

She opened her eyes and raised herself up on her elbows to take in the film.

"Oh dear," she said.

"What?"

"I've never been in the same bed as a man who watches Westerns early in the morning."

The warrior son of the now dead Apache chief was in counsel with the tribe's elders about the threats facing their ancient way of life. He was nodding sombrely while a medicine man, played by an actor of such palpably Mediterranean origins that he couldn't wholly disguise an Italian accent, advised, "Steel horse, him never eat, him never sleep, him gallop in straight line."

Kate rolled over, sat up, yawned. "Steel horse?"

"A train."

She nodded, still yawning.

"Thanks," Roddy said, watching her.

"Pardon?"

"For this," he said, indicating the bed, and him in it. "It was exactly what I needed."

"No problem. And you were too zoned out to get the wrong idea."

"I can barely remember what the wrong idea is."

"I bet you've got more recent memories of the wrong idea than me."

"What? No chance."

"Nine months, no, shit, ten months."

"Mm."

"And you?"

"About four years," said Roddy.

"Ah…"

"You can't be short of offers."

"I've got this dumb habit of going for completely unsuitable men – but at least none of them was in the habit of watching Westerns at dawn."

"It's not that early," he said, at length.

"What time is it?"

"I don't know, nine, nine-thirty."

A pause.

"Fuck!"

She was getting out of bed.

"What?"

"Why didn't you wake me up, I thought it was about six! We can't spend the whole morning in bed," she told him, absurdly aware that her complaint sounded like part of the familiar discourse between partners who had spent many mornings in bed together. He shrugged sheepishly. Kate stomped across the room towards the bathroom, Roddy watching her retreating behind with the first faint, guilty stirrings of sexual interest; she was so young and lovely. But she was right, they had things to do. The bathroom door slammed shut, and the mantra of the whales came unbidden into his mind, *man-get-man-fish-man-get…* What did it mean?

He felt that this was the key to everything. After a few moments to psych himself up, he threw the covers off and got out of bed.

The film was coming to a close with a steel horse belching clouds of steam as it crossed the American plains, awesome and relentless. The sound of the train's wheels hurtling over the rails was rhythmic and regular, became louder, merged with Roddy's thoughts until, very quickly, the noise they were making was man-get-*man*-fish-man-get-*man*-fish-man-get-*man*-fish-man-get-*man*-fish...

* * *

The seaside resort of Blackpool in Lancashire was gearing up for one of the busiest days of the year: the second Saturday in August. Pale girls in fish-and-chip shops were feeding sacks of potatoes into the chipping machines; exhausted assistant-managers of amusement arcades were opening their doors to sullen youths, to hard-eyed women clutching purses of small change; on the wide promenade the litter had long since been cleared, and old ladies were settling down to their knitting on the public seats.

The weather forecast was for a scorcher. The beach was already half full with day trippers and holiday makers. In a shabby little hut near the North Pier, Arnie the deckchair man was completing his rituals. As on every morning of the season for well over twenty years, he finished off his bacon sandwich and mug of tea, folded up the *Sun*, stubbed out one cigarette and lighted another, and – exactly ten minutes late – walked along the beach to where the deckchairs were stacked up and chained.

He was an emaciated, chain-smoking, peevish, sixty-four-year-old widower. He had the kind of face best suited to people who choose to patrol High Streets in sandwich boards that proclaim "The End Is Nigh". He had never knowingly uttered a phrase of more than four words that did not contain the word "fuck" or a variation thereof. Now he inhaled hugely on his cigarette, blew the smoke out of his nostrils for fully five seconds, and surveyed his lads lounging against the stacked deckchairs.

"Get up yer crap fuckers."

There were three of them: two hygienically challenged, shifty-looking types whom Arnie suspected of being more or less on the run from the police, and a student working his vacation. The bane of Arnie's existence was the high turnover of lads he had to endure. The work was not only seasonal and poorly paid and at the mercy of the weather, it was also subject to Arnie's distinctive management style. This made it attractive only to those who had a talent for being completely useless. Their average stint before packing it in was two weeks.

He threw keys to them. They started unlocking the padlocks and reeling the chains in. Arnie spat in the sand.

"Don't nick any fuckin' takings."

They strapped around their waists the money bags that Arnie gave them and started lugging deckchairs along the beach.

Arnie spat again as he watched them: useless fuckers, especially the long-haired one, the student.

Andrew – the long-haired one – was a Business Studies student at a further-education college in Bolton. He intended to do the deckchairs for at least three weeks. It was cash in hand, he got to swan around in the sun – assuming there was any sun, which there often wasn't – and there was the added attraction of trying to chat up good-looking girls – assuming there were any good-looking girls, which there often weren't.

He chucked eight deckchairs on to the sand and peeled his shirt off. He was not the brightest student at his college, nor did he exhibit a great deal of interest in his chosen subject of Business Studies; but his body was a good one and he was mightily pleased with it. He tucked the shirt into the waistband of his shorts. It was great to feel the sun on his shoulders and a light sea breeze ruffling his carefully scruffy long hair.

In weather like this, with the eyes half-closed and the brain tuned to ambient, Blackpool could seem like Ibiza... sort of, he amended, involuntarily registering the snowy, lard-bucket breasts of a fat man prone in the sand.

He looked out to sea and smiled again; the sun was out, his mood was up, and all was well with the world.

* * *

In the shower, Kate was rinsing the shampoo from her hair and the soap from her body. Her eyes were closed and the jet of the water was thunderously strong, so she didn't hear anything until the shower curtain was whipped open.

"Steel horse!" Roddy crowed into her face.

She screamed and would probably have collapsed in shock had he not grabbed hold of her wrists.

"Steel horse!"

"What the are you *playing* at?" she shrieked, enraged. "I nearly had a—"

She screamed again as he pulled her out of the shower.

"Get *off*, what are you doing, Jesus, will you just—"

Oblivious to her protests and now giggling hysterically, he dragged her out of the bathroom and into the bedroom.

"Look at the steel horse! Beautiful! Fantastic!"

On the television, the train steaming across the American plains was getting smaller and smaller, disappearing into the horizon as Roddy watched with something approaching pride. Kate angrily wrenched her wrist free from his grip. She picked up a throw that was draped over a chair and wrapped it around her. For the first time, Roddy seemed to realize that he had just dragged a young woman – naked and screaming and against her will – from the shower. The look of hysterical ecstasy that had been on his face faded away.

261

"How—" she looked around the room as though seeking words that could express the extent of her rage, but only came up with a cliché: "How *dare* you!"

She turned on her heel and went back to the bathroom. On the television the film's credits started to roll as an affecting, sentimental melody swelled into an orchestral lament.

"Oh shit," Roddy said.

He followed her and tried the bathroom door: locked.

"Kate? Kate!"

"Fuck off!"

"It's important."

"What?"

"I said it's important – Kate, it's the code."

"Go *away*!"

The sound of the shower stopped.

"Listen," he said into the silence, "I've solved the code."

A silence.

"So what is it?"

"Think about the steel horse!"

"Don't play games with me, I'm not in the mood."

"OK, think about a steel horse being a train, and then think about the words 'man fish' in a similar way. You hear me? The whales are saying 'man get manfish', as in MAN has to GET a MANFISH. A manfish Kate, what could a manfish be?"

An empty pause, and then rustling noises from the bathroom.

"Kate?"

The door handle shifted in his grip. She opened the door a few inches and peered out, wrapped in a towel.

"A submarine?

He grinned at her. The door was flung open and they were in each other's arms, jumping up and down and whooping.

9

They were debating what they should do next – Roddy wanted to hold a press conference immediately, Kate wanted to secure more information and proof – when the issue was settled by a call from Ally Rattigan.

"Hello?... Ally?... No... No I haven't seen the papers... Or the television news... Er, it's kind of hard to explain... I see... Christ... Hang on will you?"

He covered the phone with his hand and said, "The man's a phenomenon."

"What is it?"

"You remember what Ally said last night, about the word 'jasmine'?"

"Only that she mentioned the word."

"Well, while we were watching westerns and having showers and jumping up and down, we've missed an interesting little story about a ship called Jasmine sinking in SONAZ. And as Rattigan's a shipping man..."

"Has she got proof?"

"I don't know."

"Can I speak to her?"

Over in Hampstead, Ally was in her bedroom. Her father had always encouraged her to leave her bedroom unchanged. Posters of the pop groups and heart throbs of five years before adorned the walls, the furniture had been chosen by her when she was eleven, and a collection of cuddly toys filled the windowsill. The whole effect was like a time capsule of her adolescence.

"Oh, hi..." she said when Kate came on the line. "No, I'm OK... a bit traumatized... my mother's left him and he just can't believe she's done it, so it's a bit, er, weird around here..." Ally blinked the tears from her eyes furiously; weird, she thought – now there's an understatement. "...No Kate... Kate, I don't know… He's rattled by this story in the paper, really rattled, he's down in his office doing God knows what… I can get to him to say hello to, but that's all I can do, I'm not free to sniff around… No chance, I'm the only person on the planet who can approach him at the moment… Surely it's enough just to know that he's connected to this *Jasmine* ship… Mm… Oh…"

Ally groaned inside. Kate had asked her if she could distract her father while someone else did the sniffing around.

"I can do it… Don't ask me how I'll do it… I'm fine… I'm fine… Look, Kate, I ought to warn you, if he finds you here then, er, God, I don't know what he'll do, I mean, It sounds ludicrous but I think he'll, you know… kill you."

* * *

One hundred metres below the surface, rounding the North Channel that separates the south west of Scotland from the north west of Northern Ireland, a herd of cetaceans several hundred strong was entering the Irish Sea. The composition of the group was unique. There were minkes, seis, Bryde's, blues, fins, humpbacks, sperms, killers, bottlenose whales, Sowerby's and Cuvier's beaked whales, pygmy killers, false killers and pilots. And there were the dolphins: common, rough-toothed, bottlenose, Risso's, striped, white-beaked, Atlantic white-sided, so fast and nimble that they were able to dodge in and out of the larger animals at will.

At the head of the herd was a sperm whale. He had never experienced the suffocating claustrophobia of such shallow, narrow waters. He was a young bull from the vast uninterrupted Pacific. For days he had travelled east from his ancestral waters, until he had passed between the tips of the Antarctic and Americas peninsulas and headed north, through the South Atlantic, into the North Atlantic. He had heard and answered

Blackfin's calls. During the course of this epic journey, the others had joined him. There were more than thirty sperms now, male and female, mature and juvenile. Twenty minkes had arrived off the tip of the Americas, twelve seis had been with him almost from the start, and had been supplemented by a further fifteen during the journey. The Bryde's whales had appeared in the South Atlantic, the fins had come in ones and twos in every ocean, Northern Bottlenose whales had been picked up in the North Atlantic, the two spectral-looking Sowerby's beaked whales had come from Icelandic waters. Exotic dolphins had tagged on at every stage.

The most striking aspect of this unusual, swift-moving herd was the number of blues: fifty. These massive creatures, a thousand times heavier than the smallest of the dolphins, swam in a tight mass at the centre of the multi-species herd. The force of their motion was such that many of the smaller species coasted on their pressure wave. They had a combined weight of 6,500 tonnes.

The journey had been hidden. There had been no mass surfacing and blowing. Animals detached themselves from the group when they needed to, swam along the surface for a while, then dived.

As this phenomenon of whales entered the Irish Sea proper, and swam swiftly south between the islands of Ireland and Britain, it was joined by a second herd, even bigger, to become a herd of nearly nine hundred.

An hour behind it was a third herd. Half an hour ahead, Blackfin was heading a fourth.

* * *

Having technically resumed her rich-little-daddy's-girl lifestyle, Ally had taken possession once more of her Mercedes SLK 230, private number plate ALL 1. Now she turned off The Bishops Avenue and into the drive of the house. The gates opened slowly. She drove through, past the security guards in their lodge house, manoeuvring the car down the ramp into the underground car park.

In the abrupt quietness she sat still for a moment. Her shoulders rose unusually high and abruptly fell back as she took a deep breath to calm her nerves. She pressed the boot-release button – the boot of the Mercedes swung smoothly and elegantly open – and got out of the car.

Kate was lying on her side in the boot, her hands and feet braced against the edges, sweat pouring off her. She shaded her eyes against the light as Ally peered down at her.

"Are you all right?" Ally asked.

Kate struggled into a sitting position.

"It's even less fun than it looks in the films."

"Was I going too fast?"

"I've no idea how fast you were going," Kate answered, grabbing the hand that Ally was proffering her and hauling herself out.

"Kate, I'm frightened."

"You'll be fine. Just think that in an hour it'll all be over."

"What about you? Aren't you scared at all?"

"I'll be fine too," she said.

I'm shitting myself, she thought... She had agreed with Roddy that he should hold a press conference in the afternoon, with her or without her. If it were with her, then she would hopefully be providing hard evidence linking Rattigan to his crimes; if it were without her, if she had got into difficulties... But I don't want to think about that, she told herself.

"Give me the car keys," she said, wondering why Ally was feeling so frightened; sure, it wasn't pleasant to deceive your father, but that was nothing compared to the dangers of her own role. And what the hell, Kate thought, has she done with her appearance? That ridiculous outfit, too much cleavage, the preposterously crude make-up; she looks like a fifteen-year-old trying to get into a pub…

Avoiding the lift, they cautiously ascended the stairs from the underground car park.

Ally's stomach turned as she remembered her father's hand fondling her.

* * *

The sun was beating down on Blackpool beach as though it had mistaken the Fylde coast for the Caribbean. Thousands of punters grilled their flesh under its rays and turned complacently pink. The deckchair lad, Andrew, threaded his way through the human flotsam and jetsam. He was on the lookout for a girl. As he stepped over and around screaming kids, flabby extended legs, panting dogs, picnics, sandcastles, hyperventilating pensioners, canoodling couples and groups of rowdy lads and girls, he could see her in his mind's eye: she's alone, he thought, she's blonde, she has simply enormous tits bulging out of a tiny bikini and, er, urm… well that's about it, he concluded, pleased with his fantasy. Alone, blonde, enormous tits. Alone, blonde, enormous tits…

"All right darling," he said in a kindly fashion to a pensioner eager to pay for her deckchair. "Hot enough for you?"

"Ooh yes," said the old lady, cackling as though he had made a good joke.

"Where's your bikini then?"

"Ooh you cheeky sod!" she replied, delighted.

He glanced down at himself, admiring his pecs and stomach muscles. He rubbed his hand over his stomach, breathed in deeply, ducked as a wayward frisbee hurtled by, and saw her.

She wasn't blonde and she didn't have enormous tits – she was a redhead of average proportions – but she was alone. Her deckchair was wedged between the encampment of two large families. He traversed the obstacles in his path and stood in front of her. Her eyes were closed, so he was able to assess her body freely. She was wearing a plain blue bikini and her skin was alluringly smooth.

He grabbed hold of the leather satchel strapped around his waist and gave it a good shake so that the coins inside jangled.

"Wakey wakey."

"Huh?"

"Nodded off?"

She gazed up at him, frowning.

"How much is it?"

"That depends."

"What do you mean, that depends?" she said, shading her eyes from the sun.

"It's two quid for mingers, 50p for lookers and a quid for everyone in-between."

"Oh yeah?"

"Yeah."

"How much is it for me then?"

"For you it's gratis, uncharged, nothing, zilch, zero-rated and not to mention absolutely one hundred per cent free."

* * *

There was an image forcing itself into his consciousness repeatedly, no matter how feverishly he worked: a man and a woman, very pale, waving goodbye to him irrevocably. He wore a hat. She clutched a teddy bear... Rattigan shook his head violently. Leave me alone, he commanded of these visitations.

They were his parents. They had visited his mind in this way all through his long years at the children's home, ever since he had been orphaned. After he had escaped from the home, they came less often. Only at times like these. Rattigan was not big on symbols, but even he recognized that the image represented his terror of abandonment. And Theresa – he formulated the fact of it with careful astonishment – has abandoned me. And so the image returned, his father's expression blank, his mother's expression vaguely irritated.

"Daddy? Daddy?"

Ally came padding down the spiral staircase to her father's basement office complex, and now tried to invest concern in her intonation, if only to disguise the terror throbbing in her heart. He was sitting at his desk, writing at great speed. There were papers spread everywhere, all over the floor and furniture.

"Dad?"

He didn't answer. What had taken place with Ally represented a different order of betrayal, one so difficult to confront that so far he had blanked it out.

"Daddy."

When he looked up, his compelling eyes were aglow with intensity, but what were they saying? Nothing, she decided flatly. I can't tell if he's furious, panicked, grieving, or just… concentrating hard. At least he isn't psychotically angry, like he was a few hours ago.

"Are you all right?" she said.

His gaze absorbed her, then returned to his work. He held up a hand and finished off what he was writing, read the text through, then fed it into a fax machine. With the fax sent, he glanced around at his papers. A thought or an emotion seemed to grab hold of him abruptly; his seamy forehead folded up on itself.

"Dad?"

269

Without looking at her, he gestured for her to come to him. Stopping a few feet away from him, she examined his profile. He stared into the middle of his desk.

"You see," he rumbled, his voice entirely new and unknowable, "the other day…"

She shook her head, as if to say "don't talk about it".

"I'm under a lot of stress," he said emphatically, "the pressures have been high Ally, this last week or two… I'm sorry."

It sounded good. He was pleased with himself. Now that he had said it, it sounded not just feasible, but true.

To her surprise, Ally found herself thinking, it's hard not to feel sorry for the bastard, even while knowing what he's done to Mummy, or that he coerced someone into killing seventy-eight whales.

She cleared her throat.

"Are you still under pressure?"

He pressed the tips of his fingers to his temples.

"I'm dealing with it."

"What are all these papers?"

"It's just detail."

"What detail?"

"Not the kind of detail I usually have to concern myself with."

"But what is it?"

He sighed heavily and sifted through the documents.

"Bills of Lading, Documentary Letters of Credit, cargo transfer and pump and pipeline identification, deadweight tonnage and proof of scantling and permitted percentage corrosion, Contracts of Carriage and Certificates of Origin and Certificates of Fitness and Certificates of Officer Competency and Clearance Certificates. Lessors' Charters. Promissory notes."

"Oh."

"She's gone, you know."

"What?"

Rattigan's heavy head moved slowly from side to side. He had tried to ask himself why Theresa had done it, but it was hard to clear his head from feelings of... what? Humiliation, he admitted, full of shame. And fury. And amazement. He shuddered with surprise. Her absence undermined his sense of control.

He put his thumb and forefinger to his eyelids, and closed his eyes manually.

"Let her go," he murmured. "We don't need her, do we?"

"No," Ally whispered hoarsely.

"You'll never abandon me, will you, Ally?"

His tone of voice occupied curious territory, being something between a plea and an accusation. Oh God, Ally thought, this is the moment. She thought of Kate upstairs, waiting to descend. She watched her own hand, from its place next to her hip, make a slow and unpleasant journey, through minute fractions of time and space, to his shoulder; she saw it settle lightly on him, so lightly that he didn't feel it at first. The fingers pressed down.

"No Daddy."

Listen to my voice, she observed: toneless, dead. But he won't notice that.

His hand snaked up, palm out, and grasped her own. Their fingers interlocked, like the fingers of lovers. As Ally bent down over him – how clichéd, how unimaginative, how depressing – a memory of when she was sixteen came back to her, when he had come into her bedroom and tucked her in; he had been slightly drunk; his hands had brushed over her breasts.

"Don't worry Daddy," she breathed, getting close enough that he could smell her scented skin.

"Ally," he growled.

He tried to push her away, desperate yet half-hearted.

271

"Poor Daddy. Poor Daddy."

She was standing up straight now and cradling his head against her belly. His arms wrapped around her waist. She had to get him out of there. Patting his arms briskly, she said, "Come on Daddy, we'll go upstairs. You need a rest from all your worries."

He shook his head. His bristles scoured her bare midriff.

"Daddy, don't be silly."

"Have to wait for a fax," he mumbled.

She looked down at the top of his head in despair and loathing, suppressing the urge to yank him out of the basement by his big, fleshy ears. Now what? Now what? she panicked, glancing around desperately, looking for inspiration.

* * *

When the rumble of voices down in the basement went quiet, Kate agonized about what to do. After waiting for ten minutes, she descended the spiral staircase silently, pausing two-thirds of the way down to stare around the complex. She took in the papers spread all over the place, the computer equipment and gadgetry. Excellent. But no sign of Rattigan or Ally. Where are they? Must be behind that closed door. OK, this is it; just get down these last few steps, sneak across to the desk, find a document with the word "Jasmine" on it.

Scooping up half the papers on the desk, she took them to the bottom of the spiral staircase, so that she could at least make an attempt to flee if the man emerged from somewhere. Her eyes skimmed down the first sheet: BIMCO SHIPMAN FORM; it seemed to be some kind of contract between a ship owner and a ship manager concerning a vessel called *Baltic Express*, with provisions about crewing, bunkering, chartering. The next document was a bareboat charter registration issued from

Cyprus for a cruiser called *Grendel*. All photocopies, Kate said to herself in passing. The third document was a Documentary Letter of Credit, issued by the International Iberian Bank, providing for payment of $1,231,450 on receipt of documents representing a Confirmed Irrevocable Credit on a cargo of coffee beans carried by a vessel called *Indigo*. She flicked through the pile of papers as quickly as possible. After five minutes of skim-reading she was halfway through the documents, three-quarters through her nerve, and no nearer to finding a piece of evidence that linked Rattigan to the sinking of the *Jasmine*. Though the documents varied widely in terms of type, nearly all of them concerned the same four vessels: *Baltic Express*, *Grendel*, *Gold Rush* and *Indigo*.

It was an anxious task, when she knew that Rattigan was down there, behind that door, not ten metres away. As she sneaked back to the desk to gather the rest of the papers, she wondered what Ally was doing to distract him. What's behind the door? A TV room? A kitchen? Are they sharing a cosy cup of cocoa?

For the first time, her glance took in a monitor located above Rattigan's desk. The image was in black-and-white, the quality none too good, but scrutinizing it closely... She froze for some seconds, her expression one of disbelief.

Now she started to work more feverishly. Not bothering even to get to the relative safety of the spiral staircase, she sifted through the photocopies in a silent frenzy: Rattigan, Jasmine, Rattigan, Jasmine, the words must be here, will be here, where are they?

She was concentrating so fiercely that, when the phone rang, she almost collapsed from the shock, but fortunately she didn't scream. Air hissed into her lungs. She looked up at the monitor and its image of Rattigan and Ally.

Behind the closed door of the staff office, next to the massive bulk of her father, Ally froze. They were lying on the floor. He had dissolved into her comforting arms and stayed there. They were holding each other almost like lovers. They lay still as four rings sounded. The noise changed into that of a fax coming through. Rattigan pushed himself up from her. He was on his knees, rubbing at his eyes. Ally looked up at him, wondering what thoughts were moving in his mind. Don't leave this room, she ordered him silently, do not leave. His eyes were closed tight.

"Poor Daddy," she said.

When he opened his eyes and looked at his daughter, he saw two miniature reflections of himself in her pupils: a big, dishevelled man, breathing heavily. What are you doing? he tortured himself: you're obscene. He knew he wouldn't go further; but he knew that he wanted too.

"Important fax," he mumbled.

He lumbered to his feet.

On the other side of the door, gaze locked onto the monitor, Kate watched with dread: oh Jesus, he's coming in.

His hand was grasping the door handle when Ally said, "Daddy? Don't go yet. I need you."

He watched, bewitched, as she held her arms back out to him again – he couldn't resist holding her again.

Kate took a long, controlled breath as she saw Rattigan go back to his daughter. I have to get out of here, she worried. She started searching swiftly through the papers once more, wondering why they were all relating to four different ships when it was the *Jasmine* that was Rattigan's problem. The ships seemed to be remarkably similar, the same dimensions, tonnage, displacement weight, the same number of cargo tanks, the same horsepower... bloody hell, even the propellers are of the same dimensions, twelve feet four inches in diameter... Skimming the remaining papers frantically, she was thinking, why? What is the significance?

On an impulse, berating herself for not doing it sooner, she suddenly snatched up the fax that had come in:

> Retrospective registration Geronimo II complete, Indigo (March 96) becoming Geronimo II (December 98), Jasmine never officially existing as of now. Request $2mill for mopping up supporting details, in particular classification office in Belize, insurers in Monte Carlo.

The four ships, *Baltic Express*, *Grendel*, *Gold Rush*, *Indigo*… She scrabbled through some papers, checking the dates. All the *Baltic Express* papers were from the early 90s till 2002; the *Grendel* documents were from 2002 and 2003, *Gold Rush* from 2003 till 2005, *Indigo* from 2005 till December 2007… These aren't four ships, she realized, this is one ship with four names, and the documents I'm looking through are an account of its multiple histories.

She took the lot: not just the fax, but every piece of paper that was loose, using the wastepaper basket to carry them all. She also took a heavy glass paperweight. At the top of the spiral staircase she paused to let the ornament fall. It shattered onto the tiled basement floor.

With so many troubles besetting him, Rattigan had been so comforted by holding his daughter closely to him that he had been on the verge of falling asleep. He struggled to his feet, saying "Hey—"

At the top of the stairs, Kate waited just long enough to hear him blunder through the door and across to his desk. Then she turned on her heel and rushed to the underground car park. She got into the boot, locked herself in, and waited for Ally.

10

"Oh Lord," murmured Victoria Adlington, at home in her Georgian town house in Bloomsbury.

Any moment now, Downing Street would be on the dedicated line. Beyond that predictable fact, she had no idea as to what might happen next. The spectacular claims made by Ormond and Gunning in their hastily arranged press conference – and just *how* had those two individuals ended up working together, she asked herself – were too bizarre to comprehend. She replayed sections of the footage. Ormond's words struck her mind at the key points, like a stone sent skimming over water: "...my friend Derek Petersen committed suicide because he had been coerced into killing the beached whales... ...the necropsies are being sat on but we have evidence that they reveal alarming chemical contamination of SONAZ by substances so toxic as to... ...the repeated sequence of sounds made by the killer whales represents a simple code that..." Adlington winced. So much to take in, and all of it – even the really outlandish stuff – bad. The media and the general public would receive it like matter into a vacuum, that much was obvious. The pressure on the government to accept Ormond and Gunning's analysis was going to be enormous.

Now Kate Gunning was declaiming passionately about a man called Tony Rattigan – Adlington had heard of him vaguely. "... Rattigan not only orchestrated the killing of the whales, he sold the carcasses to... ...it's his ship that sank in SONAZ... ...an area already contaminated by the British government over many years is now being contaminated all over again... ...Dr Ormond and I are demanding that the whales are listened to – we want that submarine, and we want to be in it when it explores the remote ocean bed in SONAZ..."

Adlington looked at the impassioned faces of the two campaigners. Some of their allegations agreed with her own fears: the VX, the dioxin. But the rest of it was so off the wall as to make the whole seem preposterous. Talking whales? she said to herself; whales asking for a submarine? Oh come on...

Despite the pressure she was under, she had been determined to try and have an ordinary Saturday: only six or eight hours' work instead of the usual fourteen, and perhaps a concert in the evening. But now this. She looked down at her hands and noticed she was unconsciously opening and closing them. From upstairs came the sweet sounds of a violin, lingering over the melancholic strains of a piece of music well-known to her, but which momentarily she couldn't quite place. Her husband was a professional violinist, shy, loving and utterly apolitical. She never tired of hearing him practise.

She lay down on an old, battered sofa that had been inherited from her mother. There was a muted ping from within, as the elderly springs struggled to cope. Her husband played on. Placing her hands across the great mound of her belly... Elgar's violin concerto, she remembered. But it was no consolation.

Of course, if the worst-case construction were true – SONAZ horribly polluted by old British poisoning and by new Russian poisoning funded from British aid, whales leaving the sea as a protest, fish in the sea contaminated to the point of mutation – the consequences would be dire. Collapse of the North Atlantic fishing industry for one; think of the bankrupting compensation awards Britain would have to make to the northern nations. Collapse of the government even?

Her instinct was to take all the allegations very seriously, and to agree to have the ocean bed in SONAZ investigated for chemical weapons poisoning. But on the *government's* terms, she insisted to herself, in the *government's* control: the idea of this oddball couple hopping on to a submarine themselves was unrealistic, they were too unpredictable, too liable to cause trouble.

"Roddy Ormond was pilloried when he was leader of the Whale Crisis Coordination Team," an excited journalist at the press conference was saying into camera, as behind him journalists pushed and shoved and shouted, "but at least he was palpably doing something. The crisis response since he was removed from the post has been almost invisible. We await the official reaction to this press conference with the utmost interest, in particular this extraordinary request for a submarine."

The dedicated phone started ringing. She paused the footage. I wonder if I'm still a Cabinet Minister, she thought, picking up the receiver.

Five minutes later, she was being driven to Downing Street and an emergency Cabinet sub-committee to be chaired by the Prime Minister.

* * *

His wife had left him. Some intruder had stolen reams of incriminating paperwork. And as he had blundered through his ransacked office, Ally had strode past him brusquely, looking at him in the oddest way, and disappeared upstairs. It couldn't possibly get any worse, and then, it seemed within minutes, Ormond's press conference had happened. Ormond...

He watched it being repeated over and over on television, dumbfounded: Ormond has been working against me, Ormond has got at my papers... It was so unambiguously disastrous as to lead him to a sense of inevitability, as though forcing him to accept that his lifetime's battle was finally resolved, one way or the other. Because no one likes me, he thought flatly. No one ever has, no one ever will... And now I'm finished.

He stumbled around the house, looking for Ally, needing her now more than ever. And then, in the great hall, by the front door, he found what she had left him.

Half an hour later he was still there, sitting on the floor, cross-legged and slumped forwards. She had left a pile of clothes by the front door: pretty frocks, schoolgirl skirts, the long white socks and childish pyjamas. Each item was neatly folded. On top of the pile, a note:

> *Don't need these any more, keep them for your sad*
> *fantasies. I hope they lose the key.*

For a while, it was as though the body went into hibernation, as his mind tried to process this new information: she entrapped me... She despises me... He thought of her, gritting her teeth and stringing him along while that Gunning woman ransacked his desk.

His eyes, which had been closed for some minutes, opened. They focused on the note: *I hope they lose the key...* Now his desperate, habitual egoism was reasserting itself: Ormond, that bastard, who my wife once loved, always loved, still loves, Ormond got at Ally, and used her... He's ruined me. Not yet, not for months or years, not till the lawyers have squeezed their millions from it, but he's ruined me.

He was still cross-legged and motionless, like some outsized, deviant Buddha. His breathing slowed, and slowed. The focus, the single-mindedness that had marked nearly every moment of his life, seeped back into his system like a narcotic. He was going to have them killed: Ormond, Gunning and – yes – Theresa.

* * *

After the press conference, Roddy and Kate waited for the government's response. They passed a surreal hour preparing a meal and eating it at the exercise in studied modernity that was Kate's dining table, while the world went audibly mad for them: the entry phone buzzing until they took the fuse out, their mobile phones ringing constantly until they switched them off, and the yells coming up from the streets below: "Dr Ormond, a moment of your time!... Ms Gunning, just a few questions... Sir, how do you think the government will respond to your demands?" At one point the journalists succeeded in accessing the apartment block. They had stopped short of tearing Kate's door down, but not of beating on it without interruption until the arrival of the police.

Some minutes later, chewing methodically on a mouthful of pasta, Roddy looked up.

"What's happened? Everything's gone quiet outside."

Kate leapt up and turned up the volume on the television. Clive Manners, the Secretary of State for the Environment, and Victoria Adlington, Secretary of State for Defence, were conducting their own press conference.

"...exceedingly grateful to Dr Ormond and Ms Gunning for their imaginative contribution to this difficult situation," the Secretary of State for the Environment was intoning gravely; Adlington nodded sombrely. "The idea that an individual could have deliberately killed the whales on Brighton beach is almost too horrible to contemplate. I would like to reassure the whole country that we shall be examining this and all the other allegations that have been made with the utmost vigour. Now we come to the question of Britain dumping chemical weapons at sea. Let us be absolutely clear about this: this administration is not dumping chemical weapons at sea, has not dumped chemical weapons at sea, and will not ever dump chemical weapons at sea. We are justly proud of our record on the environment, proud too of our leadership in promoting a world free from the scourge of chemical weapons. But it would seem to be true that certain worrying substances have been found in those whales sent for necropsies by Dr Ormond. For this reason, the government now undertakes to investigate whether, in an earlier and less stringent era, any government – including the British government of the day – failed in its duty of care to the environment. My colleague the Secretary of State for Defence will explain how we intend to do this."

"He hasn't said anything about VX," Roddy complained.

Victoria Adlington dwarfed her slender male colleague. Without looking into the camera she read from a prepared statement. Thrashed out in the panic-stricken Cabinet sub-committee meeting, it was designed to satisfy the public clamour for results while protecting the government's back.

"The government is not inclined to believe that whales can talk to humans, or that the whales are acting in some kind of organized fashion in order to make an environmental protest..."

"Oh no," Roddy groaned.

"At the risk of stating the obvious, whales belong to a different order of the Animal Kingdom, and the creatures of the natural world, for all their many wonders, do not form into radical pressure groups. Notwithstanding this, we recognize our responsibility to do everything in our power to resolve what has become known as the whale crisis. Although the government cannot accept that the whales are somehow asking for a submarine, we nevertheless agree that a submarine investigation of the environmental condition of the sea bed in that part of the North Atlantic known as SONAZ is an appropriate action. I will shortly be instructing my Chiefs of Staff to send an appropriately equipped Royal Naval submarine to this place. But the people of Great Britain will understand that this will be a highly serious undertaking, and not one that allows for the participation of civilians. The best contribution that Dr Ormond and Kate Gunning can make will be to stay on land and meet with me and other officials to explain in detail all the points they have made. For this reason, we have decided not to grant them access to the submarine that will be sent to SONAZ. I can assure the people of Great Britain that this mission will be undertaken urgently, with the utmost seriousness and a real will to discover the truth. Its findings will be reported in a full and transparent fashion at the earliest opportunity. Let us hope that this undertaking will lead to the beginning of the end of the whale crisis. That's it. Thank you."

Reporters started yelling out questions, but the two Secretaries of State were already up and exiting the forum, Adlington with unlikely speed.

"Well they seem to be doing something, at least," Roddy conceded, grudgingly.

"Christ Roddy."

"What?"

"You're so naive."

11

Andrew lasted until lunchtime. Arnie's exact words to his newest and most useless deckchair lad were: "You're here to fuckin' work, not fuckin' pick up birds, now fuck off." It was true that Andrew had not been the most diligent of employees. He had spent most of the morning chatting up the redhead, Amanda. Now, wedged between two families on the sweaty, noisy beach, they were eating ninety-nines. He held out his ice cream for her to lick, and contrived to drip melted vanilla on her chest.

"You know what that looks like!" he leered.

"Give over."

"Shall I lick it off?"

"Get lost."

"Suck on my flake if you like – go on!"

"What's all that noise?" she said, looking towards the sea as she pushed him away.

The tide was coming in. A freak wave had ambushed the people closest to the sea, sending them to their feet cursing or laughing. They scrambled to gather up their belongings, holding up sodden towels and dripping bags. In the sea itself, the children and adults were shouting excitedly. It looked like another one was on the way.

A middle-aged woman at the very edge of the tide's line observed the wave from its formation. It became visible about fifty metres out. Not only was it a good foot higher than the average, it was a good deal quicker too: she saw it overtake two regular waves. When it reached her, it came up to her knees and rocked her legs. Her hangdog face arranged itself into a perplexed expression as she tried to figure it out: waves can't come in at different speeds, she thought.

Further along the beach, quite close to the pier, was the short, emaciated, berry-brown figure of Arnie. In a working life that had spanned fifty years of discontent, he rated this day as one of his worst ever. It was too hot, there were too many people, he was one lad down, and his back was killing him.

"Fuck off and go home the fuckin' lot of you," he muttered, then he spat in the sand.

"Oi!" shouted a man holding a frisbee, "that could have landed on me foot!"

"Well it fuckin' didn't so what are you fuckin' moaning about?"

Emphatic screams and shouts along the entire length of the beach caused them to look sharply towards the sea. Though the water was obscured from their vision by twenty yards of tightly packed humanity, there seemed to be some sort of mini panic going on. People were scrambling back from the sea, so that Arnie and his antagonist were jostled back too; shouts and wails filled the air.

"That was a bloody whopper!"

"Me towel's wet!"

"Mam! Mam!"

"Where's the bloody dog?"

Arnie retreated before the surge of people, getting an elbow in his ribs for his troubles, then stood on a huge paper cup of coke that exploded all over his feet. Unbelievable, he moaned to himself.

The pier stretched well over 400 metres into the sea. At the end of it, an elderly man with an apparent dispensation from feeling hot – he was wearing a thick suit, under the jacket of which was a knitted sweater, and over the top of which was a raincoat – pointed out to sea. His wife shielded her eyes as she looked. She saw what he saw, and exclaimed softly. Other people were becoming aware of it. All down the side of the pier they pointed and shouted at the phenomenon. It was getting closer, and bigger. They looked between it and the beach, calculating the distance between the two.

* * *

Blackfin is fatigued and ill beyond endurance, but in these last minutes adrenaline sustains him. His battered body blasts through the water. He is leading three and a half thousand whales.

Many animals are desperate to breathe, but none has broken the surface for half an hour. Each whale is like one stone in a moving wall of underwater life. The wall is huge, and it powers the pressure wave in front of it; the wave which the tourists of Blackpool are even now pointing at in astonishment. These same tourists know nothing of what lies behind the wave, a few metres under the sea's surface: three hundred blue whales, five hundred sperm, six hundred fin... creatures weighing a thousand times more than a man, assembled in numbers never known to nature, joined in a common purpose. They are so tightly packed that their flanks glance off one another, their heads jerk up and down with the exertion, dolphins cluster near their tails and tailstocks, risking a fatal buffeting.

Blackfin can no longer swim hard enough to maintain the pace, and yet his pace doesn't slacken. The force behind him is such, the whales around him are so dense, that he is half carried along by the combined momentum of both. The tea-coloured water is beginning to lighten, and now for the first time he simultaneously sees the surface and the sea bed. To his left is a sperm whale, to his right and slightly below him is a fin whale, while above is a mini school of flashing, pulsing white-striped dolphins; again and again he feels the hard bodies of his brother creatures supporting his own. The magnitude of the power assembled behind him is physically palpable: he feels it in the dancing, extreme patterns of water movement around his sensitive blowhole. This force is too big for the shallowness of the waters; its excess overtakes the head of the whale formation and feeds the ever-growing wave in front of them, that moves almost as fast as they do, outstripping the ordinary forces of the sea.

The beach approaches. Under the pain of his wounds, in the adrenaline of his excitement, over the consciousness of consequence, there is a kind of peace for Blackfin. He has the conviction that this time – his head breaches the surface of the water, a bottlenose dolphin leaps wildly in the air, just ahead he can see the artificial wave beginning to collapse on itself – this time, the humans will listen.

* * *

The wave was creating a sensation on the beach. It appeared to be about eight feet high; hardly a tidal wave, and yet big enough to cause a great deal of uneasiness. As it got closer, its speed became evident. Most people hurriedly moved up the beach, exclaiming and shouting. Others, mostly young lads addicted to the approval of their mates, rushed in the opposite direction, struggling to force their way through the retreating surge of people. When they arrived at the meeting of sand and sea, and observed the wall of water advancing towards them, their bravado caught in their throats. Some of them turned on their tails and fled. Others grinned at each other inanely, and held their ground.

Andrew and Amanda had stood up to see what was going on. They were about forty metres away from the sea, and seemed to be occupying the unofficial border behind which people had retreated. Andrew felt irritated by the spectacle of the wave. It's interrupted my flow, he complained to himself, by which he meant his seduction of Amanda. Slipping a hand around Amanda's waist and pulling her into his side, he allowed his fingers to slip around the curve of her bottom.

"It's *massive*," Amanda exclaimed. "It won't reach us here, will it?"

"Course not, we're halfway up the beach."

"What's going on there – on the pier?"

"Dunno."

The people on the pier appeared to have gone mad. The wave having reached the pier's outermost extent and then washed under it, they were screaming and shouting at everyone on the beach, gesturing frantically. Those on the beach looked at the wave, now just a few seconds away, looked at the desperate antics occurring on the pier, looked at the wave again, and were none the wiser.

The elderly, over-clothed man who was standing at the pier's end stared in disbelief and dismay. The sea behind the wave was a cauldron of violence and dark forms, extracted from a dream so weird that no one had ever dreamt it before. Whales, thousands of whales. His appalled face turned to the beach and the poor souls on it.

"They're all going to die!"

His voice had a note of naive surprise in it, more suited to ordinary and banal phrases: "It's raining", or "What time is it?" He clutched at the railings with his rheumatoid fingers, oblivious to everyone around him, even his wife, who had abruptly sat down on the bare planks. With frightened old men's eyes he saw massive bodies rising out of the sea like mythical beasts, grey and black and mottled, surging with horrible synchronization towards the sightless people on the sand. He saw the bizarre spectacle of small silver dolphins leaping and jumping between the dark shapes, pinging off the backs of the huge animals they were accompanying, looking like leaping salmon in a stream. He saw whales of every size and hue, packed into a formation of a shallow diamond that from tip to tip had to be three hundred metres across, swimming to the shore.

The wave is about to break on the sand. The thousands of sun bathers on Blackpool beach emit screams of terror and exhilaration. The brave young show-offs in their pink, sun-burnt skins and footballers' haircuts run to meet it. As the wave crashes down, propelling ahead of it a three-foot surge of dirty, foaming water up the sand to the watching masses, the first whales break through. A young lad who, with a whoop, dives headlong into the wall of water, at least has no time to experience his own death as the pointed snout of a fin whale impacts with him; his head and neck crumple in a fraction of a second before his body is flipped up and out of the water, turning in the air, already dead, but to be crushed and mangled by the much smaller killer whale following on. Now the beach is the meeting of an unstoppable force with primal terror. As the boastful boys and young men disappear from their own lives, the crowds shriek their fear. Like some kind of surreal, mocking sideshow, dolphins are shooting out of the base of the wave and riding its wash, ploughing into human beings in the manner of vicious skittles. Andrew has turned on his heel. He runs four paces, tramples over someone, a child, he doesn't know, oh Christ, oh sweet Christ. A dolphin flashes past him and clatters into half a dozen screaming teenagers, then he is on his knees, another dolphin skids past, he is panting incoherently and somehow his head, his mouth is pressed into the sand, his limbs are scrabbling ineffectually, and half upside-down like this he sees much bigger creatures skidding up the beach, sees the one that is coming for him, tries shaking his leg desperately to free himself from something – Amanda's grip – sees it glide over her and on him and hears the sounds of bones breaking and sees nothing ever again.

The noise is that of a great killing machine shearing up the sand to the accompaniment of human suffering; human bodies are being driven into the soft sand, flipped into the air, crushed in a moment between huge moving beasts that have only inches between them. The larger whales ride over smaller whales that virtually explode under the pressure. A still moving, quivering, bloody Northern Bottlenose Whale rolls gently onto a motionless three-year-old girl. All that remains visible of her are her little feet, projecting pathetically from under the animal's milky, muscled flank.

Most deadly are the blues. These massive creatures, like the projectiles of a tribe of giants, catapult themselves out of the sea further than any other species. Their long, streamlined bodies skim up the sand with the superior momentum of the largest mass moving at the greatest velocity; they plough through the half-naked innocents, leaving in their wake wide and dead-filled gutters of sand.

Arnie is at least thirty metres up the beach, far enough to escape. While all around him are keening for life, he stands like some kind of fanatically possessed captain going down with his ship. His lower jaw hangs down. The knotty, weather-browned legs on which he could run away don't move. His eyes are fixed on what is coming. It is sweeping up the beach and over the panicked masses like a runaway juggernaut careering through a football crowd. By now many whales are being prevented from getting so high up the beach, slamming into their own kind, but this one has a clear passage. Arnie witnesses its slowing down, slowing down; he sees with his eyes, but somehow doesn't register with his mind, how people are succeeding in diving out of its way, it now has but a few metres until it will grind to a halt. Arnie's old eyes lock on to the sight of the creature's snout. He feels it slam directly into the centre of his chest. He goes over, lying on his back with his arms stretched out horizontally. He looks straight up as the blue whale edges forwards, and he watches the massive head eclipse the sky.

Not silence, when so many thousands are wailing; but in the seconds after the last whale slides to a stop, there is the terrible time-stopped aftermath. In this transitional state, shared by humans and whales alike, Blackfin strains for his senses. Just as he had beached, a blue whale had collided with him. The bigger creature had upturned him, so that he had been sent sliding and rolling up the beach, completely out of control. He had skidded and sheared, seen humans spin around him, heard high-pitched shrieks as they flashed by and beyond his ear. He doesn't remember stopping, but now he finds himself, winded and disoriented, half-keeled over to one side, towards the back of the thousands of beached sea mammals. He is facing the sea.

12

It was the day on which 3,491 whales and dolphins launched themselves onto a beach teeming with holiday makers, killing approximately 5,500 people – the fatality count would not be confirmed for several days – with a further eight to nine thousand injured. The never-to-be-forgotten day, the day of death, the worst and strangest civilian disaster in the history of Britain, was drawing to a close.

11.25 p.m. An official car was waiting for Roddy and Kate when their RAF jet touched down at the small military airstrip in Lancashire. Within a few minutes the driver of the black Toyota Prius, preceded by six police outriders with sirens wailing and lights flashing, was screeching them across the tarmac and the night. It was all evidence of Roddy's new status. Within minutes of the awesome Blackpool beaching, a government in disarray had reinstated him as the Emergency Coordinator and given him free licence to act as he saw fit.

On the outskirts of Blackpool they passed a mile-long tailback of cars queuing up at a roadblock. Roddy and Kate stared through the dark-tinted windows of the Toyota at the people in the cars. They were the relatives. Roddy peered at faces stricken with grief or numb with pain: poor bastards.

Joining the end of a convoy of seven ambulances, the car was ushered through the roadblock. There was no ordinary traffic on the streets any more. They overtook a lumbering convoy of army lorries, the headlights of each truck illuminating the troops in the back of open wagons, who were looking out blankly.

"It's unreal," Kate said.

At five minutes to midnight they arrived at the promenade, near the entrance to the North Pier. They were out of the car before the driver could open the doors for them. The first thing

Roddy noticed was the noise of helicopters in the sky. He walked the ten short metres to the railings, feeling odd and dislocated from himself. Two paramedics hurried past, ferrying a corpse on a stretcher. Then he was at the railings, clutching the cold metal, looking down.

His mind absorbed the glaring floodlights, that tore the beach from the night and exhibited it like a nightmare made real; soldiers, hundreds of soldiers, standing uneasily at ease, facing the land. And behind the soldiers... whale after whale after whale, the huge and sleek blues, the mighty and ugly sperms, the dwarfed dolphins, prostrated across a human environment. They were on their sides, their fronts, they were upside down, in places they were even in heaps, so densely packed had they been when leaving their water world for the shallow sands of Blackpool. Many were dead and many were injured.

Roddy's gaze moved from right to left, and he saw that the beached whales stretched hundreds of metres along the sands. This is chaos, he told himself, this is anarchy of the natural world, and totally different to Brighton. There was nothing familiar on which to hang his responses, just a scene beyond imagining, set off by small and absurd details: a man in suit, tie and bright yellow wellingtons, tramping through the sand; a pale Risso's dolphin perched on top of a blue whale like an oxpecker on a water buffalo.

Roddy struggled to concentrate as someone spoke to him. He gathered that he was being briefed by a Chief Constable. He continued nodding as the man explained how the last of the injured had been taken away by 10 p.m. to hospitals in ten different counties, to clinics and makeshift treatment centres in schools and leisure centres; the accessible dead, too, were no longer on the beach, but lying in a vast temporary morgue set up at the football stadium.

"I see," Roddy said. But he didn't. What he actually saw were the inaccessible dead who were still on the beach: portions of body sticking out grotesquely, and with a cruel comedy, from under the forms of sea creatures.

The Chief Constable's grim, toneless monologue was stumbling, petering out. Next to them Kate had started to swear horribly, a stream-of-unconsciousness soliloquy that was entirely unfettered by decency or sense, and that had inhibited the Chief Constable. Roddy listened to it for a few moments; he deliberately used it to distract his thoughts.

"Kate?" he said.

"The bastards," she said, in the tiniest voice Roddy had ever heard. "The bastards."

"Who?"

"The whales," she said, almost inaudible with anger.

The air in Roddy's lungs was exhaled in a heavy sigh of grief; I don't, I can't blame the whales...

She turned on her heel and got back into the car, slamming the door.

Roddy still stared into the millions of tonnes of beached cetaceans. Blackfin, where are you? Why did you do this?

"Sir? Dr Ormond? Are you ready?"

Their military driver was anxious. It was his job to get them to and from the airstrip as quickly as possible. The pair were bound for RAF Brize Norton in Oxfordshire, and a briefing with Flag Officer Submarines.

"Let's go," Roddy answered.

He had insisted on seeing this scene before joining the submarine in the Atlantic which, even now, was travelling towards SONAZ at thirty knots. He frowned bleakly, and followed Kate into the car.

On the beach, an old sperm whale with a black blotch on his rounded hump blows weakly.

* * *

No lights were on in the huge house on The Bishops Avenue. Rattigan had been watching television for six hours. He sat sullenly in front of the TV screen, radiating contempt as the Prime Minister, wearing black suit and tie, looking shell shocked, addressed the nation:

"...I stand in front of you without any prepared text or thoughts. I bring only my sadness..."

The unchanging glow from the screen cast a dim, bluish light over Rattigan's unshaven face. Peering down into the pit of his personal catastrophe, his extraordinary eyes had gone into an extraordinary mode; they scarcely moved; they hardly blinked.

"It is midnight," the Prime Minister continued, "and our nation is numbed with grief..."

But Rattigan was not listening to the Prime Minister's statement any more. He had lost his wife, his daughter, his business, his position, his future – all the props with which he held at bay the misery of being him. As in the manner of a small boy watching an exciting cartoon, one of his legs started to quiver up and down: Christ, they'll wish they'd never hated me... Ormond, Gunning, Theresa. They're dead.

His mind, now uncoupled from the fear of consequences, went delving into its own skewed creativity. Ormond, Ormond... His quivering knee gradually ceased its motion. Like some kind of chess grandmaster in a position of mortal weakness, he relentlessly sought the most effective solution to cripple his opponent, as the flickering TV light passed over his heavy face.

* * *

In the skies above a dark and bewildered England, Kate and Roddy were bickering miserably on their flight to RAF Brize Norton.

"You're terrified of having to confront it," Kate said emphatically. "They have deliberately killed a beach full of innocent people, why can't you accept that they've done a terrible thing?"

"They could kill that many people every week for the next ten years and still not even approach the number of whales killed by man, we've practically exterminated many whale populations, and for what? I'll tell you for what—"

"I don't want to know for what, I want to know—"

"—for soap, for oil, for fake ivory, for cheap dog food, for fertilizer, for candle wax, for lubricants, for aphrodisiacs, for *money!* We don't know why the whales did it, but believe me, there'll be a better reason than we ever had!"

"Er," said the co-pilot, appearing from the cockpit, "is everything all right?"

Roddy nodded and slumped back in his seat. Kate made as if to say something, but he held up a weary hand. She muttered some comment that had the word "stubborn" in it. She was feeling mounting stress: soon she would be going inside a submarine, an idea that terrified her for reasons she was so far keeping to herself.

Fuming in his seat, Roddy was thinking about the qualities by which humans elevate themselves above animals: the conscience, for one. But what about sentimentality, hypocrisy, he fumed to himself: qualities so distinctly human that they allow a human being to lavish care on a single cat or dog, while ignoring the baleful union of animal life and industrial efficiency that is modern agriculture; qualities so distinctly human, that they allow a human being to coo with fondness over the sweet and winning tricks of a whale or a dolphin in a swimming pool, while being utterly unmoved by the thousands of dolphins massacred each year in drift-net fishing. Such wilful ignorance of the connection of one thing to another – such sentimentality and hypocrisy – are not features of the whale… He turned back to Kate.

"Those whales have endured hundreds of years of persecution, they're down to pitiful fractions of their original populations – you'd call it genocide if it had happened to people, it would be the equivalent of ninety percent of the earth's population being wiped out. Understand? Not once have they done anything like this before. Now they're launching themselves onto crowded beaches, and that tells me that something truly horrendous must be going on in their world, but no, according to you it's because they've suddenly turned into psychotic murderers! What tosh!"

Kate whipped around in her seat and hurled her glass of water at him. The shock of the cold water winded him; he took several breaths, his chest heaving up and down. They looked at each other, Kate as incredulous as he was over what she had just done.

"What did you do that for?!"

"Because you completely, completely, you, *infuriate* me!"

He rubbed at his dripping face with his hand, then pinched the material of his shirt between his thumb and forefinger and peeled it away from his skin.

"Sorry," she said.

He shook his head.

"I'm stressed out," Kate said, "completely and utterly freaked out by all this. Roddy? I'm sorry. Roddy, what are we going to find at the bottom of the Irminger Basin?"

"I don't know."

* * *

At RAF Brize Norton they were met by the Station Commander and his retinue, who quickly escorted them to the Operations Rooms of No.10 Squadron. Inside the Ops Room two men were waiting: Squadron Leader Timothy Handsworth, and Rear Admiral Jeremy Noades.

The Rear Admiral held the position of Flag Officer Submarines, and was responsible for the Royal Navy's thirty or so nuclear-powered and diesel-powered attack submarines. He took the two of them through a twenty minute briefing: the location of HMS *Tenacious*; how long it would take the submarine to reach SONAZ once they were aboard her; safety procedures...

"Any questions?"

"We requested filming equipment," Roddy responded.

"Remote deep-sea-pressure cameras and lighting—"

"Yeah."

"—are already on the plane. When you go aboard *Tenacious* there'll be a wait of at least two hours while the equipment is mounted on the hull, weather permitting. As for the satellite equipment, the ship has her own gyro-stabilized portable satellite dishes with which you'll be able to transmit – both recorded and live."

"What, from the bottom of the sea?"

"No no, at those depths you can't even use radio, unless it's to another submarine at a similar depth. The satellite dishes are portable, they're set up on the conning by the Sounds people when the ship surfaces."

"What's the conning?"

"Conning tower. The sail. The structure that sticks up out of the middle of the boat."

"How big is this thing?" Kate asked.

"The conning tower?"

"The boat."

"She's about eighty metres long and about ten in the beam."

"I mean, inside."

The Rear-Admiral shrugged.

"She's a submarine. There's not a great deal of space."

Kate nodded unhappily.

Squadron Leader Timothy Handsworth briefed them about their journey to *Tenacious*. A VC10 would get them to Reykjavík in Iceland in about six to six and a half hours; there they would board a Royal Navy Sea King helicopter; the craft would fly them first to an offshore oil installation for refuelling, then to the aircraft carrier HMS *Invincible*, on exercises in the North Atlantic; after further refuelling they would continue on to a rendezvous with HMS *Tenacious*, which would pick them up about four hundred miles south of the Norwegian coast.

"Problems, questions?"

He looked at them brightly, eyebrows up and earnest. Kate hesitated before speaking.

"Does the Sea King, like, land on top of the submarine?"

"Good God no, you could hardly land a paper aeroplane on a submarine."

"So how do we get, you know, out of the helicopter and onto the submarine?"

"They dangle you out of the door on a string."

"Ha ha."

"Sorry?"

They stared at each other. She thought, oh, he's not being funny.

* * *

The private detective, one of the many little people in the bottom of Rattigan's pocket, had tracked Theresa down to a remote cottage on the Isle of Raasay in the Inner Hebrides. The killer had then been contracted immediately. But a few hours later, further information had come through from the private detective: Theresa wasn't alone, Ally was with her.

Rattigan's mind, which had been locked on to the problem of

getting at Ormond, struggled to free a part of itself to process this new detail.

It was in the early hours of the morning and he was in a car, but not the Bentley. That had been sent shrieking out of the drive and on to The Bishops Avenue as a decoy for the reporters waiting at the gates. Later his driver had slowly manoeuvred past the depleted throng in a people carrier. Rattigan had been hiding in the back in a huge cardboard box from a recently installed fridge-freezer. The rudimentary ruse had been humiliating but successful, and now they were randomly cruising around the West End. Soho was dark and nearly deserted. Most people were still glued to their television screens, and waiting for the submarine excursion to commence in earnest.

The car turned into Greek Street. On the radio, the presenter was detailing the specifications of HMS *Tenacious*: "Claimed to be the quietest submarine of any navy in the world, the Royal Navy's Trafalgar-Class Hunter-Attack SSN submarine is ideally suited to engagement with enemy craft."

Enemy craft. The words slipped into Rattigan's thoughts, and rested against his hatred of Ormond for a few seconds.

His driver, used to having an opaque partition between him and the boss, was constantly glancing in the rear-view mirror. He frowned nervously, looked forwards, swerved to correct his course, then looked at Rattigan again. A hint of a smile had appeared on his employer's lips.

Rattigan was thinking about the Russians. All this was a disaster not just for him, and not just for the people he had been dealing with – those powerful crooks within the power-broking, corrupt, competing factions of Russia's political structure and military hierarchy – but also for the real big players, criminal and clean, who were running the Kremlin. They had much to lose should a British submarine explore the ocean bed of SONAZ. Russia's ambition to secure her place in the new world order would be set back by a decade. They wouldn't just sit by and let it happen, would they? Surely there'd be some kind of rearguard action?

It's my last hope, Rattigan thought.

* * *

For twenty-four hours Kate had kept her fears to herself. On the plane to Reykjavík and on the Sea-King flights across the Atlantic she had immersed herself in operational detail. When the Sea King had refuelled at an offshore oil installation, landing in a brisk wind on what had seemed a toytown landing platform, she had shut her eyes tight, gripped the aluminium frame of her canvas seat, and performed long division sums in her mind. Even when they had made the rendezvous with HMS *Tenacious* she had not cracked. Dangling on the guideline in a bright-orange rubber immersion suit, with a life jacket pressing up on her chin and a trillion tons of sea water churning below her, she had hung limp as a rag doll. Ratings on the deck of *Tenacious* had reeled her in like a fish on a line. "Miss!" they had shouted, "Miss, open your eyes!" When she had done so, she had found herself propped up by two burly, grinning men, as the black bulk of the submarine lurched in the water. Roddy was already climbing the ladder to the conning tower, where Commander Gerhardie was waiting.

It had taken an hour and a half for the divers to mount the equipment on the vessel's hull. During that time she had stayed on the conning tower. Roddy had been down below in the control room with the Commander and a complement of officers. Three times they had sent a rating to ask Kate to come down, and once Roddy himself had emerged to say, "What are you doing? Come down." "I'm coming," she had answered with a weak smile, then, when he had gone back down, she had gripped the rail tighter and stayed put.

Roddy came up again when the submarine was ready to dive.

"What's going on?"

They stood next to each other in the middle of the wide and pulsing sea. An officer and two ratings were also on the tower.

"It's my phobias," she whispered.

"What phobias? You didn't tell me you had any phobias."

He put an arm around her. Silence, but for the surge of the sea and the wind whistling past their ears. A head popped out of the hatch.

"Commander Gerhardie's respects sir, ma'am, we need everyone down below."

"Shit!" Kate whimpered.

"Tell me what your phobias are."

"Water," she admitted, turning to face him for the first time.

"Water." He looked around at the ocean surrounding them. "There's lots of water out here. Come down there and you can't see any at all."

"Because it's all on top of you!" she shouted.

"All right, keep calm. What's the other one?"

"Confined spaces."

"Water, and confined spaces..." he said, nodding glumly.

"I can't go down there!" she hissed.

"Kate, this is the big one you've always wanted, you're going to make a broadcast that the entire world is waiting for. But the story is at the bottom of the sea. You just have to get on with it."

"I understand," she said through gritted teeth, "but if I go down there then I'm scared I'll go hysterical, I might not be able to stop myself."

The officer next to them on the conning tower said, "Excuse me sir, I'm sorry, but can you tell me what the problem is?"

"She won't go down," Roddy said. "Phobia."

There was a pause, the officer nodding uncertainly.

"Happens from time to time. I'll get the alcohol..."

300

Part Three

1

The periscopes in the centre of the control room, shining in their deck housings, had been downed. At the control console the Planesman was guiding the billion-pound machine through the Atlantic waters, operating a single joystick. The navigator, a young lieutenant, was charting their course at the navigation table. He was also Officer of the Watch for the next six hours. Ten officers and ratings were concentrating on their different tasks. Ratings too young to shave every day were hunched over the screens of the tactical systems, while engineers not much older monitored the performance of the propulsion systems; the nuclear-powered sub was served by a reactor with enough uranium to power the vessel for years.

In the adjacent sounds room, the mysterious noises and vibrations of the ocean were picked up by hydrophones installed on the bows of *Tenacious*, then converted into the infinitely variable arrangements of light showing on the flickering screens. Two ratings were monitoring the output with an extra show of diligence, given that Commander Gerhardie was in the room talking with the TASO, Tactics and Sonar Officer Lieutenant Sammy Gale. The ratings had been trained to interpret the sounds made by manmade vessels, in particular those of other submarines. They could detect and precisely identify a distant and nearly static enemy contact merely by subtle variations in sonar profile and sound waves. Now they were listening to their captain and their TASO discussing the acoustic profiles of whales.

Assured that the TASO knew what was expected of him, Commander Gerhardie returned to the control room and conferred with his navigator.

"Helm, keep course two-four-zero, maintain depth two hundred metres, make revolutions for thirty knots!" the navigator ordered after Gerhardie left him.

The commander headed for the wardroom, the officer's mess, in which the monitors and remote viewing controls had been set up. Inside, Roddy was peering over the shoulders of the two ratings who were operating the controls. Kate was setting up her own equipment. She wasn't exactly drunk, but she was undeniably humming an out-of-tune song.

Each of the four monitors could be switched between eight hull-mounted cameras. Gerhardie stared into the images of the sea, the light from the screens shining on his professorial bald dome. Brilliant underwater lamps gave reasonable visibility to a reach of ten or fifteen metres, beyond which there was a translucence for a further ten or twelve. Small, suspended organisms and particles crowded the screens, showing up almost white against the murky green background.

Gerhardie said, "I've been commanding submarines for eight years, yet I've never seen under the water before."

"Well," Roddy considered, "many whales and dolphins have the lot – sonar, acoustics and vision – but like you they're most reliant on the first two."

"What's their sonar like?"

"Better than yours. A bottlenose dolphin 'sees' every tiny detail of a shape. On a sub it would get every last rivet. They can even use sonar to differentiate between colours."

Commander Gerhardie nodded dubiously. He was about as convinced by this claim as he was by the notion that whales had "spoken" to man. As far as he was concerned, this rather strange assignment was little more than a publicity stunt forced on him by politicians who were desperate to be seen to be doing something.

"You don't believe me," Roddy said, interpreting the silence.

"Not for a moment," Gerhardie said cheerfully. "Behind my back they call me 'Captain Blunt' around here, don't they, Falkland," he continued, tapping one of the ratings on the shoulder.

Able Seaman Falkland, a shaven-headed baby-faced lad of nineteen, with very dark eyes and girlishly red lips, opened his mouth to speak. No sound came out. To say "No sir" would be to tell a lie that might not be believed; to say "Yes sir" would be to risk an insolent admission.

"Don't worry Falkland, if giving nicknames to your officers were an offence, there'd be no men in the Navy at all."

"Yes sir."

"Or women," Kate said, behind him.

"Or women," the commander agreed, turning to her. "How are you coping?"

"Well, I'm down here now, and I'm not screaming. I count that as success."

"Look, we're twelve hours away from our destination. I'd get some sleep if I were you, once you're all done and dusted in here. My cabin is yours for the duration of this little, er, escapade."

"Thanks."

"You too, Dr Ormond. You'll be sleeping in the officers' quarters. It's cramped but adequate."

"He's sleeping in your cabin," Kate said.

"No no, Ms Gunning, I said you could sleep in my cabin."

"Yes."

The Commander of HMS *Tenacious* stared at her, nonplussed. His throat contracted as he swallowed.

"You want to, er..."

"Yes." I need to, Kate thought; I'm not being alone in a tin can at the bottom of the ocean.

"I see."

He stood up straight and brushed an imaginary speck of dust from the breast pocket of his shirt.

"Well, I, I...." He suddenly grinned. "Do you know, in nearly a century of Her Majesty's Royal Navy Submarine Service, I'm pretty sure that a man has yet to sleep with a woman in a submarine."

Kate took a small sip of Bells and winced.

"Well, he's old enough to be my father but I'll do it for the Queen."

After Kate and Roddy had retired, and Commander Gerhardie had left the wardroom, Able Seaman Falkland turned his lurid baby face to his companion.

"Do you think they'll 'ave sex?" he said.

"For fuck's sake Falkland, what would you do if you were with a piece like that in Blunty's bed?"

* * *

Evening is approaching Blackpool beach. Blackfin is helpless. Being tilted over to one side destroys his sense of balance and coordination. His left eye looks into the sand a metre away. His right eye gazes at the sky, and sees curving spectrums of coloured light, whose arcs lead out of sight to the sea he has left behind: they are the spectacular artificial rainbows formed in the mist of sea water that is being sprayed across the beach.

Mechanical roars, megaphones, whales dying, helicopters, sirens... He doesn't comprehend. Sometimes heavy engines explode into life, near or far. He doesn't know what they are, or that they are winching dead whales clear of decomposing human bodies. He slips in and out of lucidity. New noises are coming from somewhere, human chants, sound waves dense with hate. Something is going on, are the humans fighting each other?

He is an old sperm whale, injured and exhausted. Three times he has left the sea, fuelled by an irrevocable determination. Now his age, exhaustion and condition assault his spirit. Sometimes an important concept floats within reach of his comprehension, an unusual image which explains – doesn't it? – why he is high and dry in this awful place... *badbright*... The humans must find the *badbright*.

"KILL THE WHALES, KILL THE WHALES, KILL THE WHALES!"

Noisy, barbaric sound pictures. What do they mean? In Blackfin's wandering mind comes the image of the first human he had ever seen, when he had been young, and foolhardy, and half stranded in a tidal estuary... The man with the warm thoughts and soft sounds... Who was that man?...

On the promenade all hell breaks loose. A swollen, enraged mob breaches the barricade of soldiers and police. Mostly young men, many with makeshift weapons – sticks, axes – they swarm down the steps to the beach. Soldiers rush to head them off, but a second breaching of the barricade further along the promenade occurs; another war party rushes down the steps to the beach and is able to puncture a weakened line. Any strategy of the authorities is quickly redundant. Virtual hand-to-hand combat breaks out across the sand. Frantic reporters gabble in high voices as the pitched battle rages.

Blackfin can hear brothers and sisters keening and weeping. He is too ill to care. Several times humans race past him. Some soldiers regroup behind him, as though he were some kind of defensive emplacement on a battlefield, then move on. And now two young men and an older one are lined along Blackfin's left flank. One has an axe, one has a machete, one has a garden fork. The youngest man raises an axe over his head. Shouting like an athlete, he lurches it down with as much power as he can muster.

"Fuck it," he grunts, struggling to pull it out of the flesh.

They hack at him feverishly, like incompetent whalers, their makeshift weapons separating blubber from blubber and blubber from muscle. The short red slashes decorate him and ooze blood. Blackfin's body pulses and spasms.

* * *

Able Seaman Falkland and his mates would have been disappointed to discover that Roddy had not made full use of "a piece like that" on retiring to the Captain's cabin. Kate had been touchingly desperate to cling on to him, as a form of insurance against the power of her phobias, but that was about as far as it went. He woke up some time later, with little idea of how long he'd been asleep. He didn't have a watch. He wasn't really a watch sort of man. Kate slept on. A small red bulb, always on, cast its seedy light across the tiny cabin.

He shifted slightly. Kate stirred and made an unfortunate snorting noise, which made Roddy smile. His right hand, draped over her back, felt her muscles move and tauten as she changed positions. She rolled over, and suddenly he found his hand resting over the soft curves of her. The urge to hold her more tightly was almost irresistible: to hold her breasts from behind and sink his face into the back of her neck. And he had a feeling that any such action, at least at this time and in this place, would be reciprocated. But...

He took his hand away from her breast and shuffled away from her.

A knock on the door.

"Yes."

"Commander Gerhardie's respects sir, er, ma'am," called a young submariner, "You've been sleeping for ten hours. We're less than two hours from SONAZ and there's a whale on the monitors."

A few minutes later when Roddy and Kate entered the makeshift video suite in the officer's mess, Commander Gerhardie said, "It appeared from the port side. We've had to slow down to eighteen knots but it's still cracking along at a fair old speed."

Roddy stared at one of the monitors, noting that the camera view was "front ahead". He saw the great tail flukes shifting up and down, gleaming grey and bright in the light of the powerful lamps.

"What is it?" Kate asked.

"Female sperm whale. Show me all the other camera views," he instructed the ratings.

From the stern, port, and starboard angles, screens of empty ocean succeeded one another.

"Zoom past her and see if there are any more ahead."

In the thick gloom in front of the sperm whale, a school of fish was seen to shear off to the side.

"Nothing," said the rating, Falkland, who was back on duty after six hours off.

"It's turning off to the left a bit," Kate said.

"It keeps doing that," answered Gerhardie. "Then it comes back."

As the whale moved further to the left, the operative shifted to a camera on the port side and tracked it.

"Follow it," Roddy rapped.

"Yes sir," said Falkland.

"Not you, the boat."

Gerhardie raised his eyebrows.

"You want us to determine our course according to a whale?"

"Yes."

Gerhardie picked up a microphone to the control room.

"Captain. Starboard three."

Slowly, the whale came back into view until it was once more directly in front.

"Now let's ask the navigator where we'll end up," Roddy said.

He and Gerhardie left for the control room. Kate went to the camera that she'd set up on a tripod in the corner, and set it running. She stood in front of the lens.

"It's ten thirty p.m. on the 22nd of August, some thirty-six hours after the appalling catastrophe on Blackpool beach. I am aboard HMS *Tenacious* with Dr Roddy Ormond. Behind me you can see the monitors that have been set up. Every second of their footage is being recorded and kept. We are two hundred metres down, approximately ninety minutes from SONAZ or the so-called 'Forbidden Zone', and a female sperm whale is in front of the submarine. We have just altered course slightly in a bid to follow her. Who knows where she will lead us..."

In the control room, Commander Gerhardie and the navigator were showing Roddy where they were now heading.

"The geometric centre of SONAZ is here," said the navigator, pointing, "but obviously that's nothing but a notional concept. The course we're maintaining now would lead us through the zone on this line here, to the east."

"Over that trough?"

"That's right. There's thought to be a very thick and turbulent benthic zone at the edges. Subs have to be careful in those conditions. Sedimenting from the abyssal waters above can play around with the sonar and other bits of kit. This trough is about a mile across. It's five hundred metres deeper than the surrounding basin, and is believed to exhibit volcanic activity and geo-thermal emissions. With the benthic layer over the sea bed plains to each side being so dense, it's a real cocktail."

"A good place for dumping?" Roddy asked.

"I'm no expert, but if I had something to hide then I wouldn't mind whacking it in the middle of that trough."

Kate stepped into the control room.

"More whales."

"How many?" Roddy asked, following her back into the sounds room.

"Six."

"Six," he repeated, so absorbed in the images on the monitors that he didn't realize he was gripping the shoulder of one of the ratings operating the cameras, Able Seaman Drew; the young rating, similarly absorbed, didn't notice Roddy's touch. "What happened to the original whale?"

"As these six came into view the other one headed for the surface."

"I suspect she'll be back soon after taking in oxygen."

Over the course of an hour more sperm whales joined the party, until there were upwards of twenty. They swam ahead of the submarine at a constant speed. Occasionally one of them would break for the surface, reappearing five or ten minutes later. Once, one of them drifted back towards the submarine until it was level, then maintained an equal speed.

"Fuckin' 'ell," Falkland said, as the sperm whale's eye loomed large in one of the port side lenses. He focused on it. Roddy watched, fascinated. He saw the dark globe swivel as the whale scanned the hull. For some ten or twenty seconds the creature swam close by – trying to see us, Roddy guessed, understand us, gauge whether we're up to the job.

Simultaneously, all but one of the whales started to ascend.

Roddy watched them merge into the ocean's opacity, though they never completely disappeared; their shapes remained faintly visible against the distant light at the surface.

"And now?" Gerhardie asked.

"I think they must be getting ready for a big dive. Just maintain this course with the single whale. We'll keep one camera tracked on the ones at the surface. Can we be on standby to dive, steeply?"

"We can be on standby. We can't dive steeper than forty-five degrees."

For twenty minutes there was no change. *Tenacious* glided at eighteen knots through the North Atlantic, a single whale in front of her, twenty or more far above. Kate made another report. Roddy's eyes were permanently fixed on the monitor of the camera trained above. Hunched behind the seats of the two ratings, his angular frame looked like a permanent fixture of the room.

"Here we go," he whispered.

The waters far above were showing signs of movement.

"Dive dive dive!" he called.

Even at her steepest descent, *Tenacious* was inadequate to the task. The score of whales above came into sharp relief within thirty seconds.

"What a sight," Able Seaman Drew croaked to himself, guiding the joystick of his remote camera.

"It's snowing whales," Kate said into camera. "On every side of *Tenacious* the sperm whales are descending, head first, sinking like stones, here they come, one past, two past, it's an amazing sight to see these huge creatures dive vertically downwards, now the screens show ten or twelve massive bodies falling like giant water drops beyond *Tenacious*, just metres away from the hull, the cameras track them, the whales are below us now, all of them, their tails scarcely move as they disappear beyond the reach of the flood lamps into the green blackness beneath…"

Kate stopped broadcasting. The wardroom fell quiet. At regular intervals, they could hear the pilot in the control room calling out their depth.

"Five hundred metres... ...Six hundred metres... ...seven hundred metres..."

Tenacious was alone at the edge of the Forbidden Zone.

"One thousand eight hundred metres... ...One thousand nine hundred metres..."

"What are you doing?" Roddy asked Kate, suddenly noticing that her eyes were shut, and that she held her hand over her sternum.

"Breathing exercises."

"Are you OK?"

"I'm OK. It's the depth we're at, the idea of it."

Commander Gerhardie bustled into the wardroom.

"Sounds men say the whales are a mile ahead, almost stationary, and between twenty to forty metres above the sea bed. I'll be levelling her off with a hundred metres below the keel," he told Roddy.

"That's no good."

"I'm sorry?"

"We've got to go as deep as the whales. We're here to examine the sea bed. The lights can't penetrate beyond thirty metres, or even twenty with any degree of clarity."

"We can't go at eighteen knots with anything less than a hundred metres under the keel."

"Go at ten knots, go at one knot, it doesn't matter. We must be able to see the sea bed."

Gerhardie picked up the microphone.

"Captain. Reduce speed to ten knots at two thousand two hundred metres. Reduce speed to three knots at two thousand three hundred metres, level off, await further orders."

At two thousand three hundred metres, sonar soundings

revealed that the whales were, as Falkland put it, "still waiting". They were half a mile ahead. *Tenacious* reduced speed to one knot and went deeper. Gradually, at first too faintly to be sure of, the bottom of the sea came into range of the deep-sea-pressure flood lamps.

"Mud?" Kate asked, peering at its dirty, soup-like appearance.

"This is the benthic zone. All the flora and fauna and matter that dies and decomposes in the sea, that isn't eaten on the way down, finds itself here. It provides for a very rich, specialized eco-system. There's more life in the twenty to fifty metres of water below us than there is in the mile of water above us."

"What kind of life?"

"Mostly microscopic, single or multi-cell, but absolutely seething. There's also lots of bigger stuff like, I don't know, copepods, ostracods, chaetognaths, polychaetes, deca—"

"Whoa whoa whoa, in English?"

"Worms and crustaceans."

"Well why didn't you say so in the first place?"

"And there are fish too," he added, ignoring her complaint, "*Bathypterois longipes*, *Echinomacrurus mollis*, rat-tailed fishes such as *Coryphaenoides rupestris*."

"We are now officially in SONAZ," Gerhardie announced.

Tenacious edged forwards, her prow churning up the topmost layer of the benthic zone. The ratings flicked between the camera angles. Roddy caught a glimpse of something just before the screen he was looking at changed to another angle.

"Wait, go back to the previous camera, which one was it?"

"Stern sir."

"No, nothing," Roddy said, peering.

"There's something to port sir," Drew said.

An amorphous shape tantalized their vision, monotone, barely distinguishable in the murk of the sea bed.

"What is it?" asked Kate.

"I can't tell, it's not near enough or clear enough."

There was an uneasy silence. Roddy wondered what creature he had glimpsed, and strained to see another one. Captain Gerhardie reappeared in the wardroom after a brief visit to the control room.

"We're just a hundred metres from the whales."

"OK," Falkland murmured a few seconds later, "there they are."

The sperm whales were stationary at the top of the benthic boundary layer, their undersides obscured like the keels of boats in a murky lake. When *Tenacious* was within fifteen metres of them they started off – and glided into a new dimension. For the submarine was nudging her way through a seascape that offended the sense of the possible. Someone said, "I don't like it." Commander Gerhardie's eye's narrowed. The palms of his hands oozed sweat. He thought, no one mentioned the possibility of this, it wasn't in the briefing...

Sammy Gale, the Tactics and Sonar Officer, came into the room.

"All sonar and radio systems down sir. It's as though we're going through custard." No one answered him. He looked at the monitors, and made a sound that was something like an exhalation of a breath, and something like a low whistle, but which was neither.

"Roddy?" Kate asked.

Roddy's hands, limpet-like on the back of Falkland's seat, spasmed in a nervous tic. He cleared his throat nervously.

"Very common, very primitive, four-cell micro-organisms, just visible to the naked eye in, er, normal conditions."

But these were not normal conditions. Suspended in the water as densely as apples in a bucket of water, these organisms were up to two metres across. Their red, gelatinous forms looked like obscure cuts of meat, or vital organs cut loose from massive bodies; their simple mechanisms, telescoped to hundreds of times the usual size, throbbed. The whales, and *Tenacious*, nudged delicately through their tender tissues.

"Look there," Falkland urged, "a fish."

Emerging from between the pendulous, undulating fauna came a *Coryphaenoides rupestris*, a rat-tailed fish, but one such as Roddy had never seen or imagined. It was perhaps some ten times bigger than the typical size, and grossly misshapen. The tail for which it was named swelled bulbously in several places. As the creature listlessly approached, it gave a flick of an overgrown, lobe-like pectoral fin; the movement turned it round, to reveal that its eye on the left side seemed to grow up across the head and along the back; if its other eye could be compared to an ordinary light bulb, this one was more like a thick, uneven strip of neon tubing, surrounded by fleshy bulges and polyp-like growths.

"Mutations," Roddy whispered to Kate, thinking about the whistle-blower's letter from the fisherman.

The hanging cell structures were thinning out. More fish came into view, hauling their grotesque forms through the water like cripples swimming in a vision of hell. An entire school of one species oozed across the sub's path. Their heads bulged fleshy and bright, bubbled with excrescences and knuckles that grew one on the other. Some were so wrapped in deformity that they dragged streamers of grotesque pink flesh behind them, long chains of undulating, stomach-churning growths three times the lengths of their bodies. Like a party of war-wounded, the fish propelled themselves as best they could. Some swam with largely unaffected tails; others had tails so weighed down or obscured by knobbly lumps that they used their pectoral fins as primitive paddles. Glowing oddly pink, looking – or not looking – from eyes still visible or eyes covered over by malformations,

316

the school dragged itself into the unilluminated mysterious deep.

Ahead, the escort of sperm whales was becoming more visible. Now there were fewer tortured marine life forms to obscure their passage. The monitors were clearer.

"So now we know," Commander Gerhardie said gravely, as though summing up the mission.

I hope you're right, Roddy thought privately, but he was convinced that the worst was to come. The mile-wide deep-sea trench that bisected the eastern side of SONAZ was the focus of his private speculations. The whales were still leading them there. It was about seven minutes away. Housing her fragile cargo of human beings, *Tenacious* approached closer.

"Er," Kate said, squinting as she peered into a monitor.

"There's something different, sir," Drew commented.

It was some moments before their brains caught up with their senses, and were able to put an explanation to what their eyes were looking at. The flood lamps seared ahead with their brilliance, but beyond their range was another light source. It strengthened. It became general. It became bright, and Commander Gerhardie found himself looking through half a mile of water, with twenty whales immediately ahead, and, in the distance...

In an awed voice, Kate added to her running commentary.

"We have descended into the utter deep-sea dark, escorted by sperm whales. We have seen giant, grotesque creatures packing the ocean bed like marbles on a plate. The whales have lead us through that disturbing scene to this one – different, but equally inexplicable to me. In front of us, getting closer as we glide on at three knots, is what I can only describe as a brilliant wall of light..."

Exactly that, it stretched across their submarine horizon. There was nothing between them and it except the whales and the cloudy rolls on top of the benthic boundary layer, which were eerily illuminated like a thick, early morning fog by a low, winter sun.

Roddy's bewildered expression changed to one of animation as he realized that the whales were coming to a halt.

"Slow us down," he urged, "no, stop, they're stopping."

"Captain," Gerhardie exclaimed into the microphone. "Speed zero. Repeat, speed zero."

Machine and whales glided to a halt, just a few hundred metres from the wall.

Roddy left the wardroom and took the half-dozen steps needed to get to the control room.

"How far are we from the trench?" he barked at the navigator.

"We should be pretty much on it," came the reply.

At that moment, "Sir, come quickly!" shouted a voice from the wardroom. He got there just in time to see a single whale, that had detached itself from the main group, disappear into the luminescence. Roddy stared into its absence, into the light. Around him he could hear talking, orders, exclamations. But his eyes were still fixed on the wall of light. He had noticed something. Like a bulge of red hot lava pushing slowly down a shallow slope, the light was visibly expanding over the ocean bed.

2

A second and a third whale had disappeared into the light before *Tenacious* was ready. But when the fourth sperm whale detached itself from the group and headed for the brilliance, "Pilot go go go!" Gerhardie rapped into the microphone. "Good luck everyone!"

Tenacious passed through all the remaining whales; they sheared off to the sides as the great black machine flashed by. The sub could go twice as fast as the whale it was following, but its acceleration wasn't half as effective. All eyes squinted ahead at the blinding light into which the creature had disappeared.

"Ow!" howled Able Seaman Falkland, involuntarily, as the monitors turned painfully white

"...following one whale into the light, light at the bottom of the sea which we plunge into with a frightening ignorance... ...I can, I, we're through it, we're in it, we're in the middle of the light, it's as though the water itself carries the luminescence, ahead I can see the whale, the whale is diving slightly, below us we know there is a deep sea trench and... ...now one of the ratings is searching below us with a remote camera, it's like standing on a cliff top and looking three hundred metres down at the ground, I can't see anything extraordinary but it's extraordinary I can see at all..."

Roddy had his eyes fixed on the solitary whale; what's going on? She was swimming at around nine knots, eight knots, seven knots, and angling down. She was slowing as she got closer to the bottom of the trench. *Tenacious* came within one hundred metres of her, eighty metres, fifty. Now whale and submarine were less than a hundred metres from the bottom. Their speed had reduced to a couple of knots.

"Something's wrong," someone said.

The water immediately around her seemed greenish in hue. She was still managing to swim, but her tail moved heavily in the water. With the submarine just metres behind, scraps of skin and flesh were brushing over the hull, hitting the camera lenses, washing away; strips of whale were peeling off. Already her tail flukes and pectoral fins were red, bleeding paddles devoid of skin and tissue. The blubber was coming away from the body. It's grey-white layers broke up into gory blobs. A thin

319

jet of blood suddenly spurted from her side, as though from a laceration; more followed. For a few seconds there were scores of jets of blood pumping out of her at crazy angles. She was purple, she was livid, she was visibly diminishing to layers of muscle, but somehow she swam on as though through acid. The very tendons, as huge as knotted rope, were stripped bare and there to see on her tailstock. She was disintegrating. Something came away from underneath, her intestines; they floated away to the side, unravelling, diminishing. A few last feeble pushes of the tail flukes, a spasm... the whale was little more than a chassis. It descended gently under them, looking as though it had been ripped apart by a pack of sharks.

Able Seaman Falkland's baby face was trembling. Gerhardie was voiceless with dread and wondering whether *Tenacious* was capable of withstanding whatever chemical soup it was passing through. And Roddy...

"Talk," he hissed at Kate, who seemed to be in shock; "*talk!*" he yelled. "Describe what we've done to the sea, then tell me that those whales on Blackpool beach weren't driven to it." He turned to Gerhardie. "She was taking us somewhere. We should maintain her course."

Gerhardie nodded. *Tenacious* crept ever closer to her unknown destination. She was now navigating as though up a river, passing up the middle of the mile-wide marine canyon. There was no benthic material to obscure the sea bed beneath them. Underneath was rock. The all-pervading light illuminating it seemed to emanate from the water itself, like some kind of phosphorescent dye.

Under Roddy's arms were rings of sweat, saucer-sized. He retreated slightly from the monitors, his arms folded tightly across his chest, his hands clenched into fists. His horror was such that his first thoughts were expressed in banalities: *Oh Jesus, Jesus Christ, what the fuck, my God...* What kind of gross abuse of nature, he agonized, what kind of criminal chemical cocktail can do this to an environment? It's more, much more than mere pollution; that would be diluted across the ocean. Something active's going on, some ongoing chemical reaction, some process we don't know about. The unknown compounds... perhaps chemical weapons and benthic matter are feeding each other, perhaps there's a freakish set of environmental conditions – volcanic energy and matter? Hydrothermal toxic emissions? God knows. I don't. In Roddy's mind, a weak little voice that spoke for all humanity asked a pathetic question: *what have we done?*

Falkland's pink, immature face was dotted with shiny drops of sweat. He kept moistening his lips with his tongue. His fingers delicately nudged at the joystick of the remote cameras, searching this lit-up underworld. Roddy sat down at the empty seat next to him – Commander Gerhardie, anxious about how the sub's exterior might be reacting with the contaminated sea water, had assigned Able Seaman Drew to damage assessment duties – and started to operate two of the cameras. He swivelled the starboard camera through sixty degrees, and looked out across a seascape almost lunar in atmosphere: pale and bright and corrugated with geology. He thought he could see the limit of the trench, a hazy vertical plane in the distance. But there was nothing else in sight. Three minutes previously there had been the disintegration, the *dissolving*, of the sperm whale; and before entering the trench there had been the mutated fish and inflated simple organisms, hanging in the water like grotesque decorations. It was as if *Tenacious* were passing through different zones on her way to the epicentre of the evil. So what next? Roddy thought.

He could hear Kate's broadcast, low and urgent, but in the intensity of his concentration couldn't distinguish the words. In the other world that lay outside the metal tube, the quality of the light was changing. Ahead, there was an added lustre to it, an extra energy. It was not unlike looking east half an hour before dawn, when the light that is about to coat the earth can be felt and anticipated, but not seen.

"Are you all right?" Gerhardie asked, stepping into the room momentarily.

"Yes," Roddy answered, startled.

"There's no major damage. We think we're easier to ping."

"What?"

"Subs are coated with special substances that radar and sonar don't like. It's all been stripped away, so other subs would find it easier to ping us, meaning locate us. But the main thing is, the metal isn't degrading."

"Good."

Gerhardie paused a moment, weighing up some words.

"When I saw that whale break up into bits in front of our eyes…"

"Yes?"

"That's when I realized you weren't a lunatic being humoured – or used – by a weak government."

The different quality of the light on the sea bed became more apparent as *Tenacious* glided on. It had a bluish cast to it. It sat on the sea bed and threw its light above, so that the blue of it mingled with the colourless light that seemed to emanate from the water itself; it appeared to stretch the width of the trench. It had a heavy texture of doom that only increased the closer they approached. Roddy didn't like it; he almost felt compelled to say so aloud, like a child who articulates every whim. *Tenacious* drew closer at a miserly half knot, approaching ever nearer to the blue – the *badbright*.

"It's like a, it's like it's coming from a sludge, or something…"

An unpromising description by Falkland, but he was right.

322

Now only two hundred metres ahead, a thick, translucent ooze could be seen. Glutinous and viscid, it smothered the sea bed. It was clotted into lumps, a colloid, bluish, phosphorescent slime in which could be seen – *Tenacious* was passing gingerly over the outermost edge of the stuff – amorphous shapes and blobs and darknesses, all suspended in the glutinous mess.

"Sir," Falkland said tentatively.

The camera winkled it out: a man-made artefact submerged in the slime; metal. The monitor lingered over it. Soon there were more. They discovered them deep in the ooze and scarcely discernible, and they discovered them half in and out of the blue. There were new ones and old ones, ones that were corroded by tranches of time and others that looked untouched: canisters large and small, metal drums, lead-lined vessels, shoebox-sized capsules. In places they were virtually stacked up, so that the blue ooze formed into small peaks around them. In places big, fat bubbles spat from the substance, like air hissing out of a hot mud geyser.

"It's been going on for years," Roddy said, "they must have put all sorts of filth down here."

"But how can you explain what it's... done?" Kate asked, peering in horrid fascination at the obscenity on the monitors.

"I can only speculate. If everything's been dumped, from Agent Orange to rampant toxins and pathogens, VX nerve gas, hell knows what, I mean... there might be reactions between different types of chemical weapon, there might be substances from biochemical weapons reacting with substances from chemical weapons, and no one can say what the processes might be. And it might be going on alongside other stuff, you know, for example where's the bloody benthic matter down here? The benthic zone is billions of tonnes of dead flora and fauna, it's pure fuel, so where is it? It must have been consumed or colonized... and then there might be unforeseen reactions due to the pressure down here – the pressure is a hundred atmospheres – there might be volcanic activity, hydrothermal vents at temperatures of up to four hundred degrees centigrade..." He breathed out slowly. "I can't explain it at this stage, I can only guess. It's for the guys in lab coats to work out."

Falkland was zooming in on another canister. Commander Gerhardie peered forwards and squinted.

"Get in closer," he said.

The container was sitting on top of the slime, its base hardly covered at all. About the size of a suitcase, its grey metal reflected the blue sheen of its unnatural bed. There were skull and crossbones all over it and, in the right-hand corner, Russian text; along the bottom, "European Union / St Johnston Atoll CW Disposal Plant".

"An inspired use of British taxpayers' money," Gerhardie said in disgust.

* * *

Some eighteen kilometres away, a black shape probed the inner space of the ocean on five-kilometre east-west lags. Her bow and dorsal fins parted the water almost apologetically, so slowly did she glide. Behind her she was towing an extended sonar array. Like any submarine, she was deaf, dumb and blind when travelling at speed – twenty-two knots or more – but at low velocities she could ping a contact at forty kilometres. So why was she hearing nothing?

Captain 2nd Rank Mikhail Zemtsov stood in the sound room of this Russian submarine, watching over the shoulders of the sonar operator and trying to conceal his anxiety. Inside the eastern part of the so-called SONAZ area, ten or twelve square kilometres were simply invisible. In one way, loss of contact with the British submarine was the best case scenario; if only the

Trafalgar-class would disappear, for ever and irrevocably, into the abyss of Britain's own making... But what if the submarine's disappearance represented, not the demise of *Tenacious*, but a successful evasion?

The sonar operator sighed melodramatically and shrugged his shoulders, as if to say, what's the point of pinging when there's nothing coming back?

"Just keep trying," the Captain said shortly, extremely annoyed. A conscript, he fumed, poorly trained and poorly motivated – it didn't used to be like this...

The Captain's first command, a Kilo-class diesel submarine, had been at the end of the Soviet era. God knows, Zemtsov didn't hanker for the tyrannical certainties of that regime, like so many of his brother officers seemed to; and yet, how thrilling it had been to be part of a feared, mighty naval power!

He left the sound room and let himself into his private dayroom, just a small box, but his and his alone, as befitting his status. A flask of strong black coffee was waiting for him there, and he poured a small cup thoughtfully. Soon Klepko, his number two, would arrive for the meeting. He wondered how Klepko would react to what he had to tell him. He shook his head in sorrow for himself, for the Northern Fleet, but most of all for Russia. Investment in the motherland's military might had collapsed as the Soviet Union had collapsed, and the problem had only recently begun to be addressed. Hardware of all kinds had deteriorated to the point of becoming scrap metal. Even now Russia could barely maintain some of her warheads in safe conditions. During the very worst period, personnel had been halved, and there were still too many conscripts who were paid sporadically. As for the command, it had been politicized and corrupted, but then – Zemtsov rolled his eyes in exasperation – what could you expect in a country where the kleptocracy was so powerful that it routinely owned the banks? And as for his beloved Submarine Force... The Northern Fleet, which at the height of its power had boasted two hundred attack, ballistic-missile and cruise-missile submarines, could now barely muster the resources to keep thirty of those boats operational. The rest were rusting in the naval dockyards of Polyarny and the Kola peninsula. His own vessel, a PLA – Podvodnaya Lodka Atomnaya, or nuclear-powered – Victor-class attack submarine needed a comprehensive refit; *five years ago*, Captain Zemtsov raged.

"Come," he called, hearing Klepko's approach before his number two had chance to knock at the door.

"Captain."

Klepko, like Zemtsov, had served in the Soviet era, and like Zemtsov was heartily ashamed of the Submarine Force in its modern guise. They had that bond. But whereas the Captain still clung to the hope, if not the belief, that their motherland was in a painful transitional period to a mature and functioning democracy, Klepko was an unreconstructed party man, who regarded *glasnost*, *perestroika* and the free market frenzy that had followed as catastrophic.

"A strange mission," Klepko said, declining his captain's offer of coffee.

"Stranger than you think, comrade," Zemtsov answered; and he was as surprised as Klepko that he had used the old epithet. It had slipped out unconsciously. The two men stared at each other. "Listen well. I must tell you that I have received orders from certain superiors which are not known to certain other superiors." There, the Captain had said the words he had been dreading. Klepko's eyes had widened. "And so, whatever I choose to do, I will be obeying one set of masters and deceiving, or disobeying, the other. I wanted to tell you."

"Captain Zemtsov, what are your orders?"

"To destroy the Trafalgar-class submarine."

Klepko blinked.

"Whose are the orders?"

"The orders come from the Commander-in-Chief of the Submarine Force of the Northern Fleet, but not from the Commander-in-Chief of the Fleet itself."

"He doesn't know?"

"He doesn't know."

"But he'd find out within minutes!" Klepko exploded. "How can we possibly conceal the firing of torpedoes?"

"Yes yes, but once fired, the pressure to cover-up the act would be irresistible, it would stretch to the Kremlin itself."

"So the Kremlin...?"

"Not involved. Yet. Though the C-in-C of the Submarine Force claims the 'sanction' – his word – of the Deputy Defence Minister. Which doesn't surprise me in the least."

Klepko whistled. He picked up a blank sheet of paper that was lying on the Captain's table and smoothed it between his fingers.

"Such an order," he probed, "with all its attendant risks, must come with an explanation if they expect you to carry it out."

"It seems SONAZ has been an international dumping ground on a grand scale. Many nations are implicated, including our own and the British. But intelligence reveals that if Britain goes in and comes out, regardless of what they find it will be proof of Russian wrongdoing they bring back. The C-in-C indicates that our country cannot afford to let that happen."

"Meaning, his political masters cannot afford to let it happen, nor their...." Klepko paused in distaste; "their free-market associates."

"Yes yes, I know. Our country is run by the weak and the bad, hand in hand. But Klepko, that doesn't alter the fact that the British are masters at avoiding blame. The consequence for us will be to become an international pariah: international aid suspended, further disintegration and hardship for our people. But if their vessel were to disappear in SONAZ, then there would be…" The Captain picked his words carefully, "an alternative outcome."

"You risk an international crisis."

"There is an international crisis already, one in which we are badly implicated. And why should the West make us the scapegoat for it?"

"And what happens when they send the next submarine down? That one is 'disappeared' too?"

"They won't. Not into a place which absorbs sonar and radar in a way we can't even imagine, never mind explain scientifically; and not in a place in which their first submarine vanished. Even the West can't afford to throw away billion-dollar submarines."

"Your mind is made up."

"I wanted your opinion."

"I will follow *my* orders," Klepko said, quietly.

* * *

Bearing her precious cargo of footage that would focus the conscience of humanity on one of humanity's darkest deeds, *Tenacious* had negotiated an exit from SONAZ. There had been more mutations to record and be appalled by, but nothing to match the dangers of their journey in. They had noted the stripped carcasses of two of the other sperm whales that had entered the deep sea trench. They had emerged from the trench and nudged their way through the primitive, fleshy, somnambulant forms that hung in the water. Now that the worst was over, the fear and tension had been replaced by a kind of grief. In the Captain's cabin, Kate and Roddy were deep in discussion with Commander Gerhardie.

"The government will topple," Gerhardie offered in a wondering voice, amazed that he had been part of such a historic event.

"So what," Roddy responded, so dismissively as to be rude. He was sitting on the Commander's bed, exhausted, apparently keeping his eyelids open by the crude but effective method of propping them up with his forefingers. "The fall of a government is not what is important about this. This is about human greed, human stupidity, and the survival of life on earth. Who cares one way or the other if the government goes? There'll be another Prime Minister. There won't be another Earth."

"Wish I'd got that little speech on tape," Kate said at last.

"I'll do it again on the surface," Roddy offered, not without humour.

There was a knock at the door and the TASO pushed his head through.

"Excuse me sir, just to let you know that we've got out communications back, radar and sonar, all bar a couple of fiddly bits."

"Excellent. Anything near us?"

"A Victor III pinging us openly."

"Really?" Gerhardie stood up and considered the information. "Well, ping her back. Let her know we know she's there. Cheeky bastards."

"Yes sir."

* * *

The Sonar Supervisor was listening to the noise of the ocean on his broadband audio receiver. The pops and crackles coming through his earphones were the sounds of innumerable small marine life forms, but they formed no clear pattern on the display. After a while however a line started to form, made out of little inverted V's, representing a constant noise at 60Hz. He thumbed through his guide to check the profile.

"Contact," he called. "Discrete frequency. Suggest identity British Trafalgar-class."

In the control room, Captain Zemtsov peered at the dark screen and waited for the radar officer to get a bearing on the sonar contact. The radar's rhythmic sweep, monotonously regular, was hypnotic. And then a small green diamond started flashing on and off.

"Steer two-eight-zero, establish target bearing."

The hydroplane operator raised his eyebrows as he guided the sub to the new course. Target bearing?

Range of twelve kilometres, Zemtsov was thinking; too far for anything but a wire-guided missile. But it's essential to sink her as close to SONAZ as possible.

Ten minutes later, after the Trafalgar's bearing had been confirmed, Zemtsov and Klepko were staring at each other across the control room. Zemtsov took a last look at the target contact.

"Watch stand to, Weapons Control Operator number three tube active!"

The lack of activity which followed was motivated not by mutiny, but surprise.

"Implement the instruction!" Klepko bellowed.

"Sir!"

The Weapons Control Operator, a Muslim called Vadyaev who was one of the few non-conscripted crew members on the boat and therefore one of the most capable, hastily left for the forward-weapons compartment to oversee the opening of number three tube bow cap.

"Steer one-five-five, compute final range for target."

The short flurry of activity was soon complete. The Weapons Control Operator returned and took up his position.

330

"Starboard five," Zemtsov commanded, "wait."

There was an interval entirely of the Captain's making. His crew waited on his order. Vadyaev, hunched over his console, wrapped his thumb around his forefinger; it was his firing finger; it was twitching.

"Standby to fire," Zemtsov said.

Vadyaev nodded imperceptibly. Silence enveloped the control room of the Victor. He felt as though the fractional finger movement required to fire the missile would result in deafening noise echoing through the chambers of the submarine. For some seconds, ten seconds, longer, his hunched position didn't change. Just as his concentration began to falter, and he found himself wondering what the Captain was waiting for, "Fire," said Zemtsov in a memorably quiet voice.

Vadyaev released his twitching finger and prodded it at the firing button. From forward, the missile fizzed from its tube, trailing a guide wire.

"Bow sonar in control of the weapon," the Weapons Control Operator said. "Weapon sensors will take over in approximately sixty seconds."

His hand hovered near the joystick; in the event of the weapon sensors malfunctioning, he would have to guide the missile himself.

Zemtsov's mind entered a peculiar and distant realm. It was done now. He had taken his decision. Innocent men were minutes away from death. How would he feel about it in ten years? In twenty years? On his deathbed? He watched the screen, an abstracted frown on his brow. The target remained motionless in the centre. The torpedo – a green dot – was approaching it inexorably.

3

Tenacious ascended steadily. In his cabin, Commander Gerhardie was pouring glasses of sherry for Roddy and Kate.

"To the sea," he said, with a slightly embarrassing air of grandeur, "and to the truth about the sea."

Roddy gamely clinked his glass against Gerhardie's and Kate's; despite the devastating scenes of destruction they had witnessed, despite what was yet to be done to arrest and reverse the incalculable damage to the ocean environment, he couldn't help feeling a measure of relief. He had been proven right to an extent beyond anyone's imagining, and now, surely, the world would really listen when environmentalists spoke. He envisaged – perhaps idealistically – governments, industry, consumers coming into line, working hard to nurture nature back to some kind of sustainability.

Kate was still tense and abstracted, her part in the commander's toast less whole-hearted. The strain of suppressing her fear of water and confined spaces was taking its toll. Ahead of her, too, was a task of great importance. She was only an hour away from making perhaps the most significant broadcast she was ever likely to make. The memorable by-line that would imprint this whole experience onto history's consciousness had yet to present itself to her. Fragments of phrases were swimming around in her mind. She tried to shoulder aside her phobic tension and assess them.

"Not bad stuff," Gerhardie said, of the sherry.

From the control room on the other side of the door came a loud and unnerving "Jesus...", immediately followed by a harrowing chant: "ATTACK, WE ARE UNDER ATTACK, ATTACK ATTACK ATTACK!"

Gerhardie wrenched the door open at the exact moment that Sammy Gale barged at it on the other side; the man lurched into the little room – "Missile sir!" – and shot out again.

Gerhardie followed him out, shiny-headed, shiny-eyed, disbelieving.

"Missile bearing red zero-four-zero," someone was yelling, "true bearing two-three-five!"

"Steer two-three-five," Gerhardie yelled as he rushed to the Weapons Control Console. His quick glance at the screens told him that this was no error. "Crew of *Tenacious*, I have command! Fire a decoy!"

"Ay ay sir!"

"Keep calm, remember your training, your lives may depend on it!"

The clunk of the Bandfish decoy being launched into the water could be physically felt. The Commander and the WEO hunched over the Weapons Control Console. The pilot and other officers and ratings in the control room were motionless and alert, like rabbits downwind of a fox. There was a silence of a few seconds. Roddy and an ashen-faced Kate stood in the doorway of the Captain's cabin, unconsciously holding hands. When the WEO broke the silence, his voice presented the truth with an eerily ordinary tone.

"Tracked it, sir. Look at these bow cap transients. It's the Russian sub."

From the Sound Room came a snatch of yelped information that only confirmed the WEO's analysis.

"How long have we got?" Gerhardie asked.

"Three to three-and-a-half minutes."

One moment, Kate was clenching Roddy's hand; the next, her body shook and thrashed as though an electric shock was ripping through her.

"Not in a submarine!" she screamed, struggling against Roddy's attempts to hold her. "Oh sweet Jesus don't let me die down here!"

In her terror, her strength was almost supernatural; Roddy

couldn't hold on to her. She lashed and kicked at him, screaming and spitting. Two ratings rushed to Roddy's aid, and the three of them wrestled her unceremoniously to the ground. One of the ratings kicked the door shut so that the commotion wouldn't distract those in the Control Room.

"Kate, Kate, Kate, Kate," Roddy was saying, over and over, desperate to break through her hysteria with words of consolation and encouragement, his mouth pressed hard to her ear, but it was a useless endeavour. There were no such words.

"Missile sensors taken over," the WEO was saying grimly. "Two minutes forty-five seconds."

"How noisy is our Bandfish?" Gerhardie shouted into the sounds room.

"Very noisy."

"Noisy enough to divert the course of the torpedo?"

"It's too early to tell, sir."

"All right. Pilot, dive."

The sub angled down precipitately, everyone adjusting their balance as it did so. Silence in the Control Room again. From inside the Captain's cabin, muffled bangs and shrieks.

"Two minutes fifteen seconds."

* * *

In another control room, in another submarine, the Weapons Control Operator was relaying the timings to his Commander.

"Two minutes to impact."

"Their decoy?"

"Bandfish. We know all about those. It's swamping the passive sonar, Captain, but the active sonar's not fooled."

Zemtsov and Klepko watched as the green dot approached the cross at the centre of the screen. It was like watching some inane computer game, knowing that the result would be measured in deaths rather than points.

"One minute thirty seconds."

"One minute to impact."

"Forty-five seconds!"

"Thirty seconds!"

It's all over for them, Zemtsov knew. Poor bastards.

* * *

"Thirty seconds sir!"

"The Bandfish?"

"Nothing doing sir." The WEO gave a sad, small smile and, with supreme inadequacy, said, "Sorry."

The stillness now was of the kind that only those about to die can know. Someone proffered his hand to a friend.

"Good luck," he said.

"It's not a fucking football match," was the reply.

In the Captain's cabin, Kate's hysteria had passed. She was in shock. Limp and quivering and panting, she lay in Roddy's tight grasp. He was whispering "It's OK, it's all right, it's OK," but he was no longer aware of her. He was talking to himself.

In the wardroom, Able Seaman Falkland trained a remote camera straight ahead. He could hear the WEO's countdown, the last few seconds of his life being torn off and discarded like tickets from the stub. He licked his lips messily and strained his eyes at the screen. He was looking for a metal cylinder looming out of the darkness; a fraction of a second later it would... Oh God, oh save me God – Falkland started to pray an instinctive and primal prayer.

The sub's escort of whales appeared in the monitor connected to the front-mounted camera. Surging forwards, they left *Tenacious* behind them and swam in a tight pack straight ahead.

The whales had only been on his monitor for a few seconds, their tails lashing up and down, when—

* * *

"Four hundred metres," the Vadyaev bellowed, "TEN seconds NINE seconds EIGHT seconds..."

The men in the control room looked at each other in wonder; this is what they were trained for, but had never done.

"FIVE seconds FOUR seconds THREE seconds— impact?"

There was a anticlimactic pause.

"What do you mean, impact?" Klepko hissed furiously.

"Two seconds early," Vadyaev said, puzzled.

* * *

Shockwaves from the deafening underwater boom rippled the fabric of *Tenacious* and poleaxed everyone inside her. The blast wave struck momentarily afterwards, heaving the bows upwards and askew. Kate and Roddy were catapulted across the metal floor of the little cabin, then plunged down roller-coaster-style, leaving their stomachs somewhere else. Silence, and then from different sections of the submarine came shouts and groans.

"We're OK!"

"Aaaaaaaah!"

"He's bleeding, help me!"

In the control room, Commander Gerhardie found himself being helped to his feet. He shook his head to clear it, and noted with some surprise a fine spray of blood droplets emanate from his left temple.

"She didn't hit," said the WEO simply, still sitting at the Weapons Control Console. "She didn't hit."

"The decoy?"

"She didn't hit the decoy either."

"What did she hit?"

The WEO shrugged his shoulders.

In the wardroom, Falkland was watching the monitors speechlessly. *Tenacious* was butting through sections of whale: ragged masses of flesh hanging in the water, turning with obscene balletic grace. They were so freshly blown apart from the bodies that they oozed scarlet. An entire and enormous ribcage grazed the bows, was pushed aside, and span slowly down the side of the submarine. An absurdly detached tail lodged against the prow and became the repulsive figurehead of the vessel. Blood pumped out of the severed tailstock. Ahead, moving into the reach of the flood lights mounted on the hull, a living whale came into view, then another. A kind of muted, miserable pant was ejected from Falkland's lips; the creatures were whole, they were living, but they were mortally damaged. One was already sinking, its left flank nothing but an abstract of blood. The other listed in the water, pathetically moving a tail at the end of which were just the fragments of flukes. Other injured whales came into view; *Tenacious* struck one of them squarely, and as Falkland cried out in ineffectual protest it disappeared underneath the bows, taking the freshly dislodged tail with it. After a few minutes the waters were clear. Bloody bits of whale, dead whales, dying whales were left in the vessel's wake. Ahead were the whales which had survived intact, the ones that Falkland couldn't see, as they swam with grim purpose towards the Russian Victor.

* * *

"Missile detonated on impact, sir, but the target is still... there." said Vadyaev weakly.

"What do you mean, still there?"

"I don't know sir. We didn't hit it."

"Of course we bloody hit it you imbecile! Sounds room, what have you got?"

"I can't understand it sir," the conscript called. "The data's exactly the same as it was pre-impact. The target hasn't been touched."

"What about the decoy?"

"The decoy hasn't been touched... Numerous whales in the vicinity, sir."

Captain Zemtsov looked around him, struggling to articulate to himself what was going on.

"Give me the target's range," he commanded. He waited, but got no answer. "Sounds, I said give me the range!"

"Yes Captain. Sorry Captain. Er..."

Zemtsov's cool deserted him. He strode into the Sounds Room shouting "What is the matter with you, you fucking peasant? Give me the range!"

"Can't see the target any more, sir. There's something wrong."

The Captain looked at the screens... What a mess.

"What's going on?" he said more quietly

"I don't know sir. It's like there's something around us. We can't hear a thing."

There was a lurch in the submarine's motion, the feel of which was like nothing the submariners had experienced before. They looked at each other uneasily. Another lurch, even more unnatural.

"What's happening?" someone called anxiously.

The floor under their feet was moving.

"Hey!" Klepko called, with hopeless inadequacy, as the vessel rotated.

In the cold waters outside, whales were arranged down one side of the thirty-foot column of the conning tower. They pushed against it steadily, forcing their tail flukes against the water's resistance. Like a sodden log slowly turning in a river's current, the vessel rolled.

As frantic as hamsters in a revolving wheel, the crew, yelling and exclaiming in all parts of the vessel, found themselves clambering over fixtures and equipment as they adjusted to the changing horizontal. In the sick bay, a conscript half dead from TB fell out of his bed and slid down the floor. He lay wrapped around a bolted-down table leg as the submarine turned, groaning.

"Full speed!" Zemtsov yelled. "Pilot, fucking full speed!"

The vessel sheared crazily through the water but didn't stop rotating. 90°. Clinging to the fixtures of his Weapons Control Console, Vadyaev tried desperately to avoid activating anything. In the weapons compartment forward, a torpedo slipped from its housing and clunked against metal supports. 120°. The propulsion systems failed. The Victor glided slowly to a halt, still turning. Upside down, helpless, and resounding to the shouts of men, it was gently pushed down, down, down by the whales, until it clunked against the ocean bed to lie, disabled, on its side.

4

Ally walked into the bedroom. Her mother was sleeping. The white bedspread, the whitewashed plaster crudely covering the thick stone walls, the absence of anything fussy or luxurious, made for a peaceful and Spartan atmosphere. The cottage they were renting was on the east side of the Isle of Raasay in the Inner Hebrides, not far from the cleared settlement of Hallaig. Ally sat on the edge of the bed and listened: bleating sheep, a distant, barking dog, and the soft swish of the sea on the rocky beach; all noises that felt good and nourishing. An hour ago they had returned from a trip to the general store in Inverarish, an eight mile round walk across the island's southern tip. Each step of freshness and freedom had seemed to reinvigorate her mother's appetite for life.

"Mummy... Mummy..."

Theresa moaned and stretched.

"Hello darling."

"Hello Mummy. How do you feel?"

"Sleepy."

"They've just said that there's going to be a broadcast from the submarine in a few minutes. I wasn't sure whether you'd want to watch it or not."

Theresa sat up and dragged the tips of her fingers from just under her eyes to the corners of her mouth.

"Yes."

They went into the only other room of the cottage, a living area with a simple stove and sink in one corner. By the open front door was a small black-and-white television; outside was a straggly, untended plot, then a field that sloped down to the rocky shore.

"You seem so much better," Ally said.

"I feel it. I feel as though I might, possibly, be something like a person again."

"Of course you're a person, you've always been a person, it's him who's just... *nothing*."

She said it with vehemence. Theresa stared at her thoughtfully. Ally turned away to fill the kettle. On the television, a tense announcer was struggling to get a handle on the unfolding events.

"We believe... I'm just being informed... We are moments away from the link up with HMS *Tenacious* and – no, I'm just being told of technical difficulties, so let's now, er..."

"God," Theresa said, "I wonder what they found."

A mile away, a small, nondescript man was walking methodically towards their refuge.

* * *

The Prime Minister was a few minutes late for the meeting of his Cabinet. While they waited, his colleagues conversed with their allies – and their enemies – in a muted fashion. A few were reading newspapers, which dripped hysterical proclamations and analysis. Elbows resting on the famous table, Victoria Adlington was one of those immersed in headlines...

AND STILL THE INJURED DIE.

REVEALED: THE SHADY BACKGROUND OF THE SECRET SHIPPING MAGNATE

BEACHES CLOSED, TERROR REIGNS

PM PROMISES ACTION

MoD HINTS AT DUMPING BY PREVIOUS BRITISH GOVERNMENTS

MAN-GET-MAN-FISH – CAN DR ORMOND "TALK TO THE ANIMALS"?

SPECULATION MOUNTS ABOUT MISSION OF HMS TENACIOUS

The doors opened and the Prime Minister was ushered in.

"Good morning," he said briskly.

He sat down and poured himself a glass of water, then drank half of it in a brooding way.

"To business," he began, but immediately the doors to the Cabinet Room opened again. An aide walked across to him and whispered something in his ear.

"I see. Well do it then," the Prime Minister said. "HMS *Tenacious*," he explained to the ministers.

They watched as a wheeled cabinet containing a small television was trundled in. A few moments passed as an attendant set it up. The ministers pushed their chairs back and angled them for good viewing. A woman's face appeared on the screen. She looked so ill that at first she hardly resembled Kate Gunning. Seated on each side of her were Roddy Ormond and Commander Frank Gerhardie.

Victoria Adlington pushed herself back in her chair. The roof of her mouth was as dry as cardboard.

In the wardroom of HMS *Tenacious*, Kate willed herself on. The trauma of her phobic hysteria had left her with a debilitating migraine; the headache pounded and throbbed at her temples. But there was a job to do.

"I am about to make the most unsophisticated broadcast of my career. In place of proper preparation I have experienced an hysterical fit. Instead of slickly edited footage, there will be a transmission edited by me as I go along with no tool more sophisticated than a jumped-up fast-forward button. But I can tell you that none of this matters, because I have been to a place you can't imagine or believe until you see it for yourselves."

On a billion television screens the images materialized: the sperm whales guiding *Tenacious*; immense, pulsating organisms hanging in the sea; fish, huge and misshapen, decorated in growths and mutations; a wall of impossible light in the deep-sea darkness, edging across the ocean bed insidiously; a single sperm whale disintegrating; and the bluish, translucent, clotted ooze, that smothered the base of the trench, and contained the unmistakable evidence of sustained and indiscriminate dumping.

"Much of the material dumped here is British, from long ago. Much else appears to be Russian, ironically part of the EU's programme to render chemical weapons safe in the former

Soviet Union. All of it has been dumped indiscriminately, with a total disregard for the health of the sea and the animals who live there. We can now expect the total collapse of the North Atlantic fishing industry."

In the Cabinet Room of Number 10, no one spoke or moved. Outside, London seemed as quiet as night. Inside, these movers and shakers of government, these sound-byte merchants and political plotters and impassioned campaigners, these over-sized egos and chip-shouldering idealists, matched the city's silence. For once, the politicians were lost for words.

"But this," Kate was saying, "is not the end of the story. When we thought we were safe at last, we came under attack from a Russian Victor III class nuclear-powered attack submarine."

"What?" a minister hissed.

The Prime Minister, the Defence Secretary, everyone, blanched.

"...A wire-guided missile was launched by one submarine and targeted at another. I am not ashamed to reveal that I became hysterical at this point. As I understand it, Commander Gerhardie responded by launching a Bandfish decoy, a device that emits radio noise and can confuse the tracking systems of the attacking weapon. The decoy failed. I have to tell you that we all prepared to die. Two seconds before the expected impact there was an explosion outside *Tenacious*. We now know that a party of sperm whales swam straight at the missile and took the full brunt of its destructive powers. They sacrificed their lives. These images show *Tenacious* nosing through the bloody debris just seconds after the explosions..."

Adlington closed her eyes. Impossible. Awful. That the Russians would even contemplate such an act in peace-time... She swallowed hard, trying to retain her self-command.

"...We have survived a voyage into the centre of ecological catastrophe, biological horror, and political obscenity," Kate said.

Sitting besides her, Roddy watched her jaws working, noticed the slight trembling of her chin.

"...The British government must have been aware of their old dumping in SONAZ, but have concealed it for years. The Russian government and military, or senior elements within their hierarchies, must have been aware of their own industrial-scale dumping of lethal chemical weapons, and were prepared to sanction an act of barbaric piracy in order keep such environmental crimes hidden. And the whales – the whales sacrificed themselves so that this submarine could return from the Forbidden Zone with a precious cargo: the truth. They did it because one man, Roddy Ormond, learned their language, and listened. Now all of us must listen to those whales, and that man."

It was some moments later in the Cabinet Room when Victoria Adlington opened her eyes. Only now did she realize that the television had been off for a while. She looked across at the grey, middle-aged faces: shock; trauma. Someone uttered a cliché in a tinny voice:

"I don't believe it."

All this time the Prime Minister, ashen-faced, was arrested in some kind of absurd biblical gesture, his hands raised and held apart. He cleared his throat, but without purpose. The guttural sound hung in the atmosphere. He picked up a phone, almost rapped "Get me the Kremlin", then changed his mind. He put the phone down. His hand rested on it still. He said, "I'm ashamed."

* * *

For three hours the stricken Victor had lain on her side, 2500 metres under the sea. Inside, in the sick bay, the TB patient was lying across a hammock of cable ducts, babbling incoherently.

He knew nothing: not that each section of the submarine had been sealed off, confining men to whichever section they were in; not that Captain Zemtsov was desperately trying to launch an emergency capsule to the surface that could lock into satellite communication systems and signal a position; not that the nuclear reactor in the central section of the boat had already cracked and split in its tons of lead casing, and was getting so hot as to melt the fabric of the submarine; not that the generators which powered the oxygen recycling systems had ceased functioning, and that the emergency oxygen supply candles had been automatically activated.

In the central section, the heat from the split reactor became so fierce as to melt a hole to the sea without. It was over within seconds. Water was forced through the rapidly expanding crack by the difference in pressure within and without. Meeting the heat of the split reactor, it instantaneously expanded in volume by a factor of two thousand; a steam pressure explosion was a mechanically primitive way for a vessel of such technological sophistication to blow up, but it was effective. The Victor III exploded from the middle.

Far above, on the surface of the ocean, sperm whales listened to a low rumble.

* * *

For two days and nights Rattigan had been sunk inside an almost hallucinogenic agony of waiting. Government investigators had raided his offices at home and in the city, confiscating paperwork and computers, but Rattigan had hardly cared. He had been subjected to preliminary questioning, and barely known or noticed. Outside the gates of his house on The Bishops Avenue was a media encampment of military dimensions. It was so large as to require continuous policing; fast food vans and sandwich delivery companies were polluting the most exclusive street in the London suburbs as they catered to the hungers of the greedy journos. Inside the house, the staff had contracted to just a couple of people, and there was an atmosphere of Hitler's bunker about the place. Hunched in front of the television in Ally's room, Rattigan had been focused on one thing: the fate of Roddy Ormond on the submarine. His entire being had fastened itself to the hope of Russian interference like a fly drawn too deeply into a pot of jam. But finally, while he wriggled and flailed, the three dreadful visages had appeared in front of him – Gunning in the middle, the submarine commander to her left, and Ormond... There were no words or thoughts for the intensity of his despair. It filled him up and spilled over the edges of his sanity. For the duration of Gunning's broadcast he slouched in his chair with his chin resting on his chest. His massive arms were folded. To an observer he might have seemed dead but for his stomach rising and falling, rising and falling, in slow, steady pulses. On the television, the awesome, unimaginable images of a grotesque seascape, the warped and buckled life forms, the sheer toxic evil of it all, hardly registered in his brain. He only shifted when Gunning explained how HMS *Tenacious* had come under attack. He hunched forwards and gripped his knees. So the Russians had gone for it, but whales had met the missile? It was intolerable. Ormond was blessed, protected by Gods, unkillable. For a moment Rattigan almost smiled.

The gardens of Rattigan's house were very splendid. Rattigan himself seldom visited them. The one permanent and two part-time gardeners he employed had seen him perhaps five times in as many years. But an hour after the Gunning broadcast, the permanent gardener looked up from his work to see his lumbering employer approach. He swallowed nervously. His two colleagues had jumped ship, alarmed and disgusted by the allegations circulating.

"Yes sir?"

A song thrush sang sweetly near the top of a dwarf silver birch. Across the blue sky a plane left a pale trail of vapour. Rattigan came to a halt a few feet away. He was slowly rubbing his knuckles against his mouth. His big, rubbery lips yielded to the action, flopping up and down. The gardener tried not to seem unduly interested or put out by this, but it was difficult. His employer looked frightening, not just unshaven and unwashed – there was a keen BO in attendance – but deranged. The gardener, afraid, examined the ground and waited.

Rattigan stopped fiddling around with his lips and started to sneeze: one, two, three, four, five, six... it carried on for over a minute, more than twenty sneezes. He stood there, his body convulsed by the heaving, fat-shaking explosions. At the end he was out of breath. He sucked in the air hungrily. There was a gardener in front of him. He thought, why did I come outside, there was some reason for it...

"Yes."

"Er, sir?"

"Good..." A pause. Rattigan seemed lost in some abstraction, from which he emerged with an abrupt question: "Do you drive?"

"Yes sir."

"Do you think you can drive a Bentley?"

"I don't see why not."

Rattigan nodded and turned away, feeling mildly pleased with himself for remembering: his official driver was nowhere to be found. He walked back to the house in a straight line, trampling over a couple of flower beds. At the French windows he turned around and saw that the gardener hadn't followed him. He rubbed his eyes, puzzled. Why hadn't the man followed him? How could he drive the Bentley if he didn't follow him?

The gardener discarded a hoe and hurried up to the house.

There was something on Rattigan's mind. It prodded and nudged at him as the Bentley went up the ramp and into the drive. At the gates were hundreds of people. As the Bentley passed through them they shouted and screamed, and pounded on the roof and windows. Rattigan saw contorted faces, pale palms outstretched on the dark glass. Why are they so excited, he wondered? The Bentley cruised, in an uncertain manner, down The Bishops Avenue and turned into Hampstead Lane. In its wake, journalists were leaping into cars or jumping on to the backs of motorbikes, gabbling into their mobile phones.

"This is the Heath!" Rattigan said to himself, looking out of the left hand window.

"Yes sir," said the gardener from the front, his voice slightly detached and telephonic on the intercom.

Rattigan seemed surprised to hear the man, but not displeased.

"Where do you want to go?"

"What?"

"Where shall I take you, sir?"

Rattigan nodded in concentration. Where am I going, he wondered. He thought there was a place, but he couldn't remember.

"Just drive around."

"Sir?"

"Just drive around the Heath."

They negotiated the kink in Spaniard's Road, passing The Spaniard's Inn. There was a lengthening convoy behind them. A motorbike drew level. It was inches away from the side of the car, and the pillion passenger started to take photographs with a motor-wind camera. Blinding flashes of light rapidly succeeded one another. This annoyed Rattigan. Without malice, in a merely reactive and unthinking fashion, he opened the left-hand door and swung it against the motorbike. The machine veered off to the left and, out of control, crashed into the pavement, a signpost, the hedge, spilling the rider and passenger. Oh shit, thought the gardener.

What do I need to do? Rattigan was thinking. There's something... He shook his head, frustrated. There was a helicopter above, very noisy, and sirens going. Even a soundproofed car can only take so much, he thought. He turned the television on, only to be confronted by live footage of the car he was in it drove down the street he was on. He flicked through the channels but found only himself or whales. Leave me alone, he found himself thinking, leave me alone, and he fumbled through the small collection of DVDs, randomly inserting one. After a few moments, Ally came on the screen blurrily, the lighting low, the images poor quality. She was ten years old, dancing with her classmates in a school production of Swan Lake. Very good, excellent. But the sirens, the helicopter... He turned the sound up high. Very high. Grossly distorted music filled the Bentley. It sounded like a torture chamber. In the front, the gardener rubbed at his chin anxiously and wondered what to do. He wondered if he could just stop and bail out of the car.

They were passing through Gospel Oak at a stately fifteen miles an hour. OJ-Simpson style, there were people gathered by the roadside, watching the convoy; they had been watching the cavalcade on TV, and had rushed out of their houses when it approached. They were booing. They were angry. Half a brick landed on the bonnet of the Bentley and bounced ineffectually against the windscreen.

Ally jumped clumsily but sweetly, in unison with several other swans. Rattigan patted his thigh in time with the music, nodding. Missiles struck the Bentley, an authoritative voice was being amplified from somewhere – the helicopter? – and ahead there was a police road block looming into view. The gardener eased the car to a halt at a bus stop on Highgate

Road, opened the door, and walked away with his hands over his head. Rattigan didn't notice. The little girls on the film were curtseying and giggling, as their teacher walked up behind them and contributed to the applause of the audience. The amplified distortion hurt Rattigan's ears. Ally smiled sweetly, curtseyed again, bowed her head, and trooped off the stage. No no, don't go, he was telling her in his mind, come back, don't go. And now he knew there was something about his darling, his Ally, something important that he had to remember. Guilt and fear swamped him, made all the worse by the fact that he couldn't think of the cause of it. Ally Ally Ally.

His door sprang open, to reveal an arc of policemen standing ten metres away, shouting at him.

"Get out of the car! Get out of the car!"

He looked at them absently. So much noise. And they were waving guns around. He got out of the car and looked around him: policemen everywhere, holding firearms in double-handed grips. Four officers approached him warily. Cameras were flashing, shouting bystanders were being pushed back.

"We are going to frisk you sir. Do you understand?"

A young policeman was looking earnestly into his eyes. Of course I understand, he thought. What's wrong with all these people?

"Raise your arms please, sir."

He followed the instruction.

It was as hands explored his armpits, his inner thighs, that Rattigan remembered what had been forgotten: Ally, Theresa, the contract killer. He moaned piteously.

"All right sir, just keep calm, I'm going to read you your rights."

What's this boy talking about, Rattigan wonders? The features of Ally's sweet young face flood into his thoughts and form into her slightly questioning expression: she seems to be looking at him yearningly, helplessly, and now she's saying help me, help me Daddy, help me...

Two policemen lead him gently towards the open doors of a van. He's lost, dying, panicked. All his energy gathers and detonates, and he launches himself at one of the policemen. He drags him to the floor and starts battering him viciously, the punches thudding into the face with sickening power.

"All-y – what – about – All-y," he splutters between the blows.

The other policeman's knee slams into his cheekbone, a truncheon flails down on his crown, but the force Rattigan expends is monstrous and won't be contained yet. Five or six officers plough into the affray, two of them lashing out with their batons, the others attempting to pull the possessed man off their colleague. Rattigan's demonic strength gives out. They drag him off, collectively enraged, still administering retributive blows. Their colleague isn't moving.

Rattigan is being pinioned face down on the hot tarmac. He struggles to lift his head. He briefly sees the camera flashes going before his face is slammed back into the tarmac.

"My daughter," he begs.

* * *

It was the kind of contract "Baxter" disliked intensely – an innocent person, a harmless person. Baxter preferred killing criminals, like himself.

The distant location of Raasay was not to his advantage. He knew it was impossible to blend in easily and slip away after the deed was done; a stranger in a remote rural community is always noticed. Catching the ferry from Skye and then striking off alone across the southern peninsula, he could only present himself as a tourist – walking boots, haversack, map, binoculars.

351

Ally smiled at the stranger when he materialized on the overgrown path of the cottage, and watched him walk up to the open front door.

"Hi."

"Hello, my dear," Baxter said. He smiled in a kindly way while trying to work out who she was. Where was Theresa Rattigan?

"Are you bird-watching?"

"More of a walker," Baxter said, hedging his bets.

They looked at each other in silence. Ally experienced the abrupt realization that she didn't like the man.

"So…" she said.

"Yes?" said Baxter, as if it were he who was wondering what she wanted, rather than the other way round.

"So, what can I do for you?" Ally asked.

Baxter smiled again, and edged into the cottage.

"You're here alone?" he probed.

"No," Ally said immediately, now worried that he might pose a danger to her, "no, I'm here with friends. They're just outside. They'll be back any minute."

As she said the words, Theresa was returning from a thoughtful walk along the seashore. She walked in breezily.

"Hello," she said brightly, striding over to the TV and switching it on. "Sorry for being rude, just want to see the latest with the whales." She stretched out her hand to Baxter. "On holiday? I'm Theresa," she said.

"I know who you are, Mrs Rattigan," Baxter said with deliberation, shaking her hand with a limp, watery grasp. He looked from one woman to the other. His spirits sagged a little.

"Oh God," Theresa said, in a little moan, understanding at once. "My husband sent you."

"I wouldn't know," Baxter said. That was information he did not require. "Go and sit." He pointed to the settee.

The two women stood their ground, and a cold, doom-laden atmosphere seemed to seep into the cottage.

"Get out." Ally rapped.

She stared at Baxter warily, sick with fear, suppressing a scream. The walls of the room seemed to contract, until she felt that she was crammed into a small cage with her amazed mother. Meanwhile, despite her confusion and anxiety, something else was intruding into her consciousness. The TV. She could hear her father. "It's Daddy," she said, involuntarily.

Her father was on television, crazed and pathetic and floundering.

"The constable attacked by Mr Rattigan is unconscious, possibly badly hurt," a voice from the TV was saying.

Baxter, Theresa and Ally watched the TV for some seconds in a surreal subversion of a domestic scene. Baxter had not known who his client was. It was safer that way. But now he knew his client was Rattigan – and that his client was crazed, in custody.

"Get out," Ally said again, this time in a guttural, menacing rasp; she moved closer to him; her hands were shaking.

Baxter adjusted the haversack on his back. His commission was redundant.

He looked at each of them, once, and padded out of the cottage and down the path. Ally walked to the doorframe and watched him striding away towards Inverarish. Theresa came up behind her, and hugged her. They were both trembling.

"Who *is* he?" Ally asked. "What did he *want*?"

"Don't think about it," Theresa begged her. "It's all over now, my baby. Daddy's finished. We're safe."

5

A Sea King helicopter was hauling its cumbersome form through the sky. Its rotors whipped the air into shreds and made it roar in protest. A few hundred feet below, the Atlantic Ocean glinted and foamed, giving no hint of the trauma she was enduring in her depths. Inside the Sea King, Roddy and Kate sat strapped into the steel frames of their seats, exhausted. Their helmets incorporated earphones and microphones so that they could talk to each other through the boom and blast of the noise.

"All right?" Roddy asked.

"Yeah." The two-way radio system made Kate's voice sound tinny. "Glad to be out of that coffin."

Roddy nodded. Opposite them, the doctor and Rear Admiral who were escorting them to Reykjavík were engaged in their own earnest discussion.

"Hey," Roddy said, shyly.

"Yeah?"

"That was an amazing broadcast."

"Oh..." She flushed. She was grateful that the helmet obscured her face. "Thanks."

Neither of them said anything for a time. Once Kate looked up and caught the doctor or the Rear Admiral staring. The ocean spanned all horizons without cease. The flying machine throbbed and boomed.

"Roddy?"

"Ah ha?"

"Why did you hate the press so much? During your career?"

"Oh." Roddy closed his eyes, weighing up the question; it was funny how, during all the terrible dramas of the past few weeks, he'd been forced to confront his own past so often. "I've had so many bad experiences with them, as you know. But there was one that just, I don't know... the straw that broke the camel's back. I just gave up on the media after that one. I lost the will to respect them."

"What happened...?"

"I was in California, trying to raise funds for the promotion of a sanctuary for whales injured in collisions with boats. And I was rung up by a TV station – there was a dead pilot whale washed up on a beach, would I turn up and do an interview? I said I'd do it if they gave me a couple of minutes to talk about the sanctuary. So I turn up, there's a dead pilot there – beautiful creature – and we do the interview. It was sunset. There are two other local TV crews there by then, so I do something for both of them too. They all seem like nice people, if a little vacuous, but they seem to be genuinely interested in the issues I was trying to raise. Then I went home to get my camera, I'd forgotten it and I wanted to photograph the whale."

He turned to look at her for the first time, eyes shining. The aircraft throbbed and buzzed.

"I get back to the beach about an hour and a half later. It's dark by then, but there's a small crowd where the whale is, a couple of fires lit, music. It seems a bit odd. And when I go up, there's half the people from the TV crews, work over for the day, dancing to the music with a load of other people, swigging beer. There's an inflated beach ball in the pilot whale's mouth, its blowhole is an ashtray full of cigarette ends, and there's an empty whiskey bottle jammed into its anus. They've hacked off the whale's flippers and flukes – souvenirs. And as I stand there, amazed, taking it all in, one of the guys who interviewed me starts taking a piss on the red stump of a flipper. And then I knew..." Roddy's hand hovered in the air, helpless to find the right gesture. "God I'm tired," he said finally.

"I'm sorry. I know the type you mean. But there are lots of good people too, trying to do the right thing."

355

"I took photos of what I saw, and you know what? No one would run it."

"Oh."

"The fearless seekers of wrongdoing and injustice closed ranks like a Roman legion. And you know something else? In the news that night they edited out everything I'd said about the sanctuary for whales injured by boats. Didn't want to offend the boat-owning, news-channel-investing classes. You see? And I just..."

Moved, she waited for him to carry on, but he didn't. I wish, she thought, I wish I could express that I'm not one of those kinds of people. Maybe I was in danger of it once, but I'm not any more. She tried to find ways of saying so without seeming too mawkish, but nothing came to her. Something else did.

"Roddy?"

"Yeah?"

"I can't wait to get home, you know?"

"Yeah."

"Be on solid earth, sleep in a proper bed."

"Yeah..."

"Roddy, if you need somewhere to stay for a while..."

The offer was put in as innocuous a way as she could manage, but she knew that he knew what she was saying.

"Oh, yeah, that's really generous of you." Roddy paused. He cleared his throat. "You know, I think I'll probably stay with Whitaker for a while."

"Of course, yeah, OK."

Opposite, the Rear Admiral was scrutinizing them as though they were apes in a cage. I wish I could just say what I'm thinking, she thought, then started thinking about what she could say. Minutes passed. The clamorous rotors hammered the air. No, don't say anything, she decided. Then through the heavy-duty earphones, she suddenly registered his heavy breathing – he was asleep.

Epilogue

Forty-eight hours after Roddy arrived back in Britain, the spell of fine summer weather broke. Rain leached over Lancashire. The sky above Blackpool was dirty and dull, the sea seemed heavy and sullen, and the scene on the beach was like something out of animal hell. Of the three-and-a-half thousand stranded whales, almost two thousand eight hundred were dead. Injuries received when beaching, dehydration due to lack of misting in the first few days, and the bloody attacks of the mob had proven too much. There were fears of a catastrophic public health crisis. Already over a thousand carcasses had been winched out to sea for disposal, but the stink of those that remained was insupportable. The several thousand personnel on the scene were wearing breathing apparatus and sealed rubber overalls that were colour-coded according to function: police, army, drivers of trucks and operators of heavy machinery, vets, scientists, environmental health officers, council officials, accredited press. The stench wafted up the beach and into the town, spilling into every alley and nook. The promenade was deserted except for personnel involved in post-incident operations. The streets were nearly empty. Only residents of the town were permitted access, and those few hardy souls who ventured outside did so wearing protective masks issues by the council.

The Imperial Hotel on the North Promenade had been requisitioned by the local authority. In a small room at the back, Roddy was taking a half-hour break from his work on the beach. Whitaker, still wheelchair-bound and with his leg outstretched in plaster, was keeping him company.

"How many whales are still viable?" Whitaker asked.

"A hundred, a hundred and fifty max."

"It's not many."

"No."

Roddy was determined to return to the sea those whales that had a chance of survival. The conditions were completely different to those at Brighton. Blackpool beach was a shallow sand beach, and the whales were a long way up it. So he had supervised the digging of channels between the whales and the sea. Lined with plastic sheeting, they filled with water at high tide. The whales were then guided, backwards, down the channels. Roddy regarded it as a fairly desperate business. At times he wondered if it would be more honest to put all the whales down. He knew that the biggest deterrent to successful refloatings was stress in the animals; he also knew that the stress these animals had suffered, were suffering, was extreme.

"And Blackfin?" Whitaker asked.

"Still hanging in there," Roddy answered, trying to sound brisk and business-like. Blackfin, my Blackfin, you're dying...

"Unbelievable. How he's alive is a miracle."

"Don't you think you ought to – you know – with Blackfin?" Whitaker urged.

There was a pause. Roddy cleared this throat, leant over his laptop, started typing.

"Sure."

He knew what Whitaker was saying. The rational thing to do was to put Blackfin down, humanely, as with all the other unviable whales. But – he couldn't do it. He couldn't do it. Roddy wasn't even able to explain his reasoning on this matter; only his inarticulate sorrow understood that Blackfin was a life force, and must die when he was ready, not before. Blackfin was his friend.

Roddy contrived to wipe his eye with his shoulder as he typed. Whitaker's eyes widened. He rubbed at his nose and searched for something diverting to say.

"Oh, you won't have heard the Prime Minister's broadcast yet."

"Yeah? Don't tell me, he *isn't* resigning."

"How did you guess? Adlington's gone, and the Minister for the Environment. But he said – what did he say? – something like, 'I feel the crisis will be best served by my continuing in office'. He says the government accepts full responsibility for what's happened in SONAZ."

"How gracious."

"He's earmarking half a billion, and that's only initially, for cleaning it up."

"Half a billion, five billion, ten billion... Who knows what it will take to sort it out, if it can be sorted out. The techniques haven't been invented to clean up an environment three thousand metres under the sea. You can't just go down there with a few black bin liners and a shovel."

"Well, that's true. But he's saying, if it can be done, they'll do it, whatever it takes."

"Mmm..."

"And he announced an initiative for the ethical and sustainable exploitation of the oceans."

"Oh yeah? Meaning?"

"Well, stringent guidelines for every aspect of commercial activity in the marine eco-system, from anglers collecting lugworms on mud flats to deep sea oil exploration by trans-national corporations. He had this slogan, Nature First For People To Prosper—"

"*What?*"

"Stomach-churning, isn't it. He says that once the guidelines are drawn up, Britain will implement them unilaterally, and promote them multilaterally."

"In other words, business as fucking usual." Roddy's voice was cracked with fatigue, cynicism. "Until people accept the blindingly simple premise that a world of finite natural resources cannot sustain year-on-year economic growth, and that we have to find an economic model that measures success by quality of life rather than by increase in consumption, then it's completely meaningless."

"Well, here's your chance to put that view – you know he's gagging to meet you and pin decorations all over your skinny hide."

"Sure he wants to meet me – cameras running. I told his flunkeys to scram."

"How diplomatic of you," said Whitaker. "Hey, apart from the fact that the planet is dying, are you feeling OK?"

"Yeah yeah..."

"You don't seem too good."

"Ah, God. I feel strange, you know? Putting whales back in the sea, convinced they'll die anyway... And..."

"And?"

Blackfin. Theresa. Kate. Me. Even Rattigan... "Aaah forget it. I have to get back to the beach." He stood up and struggled into the ungainly rubber overalls. "I got a call from Ally Rattigan," he said. "She says she might ring you."

"Ally Rattigan? Ally Rattigan said that? Ally Rattigan said—"

"Christ, don't get a hard-on."

"What else did she say?"

"Nothing else."

"Come on, tell me everything she said."

"There's nothing to tell," Roddy answered. He slung his breathing apparatus under his arm and left the room.

"Well why the hell did she ring you then?" Whitaker shouted from behind the closed door. He swung round in his wheelchair and slammed his plaster-cast leg into a table. "Ow! Shit! Hey, Roddy – when is she going to ring me?!"

Boys and girls, Roddy thought: for as long as we're here, all that will continue. He walked through the lobby of the Imperial, nodding at various officials, all of whom seemed slightly awestruck by him. The stink was bad enough indoors, but outside it could make you gag; he fitted the breathing apparatus and passed through the doors of the hotel. Once, outside a different seaside hotel, thousands of protesters had spat at him and called him a murderer. But Roddy was thinking of something else. Of how Ally, after a bit of awkward chat, had revealed the real reason for her call. "Mummy wants to say hello," she had blurted; and Roddy had found himself speaking to Theresa, for the first time in over twenty years. Strange. Frightening, almost, but – he admitted it to himself tentatively – wonderful.

* * *

Blood stains the sand around Blackfin. Flies swarm up when Roddy makes his way to the old sperm whale and rests a hand on the snout. He feels weary with pity as he looks at the heavy-duty chain around the tailstock, at the raging infection over the entire lower end of Blackfin's body. He's got slashes and cuts all down one flank, Roddy agonizes, by rights he should be dead, and yet he isn't; why is he clinging on like this?

"What is it?" Roddy says, feeling desperate about something, but not sure what it is. Nothing is happening, but he feels sure that something should happen – he rips off his breathing apparatus, flinches and gasps as the stench of the beach hits him.

Blackfin has been waiting for him.

Roddy places the palms of his hands against the whale, and gazes into that enigmatic, fading dark eye. They look into each other's being. The whale is close to death. But here is his friend, who has understood him, who has followed his kind in a *manfish*, and who has witnessed the *badbright*. The oceans, the whales, might survive now.

An unstoppable tide of peace is washing over the great creature, and as Roddy watches, the brightness of the eye starts to fade further. A whale is dying, and a man is with him. Roddy's tears, pent up for days, dammed behind his responsibilities and suffering and past, start oozing out of him, coursing down his cheeks. He leans his face against the hot coarse skin of Blackfin, and gulps out his wretched male tears. Go, he tells the creature; go now.

Blackfin slowly loses awareness of the gentle man who stands next to him. His unconscious has taken possession of him, communicating certain elemental truths that only the dying are granted. Now he not only knows that the man has understood everything; Blackfin can see it. In his final moments he gets a strange vision-version of the cold valley in the ocean: *badbright*. He sees the man, his beautiful friend of the soft, warm voice, swimming easily at the bottom of the sea. The man swims into the centre of badbright, through the very vortex of the evil, and comes out unharmed at the other side, where the deep water whales are waiting for him. With great tenderness, the whales escort the man to the surface far above, back to his own world of land, where he tells his species of what he has seen...

A curious, muted clicking emanates from Blackfin, a coda, an unknowable whale prayer that sends a cold charge of energy crackling down Roddy's spine, and makes him cry out in the intensity of its signal. *Christ! What the hell was that?* The clicking slows but continues, filling Roddy with extraordinary feelings of warmth and optimism. It's a message of hope from Blackfin, and a call to carry on.

"Blackfin…"

The clicks peter out. Roddy's hand moves gently against the snout. There is a violent, juddering spasm down the whole body of Blackfin – the last pulse in the long life of an old bull sperm whale – and Blackfin no longer exists in the treacherous realms of time, suffering, land, sea.

Roddy sucks in a wounded breath, and turns away. For half a minute he stands where he is, looking down at his feet, trying to master himself. He shakes his head, as though this could shake the grief from his mind – then clamps his breathing apparatus back on and tramps through the sand to where sixty soldiers are digging a channel between the sea and an exhausted minke. Actually, he thinks, I will see the Prime Minister, and the cameras can run when I tell him a few things.

He looks back, once, through the scratched visor of his mask, at the huge dead sperm whale; then he grabs a shovel, and starts shifting sand.

Acknowledgements

With thanks to Daniel Watkins, Paul Stocks, Jonny Pegg at Curtis Brown and everyone at Alma Books.